PRAISE FOR CAMERON JOHNSTON

"Cameron Johnston is an exciting new voice in fantasy. His writing has a dark sense of humour and his debut is bursting with imagination and wonders. Fantastic stuff!"
Stephen Aryan, author of the *Age of Darkness trilogy*

"Epic fantasy meets hardboiled noir, with a foul-mouthed, seen-it-all narrator you won't soon forget."
Barnes & Noble Sci-Fi & Fantasy Blog

"I'm looking forward to seeing who and what Walker kicks in the balls in the sequel. If you enjoy clever gray characters, gritty but interesting worlds, and creepy magic, this book is for you."
Fantasy Hive

"A dark and rich fantasy with an inventive magic system that will raise hairs on your neck."
Ed McDonald, author of *Blackwing*

BY THE SAME AUTHOR

THE AGE OF TYRANNY
The Traitor God

CAMERON JOHNSTON

GOD OF BROKEN THINGS

THE AGE OF TYRANNY BOOK II

ANGRY ROBOT
An imprint of Watkins Media Ltd

Unit 11, Shepperton House
89 Shepperton Road
London N1 3DF
UK

angryrobotbooks.com
twitter.com/angryrobotbooks

An Angry Robot paperback original, 2019

Cover by Jan Weßbecher
Set in Meridien

ISBN 978 0 85766 809 7
Ebook ISBN 978 0 85766 810 3

Printed and bound in the United Kingdom by TJ International.

9 8 7 6 5 4 3 2 1

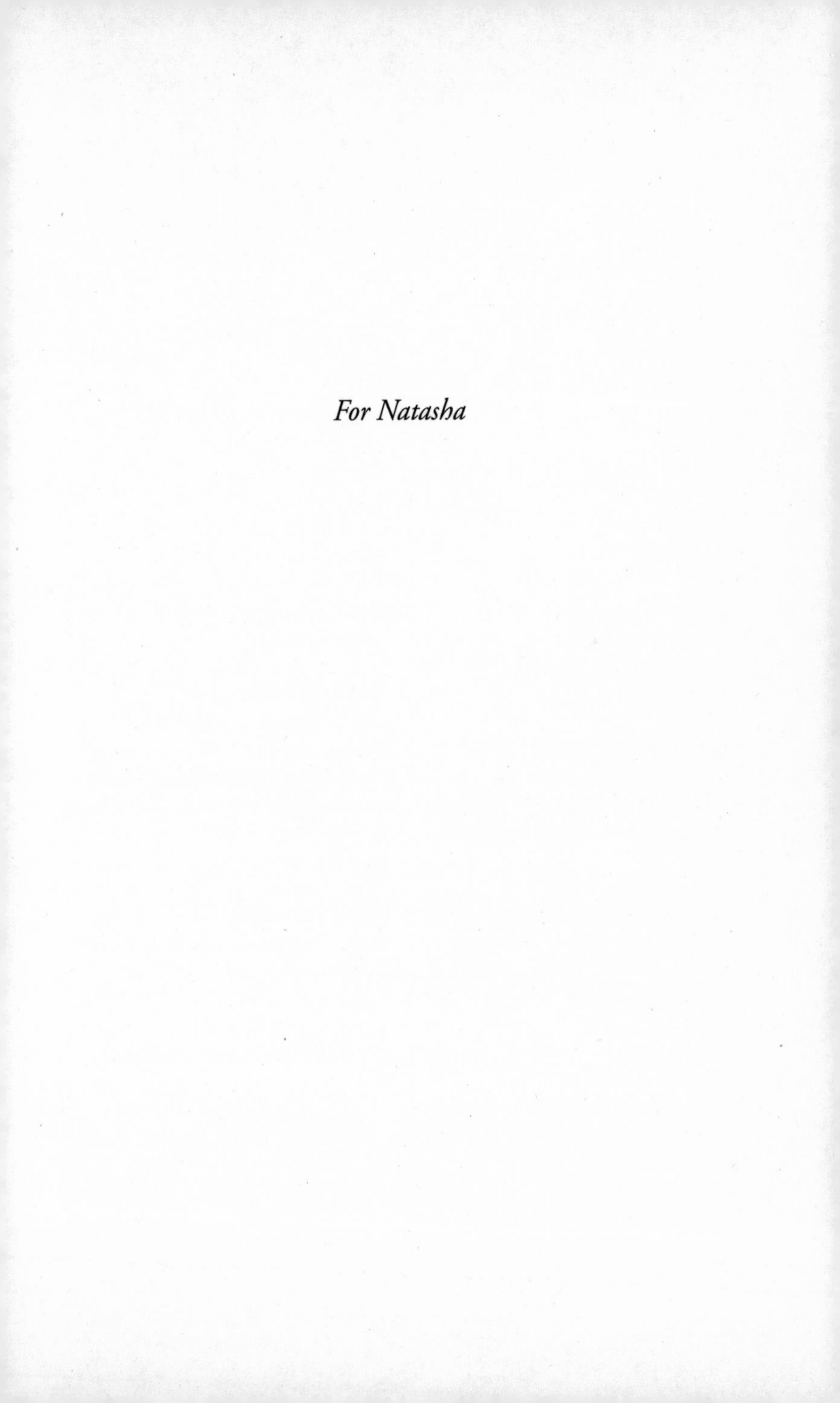

For Natasha

CHAPTER 1

From the shadows of a doorway I watched as Vivienne of House Adair – a middling House of waning influence – exited the rear of the building after a midnight tryst with her lover, a married warden captain. The hood of her cloak was up and her cheeks still flushed as she made her way down the back streets of the Crescent, intent on returning to the Old Town before her own husband became aware she was otherwise engaged. To my magically Gifted senses her unguarded mind radiated the fuzzy warmth of a lust well-satisfied.

If she was still fully human then she could spread her legs for whomever she liked; it was none of my business. But if she was infested with the same parasitic creatures that had dominated the traitor Heinreich and almost succeeded in destroying the city, then that unwitting warden was a source of information to use against us, and that was most certainly my business.

She was the least dangerous of the three magi I had marked as likely threats, an artificer more at home with her arcane apparatus of cogs and crystals than with battle. As a young and indifferent pyromancer blessed only with a truly extraordinary memory, her Gift would be weaker than mine by normal standards, but since I'd bathed in the blood of gods some of their potency had seeped into me and it would prove no contest unless I was foolish. Always a risk of that of course. Vivienne's knowledge of architecture and alchemy was what made her dangerous – and a likely partner in bringing down the Templarum Magestus. The Arcanum's seers had divined a number of unknown magi had collaborated in that betrayal and if you needed a magus to circumvent protective wardings and magic-strengthened stone then an artificer would be the obvious choice.

Those soaring spires at the heart of Setharis had fallen – and I was here to ensure that all involved paid a terrible price for their treachery.

I stepped out of the shadows to block her path, "Hello, Vivienne."

She started and loosed a little yelp. "Who–" The blood drained from her face as she realised who stood before her. Her Gift flew open and drew in magic, ready to fight even as her mental defences slammed shut. She straightened her back and stared me in the eye. "Edrin Walker. What are you doing lurking in the shadows? Up to no good I warrant."

Ah, it never got old hearing my name said like a curse. The stories told about what I'd done a few months ago had bubbled up like a blocked sewer, and every bit as foul. None of them came close to the truth. I fumbled a bent roll-up from my pouch to my lips, the last tabac to be found anywhere in the city. "Couldn't trouble you for a light could I?"

Her lips thinned and the end of my roll-up flared bright for a second, hotter than was necessary – a clear warning. I took a long drag and blew out acrid smoke. "What do I want?" I probed her defences, searching for any hint of wrongness, of anything other. "Tell me, Vivienne, are you still loyal to Setharis?"

She swallowed. Her hands trembling as her façade of strength cracked. She had probably leapt to the conclusion that I meant to blackmail her about her dalliances with men other than her husband. That was the last thing I cared about.

The cracks in her confidence let my Gift slip in. If I'd wanted to I could have torn her mind open and taken what I wanted. With Councillor Cillian's sealed writ giving me leave to do as I wished it wouldn't even get me killed once people found out. Tempting. So very tempting.

"What do you want?" she spat. "Gold?"

"Hardly," I replied. "I want to know about Heinreich. Tell me what you built for that traitorous cur."

She lurched back, forced to lean a hand on a wall to steady herself, doubled over, throat spasming and threatening to vomit. Her mind crumpled in on itself, oozing guilt.

"Did you think nobody would ever find out? Somebody always talks, even if you pay them off." Her workshop apprentices had suddenly become flush with coin and hadn't been shy in spending it. They hadn't spilled their guts willingly but I can be ever so persuasive.

She choked back a retch. "I…I had no idea. Heinreich was so nice, so…charming. How could I ever suspect what he… It was not my fault."

I stabbed into her mind, making her gasp with shock, and waited for a response to what I was about to say.

"Scarrabus."

Nothing. The name evoked no sudden firing of thought and fear. She had never heard the name before. Her mind ran clear of those creatures' parasitic taint. She was no traitor, just another dupe.

She mustered enough bravery to look me in the eye again. "Are you here to kill me? If so, just get on with it."

Oh, I wanted to. Hundreds died when the Templarum Magestus was brought down, and it couldn't have been done without the help of her and others like her. My right hand clenched, itching to dig into her throat and rip it out. Instead I sighed and let my anger drain away. She was hardly the first or finest he had fooled. My mind's eye flicked back to Eva, her face frozen in shock as somebody she had once considered a friend turned his flames on her. Yes, that twisted wretch had fooled the best of us.

I grimaced as I forced my stiff hand to open. "Not today." I raked fingers through my mop of hair. "You will drag your sorry arse over to Councillor Cillian in the morning and detail exactly what you built for that bastard. Don't dare try to leave the city." My lips twisted into a vicious grin that suggested I really hoped she'd try. "I've been given a writ that says I can do whatever I sodding want with you." People were always more than willing to think the worst of me and her own imagination would supply horrific images of the very worst tortures, personalised just for her. Cillian would roast me over hot coals if I stepped too far over the line however, and others would also likely be far from happy with me, the kind of displeasure that kept assassins in ale money.

Vivienne shuddered, then took several deep breaths and calmed as her training slid a measure of control back in place. She nodded, and if anything looked relieved that her dark secret had finally been exposed.

I didn't have time to interrogate her further, not tonight. "Go home to your family. You may yet escape this mess with your hide intact." I turned to leave.

"I'm so sorry," she said in a small, tortured voice. "It's been eating me alive...I just, I needed to forget. Just for a while. I was such a fool to resurrect that madman Tannar's designs. Those alchemic bombs should never have been built."

The last smoke in this whole sodding city almost fell from my lips. "Bombs? Plural? You built more than one?" I spun back. "What do you–"

A flare of killing intent sent me diving and rolling. The cobbles where I had stood erupted into jagged spears of stone that punched Vivienne from her feet and turned her into a human pincushion. Spikes through her heart and skull gave her a mercifully quick death. She hung suspended in the air, hot blood steaming down the winter-cold stone that had killed her.

Shite. Tonight was not going to go my way...

CHAPTER 2

Nine hours earlier, I'd been surrounded by armed men and escorted to the Collegiate of the Arcanum for an urgent meeting with one of most important magi in the city. As usual, important people made you sit on an uncomfortable seat and wait an age for an audience, but at least I wasn't suffering alone.

After a while the sound of screaming becomes white noise, a buzzing annoyance in the back of your head no worse than a yapping dog or a drunkard's droning snore from the straw pallet right next to your own. I yawned, ignored the two armed wardens flanking me, and shifted on the hard wooden bench as I stared ahead at the iron-bound doors. My eyes traced and re-traced the all-too familiar patterns of glimmering arcane wards worked into the oak. The Forging Room was far from my favourite place in the Collegiate, not least because I had been through this particular magical rite myself as an initiate. All magi had but nobody remembers it all, just the agony and the raw-throated screaming. And the needles, we mustn't forget the needles.

Inserted under the nails…slid into the eyes…piercing the tongue…the other bits…

I crossed my legs and pulled my great coat tight around me. I hated the bloody Arcanum – their brutal rules and rites had broken my old friend Lynas. He had never been the same afterwards. How dare they put innocent initiates through this! And yet… I now understood and acknowledged the necessity of magically enforcing loyalty to Setharis. You can't begin turning people into living weapons and let them do anything they wish without a measure of control. After the catastrophe three months ago that we now called the Black Autumn, there could be no denying it. It didn't mean I liked it.

The door to the Forging Room finally creaked open and I sat up straight, wincing as my spine complained. Pain was now my constant companion.

A young magus poked her head out. Her chestnut hair was pulled into a neat tail and she wore plain brown robes entirely lacking the ornamentation and wealth worn by most others – the dark stains marked her as a healing magus of the Halcyon Order. Once their robes had been pure white, but now they all wore cheap and practical brown. Me, I couldn't stand robes and the status they proclaimed. Plain old peasant tunic and trousers had always suited me just fine.

Her eyes were wide and nervous. "Councillor Cillian bids you enter, magus." She swiftly stepped back to make way for me. There was no sneaking about as an unknown face for me these days – every fucker and their horse seemed to know who and what I was. I suppose that's what happens when you kill a god and save a city. Most seemed to doubt it was true that Nathair, the Thief of Life, had died at my hands, but many magi had heard enough rumours to make them nervous in my presence. And as for those that actually knew the truth of my part in it all, well, who could blame them for being afraid.

The sour stench of blood, sweat and piss mixed with vinegar assaulted me as I stepped inside, almost overpowering a sharp clean scent reminiscent of the aftermath of a lightning storm. Behind a wooden privacy screen, the room was ornate and bewilderingly complex. Copper pipes and bundles of golden wire covered one entire wall, humming with power like a hive of angry bees. Trapped inside glass jars, lightning crackled and spat. Brass cogs ticked and turned with mesmerising regularity. Five artificers wearing odd ceramic gauntlets sat studying arrays of glowing crystals and moving rods that flickered and danced in tune with whatever was happening to the poor naked git strapped to the table in the centre of the room. To me it was all just pretty lights.

Steel manacles bound the young Gifted initiate's limbs to the table and leather straps held his head and body immobile for his own safety. His head was circled by an open helmet containing an array of needles, some of which were already embedded in his skull, connected to wires running back into the arcane machinery on the wall. A steel grate was situated directly below the table to deal with the subject pissing themselves from fear and pain. I shuddered, remembering that particular bit of humiliation only too well, and that was only a herald of far worse to come.

Cillian's demeanour was unusually severe today as she bent over the initiate and slid another needle in, this time into his chest and heart. She attached it to a wire and stepped back. The nearest artificer nudged a lever up slightly. The boy convulsed and screamed as magic I knew nothing about poured into him.

I winced, his panic and pain seeping into my mind through my cracked Gift. I couldn't keep the thoughts of others out entirely anymore, not after what I'd been through. The buzzing machinery gave off a whiff of magic that smelled reminiscent of my own. Not entirely surprising since all this weird and unsettling machinery was designed to do one thing – to burn loyalty to Setharis and the Arcanum into a Gifted mind. It was a relic built at the very founding of the Arcanum in the years following the destruction of ancient Escharr. Those refugee magi had created it using long lost knowledge for unknown reasons, and I had to wonder if this was one path of knowledge that they had purposely let fade away.

The initiate's eyes rolled to me, pleading to make it stop. Tears wet his cheeks.

"Ah, Edrin," Cillian said. "I am glad my messengers finally found you." I always forgot how tall she was, and how beautiful. She was wearing her formal azure silken robes and an elegant gold circlet to restrain her unruly mass of long dark curly hair. Her pale olive skin appeared sallow and waxy from exhaustion. Knowing her she hadn't stopped for more than a short nap every night for three months solid.

I eyed the torture table; there was no other suitable word for it. "Enjoying yourself are we?" Messengers she said! More like a pack of armed wardens hauling me straight to her whether I liked it or not.

She ignored my jibe entirely, which in all fairness is a wise tactic when faced with annoying people like me. Her lips pursed. "It is only a few hours until nightfall. I had not expected it to take quite this long to find you. I assume they checked all the ale houses first, then the brothels… which were you in?"

"Neither. I was in a hospital."

She looked concerned for a moment, but I was an experienced magus and with magic we didn't have much need for powders and potions and healing in general unless it was from enormous trauma. If it didn't kill me outright I would generally be back on my feet in a ridiculously short time.

"I work there on occasion," I added.

Surprise flickered through her expression, but not as much as I might have expected given my blackened reputation. "Well well. It is good to see you putting your unique talents to use. Speaking of which, I have a task you are especially suited for."

A ruby began blinking in the machinery and she held up a finger. "Do not go anywhere. This may take a while."

She leaned over the delirious, moaning boy and began asking him questions:

"Are you loyal to Setharis and the Arcanum?"

"Would you ever take coin or favours from foreign powers?"

"Would you ever consider using blood sorcery?"

The questioning went on for an age, and whatever the machinery and needles did to him they seemed to force truthful answers. When they uncovered an answer they approved of an artificer would pull a lever and his body would shudder with crackling energy, leaving him gasping and sobbing. They were burning it into his mind so that betrayal was not something he could ever seriously consider.

Once or twice they came across opinions or inclinations that they did not approve of and an artificer would lean forward to study the instrumentation and then call over to Cillian – who would then get to work inserting needles and applying shocks and pain and magical manipulations until those opinions were bent back toward compliance, then burned into place. I was living proof that it didn't always hold entirely, but then I was messed up in the head in all sorts of ways.

It would have been easier and less painful if I did it for them, but that was not a role I would ever volunteer for, and in any case the Arcanum would never trust a wastrel tyrant like me to make a proper job of it.

Cillian and her machines got to work on keeping away the Worm of Magic, that seduction to use more and more magic until all of your self-control was eaten away and your body and mind were warped into a mere shell for magic itself. My mouth went dry. This part was the worst. "Open your Gift," Cillian said, pressing a wooden rod wrapped in leather between his teeth and securing it there. "Let as much magic as you can flow into you." At this stage in his development nobody knew if the youth's Gift would mature enough to become a full magus, but they enforced their hidebound rules all the same. Better now than too late. When the artificers read certain arcane signs in the machinery they gave the word that the subject's Gift was straining, and then the real agony began. Needles jabbed and bottled lightning sparked into human skin, releasing a stench of burnt hair into the room. The machinery whined as magic poured into the boy's skull to stamp a single message: overextending your Gift was a very bad thing. *This agony waits for you if you try!* He screamed through the gag until blood mixed with the spittle.

My head throbbed from the poor bastard's ordeal, and I turned my back on them to study the walls until Cillian was done torturing him into unconsciousness. The artificer's machines had done their work for the day and I couldn't help but feel sorry for the boy – he had no idea the needles and bottled lighting were only the first of three sessions. A wave of nausea washed over me: I had been through this myself and knew what horrors were still to come. In the morning he would be dragged back in kicking and screaming to undergo an even worse set of procedures.

The brown-robed magus wheeled the unconscious patient out and the artificers filed out after her, leaving me alone with my old friend and ex-lover. It was only slightly awkward now that she was one of the seven members of the Inner Circle in charge of basically everything, and could order me tossed onto a pyre if she deemed it necessary.

The pretence of dispassionate control dropped away from Cillian and she sagged into a chair in the corner, ripping off her circlet to release her hair and taking a deep and ragged breath. "I hate this." She bowed her head and hid behind a dark and curly veil. I didn't play the game of politics, which made me one of very few people she could relax around.

"Don't do it then." My sage advice was not overly helpful to her.

"I don't order something done unless I could stomach doing it myself," she snapped. "But it must be carried out. We have all seen the havoc a rogue magus can cause, and there are only a few of us with the skill necessary to enact the Forging with a minimum of pain caused to new initiates. All must take their turn and share the burden, even a member of the Inner Circle."

Fair. "How are you doing? You look…" I didn't want to say 'like shite', "…worn out."

She sighed and her eyes drooped as if she would like nothing more than to sit on that chair and drop off to sleep. "As are we all. We must all do as much as we can for as many as possible. There is a mountain of issues that need attending to every single day."

This was why they put people like her in charge and not people like me. I was selfish, and after a day like hers with all that heavy responsibility I would have pissed off to a tavern and gotten rat-arsed on gutrot booze. I was far from the reliable type. Not her, she would be up at the crack of dawn and working before I fell out of my blankets with a hangover and a bad attitude.

"So why have you dragged me here?" I asked.

She swept her hair back to look me in the eye as she pulled a folded parchment from a pouch on her belt and tossed it over.

"Archmagus Krandus is in agreement."

I opened it and examined the wax seals affixed to the bottom: the seven stars of the Inner Circle and the griffin rampant of High House Hastorum.

Magus Edrin Walker acts under my command and with my full authority. Give him whatever aid he requires and impede him at your peril.
Cillian Hastorum,
Councillor of the Inner Circle,
Seat of High House Hastorum

My eyebrows climbed and I whistled in appreciation as I noted the details of the writ. They were astonishingly brief and all-encompassing: I could legally kill people with this. "Are you cracked in the head? Must be if you're authorising this."

"Don't abuse it," she said, reading my mind. Not that it was difficult on this occasion.

I nodded and tucked it away inside my coat. "The hunt is on then?"

"Yes. You have identified three other magi possibly infested and controlled by Scarrabus parasites. Do not take any unnecessary risks. Investigate and report and I will do the rest. Should things go wrong you are ordered to capture them if you can and kill them if you can't."

I grinned. It was about fucking time to dish out some payback.

She yawned and rubbed tired eyes. "Any questions?"

I thought about it, and the longer I did the lower her eyelids drooped. Her head bobbed up and down, and finally settled on her shoulder. I carefully and silently retreated. By the time I reached the doorway a soft snore came with each breath. As I left the Forging Room another magus and two scribes moved to enter bearing armloads of scrolls. Yet more work for Cillian. I barred their entry with an arm across the doorway.

I glared down at the young magus, barely out of Collegiate

training probably. "The Councillor is not to be disturbed. She is attending to a vital issue."

"But..." she withered under my glare. The scribes swallowed and backed away. The two armed wardens were still waiting for me, and they approached wearing their serious faces, hands wrapped around the hilts of swords.

I waved Cillian's writ in front of their noses. "See this? You two are to guard this doorway for the next two hours and let nobody else in. The rest of you can turn right around and go do something else for a while."

Their eyes flew wide and they leapt to obey me with a level of respect that I didn't think I'd ever experienced before. Cillian would be furious when she found out I was letting her sleep. Not two minutes had passed since she had asked me not to abuse my new powers, but oh well, at least she would be a better-rested angry councillor. Besides, she had said I could do whatever I wanted to whoever I wanted.

I loved this writ already.

Cillian was exhausted and I was rapidly getting there myself, but I had an appointment at another hospital up in Coppergate that I refused to miss. After that my real work would begin – in the deep of night I would finally wrest some answers from the Scarrabus parasites that had tried to orchestrate the destruction of Setharis.

CHAPTER 3

A couple of hours later, I was freezing my arse off hurrying halfway across the city to get to the hospital on time.

Winter's grip on the ancient city of Setharis had broken, causing her cloak of pristine white to slump into piles of dirty grey slush. Her disrobing exposed the brutal scars of last autumn: the blackened ribs of burnt-out buildings, ruined streets and tumbled monuments, and worst of all, the frozen corpses of her murdered children. Far too many of them.

I splashed through reeking pools of corpse-melt and trudged up Fisherman's Way passing patrols of armoured wardens and work-gangs of diggers carting away rubble in a long and gruelling attempt to return a measure of order to the streets. The wind bit at my skin and I tugged my sodden greatcoat tighter, for all the scant good it did. The ragged scars that cut from the corner of my right eye to my jaw and trailed off down my neck pulled tight in the cold, left unprotected by the absence of the forest of stubble which sheltered the rest.

I was bone-tired and half-starved but still had one last obligation before my hunt could begin, something that even morally bankrupt scum like me couldn't bear to shirk. I always repaid a favour – good or bad; well, to people that mattered anyway.

The street led me uphill towards the Crescent and the Old Town and in my weary state it felt like a mountain beneath my aching legs. My belly rumbled, but I could only ignore it. Food was scarce right now – even for a magus – and our paltry rations never stretched far enough. With most of the grain stores torched and the fishing fleet wrecked we were barely surviving by stripping bare the farmlands and towns beyond the city walls. I was sick to death of fish, pickled cabbage, and turnips. Still, things could have been worse: the self-obsessed Arcanum magi and the High House nobles, safe in their mansions perched atop the high rock that loomed above the lower city, had opened their stores to the war-ravaged Docklanders below them. I… had not expected that from their sort, even given the horrors of Black Autumn. The cynical side of me suspected that Archmagus Krandus had threatened to seize it by force if they hadn't taken the opportunity to flaunt their magnanimity.

As the edge of twilight approached and the sky began to darken, I paused to catch my breath and as always my eyes were drawn to the vast crater in the centre of the lower city that had once been the snarl of crooked lanes that made up the human cess-pit of the Warrens. Where I'd grown up. Where Lynas had been murdered. Much of the Docklands area had been spared complete devastation by the Magash Mora, instead being merely ransacked by Skallgrim raiders or subjected to fire's voracious hunger. The people of the Warrens had suffered a far darker fate than axe or flame. I shuddered at the memory of that mountainous creature of stolen flesh and bone erupting from beneath our streets and lanes. It had been a thing of nightmares, and visions of it plagued my nights; I was lucky if I ever managed more than a few hours of undisturbed sleep.

An old man in rags with a long straggly beard shuffled towards me. "Got any food, friend?" There was little hope left in his voice, and just enough desperation to speak. His nose was red and his lips were blue, not good signs. A duo of corvun lingered on nearby rooftops, the great black birds waiting for him to drop dead so they could feast on his warm innards.

I went to turn away and resume my journey. I meant to. But some small voice lingering in the back of my head spoke up 'What would Lynas do?' My best friend had ever been my conscience in life, and in death his memory tried its best, but it was failing. I had always been selfish, but these last few months had wrought changes in me, and not for the better. You could not go through what I had and come out unscathed; mentally, magically and especially physically.

I sighed and dipped a leather-gloved hand into my money pouch. A couple of silvers left. Enough for scraps of food and warm lodgings on a few frozen nights. I dropped them into his shaking hand. "On me, pal." It wasn't like I was going to die from missing a few more meals. Magi died hard, and after recent events I would die harder than most. My flesh was changing, and that was more terrifying to me than any hunger. I flexed my right hand, skin and leather creaking. The taint was making it increasingly stiff and painful, but under that glove waited worries best left for another day.

As I left the old man behind I searched inside myself for any sign of satisfaction, any hint of taking pleasure from doing a good deed as I had felt in the past. Nothing. Just an old friend's voice blowing away on the breeze.

Resuming my trek up the hill, I passed through palls of smoke and steam. The pyres burned day and night, sending columns of black smoke and funerary prayers up to writhe around the five gods' towers that reared up over the Old Town on its high rock, slick black serpents of stone twining around each other until their fangs pierced the clouds. The towers remained dark and silent, our gods still missing, and in one case, dead. The Fucker. I only wished I could murder that traitor god all over again! You know, without all the writhing in agony and torture I'd experienced – he had not been in his right mind and I'd still only survived through crude cunning and blind luck.

I passed over the worn hump of Carr's Bridge into the largely undamaged streets of the Crescent, slogging through rutted piles of slush towards what had been a fine inn for wealthy travellers with a gleaming copper lion rearing over the doorway. It had served mouth-watering spiced meats and fine ale, and now it served up bandages and medicine. A line of the diseased and destitute stood outside waiting for hand-outs of stale bread, smoked fish and, if they were lucky, a morsel of preserved fruit.

The burning sun dipped behind the city walls and the bells of the Clock of All Hours rang the day's last. Lanterns and candles came to life all across the city, a tide of flickering flame. I was too busy looking up to watch where I was going; my boot came down on black ice and went right out from underneath me, pitching me down on my arse. My back and side shrieked in pain from where that corrupted god had shattered my spine and torn out a rib to prove a point before putting me back together in order to start all over again. It had never fully healed, despite the best efforts of the Halcyon Order. I tried to lever myself up but my left hand flopped beneath me, taking another of its trembling fits.

"Fucking useless lump of meat, work damn you!" That damage was all of my own making, but you couldn't fight a god and come out intact. The fear that both of my hands were becoming useless was inescapable.

Anger and frustration were futile, but when did that ever stop anybody from feeling it? I'd likely never be free of pain and disability: magical healing just didn't work that way. It could only heighten what the human body could already do for itself and even a magus like me couldn't suffer what had been done and walk away. It was, I suppose, a small price to pay for survival.

I staggered to my feet, bones clicking, and kicked a wall to knock the slush from my boots before shoving open the door to the hospital. Inside, the smoky, sawdust-floored room was packed with wounded being attended by chirurgeons and nurses. I wrinkled my nose at the sour reek of sweat, sick and putrefaction. It was a scent I was still to get accustomed to. As I stepped inside I ran head-first into a wall of agony, my every nerve raw and burning. Gritting my teeth, I shoved it to the back of my mind and hung my coat from a hook on the wall, in its place donning a stained leather apron.

That's one problem with my sort of Gift: unlike the vulgar elemental magics – summoning otherworldly flames and the like – mine is a double-edged sword. While others called my mentally manipulative kind tyrants because we can get into your head and rearrange things, the men and women in this hospital could now affect me as well. My Gift had been abused and torn during the carnage of Black Autumn and I could no longer shut out all their fear and agony.

Old Gerthan looked up from the patient moaning atop his work table. His aged face was gaunter than ever, eyes red and watery, and his beard wispy and stained. "About time," he said wearily, "I'm taking this man's arm off." He stabbed a thin dagger into the glowing coals of a brazier and took a bone-saw from the hands of an apprentice chirurgeon with a wine-stain birthmark across her cheek. She gave me a nod of greeting and then busied herself setting out needle and thread and other instruments.

Old Gerthan tested the saw's teeth with a finger. He grimaced, then shrugged.

The emaciated young man on the table complained feebly and tried to sit up. The magus firmly pushed him back down – Old Gerthan might be cursed with permanent old age but his withered flesh still coursed with potent magic. I took his place holding the man down and studied the angry red and ominously black threads of infection running up the poor sod's arm and shoulder from a festering wound in his forearm. His other arm was afflicted in a lesser way. I raised a questioning eyebrow. I'd seen them heal far worse.

"I have been here for ninety-six hours," the old magus replied. "Assuming I haven't missed an extra day." He didn't need to elaborate. There had always been too few magi with the Gift of healing in the Arcanum. And now? That number was hopelessly, laughably, inadequate. Countless Setharii had already felt the touch of his healing Gift, their flesh purged of infection and mending with eerie swiftness, but now he was exhausted and strained, teetering on the edge of losing control. And if a magus lost control they were destroyed like rabid dogs. A Gifted healer like Old Gerthan was far too valuable to take such risks.

Only the very lucky came back sane after ceding control to the Worm of Magic, and even then only if quickly caught and disabled. Nobody ever came back unscathed – I was a living example. My damaged Gift throbbed with remembered pain. It had been ecstasy to be filled with such power. I was only too aware of the new and gaping holes in my self-control left from one moment's madness necessary to save a friend.

I reached into the patient's mind to tinker with his awareness of pain, dulling and diverting the flow of sensation until all he felt was vague warmth.

At my nod, Old Gerthan tightened a tourniquet around the man's upper arm and used a sharp knife to peel back flaps of skin before setting the saw to his swollen flesh. I shuddered and looked away as the saw bit through muscle and then began rasping through bone. I had never been squeamish, but it reminded me of far worse horrors. Thirty seconds later the man's arm thudded to the sawdust and Old Gerthan swiftly tied off his arteries and blood vessels with thread. Then he pulled on a thick blacksmith's glove and retrieved the dagger, the blade now cherry red. He pressed it to the other wounds. Flesh sizzled and steamed, but thanks to my ministrations the man on the table barely twitched. The apprentice chirurgeon applied pitch to keep the wounds clean but still allow fluids to drain, and then it was done. The nurses quickly set another man in his place.

There were always more in need of my numbing touch: today brought four amputations, three surgeries, and one painful investigation of post childbirth complications. It was a long and tiring day and Old Gerthan must have had inhuman willpower to do this for days on end. All magic had its limits where our bodies and sanity were concerned, even for canny old magi like him. I was a wreck after only one day here and there, but I owed the Halcyons: they had done all they could for my friend Charra and made her last days of illness as peaceful as possible. My streak of black bastardry was thick and rotten, and my friends had been all that was important to me. And now that they were dead and gone? What now? Lingering memories and half-baked promises to protect Lynas and Charra's daughter Layla…

It was late and most of the hospital staff were finishing up for the day. They washed all the bloodied tools and bandages with boiling water and vinegar and left them out to dry for use in the morning. Tomorrow always brought more to fill up the hospital beds. Old Gerthan took me to one side and clapped a hand on my shoulder. "How are you doing, my boy?" He sagged with crushing weariness. He had been a loyal friend to Charra and that earned him as much respect and assistance as a wretch like me could offer. He'd readily cashed that debt in.

"Better than you, old man. You are dancing on thin ice. You need to rest."

"Nonsense," he said. "I'm in total control."

"For now." I tapped my temple. "Who are you trying to fool? I've plunged into that icy abyss, remember? Let me take a wild guess how it's getting to you?" I cleared my throat. "Imagine how many more you could save if only you had more power. Just open yourself up to the Worm and burst that dam, let magic pour through you..." His face grew stony "...you could do so much good if only–"

"I take the point, boy."

"Do you? I'm surprised you can string two words together you're that knackered. When did you last eat a proper meal? Do you even remember?"

He grimaced and thumbed gritty red eyes. "Three months on and there is still so much needing done." His voice held that haunted tinge of people who had seen too much. We all had. This was his way of dealing with it, trying to pour a little good back onto the scales in a futile attempt to balance out so much death and despair. Me, I wasn't nearly so benevolent – I wanted to wreak bloody and brutal revenge. I still raged at what Heinreich and Nathair had done to my home and my friends, but with those two traitors dead I was left with this red mass of impotent fury eating away at my insides. Those alien parasites called the Scarrabus had been behind those two bastards, pulling their strings, and soon we would know what the creatures really were, and exactly what they planned.

"If they lose you, they lose everything," I said. "They need you more than they need somebody like me. When you are this worn down you will make mistakes, or push yourself a step too far trying to save a life and it will all slip out of control. I don't want to have to toss you on the pyre, Gerthan. Let the chirurgeons and nurses take care of them until you recover."

He sighed and nodded. "Very well. You make irrefutable sense for once. However, don't think you have dodged my question. How are you faring?"

"The usual."

He grunted commiseration.

"And Layla?" he continued. "How is she coping after her mother's death?"

I shrugged. "Not very talkative, but holding up as well as can be expected. Everything going well I will see her tonight."

He frowned. "I see. Do try and keep your head on your shoulders."

Ah, he knew what tonight held in store for me then. "I have no intention of dying; have no fears there." It wasn't surprising given his newly elevated status in the Arcanum hierarchy – I should have expected that all of the seven councillors of the Inner Circle would know exactly what prey I hunted tonight. I trusted that he had helped ensure that the information had also reached other, less trustworthy, ears.

With that I tossed my bloodied apron onto the wash pile, donned my coat and made my escape out into the night air. A chill breeze cleared the stench from my nostrils and the tiredness from my mind. I took several deep breaths, banishing the dregs of the patients' fear and suffering from my mind. There was no room for such emotions this evening. The shattered face of Elunnai, the broken moon, was visibly smaller in the night sky and with her retreat the worst of the winter storms were already ebbing. Soon the sea routes would reopen, and with that would come more Skallgrim wolf ships and war. I relished the chance to pay back all the pain they'd caused.

Cold anger bubbled up. Heinreich could not have brought down the Templarum Magestus, the heart of the Arcanum, all on his own:

he'd had Skallgrim allies without, and traitorous allies from within the Arcanum. Now I had narrowed it down to three magi.

I'd fully expected one or all of them to die tonight. First, I would be interrogating Vivienne outside a certain lusty warden's house in the Crescent... how was I supposed to know the plan would fuck up so badly?

CHAPTER 4

While I'd been tracking and waiting for Vivienne Adair, somebody else found out what I was up to and had spent those hours hunting me – my luck was as shitty as ever and I had just gone from predator to prey.

Cobbles and stone chips rained down all around me as I stared at Vivienne's twitching corpse, impaled on stone spikes that had thrust from the ground beneath us. A geomancer had just tried to murder me.

I scrambled to my feet and pulled a knife from my belt. It was merely steel, and at times like this I missed Dissever's enchanted black iron, despite the murderous and foul daemon that my spirit-bound blade had contained.

My preternatural senses felt the air stir around me and pulled my gaze up into the night sky. Two robed men dropped on swirling wings of icy wind, splashing down into Vivienne's pooling blood. One was burly and bearded, the other holding him aloft by the armpits, was freshly shaved and slim, almost androgynous: the big man was Alvarda Kernas, a geomancer of some small renown, and the other a nameless youngling freshly released from Collegiate training, new enough that I didn't know his name. Both their expressions were curiously blank and emotionless – they were exactly who I'd been looking for. It seemed they had indeed heard I was closing in on them. Perfect.

I reached out with my Gift as Alvarda shrugged off the youngling and advanced on me. The merest brush of minds was enough to know I was correct – their thoughts were tainted with inhuman influence, a rancid oily scum spread across their emotions. The geomancer's mind was a black morass of Scarrabus-stain, indicating he had been infested for a long time.

We struck at the same moment, Alvarda's power ripping cobbles from the street and launching them at my head, and mine smashing not against that experienced magus' mental fortress but instead cutting straight through the youngling's walls of green wood. I found his mind conflicted and confused, still instinctively trying to fight the parasitic creature's controlling influence. They must have taken him in the last few months else his mind would have been as corrupted as Alvarda's. I felt what could only be that creature's shock as I stormed the man's skull. I didn't try to fight it for control of his body, instead I was in and out quick as a sharp knife through the ribs, ducking and diving the flying cobbles while leaving the aeromancer to enact my orders before the Scarrabus knew what was happening.

Wind tore Alvarda from his feet and flung him face-first into the nearest stone wall – which parted and left him crashing through somebody's kitchen, pots and pans clanging. With any luck he'd landed balls-first on a whole tray of kitchen knives.

I focused my Gift and will upon the aeromancer, peeling open his mind like ripe fruit. As I struck, the Scarrabus burrowed further into his mind like a maggot through rotting flesh. We struck and recoiled, both shivering and numbed like swords swung full force colliding into each other. These creatures controlled their hosts' thoughts and feelings and twisted them towards their own alien ends, so it only made sense that they would be able to detect my intrusion and fight back. I recovered first, but then I'd come expecting this kind of fight.

I tore into the Scarrabus through the aeromancer's mind, following the flow of thoughts and spreading stain to locate the vile thing's connections to his brain. My magic burned through the mental pathways with righteous wrath. These were the vermin that had attacked my city, my people – and they had murdered Lynas. Nothing and nobody would stand between me and them. I could have killed them but we needed one alive. Man and creature convulsed and collapsed; the youngling lay foaming at the mouth, spasmodically twitching, leaving me free to focus on the more experienced and deadly geomancer.

I was a shade too slow. Alvarda had already recovered. He leapt from the gaping hole in the wall and gestured. The ground went liquid beneath me, swallowing my feet and ankles before solidifying again to pin me in place.

"Hey, hey, let's you and me make a deal," I said. "There must be something you lot want?" Shackles of stone slithered up my body to secure my arms.

His expression didn't change as he reached inside his robes and pulled forth a pale ball that unfolded into a squirming segmented beetle with too many legs and dozens of translucent threads instead of mandibles. Scarrabus. This was the same kind of vile creature I had seen torn from that traitor Heinreich. "You are correct, Edrin Walker. There is something that we desire of you."

My mouth was suddenly a desert. I swallowed and scrabbled feebly at his mind. His Gift was strong and his mind tight; he kept me out with apparent ease. "Oh gods. Please, no. How many of our magi have you already taken? You don't need me too."

His mouth ticked into a smile that came nowhere near his eyes. "You have talents that will serve us well, as they were always meant to. You will find it a most fulfilling life."

I cringed, or tried to. The stone held me secure. "The two of you can't possibly defeat the Arcanum."

"Here we become three, but already hundreds elsewhere," he replied. "Soon to be thousands. We have no intention of defeating your Arcanum. We will become the Arcanum, and so much more. Rejoice, for you will become what you were bred to be."

I grinned. "Cheers for the information you festering piss-stain. Good to know there's only the two of you here." Then I raised my voice. "Now would be good."

An arrow thudded into his eye. His head snapped back in a spray of blood and jelly. He didn't scream or snarl or make any human noise, instead the street around me erupted as he flailed and fell. Anything less than a mortal blow would just have enraged him. The older a magus got, the harder they died.

I spat at him. "Fucking parasite."

I scanned the rooftops and spotted a grey figure wearing a black leather mask perched on the roof above. My friendly assassin lifted two fingers in greeting – only a fool would hunt magi without somebody to watch their back.

My moment of victory was immediately spoiled as a pale and slimy creature the size of my fist escaped from the grasp of his corpse and scuttled straight towards me. I panicked, struggling against my prison, flooding my muscles with magic as I heaved at solid stone to no effect. My minor skill with body magics proved useless, and whatever enhanced strength I could gather was not even close to breaking free. I turned my Gift on the parasite, but the creature's mind was too alien for me to understand, and too well protected to crush out of hand. I didn't have the time.

"Layla!" I screamed, as the creature reached for my legs, translucent tentacles writhing.

A block of masonry smashed into the cobbles, crushing the creature to paste and almost taking my foot along with it. I loosed a shuddering breath of relief. Then I shivered at how close I'd come to being taken by those things. The horrors they could wreak with an enslaved tyrant would be unimaginable.

The tall grey-clad woman leapt from the high rooftops and landed with all the grace of the mageborn assassin she was. A four storey drop meant little to her magic-infused muscles and bones.

"You look a tad worried, Walker," she said from behind her mask. "I'm wondering if I should be insulted you thought me unable to squash a mere bug. Did you imagine an assassin of my skill would miss such an easy target?"

What a magus she would have made if only her Gift had fully matured! She had already mastered our arrogance. I struggled against the stone clamping me in place. "Ach, save me the lip and just get me out of this."

She removed her mask and smirked at me, brown eyes shining bright in the moonlight. Her dark skin bore numerous still-healing scars that made my withered old heart lurch. Even with her hair cropped short she resembled Charra far more than Lynas, but that was no bad thing. She noted my expression and the smirk dissolved. There were reasons we'd kept our distance these last few weeks after her mother's death. Emotions were still raw and it proved to be too much of a reminder for the both of us. Still, I couldn't have denied her this opportunity: these things had killed her father, the best friend I'd ever had.

Being what I was I harboured no illusions as to which of us hurt the most. It's hard to wallow in your own misery when you can take a peek inside somebody else's head and feel so much worse. Really, you'd expect I of all people would have more empathy for others. But this thing here and now was business and emotion had no place, not even our anger.

She picked up the block of fallen masonry and smashed it into the stone that held me. It took a few bone-jarring blows before it split in two and freed my arms. After that I was able to pry my feet free of their old boots, leaving them behind still stuck in stone. I sighed. Those comfy old boots had served me well over the years. I eyed the two fallen magi critically, then approached the corpse of Alvarda Kernas. His House were going to be beyond pissed, at least until the pungent stench of treachery rose around them. Hmm…he had some fine boots on him. I yanked them off his corpse and pulled on the soft leather. Luxury! They were a shade overlarge but an extra pair of stockings would sort that. My feet had never had it so good.

"Are you finished looting the corpse?" Layla said. There was no disapproval in her voice, just impatience.

"One second." I cut free both magi's money pouches and then pocketed them. "I earned this." Layla kept watch while I leaned back against the wall and closed my eyes, picturing Cillian in my mind.

It was still tricky for me, this new magical technique. I'd only discovered it after my body and Gift had healed (more or less) from their traumas. I no longer had the control I'd once had in keeping out other people's thoughts and emotions but I could also reach out further than ever before, but only with people I knew well or whose heads I'd already been inside.

I opened my Gift wide and the world rushed in. Layla was a snarl of anger and loss. Hazy blobs all around denoted sleepers and drunks whereas others felt razor-sharp as they padded down alleys with knives at the ready. Late as it was, the Crescent was filled with thought and emotion. Burning lust. Keenest loss. Terror. Pain. Joy. Love. It was almost overwhelming. Almost. I bit my cheek and used the pain to centre myself. I resisted the pull of myriad minds and reached up towards the Old Town on its high rock, to where the spired domes of the Collegiate now served as the beating heart of the Arcanum. I couldn't see any of that of course, it was more like blindly groping my way around dead rock up towards bright stars of living minds.

I homed in on the familiar, finding Councillor Cillian awake, and judging from the faint images flickering through her tired thoughts, in bed reading ancient stone tablets by crystal-light. She had been waiting up for me. I felt her jerk straighter at my touch, but I didn't dare do more than politely knock on the doors of her mind.

Cillian's mind slammed shut and barred the gates, only allowing us to speak through the smallest of peepholes. I couldn't blame her; Cillian knew exactly how untrustworthy I was. I'd lied to her for the better part of twenty years after all. After my return from self-imposed exile I'd earned back some small measure of respect, but then I'd gone right ahead and abused the writ she had just given me to let her sleep, but oh well, if she got some rest it was well worth it.

Alvarda Kernas is dead, I projected. *Though his parasite may still live. He murdered Vivienne Adair and tried to kill me.*

Vivienne was innocent? she thought.

Hardly. I dumped the entire confession into Cillian's mind. It really was a superior method of communication. Her immediate flash of dread was only to be expected. If Vivienne's devices had helped bring down the Templarum Magestus then the Collegiate was also vulnerable.

Alvarda was not alone, I projected. *Who is this?* I sent her the face of the youngling I'd disabled.

Rikkard, second son of High House Carse. I could almost feel the political wheels turning in her head. *Will he live?*

Perhaps, if you can remove the Scarrabus from his body. Even then I doubt he'd ever be whole again. Personally I'd use him to torture the creature for information. The infestation of his body must work both ways, and we only have the two of them.

There was a long pause as my once-idealistic and principled former friend Cillian wrestled with her role as a councillor of the Inner Circle. Duty won, as it always would with her. *Are you certain you can learn more of our foe?*

I opened my eyes and glanced at Layla. She had a satisfied smile on her face, revelling in striking a small blow against those who had murdered her father. From the darkness in her eyes and heart, it was far from enough. She was more like me than either Lynas or Charra would have liked.

At heart I would always be a creature of the Docklands, growing up running with street gangs and alchemic dealers. I'd made my first kill at an age when Cillian was still cooing over doll's pretty dresses and I'd never had any qualms doing what needed to be done to survive. *Can I be certain? No.* I mentally shrugged. *But it's not like you have any other sources of information to hand.* This magus was nothing to me.

Stay where you are. I will send wardens to bring all of you to Shadea's quarters. Quarters? Bloody politicians always had to put the best face on things. It was such an unassuming word for that terrifying old crone's dungeon. Hundreds of daemonic creatures, rogue magi and blood sorcerers had met their end in there under her questing knives. Parts of them sat pickled in jars for future research. A few months back I had almost joined them.

Your wish is my command, most esteemed councillor.

Her anger was less than I'd expected. *Don't push me, Edrin. Most of the Arcanum would sleep better with you dead. I'm still not entirely convinced they are wrong.*

But pushing it was instinctive; I couldn't help but slip that last little dig. That twisted present from my old mentor turned god, Archmagus Byzant, just kept on giving. I choked back a further needling quip. He'd meant to get me killed to purge the Arcanum of the dangerous tyrant in their midst, and I refused to give that lying old shitebag the satisfaction. Wherever he was now, I hoped he was in fucking agony. He was missing with the rest of our gods and I hoped he'd stay that way. From what I'd seen, Krandus was doing a decent job as our new Archmagus. He seemed willing to put his fear aside and give me an honest chance, which was more than most in this damnable city.

I said nothing and broke contact. We were both thankful.

Layla glanced at the corpses and the unconscious magus. "What now?"

"They're sending men to scoop up this dung and cart it up to the Collegiate. You'd better make yourself scarce – I doubt wardens will be overjoyed at the sight of an assassin standing over dead magi."

She smiled and set her mask back in place. "Always a pleasure, Walker. Let me know what you find out. I'm happy to take care of any more of these little problems you uncover."

I nodded. Sod Arcanum secrecy, she had a right to know. Layla was the closest thing to family I had left and the only person I trusted to cover my back. Old Gerthan and Cillian were friendly enough, but their loyalty to the Arcanum was burned into their minds and magically enforced by the Forging. If they truly thought me a great threat they would burn me to ash without a second thought.

As Layla slipped away into the shadows I searched the ground in vain for any sign of the smoke that had fallen from my lips during the fights. A quick search through my pockets for any other wayward smokes that might be hiding turned up empty. I cursed and savagely kicked Alvarda's corpse, then turned the collar of my coat up and stuck my hands deep into my pockets, waiting there freezing my arse off while the wardens and their cart took a sodding age to arrive.

CHAPTER 5

Shadea's workshop was built into the very foundations of the Collegiate. Her macabre collection of specimens was squeezed into a sprawling series of arched tunnels and vaulted chambers dimly lit by flickering wall crystals, where they still remained operational; Arcanum artificers were more concerned with reconstruction than replacing drained lighting in disused dungeons. Her research subjects floated in glass jars lining the walls: daemonic eyes and organs of creatures from the Far Realms sitting next to the twisted flesh of human magi who had given into the seductions of the Worm of Magic and let it change them. All were sorted by creature type and meticulously labelled in Shadea's elegant script with date and circumstance of acquisition, then their name if they'd had one.

One empty jar in the corrupted magus section caused me to misstep. I stopped and stared at the jar labelled *Convicted Tyrant: Edrin Walker*. I snorted. "Stinking old hag, getting ahead of yourself there I think." I'd always known she had her eyes on my bits and pieces.

The wardens carrying the chained bodies of the Scarrabus-infested magi glanced at the jar and then eyed me warily as they slipped past into the rooms used for dissection. I took a little diversion further up the tunnel to pay my respects, such as they were.

Most of the doors in this area were sealed with arcane locks and intricate wardings that nobody had dared to touch since Shadea's sacrifice, but the one at the far end had been taken off its hinges and the doorway crudely widened with hammers. If the old woman could see what they had done to her chambers she would have flown into a rage. The room beyond was lit by an ornate candelabra holding fat, dripping candles, the flickering light drank up by a huge and ragged sphere of dark metal that trailed snaking tubes and fibrous shreds of steel muscle. What was left of Shadea was exactly where it belonged – amongst her precious research subjects as a thing to be taken apart and studied. We were not even sure if she was wholly dead inside the wreckage of the ancient war engine. It still fizzed with potent magic that burned against my Gift like hot iron.

I suffered mixed feelings every time I saw her like this. I had always hated her elitist arrogance and exacting tuition, her foul temper and venomous tongue. Still, she had sacrificed herself without hesitation to save us all.

"Stupid old woman," I muttered. After a moment's hesitation I pulled off my left glove and placed my hand on the black metal, tracing gouges left by the teeth and claws of the Magash Mora as it tried to tear her body from the titanic war engine powered by her Gifted blood sacrifice.

I shuddered. That dread name… that monstrous thing… Bile seared the back of my throat as memories seeped out like pus.

I forced them down and focused on the metal under my hand. It was cool but not cold, and my magically-enhanced senses felt a tiny but regular vibration, as if she but slept and snored softly within. But my Gift found no hint of living thought within her metal tomb.

"Thanks for what you did," I said. "Of course, you lot had planned to sacrifice me to that titan first if you could, so a big fuck you for that. Still, as you suggested, I am trying to be something better than I was, to find another path. I have a purpose now, and in these mad times revenge is as good as any." I patted it. "You were one hard old bitch, but you spoke a lot of sense."

Soft footsteps approached and stopped in the doorway. The woman's mind was cool and calm as the eldritch waters she summoned and controlled, and harboured just as much potential for raging destruction as storm-tossed winter waves.

"Hello Cillian," I said, turning to face her. Her eyes were surrounded by dark circles and her long curly hair had been left to roam free, devoid of her usual elegant circlets. Her fingers were ink-stained from writing unending orders and missives. She was a paper soldier in this war and I thought no less of her for it.

"Are you done insulting Shadea's remains?" She was visibly still pissed off with me for letting her sleep.

"For now. But that's between me and her." I intertwined my fingers, cracking the knuckles. "As Shadea might say: we have business to attend to." Then, not wanting to draw attention to what lay beneath my right glove, I slipped the other back on.

Her lips pressed tight but she said nothing and escorted me into the antechamber of the dissection chambers, to where Alvarda's corpse was chained face down to a table ready for the knives. A bewildering array of polished tools hung from racks: blades and hooks, saws and spoons and wires and other things I had no names for. All had served some sort of macabre purpose in Shadea's liver-spotted hands. Had the city not been attacked I might have ended up here myself. I dreaded to think what other horrors lurked in the large chest by the far wall.

As she led me through into the next room a strange dislocation washed over me. My Gift was cut off from the sea of magic. I felt heavier and a fog engulfed my senses. *A Sanctor was here!*

In the centre of the next room Rikkard Carse sat gagged and bound to a bulky steel chair bolted to the floor. His hands and legs were chained to the frame and a steel band secured his throat. A metal cage had been lowered over his head and locked in place. Secure as that was, you couldn't be too careful with a magus, and so on a stool by the far wall sat an unwelcome and familiar face: the sanctor Martain, hero of Black Autumn, lauded by the High Houses and Arcanum for taking down the Magash Mora at Shadea's side – ungrateful bastards the lot of them.

The magus-killer and I bore no love for each other, but once you've dived headfirst into carnage together to save your city you do acquire a certain grudging respect. We exchanged nods.

Cillian approached the captive young aeromancer and inspected the fastenings. "Has he tried to escape?"

Martain shook his head. "He has made no attempt to open his Gift nor has he uttered any coherent words." He glanced at me. "What has been done to him?"

"That is none of your concern," Cillian replied, backing away. "The Halcyon Order are sending a magus skilled with body magic to investigate the corpse in the next room. You will keep watch over Rikkard until we are ready to interrogate him. Do not get too close and keep your blade ready for anything unusual."

Martain was no idiot. Given my unexpected presence he suspected at least some of what we were about. He stood and drew his sword. "As you wish, councillor."

We retreated to the antechamber and closed the door behind us. Outside of the sanctor's area of effect we both sighed in relief, loosing a tension that neither of us had been aware of.

I cricked my neck. "I will never get used to that."

Cillian frowned at me. "Let us hope you never have to. You sail too close to rocks for comfort. You are lucky that I don't order you kept under guard."

We spent the next few minutes snipping and snapping at each other until Old Gerthan arrived. He leaned heavily on his cane, still dressed in his voluminous striped nightclothes and floppy cap, long out of fashion before I'd been born. His eyes were red and grainy and he looked distinctly unimpressed at the sight of me. "This had better be worth interrupting my sleep, boy." He looked to Cillian. "Councillor, what causes you to haul me from my bed?"

I felt awful, particularly given it was me who sent him off for much-needed sleep in the first place!

"I do apologise, Gerthan," Cillian said, "but I thought it best to keep the circle of knowledge as small as possible." She waved a hand at the robed corpse chained to the table.

He shuffled past Cillian. Taking a look at the subject in question he shot an alarmed look at her. "Alvarda of House Kernas has been murdered? Or were you successful in your hunt?"

"Scarrabus infestation," I supplied. "We have one host alive and one dead."

He nodded, set his cane to one side and rolled up his sleeves. "Very well, then let us see what we can discover." He held his hands over the corpse, a fingerbreadth from touching the cold flesh, and slowly worked his way up the body, muttering to himself, frowning and chewing on stray wisps of beard. When he reached a soft bulge at the top of the spine he hissed, and after a moment's hesitation proceeded to scrutinise every inch of the skull.

While he was busy with his work I opened my Gift and sensed nothing from the creature. Still, even mundane animals were beyond my ken so that meant little.

When he stepped back he frowned in puzzlement and began stroking his beard. "Whatever manner of creature infests him is still alive. It does not appear to be daemonic in nature, or more accurately, it is not a denizen of any of the Far Realms we have yet documented. The creature interacts strangely with my magic, producing a sort of echo in the aether." He met and held our gaze. "I would suggest disabling it now. The body of Alvarda Kernas is regenerating despite the arrow that minced his brain. We do not wish the parasite to regain movement."

Cillian nodded and Old Gerthan picked a vicious sickle from the wall. He brought the point down through Alvarda's skull, shearing through brain and bone and Scarrabus tendrils with unerring precision, and cut down to the soft bulge at the top of the spine. He left the sickle embedded there, pinning the main body of the squealing, dying parasite to the table. Using tongs he cracked open the brain cavity and peered inside. I let him and Cillian get on with poking and prodding and chattering like a pair of fishwives in a gutting shack by the docks. I'd seen these bugs up close and personal and that was more than enough for me.

"You see these tendrils inside the skull?" Old Gerthan said. "They have burrowed into the base of the host's brain. From the many head injuries I have dealt with I can say with some surety that this area controls emotion." He buried a smaller set of tongs in the wound and tugged, making the creature squeal, though it seemed to be weakening. "Tendrils have spread from there deeper into the area that controls physical motion, and… ah yes, here – they are clustered at the front of the brain which is the seat of reason. This would be expected if these creatures control the minds of their hosts."

He looked up at me. "Would you agree with that physical assessment, Magus Walker?"

I nodded. "I know that to be true, though the why and how of it escapes me."

"As it does with us all," he replied, looking back down into the wound.

Cillian chewed on her bottom lip. "And the nature of these creatures – do they breed or lay eggs? Is there some sort of queen? How do they feed?"

"Let us see what more can be gleaned." He poked and prodded and pulled. "It seems to be connected directly into the body's blood supply, feeding from the host. I can see no obvious sign of genitalia but that may need to wait for a more detailed investigation. If this does prove to be a sexless drone then yes, I would assume there to be some manner of queen birthing them."

"Or they were created," I added. "We know the Magash Mora was born through blood sorcery."

That earned me a worried raised eyebrow from Cillian. Old Gerthan harrumphed, "Not impossible, but I detect none of the magical corruption that we sensed from that creature."

"Are you done with your initial investigation?" Cillian asked. At his nod she scowled. "Kill it."

I was glad when his knives split the creature from head to tail. As the Scarrabus died its final shriek made us all wince. The noise went beyond sound and made my teeth and Gift ache. There had been a hint of something that reminded me of my own magic…

"What was that?" Cillian asked.

Old Gerthan shook his head, looking most perturbed. He cut it from the host body, removing the remains with tongs held at arm's length, and deposited it in a metal box which he then locked. "I will gather the Halcyon Order and we will have more answers for you soon. Is there anything else you require of me?"

She shook her head. "Not at the moment, Gerthan. I apologise for disrupting your sleep. I know how scarce a resource that is for you these days."

He offered her a wan smile, and me a crafty wink. "For us all, Cillian." He looked to me. "I wish you well with your interrogation Magus Walker."

I inclined my head. "Good luck with yours, Councillor." I wasn't beyond using a bit of etiquette when it suited my purposes. I'd pissed off Cillian enough already and exhausted people made rash decisions. Besides, the old man was good people.

After he left, Cillian opened the large chest and unfurled a linen sheet to cover the body. It hadn't even occurred to me to cover the remains of Alvarda Kernas. I didn't really care if I was honest, what with him trying to kill me and all.

"Did you know him?" I asked.

"Yes."

She opened the door and we swapped rooms with Martain. Cillian entered first, and as I passed Martain his cold glare said everything he needed to. We had all lost loved ones to these horrors. I nodded and he stalked from the room. Martain knew my character well enough to realise that I would make it suffer. The shining hero of Black Autumn was darker than I'd given him credit for. Maybe there was hope for him yet.

The young magus was more awake and aware than I would have expected given the damage I'd done to his mind. His Gift was not strong enough to affect such swift recovery alone. Cillian removed his gag.

One side of his face twisted in a mockery of a smile. "Have you come to cut me from my vessel? Where is Old Gerthan and his cruel knives?"

Cillian and I exchanged glances. That door had been firmly shut. "How could you know that?" she demanded.

Rikkard – no, not Rikkard, that was the Scarrabus speaking –

declined to answer. With Martain gone my Gift was wide open and I could sense the boy's own mind was still a diffuse and disoriented mess. The creature was puppeteering his body.

"That's not Rikkard," I said, carefully slipping my feelers into his skull.

Cillian had suspected as much. "What do you want?" she demanded. "Why have you declared war on Setharis?"

Rikkard's expression didn't change. Did the creatures feel anything like love or hatred? I felt a sifting of memory as the Scarrabus ransacked the magus' mind for meanings to her sounds. "War?" it said. "Humans do not declare war on ants, you exterminate them when needed. Uncontrolled human vessels are an infestation."

I had rarely seen Cillian angry at anything other than me, but now she was brimming with cold fury. "Do you speak only for yourself or for all your kind?" I noted she did not even ask about the possibility of peace between them and us – no true Setharii would ever contemplate peace after what they had done.

"One is Scarrabus. All are Scarrabus."

"Very well. Your position is clear." She stepped back and waved me onwards. "As you will, Edrin." She watched with great interest.

I flexed my gloved hands and cracked the knuckles. "With pleasure. Do you know who I am, Scarrabus?"

Rikkard's expression turned downwards in an attempt to replicate some human emotion the creature did not, could not feel. "Tyrant," it said. "Locked away in darkness." A clang of steel gate echoing from a tortured human throat made me shudder. "A half-mad and tainted aberration."

That reminder of my past unnerved me for a moment, and then anger rose. I struck deep into Rikkard's mind. His Gift instinctively rejected my power but I smashed through into his muddled human mind and slammed into the Scarrabus. I was ready for it this time, and didn't flinch back in shock. Instead I carefully mapped all the remaining routes where it influenced its host, the slimy tendrils buried through folds of brain to merge with human flesh. Focussing on one spot I let my magic build heat. My inborn talent was mind magic, with some small learned skill with body magics and aeromancy, but any Collegiate initiate powerful enough to join the Arcanum proper could learn to light a candle. Inside a human brain it required much, much less effort to cause damage. All I needed was incredible precision or I'd leave Rikkard drooling on the floor when this was done with.

The Scarrabus jerked that tendril back, the end a blackened stump. I felt a ghost of something very much like human pain. "Oh, I'm sorry. Did that hurt? I promise to do worse next time." I grinned and burned off several more, noting the physical impulses it sent to withdraw the tendrils.

"You cannot save this vessel," it said, slurring the words.

I laughed at it. "If you know about me being locked away in the darkness then you must also know what type of man I am." I spat in its host's face. "I'm half-mad, remember?"

I attacked through Rikkard's mind, trying to burrow into the Scarrabus through his. Its ability to mesh with his mind allowed the reverse to be true. Its will was strong and its control of his flesh treacherous – but I was Edrin Walker, and I'd rather have my balls smashed by a hammer than give in to the things that killed Lynas and destroyed half my fucking city. I stabbed into its inhuman consciousness, breaking through every wall it threw up to bar my advance. It tried to withdraw its tendrils, but I pulsed denial through Rikkard into its own flesh.

One last push and I was inside it, no… I was through it, past the physical and into a strange realm of the mind I'd only glimpsed once before, when I was high and near-insane from an overdose of magic.

I was fighting for my life. A thousand swarming insects stung my mind, trying to pierce me and inject their venom. Scarrabus. So many! I roared and unleashed the full force of my Gift. A few were crushed to drifting motes of dissipating thought – their slimy bug bodies rendered mindless meat, freeing their hosts from enslavement – while others were flung back, writhing in agony. Hundreds more rushed in to take their place.

In the endless darkness beyond the stinging swarm a vast consciousness took notice. It opened a single burning eye to study me, then dismissed my presence as a mere fly not worth the effort of swatting. That eye closed and another, smaller and more human, opened.

Disbelief and derision filled the realm as a potent human mind touched my own, scouring the surface of my thoughts before I forced it back. "Our intruder calls itself a magus? How very grand these crude little dabblers think themselves," he said in Old Escharric, every word perfectly formed as if he'd spoken it all his life. He even included the superior status inflections that had fallen into disuse by Arcanum scholars centuries ago.

I probed him and was slapped back, mind stinging. It was enough to realise that this was the host of the Scarrabus queen talking, the mental links between them pulsing with ropes of obscene power. My action seemed to enrage him as he rushed towards me.

I suddenly felt like a sandcastle standing before a tidal wave of magic, knowing full well that once it hit I would be shattered and spread all across this alien mindscape.

I fled back through the Scarrabus flesh and tore myself free from Rikkard's skull as they struck at me through him.

Back in my body I yelled and flung myself back from the bound magus, taking Cillian with me. Seeing my panic she caused a curved shield of stone to burst from the floor. It took the brunt of the explosion. Chucks of flesh spattered the walls and waves of fire rolled across the ceiling, then died off to greasy spirals of black smoke. We peered around the shield to see a pit filled with molten rock and blackened bone where Rikkard had sat.

I slumped and caught my breath. Shite, Cillian had really been practicing her geomancy. For somebody whose natural Gift was for hydromancy she had come far, indeed she was well on her way to becoming a full-blown adept. That massive potential was what had landed her a seat on the Inner Circle.

She stood and looked at me with shock. "In the name of the gods, what did you do? We needed him alive."

"You think I turned him into a fireball? Are you cracked?"
She hoisted me to my feet. "What then? Suicide?"
"Er, not exactly."
Martain and a squad of wardens burst through the door, all bristling with steel. She cursed them to leave and they quickly retreated in a confused mass, glancing at the mess behind them.
I explained all that happened as best I could given other magi's almost complete ignorance of how I did what I did. In some ways it was like describing flying to a worm.
"So, that quip about locked in darkness – that was referring to you being locked in the Boneyards beneath the city as a child?"
I swallowed. "Yes, and it used the exact metallic noise that has plagued my nightmares for all those years. It could only have known that from Heinreich's memories. Even if you don't believe what happened to me, if you add that to the comment about Old Gerthan and his knives…"
"A hive mind," she said. "With a queen of some sort hidden inside a magus host."
I licked dry lips. "That thing is more like a god, Cillian. And I should know. Its host seemed ancient, likely an elder magus. It adds up to bad news for us."
She paced the room, head bowed deep in thought, chewing on her bottom lip. Minutes dragged past in silence. Then the door burst open and Martain appeared in the doorway again.
"Leave us," Cillian snapped. "I am not to be bothered."
He didn't move, forcing her to look up. "My apologies Councillor, but Archmagus Krandus has summoned all magi to immediately attend a conclave in the auditorium."
"Ah shit," I said. "Today just gets better and better." What had gone wrong now?

CHAPTER 6

We gathered for conclave in a repurposed lecture theatre at the heart of the Collegiate, dawn's ruddy light only just creeping through the highest windows. Gone was the gaudy glory of the great hall of the Templarum Magestus with its marble steps and golden thrones, the crystalline art and exquisite moving statuary – now we all sat at old benches scarred with the names, sigils and graffiti of generations of bored initiates. I admired some of my own handiwork, the lines of a hairy cock and balls smoothed and darkened over the years by hundreds of sweaty palms.

We all pretended to ignore the gaps between the various cliques and factions. Even in times of war the magi of the Arcanum nursed their petty grudges. Me, I had a whole end of the back row to myself and a free space in front to put my feet up, which suited me just fine. The spaces only emphasised a sobering realisation of how few magi there were left in the Arcanum: a few hundred at most in a room built to house triple that, with perhaps two dozen more of us spread out through the other towns and villages all across Kaladon, and another hundred south across the Cyrulean Sea leading our legions in a war to preserve the last Setharii colonies in the vast Thousand Kingdoms archipelago.

Most of us had been too busy to note everybody who had died during Black Autumn, even if there had been a definitive list of those confirmed dead. Many others couldn't stomach searching the lists for those they cared about, but in my case, apart from Cillian and Old Gerthan, nobody I liked or respected could still be alive so why bother. Heads turned to and fro, searching in vain for a certain face that they were sure they must have missed during the last three conclaves. Many bore livid burns and permanent scars from the fighting.

At the front of the room sat the seven members of the Inner Circle in their finest dress robes encrusted with protective wards crafted from thread of gold: Krandus in pure white with his ridiculously handsome face and perfect blonde hair. Git. Cillian in silken blue and Old Gerthan in plain brown joined by… joined… I winced as my thoughts scattered around damaged sections of my memory. I had to work through it, trying to link faces to names via different mental routes. Stern-faced long-bearded man in green – Wyman? Crimson-robed woman – Merwyn? Yes, I was almost sure I had those two correct. The other two I had no idea about; though I knew what they were I couldn't retain who they were. I grimaced, but some damage is to be expected when you are forced to burn out part of your brain.

Krandus waited a few moments until the last bleary-eyed stragglers arrived, then launched into a series of updates on reconstruction of the city. I yawned and sat back, mind drifting off as he went through the tedious minutia of city administration. The prominent emotion throughout the room was boredom, and it had been a long night devoid of sleep for me. My eyes drifted ever lower. I rested them, just for a few moments…

A spike of danger woke me. "…accepted a request for aid from the Clanholds." I blinked and sat up, rubbing my eyes. *What was that?* The mood of the room was deadly serious and deeply worried. Shite. What had I missed?

"We cannot afford to allow the Skallgrim and their daemons passage through the mountain passes of the Clanholds. It is an open door to the undefended heartlands of Kaladon. As such, Setharis has agreed to send seven coteries to delay the enemy forces advancing westwards from Ironport. The Free Towns Alliance has also pledged to raise an army to aid this effort. The rest of us will march on Ironport from the south leaving only a skeleton force behind to guard Setharis until our legions return from the colonies. The Skallgrim will undoubtedly strive to reinforce their only foothold on the shores of Kaladon before our legions can return so it is imperative that we crush them before that happens. When their wolf-ships make the hazardous voyage across the Sea of Storms they will find us ready and waiting. They will find no safe anchorage on our shores."

Krandus took a deep breath. "The Arcanum will now ask for volunteers to defend the Clanholds." Many arses stirred on seats, ready to stand, eager for some payback. Mine was firmly planted on wood. It was still deep winter up north, and it was a death sentence to battle Skallgrim madmen and a Clanholds winter at the same time. I also had my own problems with the Clansfolk to consider. Krandus continued, "However, the Clanholds have requested that one specific magus leads this expeditionary force, and the Inner Circle has acceded."

Cillian's eyes sought me out. *By the Night Bitch, don't you dare!*

Krandus pointed straight at me. His gesture stabbed me in the pit of my stomach and pushed it down into a black abyss. "Magus Edrin Walker will lead this force." Arses thumped back down on seats with enough force to rattle the benches. I started to sweat as disgusted faces turned to glare at me. "Do we have any volunteers to join him?"

Silence.

Ah, it was nice to feel so loved. Or feared; there was always that more enjoyable option. I was quite literally the stuff of childhood nightmares. A big bad tyrant come to enslave them all. I regained my composure and met their gazes. They quickly turned away. Slimy cowards the lot of them.

A hooded figure stood. The magus was dressed all in black, and wore plain trousers, shirt and cloak rather than traditional robes. I thought them a woman from the hips and body shape, but broad shoulders cast some doubt on that. They glanced back at me, and whoever it was wore a plain steel facemask beneath a deep hood to hide their scars. How vain; you didn't see me hiding mine. The magus said nothing.

Krandus smiled, dazzling us all. Slimy git. "A knight. Excellent. Your strength will be sorely needed in the mountains. Do we have any others?"

A man sporting a bushy red beard stood: Cormac of House Feredaig if my faulty memory was correct, and a skilled geomancer. "I'll stand." His tongue held a mere hint of Clanholds accent, long submerged beneath the Setharii. "I have kin in the holdfasts and you'll need one of my sort in the mountains."

Krandus inclined his head, then waited again, his eyes sweeping the benches.

A slender young woman I didn't know, wearing unusual black and white hooded robes, rose to join Cormac.

Krandus smiled and nodded. "An illusionist will prove most useful in warfare."

Nobody else stood with us. I wasn't surprised in the least – who would want to head off with the likes of me to die on frozen hills protecting heathens. They would much rather take their chances with the Archmagus and the rest of the Arcanum. We would be outnumbered and facing the worst magics and daemons that their accursed halrúna shaman could summon up, but it was me they feared and distrusted the most. Gods, even I had no intention of going if I could weasel my way out of this midden of a situation.

Krandus sighed and shook his head. "We are disappointed. The Inner Circle will deliberate and appoint three of you to join them. For the rest of you, report to your coteries if you have existing assignments. If not, you will each be assigned ten wardens to serve you later this evening. This conclave is now broken, be about your work."

I sat and ground my teeth as the other magi filtered from the auditorium. It took all my self-control to hold myself back from storming down and demanding answers or telling them to fuck off and find some other pitiful sacrifice. This was just another attempt to get rid of the vile tyrant in their midst and I wasn't about to die for them, or for anybody. Burn them! I'd suffered more than enough for our oh-so-precious Arcanum. If they thought they could compel me to go then they would be in for a very nasty shock.

Cormac exchanged a few words with the Inner Circle and then left without so much as a glance in my direction. The magus in black turned to regard me and her single green eye glinted behind the steel mask, the left likely lost during the conflict. Great, I was landed with a crippled knight. I was no great weapons master, but even I knew enough to realise that her depth perception was scuppered. Why had she even stood? Just as well I had no intention of going.

That eye scrutinised me with such intensity I almost felt violated. I itched to open my Gift and find out why, but unless in self-defence I was strictly banned from using my power on another magus without permission from a councillor, and somehow I didn't think my writ would hold much water here in the Collegiate itself. The knight lifted a gloved fist to her face and then slashed it downwards. It took me a moment to realise it was a salute – her sword was mine to command.

I nodded gravely in acknowledgement. Whoever she was, she deserved that much. The magus in black turned on her heel and stalked from the auditorium, leaving me alone with the seven members of the Inner Circle. They expected me to come to them. I let them keep on expecting, ignoring furious glares from Cillian in favour of picking at a hangnail.

"Magus Edrin Walker," Krandus said, his voice like gravel. "Would you be so kind as to join us."

I took my time about standing up, stretching my arms back and yawning. They were forced to wait on me as I ambled towards them. Who said petty acts of spite are overrated? Cillian's eyes burned into me, warning me to bite my tongue. I honestly considered it. It would be the sensible thing to do. But when had I ever been accused of an abundance of that commodity? I was too angry to care what any of them thought.

I looked Krandus in the eye and sneered. "How stupid do you think I am? This is just another way of getting rid of me."

"Ward your tongue," he snapped. "Or I will remove it."

"I wouldn't recommend it," I replied. "If something happens to me, well, bad things will happen to all of you."

He grabbed the front of my coat and hoisted me off my feet with ease. "And just what do you mean by that? Was that a threat?"

I just smiled, showing how unafraid of him I was, and let the git's own imagination run riot. I could kill with my Gift but that wasn't what worried the Arcanum, oh no, it was my ability to manipulate minds and twist thoughts that people truly feared.

Old Gerthan laid a hand on the Archmagus' arm and guided it down until I was able to stand again. "Cease your posturing, Walker. I promise that we are not trying to have you killed. This is not our doing." I prided myself on detecting liars, noting their dilated pupils, the sweating, higher-pitched voices and a dozen other little tells. Old Gerthan was telling the truth. Or at least a *truth*, as he believed it.

I brushed Krandus' hand away, and he let me. "Fine," I said. "I believe you. But nobody in their right mind would ever want me leading an army."

"That we can all agree on," Merwyn said.

"And yet it has been requested," Cillian said. "Demanded even."

That gave me pause. "By who?"

One of the nameless others spoke. "The druí leaders of three separate Clanholds standing in the path of the Skallgrim advance: Dun Bhailiol, Dun Clachan and Kil Noth."

I paled and leaned on a bench for support.

"What is wrong?" Cillian asked. "Are you unwell?"

"I'm far from well," I said in strangled gasps, my hand rising to feel the ragged scars marring my cheek. They waited but I wasn't about to volunteer anything else. I didn't even want to think about what happened in Kil Noth six years ago. I wanted nothing to do with any of those insane druí bastards. They were every bit as mad as daemon-worshipping Skallgrim halrúna, though in a very different way.

Krandus elaborated: "If we do not agree to their request they threaten to retreat to their holdfasts and allow the Skallgrim to march unopposed through the mountain passes. Those corrupt heathens will ravage the heartlands of Kaladon, and Setharis' grain supply will be destroyed. A second year of famine will finish us."

Old Gerthan sighed. "Without their aid we would need to divert half our forces to contain their army in the mountains and risk their wolf-ships reinforcing Ironport before we can take it."

"We have no choice," Cillian said. "*You* have no choice. At first light in two days' time you will embark at Westford Docks for the Clanholds."

"I always have a choice," I snarled. Before they could react I fled the room, head and heart churning with fear and anger. Corridors and faces flashed past as I ran through the Collegiate and out into the streets.

My scars itched as I ran. I refused to go back there! *What of Setharis?* the ghost of Lynas' voice whispered in the back of my mind, still acting as my conscience even in death. *What of your home? Your people?* I shook my head and snarled as I passed through the great gates of Old Town, running downhill for the familiar safety of the Docklands. Nobody could find me there if I didn't want them to. *What of Layla?* My steps slowed, stopped.

Carriages and carts clopped past, and the constant stream of messengers and tradesmen eyed me strangely as I stood there, motionless and conflicted. Eventually a great wallowing gilded carriage forced me to retreat to the side of the street, and from there I looked out over what was left of my city.

My eyes were drawn to West Docklands, passing a forest of blackened timbers to alight on the sturdy grey stone building of Charra's Place. I'd promised Charra that I would take care of Layla after she was gone. Not that her vicious girl needed it; hard as a steel blade and just as sharp, that one. Still, I had promised my last living friend just before her death, and welching on that didn't sit well with me. If Lynas had been my conscience then Charra had been my partner in crime, the driving force keeping me moving forward in life, to try to make something of myself. During my exile from the city I had drowned my sorrow and loneliness in cups of ale and bought affection. I would not go that way again.

"If you were still here, what would you say to me?" Charra

would cross her arms and give me one of her scathing looks. *Don't be an arse, Walker. Running away solves nothing. If there is anything left here that you love then fight for it. If not... then you won't be sad to see everything torn down and ground to dust, will you? What's it to be? We don't have all day.*

Despite everything this was still my home. All the bad didn't outweigh the good memories I'd made here; my mother and father, my friends... no, I couldn't let an enemy destroy Setharis. I'd never been much of a fighter, just one of those slippery little vermin that only fights when backed into a corner, but rats are vicious when cornered. As I felt my resolve harden I knew one thing: I wasn't that little gutter rat any more, and nor was I the wastrel magus the Arcanum thought I was, or the scum they had tried to twist me into becoming. I'd killed a god for fuck's sake! What more did I have to fear?

Besides, there was the state of my hand to consider. I peeled my right glove off and stared at the hard black plates that had recently started spreading across my skin. When my spirit-bound knife Dissever was shattered by the god Nathair during the Black Autumn – may all gods burn! – needles of enchanted black iron had pierced my skin. In the weeks of chaos following I never did find the time to get a healer to look at it, and now it was too late. Not that my pact with that daemon, or spirit or whatever it really was, had ended. In the back of my skull I could still feel a dark and hungry presence biding its time, patiently waiting for something to come to pass. It was silent now, revealing only fragments of its bloodthirsty old self.

I flexed my hand, testing the increasing stiffness. Everybody was on a knife-edge and if their gods-damned tyrant wandered up with a magically tainted hand? In their paranoia they would see it as a sign of magical corruption and put me down without a second thought. I would if I were them.

Perhaps this suicidal mission to the Clanholds should be looked on as an opportunity. The Clansfolk boasted some of the most impressive healers I'd ever known. Their methods were crude by

Arcanum standards, but undeniably effective. It was either that or hack my right hand off here and now before the black iron spread further up my arm. And with a palsied lump of flesh attached to my left wrist that would leave me out to sea without a sail, crippled and useless.

"Worth a try, eh, Charra. Never give up, never give in. You never did." I sighed deeply, pulled on my glove and began the trek uphill. Sod it, I was going to war.

I paused. Oh shite, was I now in charge of an army? Those poor bastards had no idea what they were in for. I certainly didn't.

Cillian was sat alone and waiting for me when I returned to the auditorium. "I suspected you would not be gone for long."

I thumped down next to her. "You've more faith in me than I do."

Her mouth quirked into a tired smile. "My faith in you was never what was lacking, Edrin. Besides, after recent events I know you are in need of something worthy to vent your anger." Both comments were true.

I groaned and rubbed tired eyes. "I'll do it, but I get to choose my own damn coterie to guard my back. I'll not suffer your stuck-up wardens who'd be happy to stick a spear in me at the first opportunity. And would probably be well-paid to do so."

"That sounds eminently sensible," she replied. "Something that I do not often say where you are concerned."

I eyed her. "Was that a joke, Cillian Hastorum?"

"Just because I must be serious to deal with matters of life and death does not mean that is all that I am. Besides, you are not blameless when it comes to how you have lived your life. Your status as a tyrant aside, is it any wonder that many would want to stab you in the back?"

I opened my mouth to object but she talked over me.

"Yes, yes, you have told me all about how Archmagus Byzant influenced your mind to twist you into this rogue of a man. It's all ratshit, Edrin. He may have twisted your inclinations that way but you took to it like a fish to water. Blame him all you want for that, but blame yourself for staying that way. You could have changed if you so desired."

I clamped my jaw shut before I said something we would both regret. Fuck you, I thought. How dare she sit there and be… and be right!

"Change if you want. Or don't if you prefer. But decide now rather than later, for you can never know how long each of us have left." She regarded a puddle of water on the floor, slush trodden in by the gathered magi. It swirled and coalesced into a hooded water snake that slithered across the floor and climbed up the bench to rear on her palm, menacing us with liquid fangs and hissing tongue. She stared at it and then clenched her hand into a fist. The water exploded, splattering everything but ourselves.

"My father died doing battle with the Skallgrim and their vile daemons. A halrúna shaman blinded him with vile blood sorcery and he suffered a spear through the skull before he could recover."

"I'm sorry," I said, my ire forgotten. The man had been a pompous prick, but he had loved all his daughters fiercely. This was not the politician of the Inner Circle speaking to me, this was my old Cillian, grievously wounded beyond belief. Her mask of control had shattered.

She locked eyes with me. "I want all the Skallgrim dead," she said through gritted teeth. "I want to slaughter these Skallgrim tribes and salt the earth where their villages once stood. I want to burn every single one of these Scarrabus creatures and I want to watch all of it done as excruciatingly as possible." She shuddered and looked away. "We have been through much together, some of which I have never mentioned to the others. I know that your Gift is far stronger than any of them know. Or I, come to that. It would be a fearsome thing if you unleashed it."

"What can I do for you?" I asked.

"Survive," she said. "I need you to keep their army bottled up in the mountains for as long as possible. Will you go to war, Magus Edrin Walker, for the Arcanum, for Setharis, and for yourself?" In a quieter voice she added, "And for me?"

Gods help me, I said yes.

She smiled and proceeded to inform me of all the arrangements: the ship we were taking, that our forces would gather at Barrow Hill in the North, and just how many Arcanum rules she was allowing me to break. This was war, and my muzzle was off. The Inner Circle needed their dreaded tyrant to wreak havoc. No questions would ever be asked as long as we were successful. It was almost like they trusted me.

It was a shame that trust wouldn't last past tomorrow.

CHAPTER 7

I took a whole day to rest and recover and get absolutely stinking drunk, then I was up at the crack of dawn – not a natural time of day for me. Being Gifted had many health benefits when compared to a mundane human, but my physical resilience was making it harder and more expensive to get drunk, and did little to help with hangovers. A quick scouring of blades formed from compressed air across my skin and hair left me fresh and clean for the day ahead. This simple aeromancy form had been beaten into me long ago. With my meagre talent for such magics I would never be truly proficient, but recently I had begun to train hard – again, not something I was used to. Recent events proved I couldn't always rely on my magical mind-fuckery. Black Autumn had exposed my magical weaknesses as glaring flaws that demanded correction, and the twin causes of survival and revenge proved a remorseless incentive.

I sat cross-legged on my bed and worked on the magic, twisting air into weapons that would rip enemies from their feet or blast them away – or at least that was my goal. If I was going to war I would need every trick at my disposal. I'd learnt a defensive wind-wall to divert arrows and a handful of weak offensive techniques, but with little time available I figured concentrating on mastering a handful of simple forms would prove more worthwhile than struggling with something complex. I kept up the practice until sweat beaded my brow and my Gift began to tremble from strain. I sighed and let the foreign forms of magic lapse into swirling motes of settling dust. I could hold them for longer now, but it still required gruelling effort to twist my own mental magic into such unnatural physical shapes.

I found body magics far more intuitive, the techniques of flushing away weariness, strengthening muscles and heightening senses came almost naturally. I could hold the basic forms for a goodly length of time, though I could never seem to harden my flesh enough to turn blades or toss boulders about like they were pebbles as a knight like Eva could.

Unbidden, my mind's eye flashed back to Black Autumn, to Eva raging amidst crystalline shard beasts, tearing razor-limbs apart with her bare hands. Then Heinreich's flames engulfed her and I was forced to abandon her charred body and run for my life. I swallowed my guilt and shame. I had done what I had to, but I would have died without her help. We all would.

Banishing all that pointless brooding, I quickly threw on clothes and raked my hair back into some semblance of order. I pulled on my coat and gloves, shoved my meagre belongings into a single backpack and stepped out into the chill morning air of the Crescent. The once-portly landlady was already out and brushing the front step free of slush and mud. Over the last two months I had watched her slowly slump in on herself, drained of life until she was not dissimilar to an artificer's automaton made of wax and wire. She had lost her husband and two sons and they were everything that had mattered to her.

"Good day to you, magus," she said by rote, not even looking up.

"Good day," I replied. "I have some news for you. I won't need my room anymore."

"I see."

"I'm off to war."

That got her attention. She looked up from the step and her eyes were red from crying again. "Where are they sending you?"

"North, to fight the Skallgrim."

Her eye ticced. She spat on her clean step and dropped her brush to grab the front of my coat. "You kill those vermin," she snarled. "No prisoners, you hear me! I'd pick up a knife and march with you if I could, but the likes of me can't do anything so you need to carry our vengeance with you. Never forget the fallen." She hastily let go of my coat and smoothed out the cloth. "I… I apologise, my lord magus. I didn't mean no harm."

"Never apologise for that," I said. "Do you know what I am?" Many people did these days.

She nodded, but was fearful of saying it out loud.

I grinned evilly. "That's right. I'm a vicious tyrant, but I swear that you and yours will have your vengeance. They killed my friends too."

The fear drained from her, replaced by cold anger. "The slicks up in the Old Town might be calling you a nightmare given flesh, but–" a ghost of a smile appeared, the first sign of pleasure I'd ever seen from her, "–you're our nightmare I guess."

It was oddly touching to be claimed as one of their own rather than the shunning I was used to, even if it was as their monster. I nodded and turned to go.

"Gods bless you, Magus Walker. May they keep you safe. I'll keep the room made up for your return."

Neither of us expected me to live for long, but it was nice for the both of us to keep up some sort of pretence.

Right in the centre of the very poorest area of East Docklands, down by the city walls and open sewers, squatted the grim stone cube known as the Black Garden, which most Setharii were proud to declare the harshest prison in the world. I'd visited a few in my years of exile, briefly, and it was certainly up there with the worst.

A moat of half-frozen sewage surrounded it, oozing downhill with the meltwaters before eventually flowing out into the bay beyond the city wall. I carefully wound my way across a charred wooden bridge that served as sole access and then pounded on the single small iron door. The thick walls bore the scars of battle: chipped stone and sooty smears, but that heavy door etched with potent wardings bore not a single mark.

Eventually a slot opened and a set of bushy grey eyebrows appeared. "What you wantin'?"

I held up Cillian's writ and smiled. "I'm here to recruit for the army."

He let me in, and I entered a gloomy building heaving with a rancid mass of pain, anger and despair. After a bit of wrangling the guards agreed to take me down to the deepest cells where they kept the worst of the worst: the mad and the bad and exceedingly dangerous mixed in with the folk whose only crime had been pissing off the wrong people. It was joining my coterie or this. A magus' coterie stood between us and danger, keeping us alive while we worked our magic, and I didn't trust my life to Arcanum cronies – they would be just as likely to stick a knife in my back as the enemy would in my front. I had my ways to make this lot of scum loyal, and nobody would ever care what I did to the likes of them.

The jailor handed me a list of inmates and I stared at one of the names. Jovian? How could my old drinking companion be here? Still, if it was indeed him and he was still whole then it meant I would be out of this dark pit sooner rather than later. My nerves were stretched thin, this gloomy prison far too similar to being buried underground again. "Him first."

They opened the door to the depths and moist air rose to envelop me in damp, decay, and cess-pool scent. They led me down into the tunnels, passageways lit only by lantern light. I shivered and held my fears tight as the darkness and stone closed in around me. I wouldn't be in here for long, and the way back remained open – I wasn't trapped this time.

The jailer showed me to a hulking oak and iron cell door that looked like it could have withstood a battering ram. He pulled a large brass key from among the two-dozen others hanging on a thong around his neck, and unlocked it with a grinding clunk. The door swung open and a dozen filthy figures squinted against the lamplight, all naked and chained to a massive steel ring embedded in the centre of the floor. Several bore black eyes, bite marks and broken noses. All but one – the smallest – were pressed up against each other, edging as far away as they could get from the feral little bastard at the other side. My eyes watered at the smell.

"You don't want this foreign scum, my lord magus," the stony-eyed jailor spat, "this little copper-skinned bastard is a black-hearted killer through and through." And he would have seen some dark as fuck things in his time. "He ate one of the other prisoners so he did."

"What now, you merda," Jovian said. "More secret assassins? Or are you finally here to sentence me and cut the head from my shoulders?" He clicked yellow teeth together and then grinned.

The slender Esbanian was a shadow of his former self: sallow-eyed and hollow-cheeked. His once-luxurious mane of black hair and glorious waxed moustache had both been shorn to stubble.

I laughed at the bold little shite. "Jovian of the Sardantia Esban – never thought I'd see you bald and wallowing in filth like the swine you are."

He squinted into the light. "Who is that? I shall ram my hand up your bottom, rip out your heart, and you shall watch me eat it."

"That's no way to greet an old friend," I said. "I'm looking for hard men and women who want a chance at freedom." And inside his head I added, *Stop being a giant cūlus you pedicator and get to your feet. Do you want out of this pit or not? I have a job and I need a second.*

"Walker? You pēdere! You live? Been twelve years, no? I say yes. A most enthusiastic yes and please. Thank you."

"You are the best sword master I've ever seen, so what did you do to end up rotting here instead of swanning about the Old Town draped in silk and gold?"

He shrugged. "I stuck the wrong nobleman with my sword."

"You killed him?"

"No, no. My other sword." He thrust his groin at me. "His father was, hmm, unimpressed at the sight of his heir with his bottom in the air and me with only the hilt showing."

"He was one of those sort, eh?"

"Not at all, I had been sticking him too. A mistake, I admit."

I groaned and turned to the jailor. "Set him free. And for all our sakes get the man some clothes, and a steel chastity belt if you can find one."

After a few moments they found him some clothes. As the shackles came off Jovian snapped his teeth at the cringing jailor. He laughed, catching and donning a long shirt taken from the prison stores. He rubbed the sores on his ankles and eyed me thoughtfully. "This will be suicidal, yes?"

"Probably."

He sighed and shrugged. "My gods-given luck has not changed." He looked me up and down, noting the vicious scars that now marred my face. "Nor yours."

I snorted. "Never will. If anything it's getting worse." Looking around at the other prisoners, I asked in Esbanian: "This lot any use?"

He spat on the filth-crusted stone and then glanced at one of the more attractive men before replying in his native tongue. "Depends what you mean by use." He grinned. "But if you want good killers, I have better suggestions."

We went from cell to cell collecting the names that Jovian reeled off, those that still lived. The guards hauled them all into a single large cell and locked us in there. I examined my haul: Jovian, five murderers – Coira with cheeks showing the scar-sign of the Smilers street gang; a big brute named Vaughn; three cold-eyed killers named Adalwolf, Baldo and Andreas who were all missing bits of ears – one hired killer and skilled poisoner named Diodorus who specialised in bow and arrow, and one mad-eyed, flame-haired habitual arsonist called Nareene. They were some of the foulest, most disreputable scum this city had to offer, myself excluded.

I opened my Gift and burrowed into their heads to see what use I could make of such terrible creatures.

Diodorus wasn't evil or insane to his mind, it was simply that he valued gold over useless human lives. Casual atrocities were nothing to him. The hopes and fears and daily life of others were only an irritating irrelevance. He was perfect for my needs.

Nareene was a simple creature. She just loved to watch things burn, the dancing flames and roaring inferno causing an almost orgasmic euphoria. It was infectious and I'd probably have to resist the urge to torch something for hours afterwards.

The others were a mixed bag of bad and brutal with Coira the best of the bunch having taken the fall for her fellow Smilers after being cornered by wardens. Brutal but loyal.

Adalwolf had been a hunter and tracker in the wilds around Port Hellisen, happily married with two sweet daughters until he succumbed to the lures of drink and alchemic highs and needed increasing amounts of coin to feed his addictions. Barred from his own home, he'd fled to the big city one step ahead of hired thief-takers. Something had caused him to snap, a bad batch of alchemic perhaps, and he'd murdered indiscriminately until the wardens found him unconscious and choking on his own vomit and took him in.

Vaughn, Baldo and Andreas were your everyday hired muscle that communicated their employer's displeasure with their fists and knives. They were painfully dull. Brave in their own way, but dim-witted. Vaughn was kind to animals, so there was that in his favour I supposed.

Then there was Jovian. The enigma. His mind was still and empty of all conscious thought, just a flow of experience and immediate goals. It was worrying in a way, but I knew from the old days that if you promised him an interesting time he would run into a burning building with you and laugh all the while. He was a simple man, and yet utterly unfathomable. Nothing ever dented his supreme confidence. I'd never been able to figure out how he did it. He had that twisted sense of Esbanian honour and would at least warn me before sticking a knife in my back.

I could use these killers. They had the wrong stuff. They would kill without hesitation, and as for morals, what little they had would not hold me back.

The big, dumb, hairy brute went for me first, as I knew he would. The others were sly predators, waiting and watching for weakness.

"Get us out of this festering pit," Vaughn snarled, "and I'll kill whoever you want." In his mind I could already see my skull crushed and him off enjoying his new-found freedom in the taverns and brothels of the Warrens. Shame those establishments no longer existed. He'd heard rumours of the devastation topside but couldn't quite believe it.

I shook my head sadly. "Sorry to disappoint, but you won't be crushing my skull, Vaughn. And you won't be enjoying any taverns and brothels unless I say so."

He stared in shock, which flipped to anger and a raised fist. He tried to punch me but his arm refused to move. I was already in his head pulling his strings. He tried to swear, and failed there too. Instead I made him slap himself, a loud crack that reddened his cheek and shocked the others.

"You don't know who I am yet," I said. "But you do know Jovian here." They shifted nervously, knowing the feral little bastard only too well. "Jovian, would you fight me?"

"I would rather rot here in the Black Garden," he said with total honesty. "Worst magus ever made."

"Why's that?" Coira demanded. I was sifting the group's thoughts and feelings on the matter and made a mental note to make her my third in case Jovian bit the mud. The woman had tits of steel to face down a magus without blinking.

"My name is Edrin Walker," I said, smiling. "You might have heard rumours about a tyrant magus saving the city."

The prisoners stared at me blankly. That was a no then.

"Well that tyrant was me." I could tell some of them knew what a tyrant was. The fear blooming in their eyes always gave it away without me even needing to dip into their minds. They shifted uncomfortably, seriously considering shouting to be dragged back to their dank and festering cells. "And yes, I can get inside your head and make you do whatever I bloody well want." I paused to raise the tension. "But I would rather not have to."

That got their full attention. "Here's the deal. We are off to war up north in the mountains of the Clanholds and I need a coterie

I can rely on – and I don't trust wardens. You lot are vicious and cunning bastards just like me, and I need that. What do you say? In or out? I don't have time to play games and make deals."

"And after the war?" Coira asked. "What's in it for us?"

I shrugged. "Bound to be lots of corpses and lots of loot to be found along the way. Couldn't give a rat's arse what you lot do afterwards. Go wherever you want."

Plans for my eventual murder began budding in several minds. In Diodorus' imagination I choked on my own lungs, dissolved thanks to some rare poison he'd made from a particular breed of frog smeared on an arrow. In Nareene's I was a human candle, my flesh bubbling like wax while she danced around me.

I shook my head sadly and gave them a mental prod. "Are you lot stupid? I can read your minds. And I can do much, much worse. How much do you value your secrets?" I looked at Baldo. "Some of you have stashes of coin." Then my eyes flicked to Adalwolf and Diodorus. "Others have innocent family or journals full of invaluable alchemic research. It would be a real shame if anything happened to them."

They got the idea.

All signed on and I requisitioned clothes and weapons from the prison's armoury. I really loved Cillian's little scrap of paper and it was so very tempting to have a lot more fun with it before I marched off to almost certain death, or at least a good maiming and being abandoned in a ditch if I was thinking positively. We made one last stop before leaving, a wing of cells containing Skallgrim prisoners.

"I've come for my boys," I said.

The jailor scratched his head skeptically as he looked at the cells. Two filthy, bearded and emotionless faces stood staring at me where there had once been three.

I made them clang against the cell door in front of us.

"Them idiots?" he said. "Those are no use to anybody. Feed and water themselves and that's all they do. Don't even talk. Rats bit one's leg and it rotted right off; he didn't even make a sound."

"They are coming with me." I glanced back at my newly formed coterie. "These two are not idiots, just broken. They tried to kill me during the stinking Black Autumn. I broke their minds and enslaved them to my will."

Fearful silence spread and deepened. "Harsh," Jovian said, finally. "I would prefer death."

I felt the same, but put on a show of sneering at them all. "I don't need you intact. Are we clear?" We were very clear.

My coterie had swelled to ten, the traditional number assigned to guard a magus. They were now my shield, freeing me to be the sword.

Out on the streets, my pale and filthy conscripts were overjoyed at seeing the sun again and I couldn't resist having a little more fun on their behalf. We walked up to a group of wardens and I essentially stripped them and stole all their equipment. They protested vehemently of course but Cillian's wonderful little writ left them with no option but to complain to their captain later. Very satisfying it was to send them scampering off up the street in their undergarments. I settled Jovian and the rest of my coterie into the back room of a tavern to sort out all the armour and weapons for themselves. I slid over a small bag of coin and they all eyed it like corvun on a cat.

"Best buy warm winter clothes and boots two sizes too large or your bits will snap off like icicles."

Jorvan pursed his lips at the comment on boots. "I am missing something, yes?"

"I doubt you've experienced a Clanholds winter. It's a frozen wasteland up there. Stuff your boots with wool and you might not lose your toes."

He nodded in appreciation. "Toes are useful things."

On my way out I paid the innkeep for a mound of meat and two rounds of ale – and strict orders to provide only two, though I'd no doubt they would find ways around that. Still, it would hopefully serve to minimise the damage – and then began the long slog uphill to West Docklands and to Charra's Place. I took

Fisherman's Way, curving west along the path of the city walls rather than cutting through the devastated Warrens. I had no desire to be reminded of that yet again.

It was early afternoon by the time I arrived at the brothel. Layla hadn't seen fit to change the name, or seemingly find the time to repair the churned up gardens and trampled moonflowers. The two hulking tattooed clansmen, Nevin and Grant, still guarded the doorway. These days they wore heavy chain and carried spiked axes instead of cloth and clubs. Nobody had time for the old armament laws and everybody from old women to the more sensible children were allowed to roam armed and dangerous.

"If it ain't Walker," Nevin said. "The big ugly tyrant himself."

"Shut yer trap," Grant said to him, opening the door for me. Seems there was still bad blood there. "Been told to expect you sooner or later."

"Wish it were later," Nevin said as I passed into the sumptuous interior with the tinkle of a bell to announce my entry.

Grant was having none of his brother's lip. "See you, I'm gonna–", his words were cut off as the heavy door slammed shut, leaving me to admire the fine oil paintings until Layla herself appeared, dressed in a soft grey silk dress and silver necklace studded with sapphires instead of her usual more functional garb. Her hair was short and spiky and showed off the silver hoops in her ears nicely.

I whistled softly. "Entertaining are we?"

"None of your business, you disgusting old letch." She gave me a twirl. "How do I look?"

She looked better than I dared admit. "Beautiful. Who is the lucky git? What do they do for a living?"

"It really is none of your business," she replied. "You don't have the right to take the protective uncle stance with me."

I held my hands up in surrender. "Fair enough. I'm just here for my chest."

She slipped the key into my hand. "I assumed so. Help yourself. Good luck up north."

"Seems everybody knows now. I guess bad news travels fast."

She smiled and patted my shoulder. "If all Clansfolk are half as troublesome as Grant and Nevin then you'll need it." I pulled a face and she laughed.

"At least keep a weapon handy," I said. "Can't be too careful these days."

She smiled again, but this time it didn't touch her eyes. "I am a weapon, Walker." With that she waved me onwards and climbed the stairs to return to her man, or woman come to that. I realised that I didn't have the faintest idea about her personal life. I suffered sudden and extreme curiosity: what sort of exceptional person had raised such emotion in Layla of all people? And should I threaten to hurt them if they stepped out of line? Huh, feeling protective were we? Interesting. If I still cared about a few things then I was not completely lost.

It was mightily tempting to meddle and go find out, but I bested it and descended to the cellar instead. I was just jealous of her happiness, needled by the knowledge I would probably never have that myself. Still, life goes on despite all the crap the world throws at us. I dusted off my old heartwood chest and examined the arcane wards I'd set to protect it. They were already decayed and useless, their intricate arcane structures eroded away by the raging power contained inside. I cracked the chest open and white light flooded the room, a liquid spilling of magic that seduced my Gift and sizzled against my mind.

Inside the chest lay a blinding shard of crystal that beat with the most potent magics imaginable – a god-seed, ripped from the living heart of a corrupted god. My gloved hands trembled as I picked it up and gazed deep into the faceted depths. I had almost forgotten how right it felt to hold this. My whole body itched and sparked with stray power, and the Worm of Magic urged me to take it, to subsume its power and ascend to godhood. My hands trembled on the edge of stabbing the shard directly into my heart.

I took a deep breath and let it out slowly. "And be chained here forever? Sod that. Bloody gods and their stinking arrogance."

I slipped the shard into the inside pocket of my coat and gave it a pat. There must come a day when you grow weary of the world and just want to sleep and never wake, but from what I'd gleaned of the gods of Setharis there was some horrible, endless duty involved meaning no time to relax and enjoy all that lovely power. I wasn't all about the duty. I was a lazy bastard at the best of times. This power and this responsibility were not meant for the likes of me, but nor could I leave it lying about for any old piece of pond scum to pick up and wield. The god-seed wanted to be found and needed to be used, it would find somebody sooner or later. That was probably how a rat-hearted bastard like Nathair had got a hold of it in the first place.

I couldn't protect the god-seed while I was away, or if I died, and I dared not risk taking such a potent artefact anywhere near the Skallgrim and Scarrabus. Which left me only two choices. To become a really crappy god myself, or to choose somebody experienced that might make a half-decent one. Only two sprung to mind, and I reckoned Old Gerthan was too focused on healing people to want any other job. Which left somebody that I really, really dreaded becoming a god. Even being mostly dead, she still scared the piss out of me.

Here it was, the point where that sliver of trust I had earned with the Arcanum was torn up and burned before my eyes.

I stood before Shadea's black metal tomb and searched again for any sign of thought inside. Nothing that I could sense, and yet there was still an odd vibration in the aether. Elder magi did not die easily, and she was one of the most potent to ever live.

I was never one for pointless ceremony. I yanked the shard of pulsing crystal from my pocket and stuffed the god-seed deep into a crack in the metal shell, then hammered it in further through metal and strands of flesh. The room filled with stray magic that began lapping across the entire foundation floor of the Collegiate. It wouldn't be long until the other magi felt it, and already those with the seer's Gift would know something was amiss down here. I hadn't dared tell the Arcanum what I was up to of course; they would never let something this powerful out of their hands, not until some power-hungry prick stole it. As they would. Such power was far too tempting. The Arcanum's previous archmagus, Byzant, was a living example of that – that fucking Hooded God… I'd happily kill him too if I could.

"Come on Shadea. Wake up and absorb the damn crystal will you! Think of what you can learn, eh, lots of juicy secrets beyond the ken of mere mortals."

A door opened and worried voices trooped into Shadea's quarters. I booted her metal tomb. "Hurry up, you ugly old hag! Want me to go piss on all your scrolls and take a great steaming shite on your antique mahogany desk? I swear I'll do it."

I turned at an intake of breath to see a pack of armed magi racing towards me. I fumbled for Cillian's writ, "Er, I can explain everything." Sometimes a paper shield was just paper.

At which point an irresistible force picked me up and slammed me face-first into the wall. *Oh shite, it's happening. Shite shite shite…* The other magi stumbled back and erected walls of stone, water and air as raw magic blazed white-hot against my Gift. Enchanted black iron that had resisted repeated blows from the most dreadful creature ever known to man cracked like an egg and ran like molten wax to sizzle on the floor, revealing a nightmare amalgam of flesh and metal inside.

I could only glimpse it from the corner of my eye, but whatever was left of Shadea was not even remotely human. Shreds of flesh and steel, bone and cable, blood and lubricant churned in a sphere around a human skull pierced by a halo of golden wires.

Her voice rang and reverberated, metallic and inhuman. "Boy."

"Shadea?"

"Dare to ruin my research and I will rip your lungs from your body."

I laughed, a wheezing gasp.

"I feel the call to duty," she said. "Power. So immense. Such… effort. The chains that bind. Ah, Byzant, we shall have words, you and I." Her attention focused on me like I was an insect and she a glass lens held up to the sun. "I feel you, Edrin Walker…and your pacted daemon. When the time comes do not run from the joining. Fight or be consumed."

That small place in the back of my skull where the last part of Dissever still lurked throbbed in response. Something passed between nascent god and fragment of deadly daemon.

I grimaced. "I don't understand."

"You never did."

Flesh and metal began to coalesce into a semblance of human form, her bare skull growing a long mane of gold hair and shining metal orbs for eyes, steel wire and pulsing veins writhing through the jawbone to form cheeks and a tongue. A smooth steel face bubbled into place showing a likeness of Shadea as she might have looked in her younger days, as her self-image evidently still was. She floated naked and metallic a foot off the floor.

"What have you done this time, you foolish boy?" she said, her voice only a little more human.

"What I had to," I gasped. "Can't have another Nathair disaster can we? Had to have somebody trustworthy this time around, even if it's you. Or would you rather it was me?" The unseen force let go and I dropped to the floor to sit gasping, my Gift blinded by the god being born before my eyes.

Her metal orbs scrutinised me. "You go to war and could not leave the seed unguarded. I understand and approve of your logic. Arise magus."

Invisible hands lifted me back onto my feet and dusted me off with meticulous care. She waved at the defensive barriers blocking us in and they disappeared. The gaggle of magi on the other side were shrouded in power and ready to strike – they did not see Shadea, just a magus twisted by the Gift into something monstrous. Fire and lightning and stone spikes blasted toward us. Magic itself twisted as Shadea countered, dissolving and dissipating their attacks.

"Yes, yes," she said. "You are all very scary and powerful." The force that had previously held me in place now picked them up and pinned them to the walls of her quarters, carefully positioned to avoid any damage to her specimen jars. "I do apologise but I cannot afford the time to teach you properly."

She drifted down the corridor towards the stairs up into the Collegiate and I reluctantly scrambled after her. The terrifying thing about Shadea was that she didn't need any godly power to beat us all down. Elder magi like her made me want to run and hide, but there wasn't any other way out and being behind her was far better than being in her way.

Somebody stepped into the doorway and a wall of hissing energy blocked her progress, giving even whatever Shadea was becoming pause. Krandus, the Archmagus himself, had come running. I probably should have given them some sort of warning beforehand, but honestly, how could you tell people you were about to make a god without pointed and painful questions being asked. Ones I had no intention of answering.

"Shadea?" he gasped.

"I have no time to explain, Archmagus. Only a short time remains to me here."

"A tower is lit!" Cillian shouted as she pounded down the stairs. "A god has retur…"

Shadea inclined her head.

Cillian blinked. "Oh." Then her gaze snapped to me and her eyes narrowed. I shrugged guiltily.

Krandus understood immediately and got straight to it. "Welcome back, now how can you help us?"

Shadea grimaced in pain, flesh and steel sparking. "There are things you need to know. I must speak to the Inner Circle while I still can. I have called them to attend us."

"Clear this floor," Krandus ordered.

The magi were released from the walls and swiftly fled the room. I made to follow them, back burning under the stares of Krandus and Cillian. Shadea offered me a deadly parting shot, "Give my regards to Angharad."

I left, bile rising and heart pounding. *How? How did she know that damned name?* My scars itched as I pounded up the stairs. *Was she mocking me?*

Chattering, frightened magi thronged the halls and many turned, questions half-formed on their lips as I emerged from Shadea's quarters.

"The Iron Crone is back," I said, taking some satisfaction in the knowledge that the unfortunate but fitting nickname would stick. I shoved through and lost myself in the crowd.

I needed to gather my coterie and get out of this place while I still could. Many in the Arcanum had heard I'd had a hand in killing a god during Black Autumn, but most didn't believe it, not really. Now, things were very different. Worse than killing a god: I'd been seen making a god, and that meant the hated tyrant really did possess knowledge that others would kill for. I was stronger than ever – more than I had any right to be – but I was still a pale shadow of an elder magus. I was vulnerable, and that stuck in my craw. Amidst the chaos and morass of spreading rumour I made my escape before anybody could think of stopping me.

I wound my way through byways and thieves' lanes to the tavern where I'd left my coterie. If I could lie low for one more night then I would be able to avoid all those awkward questions and invasive tests. They wouldn't dare hold up the campaign against the Skallgrim just to interrogate one stubborn bastard. My right hand was another matter. I couldn't allow them to see the blackness spreading through the flesh – they would never suffer a corrupted tyrant to lead an army under any circumstances. No matter the cost to the war, or to the world.

CHAPTER 8

The thing that hobbles the Arcanum the most when it comes to dealing with people in the less reputable areas of the city is that they love to keep their secrets strapped so tight under their robes that it cuts off their own blood supply. They never trust 'simple-minded' wardens with the truth, and their… our members overwhelmingly come from the noble Houses, which also means they have no sodding clue about where to begin looking for miscreants holed up in Docklands. No, they rely on the wardens for that – those very same soldiers they habitually withhold information from. Which meant the fools wouldn't even tell the wardens why they wanted me.

On the eve of them marching to war and death, the wardens didn't care a whit about trawling the arse-end of Docklands hunting a single magus on vague reasons and unknown purpose. Understandably, they wanted to spend that precious time with their loved ones. Jovian still knew a few of the wardens, indeed he had trained some of their best, and a bag of coin donated by the late Alvarda Kernas helped them support their families in their absence. It left us free to stuff our faces with the last decent food and booze we'd see this side of the war, and after lingering in prison my coterie needed a damn good feed.

Vaughn still had plans to flee into the night and when I went to drain my bladder he made his move, or tried to. For some reason he couldn't seem to find the door, running round and round the room futilely pushing and pounding on the walls.

When I returned the others were all laughing at the big, stupid brute. One by one their laughter died as they realised he wasn't that drunk and he really couldn't see the door. Then they turned to regard me nervously and I raised a jack of ale in salute. They didn't seem to want to meet my gaze after that.

As the night wore on I slipped into each of their alcohol-mudded minds and twisted their thoughts and feelings to make sure they could never betray me, even Jovian, especially Jovian. He was changeable as the wind, that one, despite his Esbanian sense of personal honour. None of them would ever have any idea of what I'd done, or why they were developing this grudging loyalty to me. Their loyal service for a single season and a little mental manipulation was a fair trade for freedom in my opinion, which was the only one that mattered.

As my last night of calm and comfort drew to a close I had time to sit and think. I nursed the dregs of my ale and pondered the morality of bending these vicious killers to my will. How did I feel about that? Once I would have felt bad. It was certainly a sensible precaution but "because they are scum" was more justification than I needed right now. I didn't need any at all in truth. They were just tools to me, things to be used and tossed aside when I was done. *That's bloody cold, Walker, too cold.* Was it due to my growing power as a magus? Or was that simply being an efficient commander? Or did I just not give a shite about folk I didn't know and like? I was growing cold and callous and that made me uncomfortable when I preferred to think of myself as a man of the people that cared for my own.

Jovian leapt onto a table and a jug of wine appeared in his hand as if by magic. He began dancing with Nareene, leading the others in an Esbanian drinking song about bawdy wenches chasing bare-chested young men. They didn't understand the words but quickly latched onto the tune. I didn't much care for the others but I'd shared wine and crude jokes with Jovian many a time back in the old days. I liked the mad little Esbanian and as a rule I didn't warm to many people. Mostly, I found them and their unguarded thoughts insulting and irritating.

I would need to watch that callous side of myself carefully. I was growing into the sort of magus I had railed against all my life, those cold and calculating elder magi that were everything I despised in the Arcanum. Or they had been. Now their mindset seemed to be making a lot of sense. The lives of mundanes were fleeting and fragile things and so very limited in scope, but they had fire and passion, and I refused to let that side of me slip away without a fight. But magic changes a man.

"Be ready, we embark at dawn," I said. Then I took my two Skallgrim thralls and retreated upstairs to a free room, leaving my people to bond without the big ugly tyrant and his broken toys looming over them. I bid my thralls to take turns keeping watch and then collapsed onto the soft bedding.

I was exhausted and at first light my war would begin, but sleep proved a flighty and fleeting prey filled with all my old mistakes resurrected to join forces with the horrors of the recent past.

We were up and boarding a rugged Ahramish sloop named Y'Ruen's Revenge before anybody could report my presence back to the Arcanum. The surly hydromancer assigned to smooth our ship's passage through the still-stormy winter sea was scandalised at being forced into close quarters with the likes of me, but he wisely kept his jaw shut. Didn't stop him thinking about it though. Unlike most magi, his mind was like a leaky bucket, one brimming full of self-entitled shite. I gritted my teeth and suffered the silent insults. For now.

I stared out at the docks watching the passing carriages, waiting for one to stop and disgorge a high ranking magus to deliver my inevitable dressing down. The deck lurched beneath me and my stomach went with it. Fucking ships!

Hot breath on my ear: "Good morning, Edrin."

I yelped and flinched as Cillian stepped aboard right in the middle of my coterie. Steps formed from water splashed down behind her as blades whispered from sheathes all around us. She looked powerfully official, wearing warded blue robes and a golden circlet adorning her brow.

"Stand down you dogs," Jovian cried. "Don't you know a magus when you see one?" They grumbled but did as he ordered. Not that they posed any real threat to Cillian of course.

"I do hope you stay more vigilant when you arrive in the Clanholds," she said, earning only a grunt from me. "I have come to wish you well, Commander Walker. The others have already set sail for Barrow Hill."

She lowered her voice so that only I would hear, "Be careful, I have heard whispers that lead me to believe many magi wish you ill and would perhaps kill you should they get the chance."

I snorted. "Oh really? I had no idea. Are you only just realising this?"

"Before, I think most viewed you as an inconvenient and dirty little problem. What you did during the Black Autumn, and now with Shadea, has driven many towards terror, which breeds stupidity. Some who feel similar may be among those magi and wardens who will accompany you." She sighed. "Those who play with gods will inevitably get burned. Should you return I will have many, many questions for you." Then she smiled at my guards as I stood sick and frozen. "I wish you all the best of luck." She descended the gangplank and entered a plush carriage.

It was a shitty send-off and no mistake, but it was about all I had expected really.

The accursed voyage passed in a blur of nausea and white-capped waves crashing across the deck. Every hour of every frozen, salt-sodden day I wished an agonising death on the spiteful hydromancer, convinced he was making the trip rougher than necessary. We sailed for four interminable days and then spent a night at anchor in a rocky bay sheltering from black waves high as mountains before continuing on. Over the next two days the only human interaction I had was exchanging green-gilled looks of misery with Nareene and Baldo as we leaned over the rails to spew our guts overboard.

After an age, we finally reached our destination. Barrow Hill was little more than a glorified fishing village with crap drink, crapper food and worse people, but it boasted an impressive collection of ancient snow-capped cairns and stone circles scattered across the surrounding hillsides. The stone monuments bore undecipherable carvings that pulled in curious travellers and scholars from all over Kaladon and beyond. Despite the town's innate and inescapable crapness, on sighting the smoke rising from warm dry buildings Barrow Hill suddenly seemed like a golden summer land of joy and honey. Dry land. Blessed, solid, dry land!

We dropped anchor just before dusk, sodden and shivering bodies greeted by glowing lanterns that beckoned us onwards. I would have sold my entire coterie for a mug of hot wine, a dry blanket and a seat next to a fireplace. My legs were jelly as I grabbed my pack and lurched down the icy wharf towards the town's only inn, my arms outstretched for balance like a pup of a boy just learning to walk.

Glorious warmth rolled over us as we staggered into the inn's common room and stamped off slush and snow. All talk and laughter ceased as our bedraggled group dripped our way over to a sparsely occupied table of locals. Stools scraped backwards as they made way for us. We were not the first Setharii here: three groups of uniformed wardens cast baleful and disparaging looks over our little pack of villainy, and three robed magi sat alone at a fine table by the fire. I left my people to do their own thing and trudged my way over. I wouldn't have bothered but the magi were next to the fire. That and at least one of them might try to kill me at some point if I didn't figure out who was against me.

Red–bearded and ruddy-faced Cormac gave me a perfunctory nod of greeting, but the other two didn't even make that small sign of acknowledgement. One I knew, a balding grey-robed artificer with hooked nose and bushy eyebrows named Granville Buros, a 'proper nobleman' and a real stickler for the rules, but superb with all things mathematical and metallic. None of which endeared him to me, but a second geomancer would certainly come most handy in the mountains. He was one of the senior artificers in the Arcanum, and was in charge of maintaining the Clock of All Hours and its associated mechanisms. He was both potent and a giant prick, which made him a prime suspect for trying to knife me in the back given half a chance.

The other magus was a pale woman with delicate features and long dark hair enveloped by an unusual black and white hood - the illusionist who had volunteered during conclave. She sipped nervously at a small cup of red wine. Her eyes flicked around the room and studiously avoided meeting my gaze.

"Good evening," I said to them, trying to be polite despite my decrepit state. "I hope you had a better voyage than we did."

"Fair to middling," Cormac said. "Granville and Secca were already in the north so I suspect they had a more pleasant journey."

"Granville Buros," I said by way of greeting.

"Edrin." It was a calculated insult to omit Walker. My legitimate claim to the surname came from my mother's folk in the Clanholds, but he'd never considered it proper in the manner of Setharii Houses.

I didn't give him the pleasure of annoying me, instead I ignored him. "Secca is it? I don't think we have met before. I am Edrin Walker, and I would clasp hands but I think I need to bathe first." She did look slightly familiar somehow, but I couldn't place it.

She offered a faltering, forced smile but her eyes burned into me, examining my face. "Well met, commander." She didn't offer her own House name, if she had one. Granville and Cormac's mouths twitched, resisting the urge to scowl. Oh I liked her. "I am an illusionist by trade and if I am honest, I am not entirely sure how I can assist you." She did look bewildered and out of place amongst armed wardens and older magi.

"I'm sure we will find many ways," I said. Depending on how proficient she was, I could come up with any number of sneaky, underhanded uses for a magus of light and shadow. That black-clad one-eyed knight could undoubtedly think up many suited to warfare.

Weak and woozy, I exchanged a few more words and then I

took my leave to wash and sup a little bland cabbage soup to settle my stomach before collapsing into a pallet of straw up on the second floor of the inn. I lay there curled up in a ball beneath a dry blanket, the ground still undulating and my nausea plaguing me until exhaustion finally claimed me.

I woke with a hollow gnawing pit where my stomach had been, a raging thirst and a pounding head. Somebody handed me a cup of cold water and I gulped it down. "Thank..." my words dropped off as I realised that one of my mind-broken thralls had handed me the cup. I'd commanded him by instinct before I was properly awake. I stared into the bearded husk's blank eyes for a moment and saw myself through his mind, then shuddered and hauled myself upright. *Dangerous, very dangerous.* I clenched my Gift tight as I could. Other people were not mere extensions of myself. For a moment there he had been a part of me, a second pair of eyes.

Every tribe and people across the known world had their own myths and legends from the distant age of tyranny, when magi like me ruled. They were misty memories of an age of nightmares, and thousands of years later it was impossible for modern people to really imagine what occurred back then. But now I was beginning to grasp those true histories only too well. They must have been every bit as horrifying as the Magash Mora, and where that abomination had absorbed flesh, blood and bone into a single amorphous monster, those tyrants had taken minds and done the exact same. If I wanted I could take every warden in this inn and enslave them. I didn't need to leave them in the same completely broken state as my two Skallgrim raiders but they would be mine all the same in both body and mind. Their eyes would be my eyes, their hands my hands. It was not surprising I was considered a nightmare to the Arcanum.

I broke out in a cold sweat – was it any wonder that Alvarda Kernas had wanted to put one of those Scarrabus into me? I was no hero eager to sacrifice myself for fame and a fancy memorial but I vowed to slit my own throat before allowing that kind of atrocity to happen.

Contemplating suicide was a shitty way to start the day. I cheered up by telling myself that I'd just need to have all my enemies slaughtered before they ever got that close.

I got ready and kicked the rest of my coterie awake. By the time we dragged ourselves down to the common room the wardens had been up, washed and breakfasted and were already outside training in a lazily drifting snowfall. The clangs of steel and muted cursing did nothing to help my headache.

After lingering in the Black Garden my guards were more in need of meat on their bones than weapons practice, so I ordered up food and we ate in the dry and warmth watching the other coteries in full mail and gambeson drilling and sparring with shield, spear and dagger.

I frowned. "Where are all their swords?"

Jovian raised an eyebrow. "You are too used to the narrow lanes of towns and cities perhaps. What use would spears be there? In open battle the reach of a spear is superior. Swords are, hmm, secondary weapons you might say. I expect our bows to take the most lives." He eyed their large and heavy tower shields stacked off to one side. "Excepting magery of course. Most die to magic while we shield you."

"I see." My knowledge about battle was pathetic, mostly consisting of brutal knife-fights in dark alleys. Let the knight and the wardens deal with everything around tactics and warfare then, I would do what I was good at – sneaky bastardry and fucking people up when and where they were least expecting it. The wardens were all very competent but I didn't need more men and women who fought by the book; no, I wanted stealth and vicious cunning. If the Skallgrim and their summoned daemons got close enough to me then a few extra hands wouldn't matter.

A note from Cormac left with the innkeep this morning advised that a ship bearing two more coteries and the bulk of our supplies had arrived in the early hours but that we were still missing the last ship, delayed thanks to damage from the storm that had caused us to shelter in the bay. I hoped the last magus and their coterie would catch up with us before we marched tomorrow. The odds were bad enough. He had left a whole bunch of other papers with names and lists but I couldn't be bothered reading them right there and then. I had a whole day to do that, and I wasn't needed until we arrived in the Clanholds. The Arcanum had already arranged everything and I was just an inconvenient figurehead.

I asked Jovian to begin teaching my coterie some of his dirty tricks after they were all fed and watered. It was a better use of his time than trying to teach them to fight like wardens. He seemed eager to begin, but also insisted on foisting a long dagger upon me, a sheathed Clanholds dirk to replace the puny knife I always kept handy.

"Mighty magus? Yes, yes all very powerful, but so is a blade in the back, no?"

It was hard to argue with that logic, so I let him tie it to my belt and then slid my smaller knife into my boot before climbing the nearest hill to take a look at some of Barrow Hill's standing stones. I wanted to be alone, and after today I wouldn't get another chance for months. I'd been through the town twice before during my long exile and I'd thought nothing of them at the time, but after what I'd seen in the Boneyards below Setharis during the Black Autumn I had some worrying suspicions that called for further exploration.

For all her filth and smoke, unique stench, terrible crime and surly big city populace, I loved Setharis. It would always be a large part of my black and battered little heart. But here and now, tramping through pristine white snow and breathing fresh crisp air, I would rather be nowhere else. The town below was overrun by soldiers and every cart, horse and donkey in the area had been requisitioned to carry our supplies. Messengers came and left, carrying reports and orders. The wardens' thoughts buzzed like a hive of angry wasps in the back of my brain, a constant annoyance. As I climbed higher the shouts and clangs of my small army faded on the wind, and the wardens swarming all around Barrow Hill reduced to dots, the buzzing dampened to a soft background hiss.

I felt cleansed; my pain, despair and loss all scoured away by icy wind. My troubles seemed lessened by distance. I left it all behind and climbed the path to the flat top of the hill and stood alone in the centre of a circle of tall grey stones that predated the town: ancient rocks standing in defiance of rain, wind and ice for years beyond record. The stones were half buried in snow and wore white caps. Three squared obelisks reared larger than the other, rougher stones in the outer circle: the largest to the north, others forming a triangle to the south-west and south-east.

From the centre of the monument, the view over the whole valley was every bit as majestic as I remembered. A slate-grey river serpentined north and west back to its source in the rugged white peaks of the Clanholds, still deep within the clutches of winter. Across the river and twenty leagues directly north along the rocky coast squatted the mining town of Ironport, from where the Skallgrim practiced blackest sorcery and prepared to invade all the lands of Kaladon.

I wondered if they'd left anybody in that town alive after I escaped onboard the last ship out. Did Old Sleazy and his serving girl still serve up fine drink and their lumpy grey special stew? Probably not. The tavern had been aflame and that sour-faced one-eyed git had meant to fight to the death, and as for her, I'd left her face down in the mud with her dress burning into her back.

I sighed and let it go. I had 'not caring' down to a fine art, mostly. That was another life, one before I crippled myself to kill a god. I opened up my Gift and let my consciousness spread out, fingers of thought drifting across the whole valley, further than I'd ever imagined possible. In the town below the anxious minds of the wardens churned, and when I focused on the eyes and ears of my two thralls I discovered my coterie plotting and planning how to survive the coming war, and me. An old couple hosting several wardens radiated annoyance at the disruption to their lives. A warden and a local girl behind the stables were having frantic, and probably final, sex.

I was too busy looking into the distance to notice the small, quiet presence until it was right next to me. I snapped back into myself and spun. The black-clad knight present at the conclave cocked her head, single green eye studying me from behind that impassive steel mask. There was something eerily familiar about the way she felt, that mind curled up tight and strong as anybody I'd ever encountered.

A grainy, broken, female voice from behind the mask: "Here to clear your mind?"

"I'm here to examine the stones," I replied. "You?"

She shook her head. "Didn't take you for a scholar."

"We haven't been properly introduced," I said. "You know who I am, but who are you?"

A dry, rasping, humourless laugh. "I should have expected you hadn't read your papers. I would hope you might remember me."

I pulled Cormac's crumpled notes from my pocket and hastily leafed through them until I found the list of magi assigned to the expedition. Breath caught in my throat. My left hand spasmed and the papers fluttered to the snow, forgotten.

"Eva?"

Impossible. She died! She must have. And yet the name Evangeline Avernus was there, inked by Cillian's own hand.

I staggered back, tripped and landed arse-down in the snow, staring up at her. Those broad shoulders and green eye, the other gone where Heinreich had burned it away… Sweet Lady Night, Eva was alive! And I had left her there to die.

"How?" I choked out. "I watched you…" The word burn caught in my throat. "It's not possible."

"I lay abed for weeks after they dragged me from the street, voiceless, healing and hurting, unable to even say my name." She placed a gloved hand on one of the great stones. Her voice took on a bitter tone, "A gods-given miracle the Halcyons called it. I suspect that I wanted revenge and my Gift made it so, whatever the cost in pain. I always did have a bad temper."

Her agony must have been unimaginable. "You saved my life," I said, skin crawling with self-hate. "You saved all of us. And I left you behind."

"Whatever is left of me now, Walker, I am still a soldier. I would have told you to go, and I would have left you there had our positions been reversed. If you had stayed we would all be dead. Martain told me everything."

"Even so, I should have been there when you woke. I didn't know…"

"We are not here to reminisce and recriminate. Guilt is a useless commodity. We are at war and it is likely we will all die in these mountains. Don't waste our time."

I got to my feet and reached for her hand. "I'm still sorry."

She flinched back. "Don't touch me."

I swallowed and nodded. She might be alive but her body would be a blackened mass of scar tissue and exposed bone – her armour had glowed red and run, melting onto the flesh beneath. Even a knight's magically reinforced body could not have withstood that. I couldn't imagine what it would do to a person's mind, and beyond confirming that she was stable and sane enough not to be a liability, I dared not delve too deeply.

"The stones," she rasped. "Why are you interested in crude rock?"

It was a welcome change of subject. I beckoned her over to the largest lichen-covered stone that faced north. "I came through here a few years ago and didn't think much of it then." I glanced at her and quickly looked away again, "However, recent events have reminded me of something from my childhood."

I dug snow from the base of the stone and scrubbed it from the shallow troughs of time-worn markings. A winter morning offered the perfect low angle of sunlight to view the carvings.

She crouched next to me to examine the symbols. Her presence – so close – burned into me. I wanted to wrap my arms around her and shout with joy, and I also wanted to crawl into a hole and hide from the writhing guilt. Instead, I did nothing.

"What are they?" she rasped. "All I see are vague shapes."

"That's what I thought the first time I visited. But I had forgotten the things I saw in the catacombs of the Boneyards." That earned me a sharp look. "Just before the Magash Mora emerged you carried me from the river up to the bridge to meet Shadea. Do you remember what she told me I found down there as a pup?"

"Something about ogres," she said, impassive steel mask revealing no trace of expression.

I took three fingers and made a triangle, pressing them into three tiny pits in the rock. "These are eyes. Three of them." I traced the surrounding shape. "This represents a sloping head, and here a bulky body like a bear or a great ape from the Thousand Kingdoms. The shape is all wrong for a human. Clansfolk stories call them the ogarim, and I found the desiccated corpse of one entombed beneath Setharis. It's where I got my spirit-bound blade. And my fear of enclosed spaces." My right hand itched like it was crawling with ants, making me want to rip the glove off and scrape it on stone until my blood ran free and hot. Anything to relieve the damn itch.

"How old is this circle?" she asked.

I grimaced. "Older than history. Our race's that is."

"Makes you wonder what happened to them," she replied. "If they can erect stones they can build houses. If they can build houses they can build a civilisation."

The corpse I'd seen had been bigger than us and wearing finely crafted bronze armour, warded too if I remembered correctly. "More than likely humans wiped them out," I said. "We excel at that sort of thing."

She grunted in acknowledgement. "As commander, do you have any orders for me?"

I shook my head. "We both know I don't have any fucking idea what I'm doing. I'm commander in name only. I trust you to do whatever is necessary."

We didn't say much after that, and nothing to do with the past, just went over a few deathly dull details of tomorrow's march, logistics and whatnot. The old Eva was gone, and she would never return. It was immensely awkward and deeply saddening to go from brazen flirting and camaraderie with a young, vibrant women to facing this desert of guilt with a tortured human shell. If I'd been faster, more powerful or more intelligent, then I might have been able to do something.

She caught my look and stiffened. "I know pity," she said. "And I want none of it." She left me there amongst the stones, alone with the wind and snow and self-flagellation. Did I pity her, or pity my own weakness? I stayed there thinking until my face was numb and my body shivering. By the time I returned to the inn I found myself agreeing with Eva. Had it been me, I'd want nothing to do with pity. Now was a time for anger.

At my coterie's table I flung my sodden coat down and bellowed for ale. "Right, you pack of mangy curs. Let's chew on this business of war. How are we going to slaughter these heathen scum and head on home? The fouler the better – you won't find me squeamish like those prissy wardens."

Over the next few hours Diodorus and Nareene proved fertile ground for gruesomely effective ideas. I grinned at Jovian: we'd been wise to choose a killer for hire and an arsonist, and I was just the right sort of callous bastard to make full use of their macabre talents.

"Just tell me what you need to make this happen," I said. "Those fuckers are going to burn."

CHAPTER 9

Our small army was joined by a dozen hardy mountain ponies pulling carts loaded with weapons and supplies, and we set off up the slushy track leading into the mountainous Clanholds. My coterie marched alongside a small heavily-loaded cart pulled by a grizzled pony of more use for making leather and glue than for hard labour. It shied from every puddle and kept trying to bite me. Only me. Vaughn seemed besotted with the vile creature and it was passing strange to see the big angry brute fawning over the beast, so I happily left 'Biter' in Vaughn's surprisingly gentle hands. It wasn't like I hated horses, especially the smaller and less intimidating breeds, but they all seemed to hate me.

Fortunately for the war effort, a gaggle of merchants fleeing south from the Skallgrim advance had arrived in Barrow Hill with most of what we might need to wreak havoc: sealed buckets of quicklime, oil, sulphur, pitch, pine resin, and a plethora of other liquids and powders that Nareene immediately demanded I requisition. It was legal theft but my need was greater than theirs.

Diodorus had obtained certain dried plants and seeds from a creepy old herbalist in a shack outside of town that sent him into worrying paroxysms of joy. He had been flung into the deepest pit in the Black Garden for murdering dozens, and even the merest graze from one of his arrows had resulted in an excruciating death. Now he was being given free rein to utilise his unique talents, and in fact I was blatantly pushing him to murder and kill as many as possible. Good and evil were merely social constructs, and depended heavily on perspective.

Every night the advance scouts (I assumed, given that Eva was taking care of the logistics and, well, everything else) staked out where our tents were to be pitched and where the cook fires and latrines were to be set. At least somebody knew what they were doing. I'd never considered all the details of what was involved with an army on the march. Then disaster struck! I hadn't thought of recruiting somebody that could cook. I was forced to do it myself and use my Gift to 'borrow' a pot and steal the secrets of campaign cooking from members of Eva's main battle coterie – a force easily four times the size of the rest of ours, designed to take full advantage of a knight's skills: Eva was pretty much invulnerable to normal weapons after all, unlike my squishy hide.

I did all the cooking myself because it was safer than accepting Diodorus' offer to lend a hand. My new knowledge was not complimented by any acquired skills but at least the food turned out edible, if a little burnt.

A constant march through snow and across frozen ground created bone-deep exhaustion and aching muscles in my whole coterie, and invited scathing looks from the better-fed wardens who were stronger and more erect than my drooping penal force. At least I had magic to stiffen my resolve, and bad jokes to fall back on.

When we reached the foothills of the mountains we pitched camp and awaited the arrival of our Clansfolk guides. Only fools ventured into that natural maze of river valleys and mountain passes without a local to lead them, doubly so in winter. Centuries ago an entire army led by the Arcanum elder Rannikus had marched into those valleys, never to be heard from again. The frozen, rocky, barely fertile area had been more trouble than it was worth to the expanding Setharii Empire, especially when greater riches and exotic goods awaited them south across the Cyrulean Sea.

With nothing better to do, I called a conclave of magi. We had all been happy to avoid each other, but now that we were entering the Clanholds I couldn't afford their blind arrogance getting them killed before we even faced the Skallgrim and their pet daemons.

It was a freezing night under a clear, star-speckled sky when the seven of us gathered in the command tent with furs and braziers to keep the chill outside. Joining Eva and Granville, who I already knew, and Cormac and Secca that I'd met, were a tall, dark and ugly aeromancer named Bryden and a greasy pyromancer named Vincent with a long nose and sneering, narrow face I immediately wanted to punch. Both were young magi with no House name. That made four of us born from the lower classes: lesser magi in the eyes of noble House-born like Granville, and without any of the political ramifications if we got butchered on this suicidal expedition. Which begged the question, since Granville hadn't volunteered, who had he displeased to be stuck here with me? Not that the proud git would ever deign to tell.

"I don't know how these things tend to go," I said, "but let's dispense with pointless pleasantries. We are heading into the Clanholds where your smooth words and political slitherings won't be worth a rat's arse." That one was aimed squarely at Granville.

"I'll begin by saying that the Clansfolk put great trust in their reputations and in their honesty, so unless you want your face smashed in I suggest you don't outright call them liars. Even if it's true. Especially if it's true."

I rubbed my hands and warmed them over a brazier. "The other thing you need to bear in mind is that they are highly religious, and not in the same loose, indifferent way as the Setharii."

"That is true," Comrac added. "Every holdfast from the oldest and grandest dun to the remotest farming croft boasts its own spirit of the hearth, and every clan also makes offerings to an ancestral guardian spirit. It would be considered a grave insult not to make a small offering if you are invited to enter their homes."

Granville huffed. "I shall not worship any crude spirit. I am not a heathen."

"You will pay your respects if you want out of the wind and snow," I snapped. "But you are perfectly free to freeze your balls off."

"The ancient spirits of the Clanholds are most unpleasant if offended," Cormac replied. "In the old places of the world they are still strong forces."

"This is not Setharis," I said. "Spirits don't wither and die here, devoured by–" I had my suspicions but didn't want to voice them, "–the very air of our home. Spirits are plentiful hereabouts, some small and weak, and others vast and mighty. Some might even be considered gods."

"Heresy," Vincent hissed. "How can you compare them to Lady Night, the Lord of Bones or gilded, glorious Derrish?"

I shrugged. "At least they are still here." The long-faced prick didn't have an answer for that, and settled for clamping his jaw shut and grinding his teeth.

I couldn't help but needle him some more. "You also missed out Shadea, the Iron Crone."

"And let us not forget the Hooded God," Granville said. His glare suggested that was not for my benefit, more that he disliked sloppy and incomplete answers.

"Yes, there is that murdering prick too," I growled, earning a few raised eyebrows. "Oh please, how do you not know that so-called god is our old mentor, Byzant?"

They all stared at me.

"What? I thought everybody knew his crimes by now." In his enforced absence I'd done my best to ruin his previously glorious reputation, but apparently had not been quite as successful as I'd hoped. It was petty revenge, but for now it was all I could do in exchange for ruining my life and trying to get me killed when I was younger.

Eva cleared her throat. "Be that as it may, Walker, do you have any knowledge of their magi or military insights into the Clanholds you would care to share?"

I nodded. "Their magi are known as druí, but they do not use their Gift in our manner. Instead they make pacts with spirits who do as the druí ask in exchange for a portion of their magic."

Granville and Vincent exchanged horrified glances.

"As for the terrain," I added, "it is rougher than the ale in the Warrens and armies travel slowly through the valleys, but the Clansfolk know all sorts of secret paths through the mountains.

A few locals can easily stay ahead of any foreign army. You will see farms here and there on the valley floor, even small villages, but the actual Clanholds are burrowed deep into the stone of the mountains for safety. The Skallgrim won't be able to overrun them easily or quickly and they will pay a heavy price in blood if they try."

"What about their daemon allies?" Secca asked.

I looked to Eva, who answered for me. "The breed and number remains unknown to the Arcanum at this time. I expect the Clansfolk will be able to provide more details."

"Speaking of numbers," Bryden said. "How many of the disgusting overseas savages do we face?"

"Our seers estimated a Skallgrim force numbering four to five thousand," she replied. "With at least a handful of halrúna shaman and an unknown number of daemon allies."

"And how many do we have?" I asked.

"Seven magi and a hundred wardens."

A magus could be worth over a hundred armed wardens at times, but still…ouch.

"Pardon?" Granville said. "I thought the Free Towns Alliance was sending an army?"

Eva unfurled a scroll. "Still ten days off according to the messenger this morning. Doubtless they will not mind us killing each other before they arrive in time to drink up all the glory."

That silenced us all for a few stunned moments, then Secca spoke. "Their own towns stand directly in the path of destruction should the Skallgrim be allowed to pass through the Clanholds. Why do they still choose to play these petty games of politics?"

Granville scowled and ignored her, "How many warriors can the Clanholds field?"

Cormac answered: "Dun Bhailiol and Dun Clachan are regarded much as we in the Old Town view the inhabitants of the Warrens and East Docklands. The other nearby holdfasts will be unlikely to offer up any sizeable force when they can fortify their own holds instead. Combined, these two holdfasts can field a thousand at most. As for Kil Noth…" He glanced to me, unsure of how to phrase it, given my family name.

"Their army cannot take Kil Noth," I said with finality.

"How can you be so sure?" Eva said, her eye scrutinising me behind that impassive steel mask.

"I've been there," I replied. "No army can take it, not even one backed by halrúna blood sorcerers and daemons. There are worse things than those dwelling in the darkness beneath Kil Noth." My mother's ancestral home was a fucking death-trap and the place where the first druí made their pacts with ancient spirits. It was a sacred place inhabited by fanatics.

"They may have more of those devices that brought down the Templarum Magestus," Eva countered. "If they do, then no fortress can be safe."

I had to concede the point. Not even ancient holdfasts cut deep into the stony hearts of mountains would survive that. We discussed the known details of the expedition and learned much from Eva's experience. She was young as magi went, but as a knight she had already seen more conflict than most wardens ever would, and a few summers campaigning with the legions overseas ensured she was one of the very few people this side of the Cyrulean Sea with any actual experience of full-blown warfare. Or she had been before last autumn.

"We are not here to win," she said as a parting statement. "All we have to do is delay them long enough to allow Archmagus Krandus to take Ironport and advance on their rear-guard. Then the enemy will be stranded in the Clanholds with no base and no supplies, with the Setharii army behind them and the Free Towns Alliance ahead."

It sounded like a desperate and dangerous plan, but it was all we had. Come tomorrow we would be led into the heart of the Clanholds, and there were only a few on my own side I trusted not to stab me in the back.

Surprise! Nothing ever goes to plan where good things for me are concerned: our guides never arrived.

While I trained my aeromancy, the wardens and my coterie spent their time at weapon practice and working out cramped and stiff muscles. We waited all day, and half-way through the next again before Eva called it. She didn't even ask for her commander's opinion, not that I had anything worthwhile to add.

"Something must have happened to them, but we cannot afford to wait any longer – we must advance into the Clanholds under our own guidance. Walker, Cormac, do you know anything about this area?"

Cormac shook his head but I grimaced and gave a hesitant nod. "I might know the way from here to Kil Noth." The memory was mostly of a blind and bloodied flight to freedom heading in the other direction. "I'd rather head for Dun Clachan or Dun Bhailiol."

"I'm sure we would all rather be heading somewhere else," she replied. "But unless you know the way then we have no other option."

I couldn't think of any polite and reasonable response, so despite my fears, it had to be Kil Noth. I consoled myself by remembering that I was not the weak and whining man I once was, nor was I wearing the mask of a drunken wastrel that had in truth grown into far more than a mere mask. I had killed a god and destroyed monsters. Surely now I could face down my own grandmother?

I flexed my right hand, testing the increasing stiffness. There would be a steep price for her help. And if she refused, well, then I would just have to force her in my own dreadful way. That malicious viper deserved everything I could inflict upon her.

And so we entered the Clanholds without a guide.

CHAPTER 10

My coterie and I pulled up the hoods of our cloaks and went forward with the scouts, following the course of the half-frozen river that cut through valley floor, deeper snow crumping underfoot. The rest of our force snaked out in single file a long way behind us as the foothills grew into looming grey mountains on either side, the sheer cliff faces appearing as if icy giants had carved passages through the mountains with their bare hands back in the dawn days of the world.

All was still in the valley ahead, with only the gush and gurgle of water and the mournful, distant cry of a lonely hawk to break the silence. It felt good to be away from the bulk of our army, as if a huge mental pressure was dissipating. My coterie's thoughts were only a muted buzz in the back of my mind, peaceful compared to the deafening hubbub of Setharis or the middle of camp. I had almost forgotten what it felt like to be alone with my thoughts, and I picked up the pace to gain even more distance. It was so wearying to constantly keep from clamouring in my head.

The scouts signalled they had found something and led me to a squat stone farmhouse every bit as drab and gloomy as most Clanholds homes. Above the mossy turf roof no smoke drifted from the chimney, and there was no sign of sheep or goats within the fenced garden or barn. The place was abandoned, but signs of recent habitation were everywhere. Iron tools had been left to rust out in the snow by the doorway, something no poor farmer would ever contemplate unless their lives were in immediate danger. A swathe of snow had been cleared from the doorway within the last few days, and footprints led to and from the barn but nowhere else.

I opened my Gift and searched the area for living minds, but found only those I'd brought with me. "Place seems safe," I said. "Baldo, Coira – check inside."

Seconds later Baldo came lurching back out. He doubled over and spewed steaming brown gunk across the white snow. Coira merely looked a little pale. "Chief, you'd better eyeball this mess."

The iron-tang miasma of days-old blood hit me as I ducked under the low lintel and stepped inside. If this had been last year I might have joined Baldo outside. But I'd seen much worse. My right hand started itching something fierce and I absently scratched beneath the glove while inspecting the wrecked home. A table lay overturned and broken in half amongst shattered pottery and a pool of iced stew. We found the sheep and goats, and the farmers too judging from the gnawed human hand by my boot. Gore and chunks of congealed flesh coated the walls, now frozen solid. It was some sort of beast's macabre den.

"Send somebody to fetch Magus Evangeline Avernus," I said to Jovian. "The rest of you stand guard outside." My people looked grateful for that but the scouts hovered by the door, indecisive. "Well? Spit it out?"

"Begging your pardon, M'lord Magus," a grizzled veteran in thick white furs said. "We was wondering if we should go on ahead, see what else we can find. Look for ambushes and tracks and suchlike."

"You're the bloody scouts," I said. "You know better than anybody what needs done. That's probably more use than standing around here."

They were clearly not used to making their own orders, but after a moment's confusion they bobbed their heads and then resumed their trek up the valley.

Alone in the house, I looked for signs of what had occurred. On impulse I slipped my right glove off and put my palm against the wall, pressing hard. Frost crunched but it was solid blood-ice beneath, and didn't melt immediately at the touch. The back of my hand was now a hard black mass the colour and feel of wrought iron, and it was spreading up my fingers. As the frozen blood began to melt beneath my palm the itching disappeared and I felt a little faint, and a little hungry. I really didn't want to think too deeply about what that creepy-as-fuck sensation meant.

Heavy footsteps crunched towards the doorway in a hurry. I wiped my hand on my coat and pulled the glove back on just before Eva arrived with a naked sword in her hands. The blade was just normal steel rather than her old spirit-bound blade that had shattered on the heart of the Magash Mora – a blade that could cut through normal steel like it was soft cheese was a sore loss for anybody, as I knew only too well. She sheathed it and surveyed every inch of the slaughterhouse, pausing to examine scores and marks in broken wood and walls, and the wounds left in frozen flesh and bone.

"Daemons," she pronounced.

"I've seen madmen do much the same," I said.

She pointed up to claw marks either side of wooden beams. "Did they also hang from the rafters like a bat?"

"Ah. That might explain our lack of local guides then." Great. Flying daemons were just what we needed.

"Indeed. I will pass the word to watch the skies." She made to leave but I stepped to block the doorway.

I grimaced and scratched my bristly chin. "I'm sorry for before. Nobody wants to be pitied. I was just lamenting my own lack of power. You're a bloody fierce fighter and I'd rather have nobody else fighting at my side. I hope we can still be friends."

Her green eye stared at me, face hidden behind the impassive steel mask. "When did we ever start?" She brushed past me and marched away to reorganise our army. In her wake she left a lingering aura of pain in my head, a weak taste of what she suffered every hour of every day.

What I really wanted to say was how bitterly I regretted what she'd had to suffer through, and how sorry I was that I didn't, somehow, prevent it. But she didn't need or want that. What would it solve? No, what she needed was a purpose – what's the point of enduring all that pain and surviving for no good reason? It also might help if I wasn't such a ham-fisted clod about it all.

I stepped out and eyed the wooden barn and fencing, then nodded to the farmhouse. "Burn it," I said to Nareene. She whooped with joy and set about incinerating what was left of those poor bastards' bodies coating the walls of their home.

The scouts found the remainder of our Clansfolk guides half a league further up the valley. Or at least we assumed the scraps of bone, chewed furs and broken steel laying in red-spattered snow were theirs. There were no other tracks, just the boot prints of three men churned up in a circle. One of the scouts pointed to a line of red stains heading towards the sheer cliff walls, and then continuing straight up sheer rock. Red icicles hung like bloody fangs from an outcrop far above our heads.

That night we set camp uneasily in a moderate blizzard, sipped our ale ration listlessly and slept fitfully. The sentries scanned the sky as much as the valley ahead. Despite our precautions, in the small hours of night I woke with a death-scream ringing in my ears and mind. On my travels I'd long ago grown accustomed to sleeping fully dressed (you never knew when you might have to slip out a window and leg it) so I grabbed my dirk, flung the sheath aside and raced out, magic surging through muscles and into my eyes, a little trick of body magic that granted keener night sight.

Bryden lurched barefoot from his tent, the lanky young git wearing a hideous yellow padded nightgown that moonlight stained the colour of piss. His head whipped to and fro, mouth gawping. Looked like he'd never been in a proper fight in his life!

My Gift located a fading mind all the way up the cliff face. It was accompanied by something inhuman, and my sharpened eyesight picked out a black shape clinging to the rock, tearing at something with its glistening beaks.

The armoured form of Eva was already blurring towards me, a

heavy war-bow fully as tall as herself already strung and an arrow nocked. She skidded to a stop, engulfing me in a wave of powdery snow. "Where is the enemy?"

I pointed to the black mass clinging to the rock far up out of our reach. As a knight, Eva's physical senses and sight were superior to mine. She grunted. "Bone vulture." In a single smooth motion she drew and loosed. A distant screech announced a hit. Pebbles clattered down the cliff, followed by a tumbling mass of feathers and snapping beaks. With only a single eye she was a better shot than I would ever be with two.

A shredded human corpse thudded to the earth beside us, the man's hairy arse jutting naked from the snow. Our missing sentry's trousers were down around his ankles from where he'd been squatting to dump a shite. It was a fucking embarrassing way to go.

The daemon fell nearby. Eva waved the wardens back, threw aside her bow and advanced on the squawking creature. She didn't draw a weapon and she didn't need one. I followed her, keeping her between that thing and me. I was squishy and soft and she was most definitely not.

The bone vulture wasn't close to being a native animal. The thing's bones were a hard outer sheath covered in iridescent feathers, and it had vibrant purple knives for claws. It looked more like a four-winged, feathered insect than a bird. One of its two heads shrieked and snapped at Eva, while the other lay limp and motionless with an arrow through its eye.

"They normally appear in flocks," she said. "Many were summoned during the invasion of Setharis." She backhanded the snapping beak and it shattered like glass. The daemon bubbled and writhed in the snow.

Before Eva could finish it off I stepped in. "Hold, I want to try something." It was the first time in my life that I'd had a daemon at my mercy. I'd always been fleeing for my life, always the prey and never the predator. That had to change. Now was the time to see if I could get into their heads like I could with humans. I'd never been able to do it with animals, but this was worth a shot.

I stood motionless and looked inward, probing with my Gift. Its mind was a confusion of half-formed thoughts and slippery as an oiled whore on silken sheets. It was every bit as impossible as trying to get inside an animal's mind. Perhaps this bone vulture was just an animal hailing from some strange and distant realm.

All the same, I gathered my power and attacked it with crude force, taking a mental battering ram to a nut, again and again in different ways until I found one that appeared to work for these particular daemons. The creature convulsed, stopped moving and lay there drooling green blood and black bile, its mind beaten into scrambled eggs. "I'm done with the fucker now." It was good to know I could use my Gift in this manner, but frustrating that each type of daemon's mind would be very different and require unique tactics.

Eva watched me from behind her impassive mask, and I imagined her eyebrow lifted in that suspicious way she used to. She shrugged and kicked the thing. It exploded against the cliff wall in a cloud of feathers and stone dust. "These things are an insult to proper birds."

That was our first night in the Clanholds. I suspected that warm welcome was just the start of our troubles.

CHAPTER 11

After a hurried breakfast of bread and cheese and a brief spell of morning weapon training, we packed up and hiked through a gentle snowfall up into a wider valley dotted with small farmholds like the one we had passed earlier. All were deserted with no livestock to be seen. Ice-rimmed streams gushed from clefts in the rock face and gathered in the centre of the valley to form a long, narrow lake before taking the lengthy and winding route southwards to reach Barrow Hill and the sea beyond. Tall weather-pitted standing stones jutted from the earth in an apparently haphazard fashion, monoliths left in their ancient seats by superstitious Clansfolk despite taking up prime farmland on the fertile valley floor.

Being geomancers, Cormac and Granville took great interest in the stones, but didn't have time to do more than a cursory inspection with their magic. Whatever they did find troubled them, and as we marched they remained deep in conversation for several hours.

We kept a wary eye on the handful of bone vultures circling on the air currents high above the valley, watching us. Eva had to restrain our aggravated aeromancer Bryden from using his power to pluck the creatures from the sky. "Not yet," she said to him. "Never show your hand until you have to." I caught her glance in my direction as she said it.

I flashed a grin. The mask made it difficult to gauge her

expression but she withdrew from my presence and kept her distance. It was probably another mistake, but why should I treat her any different now just because of scars and physical damage? I knew exactly how shallow the flesh was, and I'd liked *her*. Wasn't normality what she wanted? I sighed and as we marched onwards I stared up at the fat, drifting snowflakes. If the ordeals of the Black Autumn had taught me anything, it was to cherish every enjoyment you could, while you could.

The valley splintered into four smaller, craggier paths, the widest route heading north east towards Kil Noth and eventually Dun Bhailiol. This was where my knowledge of the geography of the Clanholds ended. Of the valleys and holds located further west and north I had no real idea beyond a handful of names attached to barrels of ale and fine whiskies.

Eva sent scouts racing along every route while we waited, concerned that our larger force might be attacked in the rear by Skallgrim skirmishers. A half hour later word came back that no enemy had been sighted, so we began the advance. Eva and her heavily armoured battle coterie took the spearhead, marching two-abreast through deep snow, followed by Bryden, myself, Cormac, Secca, Granville and then Vincent bringing up the rear.

Even with Eva's force ploughing a path through the snow, we found it slow, hard going. After an hour the wardens in front of us stopped dead and my nerves jangled as they readied weapons. The sky ahead was black with bone vultures.

Bryden looked to Eva, who nodded. His face burst into a wide grin. "Finally!" Wind whipped past and carried the lanky form of Bryden into the air at the centre of a swirling blizzard. He soared above the cliff walls, then higher still to survey the terrain ahead. The flock of bone vultures dived to attack him. He laughed as invisible fists of wind seized their wings and pinned them together. The things dropped like hailstones to smash against the mountainside somewhere above us, a drumming of dull thuds and very brief squawks.

A few scattered cheers erupted among the wardens. Even such a small victory lifted their moods, but for me every step just took us closer to Kil Noth, and to my grandmother.

I wasn't nearly lucky enough for that spiteful old crow to be dust and bones in her family tomb. She was no kin of mine, whatever she claimed. My mother had fled Kil Noth as a young woman and hadn't returned even when the madness of the voices overtook her. And six years ago I had finally discovered why.

A pulse of fear interrupted my thoughts. Bryden's grin had vanished and he was staring hard at something in the distance. He plummeted towards us, slowing at the very last moment to land in a swirl of snow. "I see plumes of black smoke to the north east."

I couldn't be sure but from what he was describing it sounded like it was coming from Dun Bhailiol, the furthest east of all the Clansfolk holdfasts, and consequently the closest to occupied Ironport. It was right in the path of the Skallgrim advance, and only three days' steady march away from us.

"Then that is welcome news for us," Eva said. She had the good grace not to sound happy about it. "If they have stopped to siege the holdfast then it grants us more time to fortify the area around Kil Noth. Every day they delay in the Clanholds grants the Arcanum more time to take Ironport and come to our aid."

With that we shouldered all our gear and marched quicker than ever before. At least our effort kept the winds from biting too badly, though already one or two wardens seemed to be suffering the beginnings of frostbitten fingers and toes. My group remained hale and hearty, and during a rest stop I ignored Adalwolf surreptitiously passing around a flask of cheap Docklands rum. I wasn't about to take the last of their drink off them, not when I might have to share my own hidden flask of fine whisky in return. I took a belly-warming sip and slipped it back into my coat pocket.

We camped only a day from Kil Noth and we had still not uncovered any signs of life, just hastily abandoned homes and empty barns. Huddled around our fire, bowls at the ready, I doled out salt-beef broth and hard bread before settling down with my own. There was a little left over, but I'd leave them to argue over that. I could do without, mostly because I had a private stash of dried meat and fruit they knew nothing about. If there was one lesson that life had beaten into me, it was to look after yourself first before trying to look after others, and to always keep something back for when Lady Night's luck flipped to the Night Bitch's misfortune.

Dusk arrived quickly in the Clanholds, the sun dipping below the mountains to paint the snowy slopes a burning bronze. It was breathtaking; you had to give these barren and icy lands that. With the sun slumbering, Elunnai's silvery light sparkled all along the valley, a silvery path enticing us onwards to Kil Noth, the accursed holdfast of the druí.

The campfires were eerily quiet tonight, devoid of the music and song I'd been led to expect of armies on the march. I opened my Gift to seek out the answer – they were dwelling on the enemy's massive numbers, and after seeing the work of their flying daemons our men were now also nervous of the open sky. My leadership only made things worse, but Eva's relentless efficiency and martial power seemed to counter that in their minds. I knew that I was pretty much just here as a sacrifice – Kil Noth wanted me back for some reason, and they were happy to use this war as leverage. They knew I would never return willingly, not unless the fate of all Kaladon hinged on it. I was a confirmed black-hearted bastard but even I wasn't that selfish.

I couldn't get to sleep, tossing and turning and mind racing with a thousand different thoughts; mostly dreading tomorrow. I gave up and threw on my overcoat and thick cloak, then pulled on my boots and gloves and headed out into the snow. With my Gift it wasn't difficult to move unseen, or rather, disregarded; I wasn't actually invisible. My footprints in the snow proved the only troublesome aspect, convincing the sentries to continually ignore them while I was away.

It was undoubtedly a stupid decision to leave camp without my guards, given we were at war and daemons were loose in these hills. But I didn't give a rat's arse, I needed to be alone and free of the morass of stray thoughts pressing in on me. People kept so much locked away in their heads, unsaid and unacted: flashes of anger and disgust, images of punching some annoying git in the face for scraping a metal spoon across a pot or for chewing too loud, hints of lust and filthy images… all sorts of impulses that they would never act on in reality. And yet I knew it all. People were never exactly what they portrayed on the outside – Eva was not the only one to wear a mask.

I tramped a fair way towards Kil Noth until I glimpsed the mountain it was burrowed into, all limned in silvery light. A few columns of smoke rose from unseen fires somewhere deep inside its subterranean halls. I stood in the snow, thinking and occasionally sipping my whisky for warmth. Eventually I became aware of a quiet presence off to one side watching me intently. I reached out to investigate and found a human mind curled up tighter than a snail in its shell. Eva.

"Want some?" I held my flask of whisky out towards her without looking in her direction.

A white cloak rose from the snow to reveal the armoured form beneath. She took her time approaching, emotions as inscrutable as ever behind her steel mask. She took the whisky from me but didn't drink.

I yawned into a glove. "Did you expect me to run and hide?"

Her single green eye studied me. "I was ordered to stop you if you did. We made a very specific deal with the Clansfolk druí."

"Not what I asked."

It took a while for her to answer, never a good sign. "No," she said finally. "Not now."

I'd tried to flee before, more than once when faced with the Magash Mora and the Skallgrim. "And why now?"

"Nowhere to run to," she said. "Everywhere is at war, with daemons and gods and fuck knows what else popping up everywhere. You would be hunted with a ferocity that no rogue magus has ever seen before."

I grunted. "True enough."

"And you have seen true horror," she added, the words oddly soft in her cracked voice. "In the end you did not shirk that terrible task. You faced down daemons, the Magash Mora, a god, and the Arcanum itself to do what had to be done. What is this petty little skirmish in comparison to that?"

Unexpectedly, I laughed. How had she managed that? "You make it all sound so easy."

Now it was her turn to laugh, a harsh hacking. "What do you make of this place?"

I shrugged. "The Clanholds is a backwater, but not without its charms. It's an impenetrable maze to outsiders and all those stones make me nervous, especially the ones marked with three eyes. This place harbours a hundred ancient mysteries. Have you ever heard of the myth of the God of Broken Things?"

She shook her head.

"It's a local legend around these parts, but unusually this one is about a god instead of giants or spirits so perhaps the tale bears some kernel of truth. There is supposed to be a sacred valley around here that only the despairing can find, hidden from the sight of all the rest. There, a god makes its home. It is said that the broken can find succour and safety there. Wish we could find it. I wouldn't mind having a god on our side right now."

"Sounds farfetched to me." She turned away and eased her mask up to take a drink.

"There's no need to hide," I said. "I have seen horrors beyond compare and your scars were gained protecting us. Without you we would all have been lost to something worse than death. Your wounds were earned in righteous battle, not like…" I traced the scars running down my right cheek, "…not like mine, earned from naive stupidity. I appreciate a good mind more than the meat we wear."

My breath misted the air for long moments until she chose to turn back to face me. I could only see her lower face, but that was enough to know exactly what she suffered. Her nose was missing and the left side of her face was a tapestry of black and red ruin with bone peering through in patches. The lips were gone to expose bare teeth. Her right side was better, but still a mass of angry burn-scars. She opened her mouth and poured in a goodly amount of whisky. Her single eye pierced me, defiant and expecting comment. I made none.

She stoppered the flask and tossed it back to me. "So now you know."

Her scars didn't matter to me. Without thinking, I reached towards her and stroked her scarred cheek with my hand. The moment I touched her I knew it was a mistake. She slapped my hand aside, a whisker away from breaking my arm, then hastily slid her mask back down into place. Her hands shook with fury. "How fucking dare you, I should break your face."

Words were crude things at times. I let go of my emotions, Gift radiating exactly what I was thinking and feeling. She lurched backwards, swamped in my unfiltered admiration and respect. Anger at what had been done to her, yes, but not a single bloody smidgeon of pity. No, I wouldn't run, and not because I had nowhere to run to – that had never stopped me before – but because of her. I wished to possess even half of her brave heart and iron will. Again, her ruined figure clad in half-melted armour stood before me during the darkest hour of Black Autumn, spirit-bound sword in her hand and duty in her heart. In agony, she did what needed to be done. Me? I just followed in her wake. She had saved me, and I owed her. I intended to pay her back in kind. I would be something better than I was. I was here to fight at her side and her ravaged body did not dissuade me – it was her mind I was attracted to.

A strangled choke from behind the mask, and then she fled as fast as knightly body-magic could propel her, a blurred shape blasting through the snow and out of sight in seconds before the waves of snow had even settled.

"Oh well done, you fucking arse. Handled that well, eh?" I had no idea how she was feeling and as usual I'd just done whatever I wanted without a thought in my stupid head, and damn what anybody else felt about it. "Walker, you absolute shitestain." But now she knew exactly how I felt about her. Surprisingly, this was also the first time that I did as well.

Jovian was awake and waiting for me when I returned, a disapproving look in his eyes. I said nothing and tossed him the last of my whisky.

"We are in this together, yes?" he said, taking a swig. "Best you had remember that, lest I spank you like a little boy."

"I'd like to see you try," I snapped, full of self-recrimination as I replayed my mistake with Eva over and over in my head, wishing I wasn't such a cack-brained prick.

"Challenge accepted," he replied, deadly serious. "We shall see at dawn."

CHAPTER 12

This morning I had the pleasure of facing Jovian in mock battle as the wardens gathered to begin their own daily drills. We picked up wooden hafts instead of real weapons and I eyed mine dubiously, clutched as it was in traitorous hands that could now barely hold a flask of whisky. It might not be steel but it would still hurt when he beat the crap out of me, and I supposed sparring with goose-down pillows wouldn't be much of use to anybody.

Still, my own big mouth had landed me here, so I just had to shut up and take the punishment. Hopefully it wouldn't prove completely humiliating. He stripped to the waist in a circle of cleared snow, and as he rolled his shoulders and stretched, the wiry little Esbanian's impressive collection of scars earned from hundreds of fights garnered a measure of respect from the circle of wardens surrounding us. I kept my damn clothes on. Nobody wanted to see a mop-haired, rake-thin, ugly old git like me half-naked. Besides, it was bloody cold.

I cricked my neck from side to side and took a stance, right leg leading, and assumed a basic guard with the weapon held in front of me. Even I knew that much of bladecraft. Jovian stood loose and easy on the balls of his feet, giving no indication of what he was about to do.

"Fight," Coira shouted.

All I could do was desperately block as Jovian exploded towards me, sword cutting down and right towards my neck. Not that it connected. My parry sailed out to the side as he twisted his wrist, sword tip slipping up and over my haft to smack me on the forehead.

"First blood," he said, grinning. I had died in half a second.

We both took our stances, and this time I started cheating. Magic flooded my muscles as I waited eager for action. This time things would be different.

"Fight!"

I darted forward with blistering speed. Lunged and cut low at his exposed knee. He slipped his leg back out of reach and swung straight down at my head.

Crack. My head throbbed. Dead in half a second again. Duels were not as thrilling and glorious as the bards depicted.

"Second," he said, smirking.

We began again, and again I darted forward, barely avoiding impaling myself on his weapon as he did the same.

I scrambled back, barely avoiding his darting point. I was off-balance, and he was on me like a cat worrying a rat, a flurry of blows that even my magically-enhanced strength and speed barely kept up with. This was the first time I'd properly used a weapon in months and my clumsy damaged hands were betraying me at every turn. My grip slipped and he was through my guard, sword smacking me on the arse as he slipped past me. He spun back to face me, grinning insolently.

"Third," he said.

"Fight!"

He whacked my shin.

"Fight!"

He tapped my elbow, exposed by a clumsy strike. I fumbled and almost dropped the weapon and in my ire drew deeper on my magic. Frustration boiled over as he took me apart with consummate ease.

"Fight!"

He rapped my knuckles, then spanked me with his hand on the way past. The wardens snickered and whispered, mocking.

I was done playing. I gritted my teeth and waited for the next bout. My Gift throbbed with the torrent of magic flooding my body.

"Fight!"

The world slowed to a crawl as I flashed forward and tossed my sodding stick at a mocking warden's stupid face. I could barely use it anyway. I'd always been better with knives and fists. Jovian's eyes widened as I slapped his weapon aside with my gloved hand and the other found his throat. I heaved the little Esbanian up and off his feet, then slammed him down to the icy earth, squeezing.

He slapped the snow with open hands, a sign of submission. After a moment's hesitation, I let go. The magic protested. It wanted me to use even more, a greater display of my righteous might. The Worm of Magic always lusted for more. The wardens murmured amongst themselves, surprised at me putting him down so brutally, so casually.

He coughed and sat up, rubbing his neck. Somewhat chagrined at my loss of control, I offered my hand and pulled him to his feet. "A dangerous man," he said. "You were playing with me, yes? Ah, one day I will be your match, this I swear."

I stared at him as he winked. The little bastard had let me win to soothe my pride and solidify my standing as commander. In his eyes he'd done me a big favour. At that moment I knew he could have spanked me like an unruly child if he'd wanted, even with all the skill I had with body magic. It was a pointed warning about overconfidence. I nodded grimly.

At some unseen signal the wardens broke away and began packing up camp. Today we would reach Kil Noth, and for that Jovian's warning was timely indeed.

Six bodies in Clan Clachan hunting plaids, half-buried in the snow and frozen solid. An equal number of dead Skallgrim in thick furs and chain scattered on the slope below them. The Clansfolk bore ragged claw wounds around their arms and faces while the Skallgrim sprouted arrows from their backs.

Jovian sighed. "It was a fine ambush. The Skallgrim advance scouts were well feathered but those Clansfolk forgot to look up. We shall not make that same mistake, I think."

I peered into the grey sky. "Staying alive is the one thing I've proven to be good at. Despite everybody's best efforts, including my own."

Jovian grinned at that. "That, we have in common."

Vaughn abruptly dropped Biter's reins and whooped in delight as he plunged his hands into the snow, retrieving a beaked Skallgrim war axe that had to be half my height. It was a fine thing, the metal acid-etched and adorned with bronze trim. He grinned at us and swung it one-handed. The big weapon suited the huge brute and I wasn't one to complain about looting a corpse; why, it was practically a second profession for us poor Docklanders.

At least one of us was happy amidst the frigid wind and drifting snow, but then he was too stupid to worry about the coming bloodshed, or maybe he really didn't care – it was still better than rotting away in the dank depths of that prison cell.

We left the frozen corpses where they lay and kept on trudging through the snow, a long line of men, women and pack ponies. As we grew closer to Kil Noth my paranoia kept my magic ready to lash out, so I was the first to sense the strongly Gifted mind waiting for us. I gently probed, finding their mind a silent fortress immune to anything bar a fully-fledged assault. I withdrew before they felt me, and warned the other magi to expect company. Scouts soon passed back word that a Clansfolk emissary from Kil Noth awaited us further down the valley.

A mere slip of a girl, perhaps a single summer past full womanhood, sat cross-legged on the mossy back of a fallen standing stone. Her hair was white as snow and spilled over a strip of embossed leather across her forehead to hang free to her waist. In defiance of the freezing weather she was naked and her flesh inked all over with whorling blue and black tattoos. She boasted delicate, almost fragile, features and her eyes were closed, her expression serene and innocent. Her appearance was deceptive – I knew it masked something gut-heavingly vile.

"What are you doing out here dressed in such an indecent manner, girl," Granville said, shivering in his thick Arcanum robes, fox-fur gloves and cloak. His misted words hung in the still air like a bad fart. "Have you taken leave of your senses? Somebody fetch the heathen a blanket before she freezes to death."

"There is no chance of that," I snarled. "Only ice runs through the veins of this heartless creature." That earned me disparaging stares.

My maternal grandmother Angharad was undeniably beautiful – beautifully horrific. That bitch's magic-wrought facade masked one of the cruellest hearts I had ever encountered. Her unending youth made a mockery of the resemblance to my own beloved and lamented mother when by all rights this thing's inner corruption should be represented by a rotting corpse. I had to fight back the nauseated shudder and the venom clamouring to spray from my tongue. The scars running down the right side of my face and neck pulled tight and hot. This thing was no kin of mine!

The girl opened her human eyes, if eyes they could still be called when amethyst orbs sat inside hollowed-out sockets. Mercifully the third, sitting in a hole carved in her forehead, remained hidden behind its strip of leather.

When she spoke her voice was old and weary rather than youthful and exuberant, and her accent was not quite that of the modern Clanholds but of a people long since dust. "The stones welcome ye Granville o' the line of Buros, and ye also Cormac o' the line o' Feredaig."

Her face turned to each magus as she spoke and they all felt discomfort. There was something incredibly off putting staring into a blind woman's inhuman crystal eyes and knowing she could see deeper than any human should. "The winter winds welcome ye, Bryden, son o' Araeda and Emlain. The fires of our hearths welcome ye Vincent, son o' Fion and Bevan. The Sun and Moon and stars welcome ye Secca, daughter o' Grania and Turi." She looked to Eva. "No spirits welcome ye, Evangeline o' the line o' Avernus, but the hearts and sword-arms o' our warriors will praise your arrival through the coming days."

Then she looked to me. And said nothing.

I was not welcome in Kil Noth. I never had been. I was merely cattle that had escaped the slaughterhouse.

I scowled and imagined my hands around her throat, squeezing until all three sodding eyes popped out. "You lot forced me to come back, Angharad, so stick your welcome up your arse. Your face makes maggots gag in a bucket of guts."

Everybody but Secca was staring at me with mouths agape – our magus of light and shadow was frowning and scanning the steep slopes of the surrounding valley as if searching for something.

Angharad rose to her feet and felt not a scrap of shame or shyness despite wearing only tattoos in front of so many strangers. Even given the looser physical morals of Clansfolk this bitch was brazen, but then she was old and terrible and beautiful so who would dare rebuke her?

She gazed down at me from atop her fallen stone, expression inscrutable. "Ye offer your poor, lonely granny no respect, Edrin Walker, nor a hug." Her words found great purchase among our men, mostly thanks to her naked beauty.

A hug? Really? Was that the best she could do to try to alienate my army from me? It was a mere drop in the ocean of dislike. All she cared about was forcing me to become what my mother was originally meant to be.

"Oh don't pity her," I said. "She's older than any of us and her hand-me-down eyes are probably older than the bloody Arcanum itself. If you stick your cock in that foul creature it will rot off. If only this little runt of a supposed seer was better at it then she might have seen this war coming in time to do something about it."

She convulsed. Her head snapped up to face suddenly roiling clouds. When it snapped back to me her blazing eyes stained the snow purple with their inner light. Blood drained from her lips, and all colour from her tattoos until they too were white as snow. My Gift was wide open and magic poured through me, ready to kill.

"Enough." A chorus of voices rang out in unison from all sides, causing the Arcanum magi to open their Gifts and our wardens to draw their weapons. Two dozen Clansfolk druí stepped out from shadowed crevices in the cliff walls, or simply appeared in front of us, all wearing grey and green clanless plaids, all Gifted. Secca grimaced and looked most affronted at having missed whatever illusion had masked them. That was all well and good – but how in all the shitting hells of heathens had they hidden themselves from me?

Eva set a firm hand on my shoulder. "Shut your mouth," she hissed. "Please, just for once. We need to fight with these people not against them."

For her I shut my flapping jaw. She was right, here and now was not the place to rip the beating heart from my grandmother. I had to be more cunning and ruthless than I'd ever been. I hated to think it, but I had to be more like her. Anything less and she would have me tangled helpless in her web while she tried to make me into something I was not.

Angharad was studying my reactions and seemed disappointed with what she found. No change there then. "Drop your weapons and let go o' your magic. Any attempt to embrace it will result in your death, and ye will stay out o' our minds, tyrant."

I glared at Eva, *I warned you.*

Surrounded by their Gifted, we had no choice but to comply. Swords and shields, spears, bows and implementia arcana all dropped to the snow.

Angharad smiled, cold and hard as her heart. "Ye may now enter the sacred hold of Kil Noth."

Warriors armed with circular hide-covered shields and basket-hilted broadswords escorted us, and at first the others could not see our destination. Only as we grew close could they discern the lines of carved stonework blending into the natural rock, the arrow slits, windows and chimneys of the upper reaches of Kil Noth.

We were taken along a concealed pathway to a massive circular doorway carved into the side of the mountain. The stone bore ancient protective runes and wards chiselled in harmony with vine leaves and thorny thistle stalks. Some of the wardings I recognised, the usual variety granting strength and durability to withstand ice and fire and hammer. For others, even my respectable experience with wards offered no answer. Some even resembled those found on the Tombs of the Mysteries back in Setharis that no magus had ever deciphered, or broken.

Angharad laid a hand on the doorway and the stone ground back to admit us to a place where I had once been tortured. I swallowed my fear of enclosed spaces, steeled myself against the horrors of the past, and entered Kil Noth.

CHAPTER 13

In the summer of six years past, I had entered that very same door to Kil Noth with hopes of salvation in my heart instead of blackest dread. I had been ragged in body and mind from four years of constant running, hiding, and futilely hoping that the daemons hunting me would eventually give up and leave me alone. I had faked my death and succeeded in throwing the Arcanum off my trail, but even that cunning victory had not offered as much respite as I had yearned for – the shadow cats had proven relentless and would never, ever, give up the hunt.

I had been so sick of travel, terrible food and bad drink in grimy rural taverns, dicing for coin with rigged dice and then moving on – always moving on after only a few short days. All the faces and names blurred into one, and it had got to the point I'd barely taken notice of tavernkeeps and serving girls as separate people: they were all just actors on a stage playing the same old roles.

If my survival in exile had not been all that ensured the safety of my old friends Lynas, Charra and Layla, then I might have ended my life long before then. Many a time I had stood atop a cliff and looked down at the white-topped waves crashing against jagged rocks while thinking of a home I would never see again. I had often pondered taking that single short step forward. A growing part of me had urged me to do it and find some rest and peace, but I never could – I loved my friends and I was too stubborn to let the enemy win. In any case, I'd always been good at putting things off until tomorrow, always the next tomorrow…

I had been filled with despair and thought that maybe, just maybe, the Gifted of the Clanholds might be able to offer me some sort of safety and rest – after all, was I not their kin on my mother's side? I knew only a very little about my family history back then, some pieced together from the scraps my mother had let slip over the years, and the rest gathered from her ravings as madness and strange voices consumed her mind shortly before her death.

The farmers in the valley just up from Barrow Hill had eyed my tattered clothing and looked at me curiously when I asked where I might find the Gifted of the Clanholds. After a bit of word-wrangling they realised that I meant those of them born with magic. "Aye, that'll be the druí of Kil Noth then, pal," one said, offering directions.

As I gave my thanks, shouldered my pack and moved on, he had offered some parting words of wisdom that I should have taken to heart: "Be careful and make no deals, traveller. Those druí care more about their spirits than they do about the likes of us."

I arrived in the village that sprawled around the foot of the holdfast with a powerful thirst and a rumbling belly. To my surprise, I found somebody waiting for me in the tavern, her hood up, sitting in my favoured seat in the corner, the one that offered my back against the wall and eyes on all windows and doors.

Her blind and cloth-bound head turned to me, and she smiled, dazzling me with warmth. "Well met, Edrin Walker. Come sit with me a'while. No need to run, I have been expecting ye. The spirits have told me o' your troubles."

She wore robes of exceptionally fine cut, woven with wild wardings more like Clansfolk tattoos than those of carefully studied Setharii craft, but no less magical for all that. She was strongly Gifted, and knew my instinctive reaction had been to leg it right back out of the door.

"You know me, but who are you?" I'd demanded.

"My name is Angharad," she replied, pulling back her hood to reveal long snow-white hair framing features so very like my mother's. "And I am your granny. Sit here by the fire, grandchild, you must be exhausted after all your travels."

I gaped at her, my heart pounding as I thumped down opposite. She smelled faintly of lavender and pine, my mother's favourite scents bringing a tear to my eyes. Nowadays I suspected that had been a deliberate ploy, damn the vile creature, but back then I had been dumbfounded. My mother had never mentioned my grandmother was Gifted, or still alive come to that. In fact she had barely mentioned her life before Setharis at all. I was a magus, and most of us stopped ageing at some point, though usually later on in life, and as such my grandmother's youth was surprising but not shocking.

"I did not know ye existed," she said, sadly. "Otherwise I would have come for ye long ago. My daughter, is she…"

"Dead a long time," I said gruffly.

The girl nodded, forehead wrinkling with sorrow – or so I'd thought at the time. "That blessed, tormented child should never have run from here. Your mother needed the help only I could give her. And I, hers. I searched up and down all Kaladon for years, but neither hide nor hair of her was ever found. In a place as big as Setharis I suppose you cannot find one who does not wish to be found."

"Oh?" I said, my hope hardening with caution. "Why did she run in the first place?"

"The spirits," she replied. "Your mother never came to respect them as I do. Their voices only served to frighten the flighty and nervous child she was. She had such rare talent, and they offer such wisdom and power to those chosen few who share our ancient blood." She turned to look at me, her eyes blind behind the strip of cloth, yet still seeming to meet and hold my gaze. "And now in turn they offer ye safety and respite from those daemonic beasts that hunt ye. They are closing in, but there is a way to keep them from ye if we hurry. Then we will have many years to grow to know each other better. After all this time, my grandchild has come home." She sniffed and wiped a tear from her pale, tattooed cheek.

Home. The word pierced my heavy heart. Setharis was forbidden to me, but I still had family, and another place to call home if I wished it. The years of running and solitude weighed on me like a lead coat, but finally here was somebody on my side willing and able to help. I could finally rest and be happy again. Hope swelled inside me, bubbling out into a muffled sob.

She embraced me warmly, arms wrapped tight around me as if she never wanted to let go. “Hush now, child. There’s no need for that. We are kin, ye and I. Blood binds us together stronger than steel.” She placed her hand on my then-smooth and unscarred cheek and her skin felt cool and comforting. “We are kin, and that means we face the perils o’ this world together – and those perils had best be afraid. I am so sorry, my child. Ye must have been so alone all these many years. Well no more will ye have to run and hide. Ye are home w’your old granny now and she’ll take care o’ everything, never ye fear.”

What could I have done but say yes? Such a trusting fool. I had wanted to believe in her so much that even my usual cynicism and paranoia gave way before the bond of family, treacherous though it turned out to be. Finally, I’d had hope for the future.

It took my grandmother three days to prepare the ritual, in between spending as much time with me as she was able, listening to my entire life story and cursing out the Arcanum and the Setharii gods for not helping me. I had been all alone for years, but now I had my grandmother looking out for me, and that was a glorious gift beyond all compare.

When the time came she took my arm and led me into the holdfast. Her scent and slender form were again so very like my mother’s that it threw my mind into turmoil. I think that was the whole point, to keep me from thinking too much. My memory of what followed is fragmented and fuzzy, partly from pain and fear, and partly thanks to whatever alchemic she was about to pour down my throat.

It was a sacred ritual, she said, handing me a drink, one brewed and infused with special magic to call her great spirit and bestow its protection upon me. I was so desperate to believe this would solve all my problems that I did as she wished without reservation. I drank the liquid from an engraved bowl and the next thing I remember are the nightmares: the running for my life as hideous snapping monsters with too many legs and eyes tried to eat my face, the screaming frantic flight through a world that was not my own, inhabiting a body that was not quite human flesh and blood.

My magic had roared through me as I frantically sought a way to escape, and in my panic I managed to latch on to a black thread of thought that lead my mind back to the realm it had come from. It led me home to my own human body, and I woke atop a stone slab screaming and clawing at the air, drenched in sweat that sparkled with ice crystals.

"No!" my grandmother shrieked. "Ye are ruining it. Ruining it!" Her blindfold was off and her eyes – her three amethyst eyes – boiled over with virulent magic.

I sat upright, groggy, breath heaving. "What was that?" As I regained my senses I attempted to slide off and get to my feet. "What's happening? What are you doing to me?"

She placed a hand on my chest to stop me, firm as an iron bar. "Shut your mouth, ye disgusting piece o' foreign filth. We try again immediately, until it succeeds or ye die trying." I tried to move but she pushed me back down with remorseless inhuman strength.

Panic reared its ugly urgent head and I struggled. "Not a chance. I am done with this stupid ritual. Fuck this shite." It was all wrong, and she was all wrong. There was no love to be found in her twisted expression. All my dreams of home and family went up in flames, a cunning lie told to a stupid gullible boy she knew had yearned to believe it. "I am leaving."

"So be it," my grandmother hissed. "We shall do this the hard way, ye ungrateful derelict." She punched me full in the face and I slammed back, head rattling off stone. The metal tang of blood from a split lip filled my mouth. Another blow followed, then another. She leapt atop me, straddling my waist.

I tried to shove her off but my body felt heavy and clumsy, still affected by whatever alchemic she had given me. "Don't make me use my magic on you."

Her face twisted with cruel and heartless fury. “Ye are nothing, just street filth squeezed out o’ an ungrateful cunt o’ a daughter. Ye will obey me!” She looked down on me with those sinister, glowing purple eyes that saw nothing but a tool of her making. “Ye would be foolish to try your Gift. I am warded against all magic. I created your faithless wretch of a mother, boy, and in the stupid cow’s absence her vulgar whelp must take her place in the ritual. For ye the future holds nothing save a life sacrificed to serve a greater purpose. I have dreamed o’ ye wading through rivers of blood as thousands die around ye. It is better that your life ends now to usher in a better future directed by my hands. At least your pathetic life will have a point to it.”

She waved to a wall where thirty-six yellowed skulls sat in niches. “There sit your aunts and uncles, who proved unGifted and their bodies unable to withstand the Queen o’ Winter’s power. Useless wretches the lot o’ them – Gifted children are so very rare. But ah, your ungrateful mother… such promise wasted! How glad I am ye are here to take that ugly cow’s place.”

“Go fuck a goat, you syphilitic whore,” I spat into her face, along with a goodly blob of phlegm and blood. “You are insane – you murdered your own children!”

She snarled and her nails extended into claws. “Not children. Flawed spawn carried in my belly like sacks o’ gold that turned to shite when they dropped. Useless creatures. But your body will serve me well – that harlot o’ a daughter did something right after all. I shall force the pact upon ye by carving the Queen o’ Winter’s name directly into your heart as painfully as possible.” She smirked as her claws raked down my cheek and neck, ripping deep through flesh and muscle before plunging into my chest, digging through muscle towards my heart.

My face burned like the wounds had been doused with salt and acid. Blood poured out of me. Agony chased away my grogginess. Warded against all magic was she? I thought not – when was the last time a proper mind-fucker like me was around? Far beyond her lifetime. I opened my Gift and slammed into her mind, squeezing hard. I didn't give a crap if the shadow cats found my scent here and killed her because of it.

One of her wardings had some small effect on my power but it was probably a half-remembered ancient structure passed down through the centuries, one nowhere near strong enough to defy me. It wasn't like they could have tested it.

Angharad was tough, many centuries old from the stray thoughts flashing through her mind, and she resisted mightily. She gasped and drew her dripping claws back, shaking her head. It gave me enough time to reach up and grab the front of her robes. I pulled her down as I sat up, my forehead ramming into her nose.

We both screamed in pain, mine from the gaping wounds in my face and neck, and her from a broken nose and my blood in her crystal eyes.

She tumbled to the floor and I rolled off the slab to fall atop her, elbow crunching deep into her stomach. I went mad, punching her in the face, over and over until she shoved me off with one hand. I flew backwards into a wall with bone-jarring impact.

I had been too enraged by pain and panic to notice this lesser pain and surged back to kick her in the side. As I went for a second blow she grabbed my foot and twisted, taking me down.

She came at me claws bared, then slowed as I found a crack in her mind, forced myself into the oozing darkness inside and ordered her to stop. Her mind was like sticking my hand up an angry badger's arse – she fought me every step with feral rage like I had never felt before.

The door to the chamber ground back and two angry druí in robes stormed in, shouting about their spirits sensing blood spilled across their holy signs.

At my command, Angharad dropped in a daze while I faced the other two. One flung razor shards of ice at me. I dodged, then kicked him in the balls hard enough to kill his unborn children. I smashed the other's face into the wall and sprinted past, clutching my ruined cheek in one hand as she fell back spitting blood and teeth. I would have killed Angharad if I'd had the time but I could hear others stirring in the tunnels and rooms nearby. I only knew that I had to get out of that subterranean pit of daemons and take my chances under an honest sky.

The rest of that week was all a blur of blood and panic and pain, of frantic, vicious fights for survival and scrabbling down slopes of scrubby scree by moonlight as I fled on foot through the slumbering valleys.

I had vowed to never again venture anywhere near Kil Noth unless it was to kill my grandmother.

Perhaps when all of this Scarrabus nonsense was over and done with I would see about fulfilling that old promise. For now, I was here and being marched into the depths of Kil North all over again on my grandmother's orders, except this time I was the angry badger with sharpened claws and wicked teeth bared that they were letting into their home. I was sure they would end up regretting it.

CHAPTER 14

The interrogations began with Granville. A dozen druí took him to the far side of the stone hall we were confined in and sat him down in a plush chair. They asked him seemingly innocuous questions that he seemed happy enough to answer. As interrogations of prisoners went, it was strangely friendly, with no chains and sharpened knives or pliers for fingernails and teeth – instead there was roast pork and ale on the table and comfy chairs for all, but a prison it remained.

A dozen men and women in fine woollen robes sporting ornate bronze arm rings and golden torcs stood scrutinising every single thing we did, and a handful of armed warriors with wary eyes stood ready at their side. All of the druí bore black and blue tattoos, some that proudly proclaimed their original clan from before they became druí, and others with more esoteric meanings. A few were just there for plain old vanity.

At least Angharad was elsewhere; I wasn't sure I could bite my tongue and stay my hands much longer otherwise.

Bryant and Secca reached for mugs of ale.

"I wouldn't if I were you," I said. "We are prisoners, which means no guest right prevents them lacing your drink with alchemics to make you spill your guts. Or poison come to that." They swiftly withdrew their hands.

I watched carefully, wondering what their goal was here. This was no way to treat allies on the eve of war. Clansfolk druí were nothing like Arcanum-trained magi and with a few notable exceptions, relatively unaccustomed to using their Gift for direct offensive purposes. At least they had no idea what I was now capable of. I had thought myself so strong last time I was here, so very cunning. Hah! I'd been naught but a whelp then, and rudely disabused of those notions.

Despite their dire warnings, I eased open my Gift and sent out careful feelers. There was a reason this was happening, and I was certain my grandmother stood to gain something from it.

It did not take long for me to uncover the stain of Scarrabus in the room, quietly watching from inside the bearded man busy interrogating Granville. I was careful not to let it detect me as I scanned the rest of the Clansfolk. The others were clean.

The Setharii magi were interrogated and released one by one, granted guest right and leave to enter the hold. I was the last, and it was difficult to keep the anger and disgust from my face as I met the gaze of the infested druí. I pondered killing him as I answered questions on who I was, why I was here and stated that I had no intentions of harming Kil Noth or any of its inhabitants. Some druí had ways to detect lies, but there is truth and then there is the whole truth, and I was a tyrant – if I didn't want to know something for a short time then I didn't and walled it away in the back of my mind. If I didn't know, I couldn't lie. Nope, I had absolutely no intention at all of sticking my grandmother's severed head on a spike after I'd forced her to heal my hand.

He studied my eyes and face for a long moment, then nodded to the guards. There was no offer of guest right. The druí and warriors exited, barring the door after them to keep me prisoner. They let me stew there for hours while all the others were free to enjoy the hospitality and entertainments of Kil Noth's great hall. It was just like the vindictive creature that was my grandmother.

Eventually I dozed off, unknown hours passing until Angharad arrived to wake me. At least she now wore an ice-blue dress, thin and teasing though it was. I kept my Gift open and ready to kill, but she was a blank slate that offered no hint of what she was thinking or feeling.

"Well?" she demanded.

I shrugged.

"Do not play the idiot with me, boy," she hissed. "Do ye honestly believe I would not know ye searched their minds? Doubly so if I told ye not to. What did you find?"

"The bearded one you had doing the interrogations," I said. "Are we done here?"

She winced. "As I suspected. Murdoc was useful as a human, but will prove more useful still as a receptacle for disinformation before his end. Do ye ken what is wrong with him?"

"Oh yes," I said. "I know everything. Do you?"

"Everything is it?" She chuckled. "Ye have grown so arrogant, my boy. So ignorant. I am Angharad Walker and I have seen sights that would blast and burn your little mind. I know the true nature o' the Scarrabus." Her amethyst eyes swivelled to look at my gloved right hand. "I also know that ye have come to be healed."

My hand clenched into a fist. "I am here because you held every innocent in Kaladon hostage to your mad whims."

"And to have your hand healed," she reiterated.

I ground my teeth. "And to have it healed. How did you know?"

She blinked, lids slowly slicking across crystal. "The Queen o' Winter told me so. She could feel the change in ye as soon as ye entered her domain and pressed your blackening hand to frozen flesh and walls o' ice."

Damned spirits, and this was the biggest, meanest, oldest spirit in all the Clanholds, the one all clans sacrificed and prayed to, and gave power to. This was the god-spirit that she had always intended me to be a priest of, the one she tried to force upon me years ago. The scars marring my face burned, remembering that damned ritual and her burning rage when it had failed.

"I am no gullible, fawning druí," I said. "The only spirits I give a crap about are the ones I can toss down my throat. The rest can all go fuck themselves."

Her fingers twitched into claws and her eyes flared with light. Then she stiffened and looked at the wall opposite me. Something was happening; I could feel a whisper, a magical vibration in the realm of the mind. It was gone before I could locate the source.

My grandmother's anger drained. "A new morning has dawned and the Eldest wishes to see ye. If ye want your hand healed ye must come with me."

"I thought you were the eldest of the druí?" My eyes narrowed with suspicion. "Or do you mean a spirit?"

"I swear on the Queen o' Winter's name, the Eldest is neither druí nor spirit. Come." She led me from the interrogation room, down a hallway, and through a circular stone doorway guarded by two mailed warriors who stepped aside to admit her. After we entered, the massive stone disc rolled back into position behind us, sealing us off from the rest of Kil Noth.

I stamped down my welling panic. Enclosed spaces and I did not get on well, especially underground. I leaned heavily on my hatred of her as I grabbed a lantern from the wall and followed her slight form down a tightly spiralling staircase. Down and down and down for an age. She did not seem to need any light, her bare feet following a familiar foot-worn path down those ancient stone steps.

My back and pits were slick with cold sweat the time the stairs opened up into a long vaulted hall, more from claustrophobic fear and stress than physical exertion. I took deep calming breaths, glad to be in a more open space, and studied the bones laying on granite slabs in long rows down the sides of the hall, great heroes arrayed in all their finery. This was Kil Noth's Hall of Ancestors, the second most sacred room in any Clansfolk hold, a place where no outsider had ever been allowed to venture. Until me, six years ago, and then only because it was on the way to the chamber where they held their most sacred of rites. On the walls behind each tomb hung weapons and prizes they had taken in battle, or great works of artistry and exquisite musical instruments. I had been too dazed from shock to examine them on my last visit.

Behind a dusty skeleton clutching a bejewelled crown and spear sat another skull on an iron spike, a heavily warded and ridiculously expensive Arcanum robe hung on a wicker frame around it. A sigil was emblazed on the front of the robes, one that I recognised from Setharii history books. Huh. I guess we now knew what happened to Elder Rannikus and his army that had attempted to invade the Clansholds. Ending up as a prize on a wall was not how I intended to go.

This great hall was not what Angharad was interested in. She led me through at a swift pace to stop before two heavily warded doorways. She placed her hand on a gold plate on the wall to the left and the stone door slid noiselessly back to reveal a strange, angular room beyond. The floor was square but the ceiling rose from the sides up into a higher point in the centre, almost like we had entered the heart of a pyramid. The walls were slick and black.

Unstoppable terror flooded through me. It was identical to the room in the Boneyards of Setharis that I had been buried alive in as an initiate, the room I thought I would die in with only a magically reanimated corpse for company. The place I went a little mad in.

My grandmother noticed my reaction, and foresaw exactly what I was about to do. Her Gift opened and her eyes flared bright with power.

My magic roared towards her mind, frantic to tear it to shreds and escape this cursed place before I was trapped all over again. *Help!* I screamed. Somebody blocked me from ripping into Angharad, sheltering her mind from the torrent ripping at it. It was not human. This was a trap. I was a fool to think the Scarrabus would not try to infest me again.

<Peace> *<Calm>* A deluge of almost-human emotion rolled over us. Angharad visibly relaxed and let go of her magic, overwhelmed and accepting.

Not me. I drew deep, and deeper still on the sea of magic as I resisted the inhuman power trying to influence me. My right hand burned with the desire to wrap around Angharad's throat and rip it out. I would die before giving in to the Scarrabus.

Apologies, Edrin Edge Walker. I am not Scarrabus.

What the f–?

The back wall rippled and something stepped through what moments ago had been solid stone. It was huge, larger even than the great silver apes of the Thousand Kingdoms to the south that it somewhat resembled, looming head and shoulders taller than me and twice as broad. It was covered in shaggy grey fur decorated with carved bone and gemstone beads. Its large sloping forehead boasted a third eye that glimmered with human intelligence.

Heart hammering, I backed away and fumbled at my belt for a knife I didn't have.

Angharad bowed in its presence, reeking of respect and admiration. "I greet ye, Eldest. I have brought the spawn o' my spawn as ye have requested." If this was the Eldest then the creature was ancient beyond belief. Its race had vanished from history and human ken long ago, or so the Arcanum had believed.

It was a beast of legend that our corrupted Setharii myths had called ogres and depicted as mindless raging beasts. "Ogarim," I said, remembering what Shadea had called that ancient desiccated corpse in the Boneyards below Setharis, the one that had once been slain by my spirit-bound blade, Dissever.

You know of my race, broken one? it said, the words brushing against my mind like a soft breeze. Despite the mental magic involved it did not feel threatening. *How?*

A gentle urging to tell all lapped against my defences, a subtle but strong invitation. I ignored the urge and kept my Gift wide open, trickling magic into my muscles and mind ready to fight for my life. The ogarim felt almost-human, which probably meant I could kill it. "What do you want with me?"

Human words are crude, it said, and I felt its frustration with humans, or 'broken ones' as it knew us. *May I…* There was a meaning there I did not understand, some sort of linkage that felt like a lesser version of the Gift-bond I had once shared with my old friend Lynas.

"Do not dare show the Eldest disrespect," my grandmother hissed. "Do as it wishes."

The ogarim felt my fear and my hatred of her, and in response it thumped its big hairy arse down on the floor, knowingly appearing less threatening. *I would show you.*

"Show me what?" I asked, suspicious.

Origin. Scarrabus. War. Future. All were accompanied by an incredibly complex interplay of emotion.

"And the Eldest will also reveal to me how ye may heal your hand," Angharad said, grinning like a cat.

I took a deep breath and pondered it. It was a risk, certainly, but the Scarrabus were ancient creatures and if we wanted more information then what better source than another ancient monster? I eased open my mental defences and probed the ogarim's mind. It was a formidable fortress, but its gate was open, allowing me to enter the inner courtyard and communicate mind-to-mind. There was no feeling of danger, only patient tolerance.

It was pleased as I touched it, and then a river of thought and emotion flowed into me. For a moment the deluge threatened to drown me, but I quickly found my balance and pushed back. Our thoughts flowed into one another, swirling and mixing, sharing…

All was peace and joy. The ogarim dwelled in small family groups within pyramids of living black stone and danced to the music of magic in vast stone temples grown from the bones of the earth itself. There was no want, no starvation or disease, no war or hatred, and no death from age, only accident. All ogarim knew all others on an intimate level that only a human tyrant like me could truly understand. If you hurt one you hurt all. What they needed they made from the elements around them, every member of their race wielding innate magic as potent as an elder magus but without the need for centuries of training or the restrictions of the Gift. They did not have pyromancers, geomancers, aeromancers or aquamacers, seers or knights, or tyrants or anything else – they had all Gifts in one.

Broken ones…

The ogarim looked up from their temples as the music faltered and the currents of magic changed. In the night sky a star guttered and went out. A few years later, another died, and in its place a sucking pit of nothingness. They felt fear, and although not a new concept, it was an uncommon thing only experienced by individuals in unforeseen peril. The eight eldest among them set out across the daemon-infested Far Realms to uncover the fate of the missing stars…

Daemons… The ogarim thought my opinion and information on the inhabitants of the Far Realms insulting and ignorant. They were alien animals and greater intelligences to match our own, and all worthy of existing as much as we did. Other realms hosted vicious predators however, and after the first death the ogarim learned to defend themselves. Which they did with unexpected and terrifying magical ferocity, though also without anger.

Eventually they travelled to a new realm close to the missing stars and discovered an intelligent species, shaped something like bears, that were tearing their own civilisation to pieces. The ogarim watched, confused and horrified as unbear slaughtered unbear. The ogarim did not understand how war was possible, not then, thinking the violence caused by disease or poison. When portals from other realms opened and unknown daemons entered this new realm to side with one faction of unbears, the ogarim thought that peacekeepers had arrived to stop the madness and heal the suffering.

Naive… The sense of regret and loss almost drove me to tears.

How could they have possibly known that the armies of the Scarrabus had arrived to aid their already-infested allies in conquering that realm?

The first taking… Its deep anger was more human than anything I had yet felt from it.

The then-Eldest of the ogarim party went to meet with the supposed peacekeepers. Then she… disappeared. This was not death, for they would have felt her passing. This was something else – a cutting of ties. When she returned to them she was no longer ogarim but attempting to pass as one, like a predator that wears the hollowed shell of another before striking. They reached into their Eldest's mind and felt what was now in her.

I shuddered, remembering my own encounter with the Scarrabus queen and its host.

War. Conquest. They understood it then. There was no reasoning with the Scarrabus. The enemy did not value all life as they did – the life of others was just another resource to be used and abused. They were selfishness incarnate.

The six surviving ogarim defended themselves and destroyed the daemon hordes of the Scarrabus in an awesome display of power that left me shaking. They felt bone-deep sadness at causing such great loss of life. The alien sky boiled and the ground burned as they disabled their Eldest and retreated back through the realms to their distant home where others better versed in healing could remove the parasite.

So foolish…

The Scarrabus infestation of their Eldest proved to be incompatible with the incredible power of the innate ogarim connection to magic. The flood of magic was slowly killing the Scarrabus, and the decaying parasite was in turn killing the ogarim. They tried to remove it from its host and keep both alive, they tried and failed and tried again but it proved impossible. Ogarim did not kill ogarim; it was not something they were capable of, so in the end they locked their Eldest away to die an unfortunate and unnatural death.

They still did not understand the enemy's uncaring desire to possess and kill other sentient beings, so they gathered at their most sacred temple with a number of Scarrabus-infested prisoners recovered from across the Far Realms and then they forced open their minds. They discovered that there were many Scarrabus queens scattered across realms near and far, each one a hive mind controlling all the lesser spawn hatched from its flesh.

The ogarim invaded the inner mind-realms of the parasite queens, linked through the minds of their offspring. I had felt the power of a Scarrabus queen, and it was no easy feat to conquer one, but somehow they managed it and learned exactly what the

Scarrabus were. Then they experienced true terror on a racial scale that sent ripples of fear infecting all ogarim that walked this land.

The ogarim knew spirits well and saw the greatest as intelligent beings no different to beings of flesh, treating them with as much respect as they granted any other sentient creature. They knew of gods too, beings made powerful by leeching life's magic from lesser daemons and primitive races that worshiped them on strange worlds. It came as no great surprise to discover that the godlike hive minds of the Scarrabus too worshipped an even greater progenitor-being, but this entity was vast and terrible beyond anything the ogarim had ever dreamed of.

The Scarrabus hive minds were obsessed with a singular goal to the exclusion of all else – the parasites called their god-beast across the void between realms to come to them, to feed and spawn, to devour life-bearing worlds whole, then to feast on the beating crystal hearts of those realms' suns, and leave the dying husk behind to collapse into dark and dense nothingness…and it was now fully aware of the ogarim.

The peaceful giants were beyond horrified. The sea of magic gave birth to suns, enormous power flowing into their hearts to make them beat with heat and light – granting the realms around them life, whose struggles and growth fed back into the sea of magic itself, enriching all in an endless cycle of life. This natural cycle was being broken to feed that entity's endless hunger.

As the stars were snuffed out one by one, coming ever closer to their home realm, ogarim searchers went out among the realms searching for answers and allies. For the first time in their history the ogarim went to war. The gathered host of their race worked a great magic, sacrificing lives to create a Shroud around their world to stop daemons from the Far Realms coming here unless summoned from within. Then they formed an army with what few strange allies they could gather and moved from realm to realm rooting out Scarrabus queens wherever they were located, burning them and their armies of enslaved daemons with overwhelming magic and bitter regret. They were victorious on the battlefield but had forgotten a danger lurked in their very home: a young Scarrabus queen had been left behind in this realm to die, but it lingered on and had been laying eggs ever since they brought back their Eldest, and those ancient ogarim had no idea it had been learning how to use the Eldest's magic.

<Pain> <So much pain> The ogarim keened with loss and regret and withdrew from all mental contact.

Another time… soon. You must understand more.

My head pounded as the images faded. But the horror remained with me. The Scarrabus were a far larger threat than I had ever dreamed of. I leaned against the wall, panting. "Sweet Lady Night, how do we fight something that eats worlds and the hearts of stars?"

It is contained. Do not worry, it answered, though it was in fact deeply worried itself. It seemed to worry about everything. I now knew enough of the ogarim to decipher that. *Worry about the Scarrabus queen. It must be destroyed before it can free their god-beast. Now that you know the history you understand the import of this.*

I licked my lips. "Free it? From where?"

Imprisoned below stone and bone and bound in chains of gods.

My stomach lurched and fell away. I knew exactly where it meant.

Setharis.

CHAPTER 15

The revelation that my entire world was merely a bright island in a vast, dark sea, and that Setharis was the enemy's real target in this realm sent me reeling. The stone underfoot began to vibrate, a deep and distant ominous rumble that sent spikes of worry through the ogarim's thoughts.

Enough. I am pained by the memory of a time become dust, and the river of now runs low. The Eldest held out a huge furry grey hand to examine my own tainted limb.

My grandmother had barely moved and I realised that for her mere seconds had passed while I had explored the ogarim's racial history and personal thoughts. It really was a far more efficient method of communication, one where nothing could possibly be misunderstood.

What did I have to lose? I pulled off my right glove and stepped forward to let the ogarim examine the hard black metal scales covering my skin. I was tall for a human, but even sitting on the floor it was still my standing height, and my hand was as a child's in its own.

It felt strange to have so much trust in a non-human creature I had just met, especially one that could rip me apart with its bare hands as easily as I tore off cooked chicken legs. And yet I knew it on an intimate level beyond all but one past lover, and it knew me from our mixing of thoughts. There was no capacity for deception in its mental make-up. Oh, it withheld information of course, as did I. The ogarim knew what privacy was and respected the inner workings of a mind.

It carefully lowered my hand and then looked to Angharad. The ether buzzed with mental power and she swayed on her feet, crystal eyes closed as her lips twitched in pain. Then it clambered to its feet and walked right through the back wall, which rippled and solidified behind it as I stared in puzzlement.

"Is that it?" I gasped. "It just up and leaves without a word?"

"Be quiet, conceited wretch," she snapped. "Show the respect it is due. Their ways are not our ways. The Eldest leaves because it must. Ye are not the most important thing in this world and ye should be honoured it chose to bestow even a portion o' its vast knowledge upon ye."

My hand twitched, wanting to be around her throat again. Showed how much she knew – I was actually pretty damn important these days. "What did it say about my hand?"

"It is a spiritual taint as opposed to a natural one. A fragment of malign spirit grows within your flesh, and it will devour ye entire unless dealt with quickly."

I flexed my hand, forcing the fingers closed against hard skin and black iron plates. The taint had indeed taken root where the broken shards of my spirit-bound blade Dissever pierced my flesh when the traitor god shattered it. I could still feel a fragment of that dark daemonic spirit in the back of my mind. "And how do we remove this spiritual taint?"

"We cannot. It has become a natural part of your blood and bone by now. But there is another who can..."

There was always a price for her help, always an angle that furthered her own goals. "Out with it."

"To force the spiritual taint from your flesh ye must form a pact with a greater spirit. Only another spirit can expel it."

I laughed. "Of course that's the only way. I knew it would all come back to your stupid fucking ritual in the end." I pointed to the ragged scars cutting down my cheek and neck. "The last time you tried to force that nonsense upon me you did this. Why should I ever trust you?"

She sneered. "Because ye have no choice. Ye were a weakling

and a cowardly boy who ran from his fears instead o' facing them like a man. You still are."

Half a year ago she might have been right. Now I was trying hard to be different.

"Think o' the power, Edrin! The Queen o' Winter will fill ye with her might. It is a great honour."

"I piss on honour and glory. I'd rather hack my own hand off," I said, moving towards the stairs from which we had come.

"Who do you think ye are to insult me in my own hold?" she demanded. "Ye are every bit as ungrateful and wretched as your mother was. I smell your fear and know ye crave the power necessary to defeat the Scarrabus. Without me ye will never achieve anything but witnessing all ye care about burn to ash."

She dared insult my mother? "Who do I think I am?" I snarled. "I crave power do I? Here, let me show you who and what I am and exactly what I can achieve without you." I stabbed my memories into her…

Limbs of writhing flesh as large as ships crushed whole streets as an abomination of flesh, blood and bone heaved the last of its mountainous bulk from the dark places below the city. Trailing tentacles snatched up corpses and screaming people and sucked them into its churning flesh.

…I growled, heaving until every muscle shook with the effort. The crystal finally broke free in a welter of blood and the screams of thousands pounded my skull more frantically than ever, then… ceased.

…Rivers of blood and fluids burst from the walls as the thing's weight crushed down. The ground decayed quickly, making the footing slippery and treacherous, but we made it back onto solid ground before whale-sized ribs snapped and the mountain of flesh collapsed in on itself.

The Magash Mora was dead.

I did that! Coward am I?

Angharad gasped with the horror and pain and emotional

turmoil, clutching her head in both hands as my memories burned through her.

Flesh burst in a welter of blood and from his insides a god came forth. My guts churned and my Gift burned as if I stood too close to an inferno. I'd boasted that I would kill this? What hubris. It sloughed off Harailt's meat suit to reveal a male figure covered head to toe in glistening blood and slime, hairless and horrible. Harailt was left a boneless, bubbling, shivering mound of discarded flesh, and yet somehow still alive. It seemed that a god's blood and power coursing through your body for so long made you hard to kill, the Worm of Magic reluctant to let go of such a desirable host. Harailt's one remaining eye looked up at me in agony and horror.

I recognised this god and shuddered. It was something ancient, more potent by far than any poxy hooded upstart. This was my patron deity, Nathair, the Thief of Life.

...of the Thief of Life's ravaged body, nothing solid remained. A lightning storm raged in the space where he'd been sitting, bolts of incandescent energy arcing inwards to a single point of blinding light where his heart had been. The storm spun around a shard of glimmering crystal, spiralling ever faster inwards until it met a single point of brilliance that eclipsed that of the Magash Mora's crystal core. His god-seed.

I did that! Weak am I? I killed a fucking god. Then I gave his god-seed away to one far more deserving of such power. Do not dare say I crave power.

"Without you I will never achieve anything?" I left my deranged and deluded grandmother vomiting on the floor and stormed through the Hall of Ancestors and up the stairs, laughing so hard that tears rolled down my scarred cheeks. To that cold, arrogant creature laughter and derision was more cutting than any knife.

"Ye will come crawling back," she screamed between retches, voice echoing up the stairwell. "Ye will need to form a pact with a powerful spirit to prevail. I have foreseen it."

I could not escape the confines of the spiral staircase fast enough. Hot anger kept the thought of darkness and cold stone walls crushing in on me at bay until I lurched back out into the room above. Finally, some peace.

Which is when I heard the clash of steel beyond the massive stone disc-door leading to the rest of the hold. There was an iron rod set into a mechanism, allowing the heavy disc to be rolled back into its recess in the wall, and when I did I found Jovian and the rest of my coterie locked in close combat with six guards, with the two door guards already unconscious. My two thralls had paused mid-punch. Struggles slowed as the others noticed me standing in the open doorway. Vaughn ceased bashing a man's helmeted head off the wall and the big brute actually looked pleased to see me.

"What's going on," I said. "Are we under attack?"

"You are well?" Jovian demanded, eyes looking past me.

"I'm fucking furious, but unharmed. Put him down, Vaughn." The clansman dropped to the floor and staggered back into the waiting arms of the other warriors. He coughed and straightening his dented helmet.

"What happened?" I demanded.

"We heard you was in trouble." Coira said, tapping her skull and shuddering. "In here, like you were trapped with a monster and we, ah..."

"We came to smash some heads," Vaughn said, grinning.

I looked to Jovian, who glanced at the moaning body by his feet and shrugged. Thinking back through my reactions in the rooms below when I had thought myself caught in a Scarrabus trap, I did reach out for help instinctively. Through a mountain of rock they had heard my call, and they came for me, unerringly knowing the way to the place where I had been taken and beating the crap out of anybody in their path. Through them I was discovering that I was more than I had been, something greater and more terrifying than a man alone.

A clansman in bloodied plaid stepped forward "You mad bastards will be sleepin' in the snow aft' this. Yer no' welcome in the hold."

I'd had more than enough of being manipulated. Forced. Cajoled. Blackmailed. By the Arcanum. By my grandmother. By the other druí of Kil Noth. By whatever the ogarim really wanted from me. Fuck what others might think, and doubly fuck being afraid of myself. My right hand burned and I wanted to ram it into somebody's face.

I reached out and seized the Clansfolk warriors' minds tight, letting not a sound escape their mouths as I sunk talons into their thoughts. "Listen well. I do not obey you, and neither do any of the Setharii. They are mine to command and I have left your vaunted seer heaving her guts up onto the floor below. If you think you can do better…"

None of them thought they could.

"Fucking interrogations? Taking our weapons? That shite is over. We have a real enemy to fight and I swear I will take you all if you get in my way." I had an illuminating new perspective on the terrible danger facing Setharis, and the entire world from what the ogarim had shown me. I was not about to let petty rivalries and pettier people impede me.

Lynas and Charra would have been proud of me. They always thought I could be better than I was, and that one day I would be. The Clansfolk and the Arcanum claimed they wanted me to be a general did they? Well now they were bloody going to get one, but not the figurehead they had intended. What was it Layla had called herself? A weapon. And now I was one I wielded myself. I had bathed in the blood of the Magash Mora, and of two gods for fuck's sake. I held a god-seed in my hands and resisted the Worm of Magic urging me to use it. If that didn't prove I was strong then nothing ever could.

I was reborn, forged anew.

I advanced down the halls shouting "Wardens! Warriors! Magi! Prepare for battle!" With my power rushing ahead of me, none of the armed Clansfolk dared try to oppose me as I took back our arms and armour, and some even seemed eager to join me if it meant taking Skallgrim heads. I could feel the frustration and chagrin inside them at being forced by their druí to sit here on their arses while Dun Bhailiol burned.

Those druí who dared darken my path wisely retreated; that or the spirits they were pacted with were far more sensible than they were.

Eva raced around a corner ahead of a group of armed Clansfolk, having heard the commotion and the rattle of weapons. She seemed smaller without her armour, and was unarmed, but behind her steel mask the stern look in that single green eye banished any thought that meant weakness. "What is this?"

"We have been invited here to make war," I said. "Not to waste time waiting for the enemy to come to us. Get your armour back on."

The group of Clansfolk behind her froze as I infiltrated their minds. Then they lined up either side to clear a path for me.

Eva's eye narrowed. "We have been told to wait for the hold's leaders to finish deliberations."

"Then I declare them finished. They shouldn't have insisted I come here in charge of an army and expect me to do nothing. This world is heading into the pyre and we don't have time to play their shitty little games. I have something you need to see. May I?"

I reached out to her mind and politely knocked to enter. She hesitated for a long moment before grudgingly acceding. We were not friends, exactly, nor ever lovers despite a brief flirtation, but we were something to each other. Whatever failings I had, we had been through unimaginable horror together and that kindled a queer sort of trust.

I showed her everything my grandmother had said, and all that the ogarim had showed me. She was not used to my magic dumping everything directly into her mind, it was overwhelming and agonising, but Eva endured. She refused to let pain rule her life.

I showed her what my grandmother in her rage had done to my face: her nails digging into my cheek, gouging flesh and muscle, ripping down across my neck towards my chest as she attempted to carve the name of her spirit into my very heart. I showed her everything.

When it became too much for her I broke the link. She slumped against the wall, head down and gasping for breath while struggling to regain her composure. When she looked up again I thought she might be grinning under the mask, a little of the old carefree battle-loving Eva in her eye. "Let's give the bastards a bloody nose."

While Clansfolk ran to check on Angharad, the Setharii army gathered and marched from Kil Noth to slow the enemy advance. A hundred plaid-clad local warriors, members of various warrior societies, came with us determined to discover the fate of Dun Bhailiol for themselves, and to return with tales of their bravery. Hiding inside these stone halls was too cowardly for their taste.

I walked at Eva's side, by her leave learning her experience in battle directly from her own memory. I was using my Gift like never before, gathering skill and knowledge from others and making it my own. It was time for me to learn, to grow, and to fuck those invading bastards up beyond all recognition. Before it was too late for us all.

CHAPTER 16

We marched northwards through the twilight shade created by the valley's high cliff walls, uphill through snow and ice, past pools of fresh meltwater and across narrow, humpbacked stone bridges arching over swollen streams. Despite treacherous footing, we made good progress by noon with the sun directly overhead offering us a vague hint of warmth. We set camp atop a flat section of a defensible steep rise that afforded a good view over the valley to act as our command centre.

Like most of the larger holds, the seat of Clan Bhailiol had been burrowed into a mountain for defence and would be considered all but impregnable by normal means. But the Skallgrim had not employed normal means. Eva had a crystal sightglass in her pack and we took turns staring out onto a distant hillside split in half, the hold inside reduced to a shattered ruin of fallen stone. A touch of magic to my eyes sharpened my vision as I examined its innards of tunnels and rooms exposed to daemon hordes that clambered over the burning rubble like an army of ants gnawing on human bones. The farmland stretching out along the valley below the hold had been churned to mud by Skallgrim feet and was choked with rubble and hide tents.

Many of the Clansfolk with us had worried about the fate of their distant kin, and on seeing the devastation they moaned in horror and gripped weapons tight, muttering oaths of bloody vengeance to their spirits. There was no love lost between the other holds and the folk of Bhailiol, but this was beyond anything they had ever experienced. It was expected for clans to raid each other for cattle and wealth and to draw swords avenging old blood feuds nobody even knew the original cause of anymore, but this lacked all honour. This was slaughter and wanton destruction. There was no glory to be found. The enemy did not desire food or wealth or even territory; they killed because they could. The mountainous Clanholds boasted little in the way of fertile croplands so such outrageous waste was an unfathomable crime to the mentality of its native populace.

Nareene was ecstatic to see the flaming death wrought upon the whole area and I thought the crazy fire-worshipper started touching herself when I turned my back on her. I had a word with Jovian to keep her well away from the incendiary supplies stowed in our baggage ponies. There was no telling what havoc she might unleash with all those powders and resins and whatnot if the idea got into her head.

I left my coterie and was joined by the other magi as we climbed a higher peak for a better view. Flocks of bone vultures circled plumes of black smoke billowing from the burning corpse of the holdfast. Far larger winged monstrosities flapped among them, scattering and snapping at the smaller daemons. The scaly beasts resembled the dragons of old Setharii legend, though fortunately for us they seemed far smaller than those great-fanged stone bones dug from the beaches of the Dragon Coast. Now that the hold had been destroyed and all resistance slaughtered, the thousands of Skallgrim who had been encamped on the valley below were busy tearing down tents and packing away their supplies. It was obvious Kil Noth was their next target.

All seven Arcanum magi stood in silence surveying the large army we pitiful few were somehow supposed stop from rampaging right through the Clanholds and out into the flat and fertile farmlands beyond. We had to hold until help arrived, but I personally doubted we could delay them for more than a few days unless Eva's military knowledge could work miracles. I could only hope that Krandus and the rest of the Arcanum were even now levelling Ironport and would soon be speeding west to take this army in the rear.

Vincent wiped sweat from his brow as he gawped at the army. "How many had they said? Four to five thousand at most was it?"

Secca shivered and pulled her black and white hood lower over her face, as if to hide. "Five to seven more like."

Eva and I exchanged glances. "The humans are not the greatest problem," she said. "We can deal with their greater numbers for a time by bottling them up in the small passes, but those daemons are a tactical nightmare equivalent to having winged cavalry. Bryden, how many could you take care of?"

The aeromancer squinted at the sky above Dun Bhailiol, trying to count. He quickly discovered that to be futile. "Not nearly enough if they swarm us."

"That's not all we need to be worried about," I added. "If I were the Scarrabus I would have infested some of those winged daemons. They will have eyes in the sky able to see everything we do and instantly communicate it to others of their kind on the ground."

Eva cursed. "Superior information wins wars. Whatever traps and trickery we can employ would be rendered useless."

Cormac stoked his red beard and nodded to Secca. "Mayhap our colleague could help with that particular problem."

The illusionist winced. "I would have to bend light over a large area. I'm not sure I could keep that up for long, but I could try."

Granville's bushy brows lowered. "Try is not good enough. Test it, and soon. I would not wish to rely on it and have you fail. In any case, these are daemons – do any here know if these bone vultures hunt through sight alone, or do they also utilise sound or smell?" It was an unsettling detail I had overlooked.

Luckily we had Eva, who had studied fighting such things. "The bone vultures are much like our birds of prey, hunting mainly by acute eyesight. The larger flying lizards I have never seen before but I imagine they will take some killing."

As we debated, I sensed a presence approaching us from below, a druí from the magical aura around them, and one that

I recognised: the interrogator, Murdoc. It would prove suicidal should a Scarrabus-infested spy learn of our plans. I turned to the others before he came within earshot: "Watch what you say here, the druí are not to be trusted. Some among them work with the Scarrabus." As far as I knew it was only Murdoc but it suited my purposes to sow distrust of all the rest as well. With my grandmother in charge they were all against me, and paranoia had always served me well.

Eva had her steel mask and the other magi's faces adopted masks of their own. We had all been trained by the Arcanum, and initiates swiftly learned to keep their secrets close or have them used against them. Children were ruthless bastards.

"Greetings," I said, pretending I'd only just noticed the newcomer.

"Edrin Walker," he said, nodding. "My name is Murdoc. I've come tae see for myself while others dicker and flap their jaws like wee old grannies down the tavern." He stared out at the scene of devastation and disaster and I watched carefully as his expression flickered between horror and… nothing. I had witnessed this before in the traitor magus Harailt, the subtle influence of the Scarrabus inside him twisting his mind and emotions towards its own ends. When it had a need to take the reins all human emotion and compassion drained away.

"The craven bastards," he said. "This cannot go unrevenged. What is the plan and how can I help?" His voice lacked anger and conviction.

A plan? He would be lucky if I… I blinked. Actually, I did have a plan, and a really good one at that. I looked back downhill to our small army squatting in the snow taking a break while we deliberated. Vaughn had brought that evil pony, Biter, with him to carry our food and supplies. Perfect bait. This could actually work.

I pointed out the vile beast, "That was good timing. Our greatest arcane weapon is stored within those saddle bags, recovered from the vaults below the ruins of the Templarum Magestus. When dusk falls we seven will gather here again to enact a great geomantic working, one powerful enough to bring all the cliff walls tumbling down to permanently seal this valley. We'll bury all those Skallgrim bastards under tons of stone. We will win with a single strike."

He looked down to the pony and one eye ticked, the only betrayal he felt any emotion at all. The Scarrabus was paying careful attention to my words.

"While we are working we cannot be disturbed, and the nature of the magic precludes the presence of mundanes. I will require yourself and a number of your most trusted Gifted druí to guard us."

He smiled, and I thought it did not originate in anything human. "Oh aye, I think I can arrange a wee surprise for the enemy."

I clapped him on the shoulder. "Excellent, then tonight will mark our total victory." The skin of my hand crawled with revulsion at touching the inhuman creature. I pitied what was left of poor Murdoc in there, but he was not going to live through the night and if it were me I would welcome death over enslavement.

We exchanged a few more forgettable words and then he took his leave to head off and gather a number of likeminded Clansfolk for our little ritual. I waited until he was well out of sight before grinning at the other magi.

Eva didn't like my look one bit. "What are you up to, you sneaky bastard?"

Granville stiffened at the use of foul language, but as it was aimed at a low-born magus like me he seemed to agree with the sentiment. He too seemed curious, knowing I possessed no such arcane weapons and that destroying the valley was a feat far beyond both him and Cormac.

"That was no human; that was a Scarrabus wearing his meat like Eva wears a suit of armour."

The others looked horrified and Vincent gasped, sneering down his long nose at me. "You traitor! You told him about our weapon!"

Even Bryden, whose head was as filled with empty air as any aeromancer I'd ever met, levelled a flat stare at him. "Have you been at the ale already?"

Vincent flushed, but was still none the wiser.

I sighed. "Does it seem like the Arcanum would entrust me of all people with anything that could destroy an entire fucking valley? I lied to them; that's what I do and that's how I win."

"But why?" he spluttered.

Eva's eye widened. "Walker is forcing the Scarrabus to strike at us tonight, here, in a place we control. Their ground forces are too far away, which leaves only their flying daemons and whatever traitors they have within the Clansfolk. Without our coteries we will seem vulnerable, and if they kill us here then their passage south is all but assured. No other hold will dare oppose them after destroying Dun Bhailiol and the Setharii magi so swiftly and so completely."

"You did say their flying cavalry was the largest threat," I reminded her.

"So your plan is to stand out here in the open is it?" Vincent said. "Guarded only by heathens under the command of a Scarrabus-infested magus? Are you cracked? That is possibly the worst plan I have ever heard."

I scratched the bristles on my chin. "Who said we would only be guarded by them?" It was far from my worst plan ever but I wasn't about to admit that. I mean, it had taken an epically stupid moment of insanity to decide to jump down the Magash Mora's throat to cut out its heart, and that seemed to work out well in the end.

"But you said… you said…"

I smirked. "I'm a liar, remember?"

Secca cleared her throat and offered a hesitant smile. "I suspect we will not even be standing where we appear to be."

Granville chuckled. "It would seem you get to test your magic sooner rather than later."

Eva studied the area. "This hilltop is deep with snow. We will make a show of clearing a circle and pile it high. It would serve as perfect hiding places for wardens."

"We will ambush the ambushers," Vincent gasped. "That's… that's…"

"Brilliant?" I said smugly. "Go on, you can say it."

"Still stupid," he said, covering his narrow face with a hand. "How can you know they will fall for it?"

My face fell. "They have eyes in the sky and traitors within, and the Scarrabus think of us as little more than cattle. They hold all the cards and they are arrogant fuckers anyway. It will work."

The pyromancer groaned. "What if they send every single flying daemon they have? Hundreds of them will tear us to shreds. I have not magic enough to burn them all."

"Aha," I said. "I have thought of that too. You are an accomplished pyromancer, Vincent, so follow me back down to camp and I will explain everything on the way. I have a special friend called Nareene who will be so very happy to meet you."

This was going to be fun. Or the worst mistake I'd ever made.

CHAPTER 17

Vincent and Nareene were sequestered inside a tent filled with all the special alchemic supplies I had requisitioned for her, supposedly deep in discussion about how they could be used to improve tonight's festivities. Blatantly ignoring the odd and animalistic grunting they were currently making, I put the rest of my coterie to work clearing a circle of snow on the hilltop. I didn't trust anybody else, and tonight's work best suited murderers and sneak thieves used to quick and silent and unscrupulous work, not wardens who might hesitate to kill unarmed people. They began piling snow up in mounds around the circumference, large enough to hide themselves when the time came. The lanky young magus, Bryden, stayed with them to keep any flying eyes from ruining our little surprise. He seemed most disturbed by my two silent thralls, and I think it served as an unwelcome reminder of just whose orders he was following.

The Skallgrim were on the move, a long line worming through the snowy mountain valley towards us. It would be slow going, the footing treacherous and the route winding, narrow, and entirely unsuitable for an army. It would take perhaps two days for them to reach our position, or three in any great force. Assuming we survived past tonight, it offered us enough time to locate suitable sites for setting ambushes and rockslides to further delay their march south.

As the sun dipped lower and dusk deepened, we seven magi assembled in the circle at the peak of the hill. The enormous grin Vincent wore had wrought a remarkable change to his entire demeanour and his sneering long face became something approaching pleasant. At our backs stood seven Gifted druí, supposedly there to guard us from the Scarrabus' daemons. Lying bastards. Still, at their backs were ten high heaps of snow containing villainous bastards ready to slit their lying throats: Diodorus and Adalwolf bore bows and had arrows dipped in one of the hired killer's most lethal poisons, made from a little brown mushroom of all things. Baldo, Andreas and my two thralls had spears buried in the snow beside them, Vaughn clutched his new big axe and the others had knife, sword and shield. I looked forward to seeing yet another Scarrabus dead. Those things had been directly responsible for Lynas' death and each and every one of the things I could kill was another little piece of vindictive joy.

We formed a circle and linked hands around a hodgepodge of elaborately decorated magical items gleaned from Granville's personal belongings – as an artificer he created such items and was rarely without some. The druí, not being trained magi, would not have the faintest idea they were not the great and powerful weapon I had claimed they were. Our 'mystic circle' made for a decent show but the handholding also allowed my magic easier access into the other magi's minds through their flesh, making it all but undetectable to the druí. *I will let you know when they are about to strike,* I thought to the others. I wasn't inside their heads but I could still feel uneasiness welling up, mental walls raised higher and subjected to constant scrutiny. Only Eva seemed to trust me, but the others didn't even really know me and their distrust was entirely understandable. I was stained by a foul reputation that even a bout of uncharacteristic heroism could not wash away.

While we stood in silence I gradually reached out to probe the 'trustworthy' locals standing guard, careful not to push too deep lest they feel it. The thoughts of only two stank of Scarrabus, the other five simply leaking a burning hatred of everything Setharii, from our corrupt morals and Setharii-centric selfishness to our pretentions of empire. They were more than happy to stick the knife in. I wondered if the uninfested humans had been promised that Kil Noth and the Clanholds would be spared if they went against the orders of Angharad and the other druí. I didn't much care what their reasons were; only the actions they were about to take mattered. Anything that sided with the Scarrabus was just another bug I would stamp on.

We waited, murmuring meaningless arcane-sounding gibberish under our breaths. Granville and Cormac caused the ground to tremble underfoot, keeping up the fictitious story of unleashing a geomantic apocalypse upon the enemy. A short while before true night I felt Eva's spike of alarm, her eyesight greatly enhanced by a knight's body magic allowing her to spot a swarm of black dots diving from above: a huge flock of bone vultures and one of the flying lizards, a fearsome thing all fang and claw.

Not yet. Wait until we can hear them. I readied my power to give the druí a push.

It was difficult not to look at oncoming danger, not to fight against our human nature, but we were magi and fighting against our desires was what we had been trained for; we managed. When the daemons were perhaps thirty seconds from attacking us, and their squawking became audible, we looked up and gasped at the same time I gently suggested the druí's attention should also be focussed upwards.

They took their gaze off us only for a moment, but that was all Secca needed. She worked her illusionary art, magic enveloping us as we carefully stepped away from the circle, rendering us invisible and leaving simulacrums behind in our stead. The druí made ready to stab us in the back the very moment we attacked the daemons, when we would be distracted and vulnerable.

Secca made our illusions look upwards, break the circle and glow with power. False fire erupted from Vincent's hands, billowing up towards screeching two-headed daemons with snapping beaks and razor-claws. Before we could cause too much damage the druí struck. Fire and lightning leapt from their hands to turn our circle of magi into a maelstrom of death, annihilating the illusions with waves of heat and visual distortion. Daemons plunged into it to finish us off and only found themselves ripping red furrows into each other.

Vincent didn't even have to set off our little surprise buried below the cleared circle – the betrayers did that all themselves. Nareene's gift to the war effort was a barrel filled with her special blend of incendiary alchemy. The ground erupted, killing two druí outright and shredding the others with sharp stone and dirt. A fireball roared into the darkling sky to consume the diving flock of daemons.

Now! I screamed. Magic flooded through my body, sharpening senses and strengthening muscles.

My coterie erupted from their heaps of snow to thrust spears into the backs of the Clansfolk druí. Vaughn swung his big axe around his head and down, splitting Murdoc's head and torso in two with a single blow, bisecting the squealing Scarrabus inside. Nareene squealed with joy as she rammed a knife into the side of another's throat and ripped it forward in a spray of blood offered to the raging fire. Swords and knives rose and fell in bloody butchery, burning bright in the firelight. The dazed Clansfolk fell in moments without knowing who had killed them, leaving us facing only burning panicked daemons.

Bone vultures fell screaming around us and the huge flying lizard roared and plunged into the snow, scales sizzling. Its tail lashed round and caved in one of my thrall's ribs, killing him instantly. I felt his death like a distant pinprick, and just as upsetting.

Diodorus and Adalwolf loosed their poisoned arrows, having no difficulty in hitting such a large beast. The shafts plunged deep into its hide. They backed away and loosed again as it surged towards them, fanged maw snapping. Then its slit eyes clouded over with red and it coughed, spraying black blood and bile across the snow. It looked confused as Diodorus' fungal concoction spread through its body, still feebly trying to reach and eat them even as it coughed up a glistening heap of its own guts. I'd always hated mushrooms and now I felt vindicated in my belief that those foul rubbery things only masqueraded as food.

As devastating as our ambush was, it still left a large flock of screaming, scorched and confused daemons milling above us. With Secca's illusion broken they quickly noticed us off to the side and came for us, claws outstretched.

"Burn," Vincent cried, thrusting his hands up. Roiling flames again roared into the flock.

The air whirled around Bryden and lashed out, clipping wings and sending a handful of daemons plunging into the heart of Vincent's inferno.

Cormac and Granville caused a dome of stone spikes to rise around us, warding off most of the bone vultures that made it through the fire. Those that did were met by Eva, blade singing as it lopped off heads. I plunged my knife in and out of any impaled daemons, finishing them off before an errant claw could rip a hole in one of us. The flock were being driven off in frantic disarray, with Vincent and Bryden picking them off.

My plan had worked perfectly. Which, given my typically shitty luck, is when everything went wrong.

Not all daemons flew, but then not all daemons needed to walk between there and here in this realm. Some could leap through the shadows and travel through their own strange realm to emerge elsewhere…

My enhanced senses gave me a split second warning before stone spikes shattered and obsidian claws the size of knives ripped through fur and cloth on my back and the skin beneath. Without that warning it would have torn out my spine. I spun and fell, landing badly, bones shrieking with pain as my blood splattered the snow all around.

The shadow cat was the size of a horse. Impenetrable blackness boiled from its fur as those burning green eyes focused on me, lusting to kill with a very personal malevolence. I had thought the entire pack dead, but apparently this one had not been present to be slaughtered at the hands of the traitor god.

I lashed out with my mind as I had with the bone vulture.

The shadow cat hissed and shook its head. The mental structure of every creature was different and my magic scrabbled to find a way in.

I'd bought only enough time to lift my right hand up to ward it off before vicious fangs crunched down. I wasn't sure who was more surprised when its fang pierced the leather glove and then broke. Inky blood gushed over the exposed black iron plates covering my hand.

A thrill of bloodlust and power as my hand drank in the daemon's magic-rich lifeblood. *Hungry!* the familiar voice of Dissever howled in the back of my head. That dark daemonic spirit had been slumbering ever since it escaped its imprisonment in my spirit-bound blade. The taint left in me was awake and it wanted blood.

My fingers clenched of their own volition, piercing the shadow cat's jaw with inhuman strength and sharpness. It roared and tossed its head, shaking me like a ragdoll, ripping my sleeve to pieces. My hand refused to let go. Had I been a mundane human I would have died.

Eva saved me from having my entire arm ripped off. She was much smaller than the daemon but twice as fierce. She shoulder-charged it to the snow, her magic-wrought strength beyond even that of the great daemonic cat. Her sword plunged deep into its flank and then ripped out in a glistening arc of darkness.

My hand plunged deeper into its flesh, feeding as the thing died and dissipated to black mist. With the surviving bone vultures in full retreat back to their Skallgrim masters, that left Eva staring at my exposed arm. The taint was visibly spreading and black iron plates rose to cover all the skin halfway up my forearm. I couldn't move it at all, though it could still feel.

"Hide that," she whispered as she flipped me onto my front and applied pressure to the wounds running down my back.

I hissed, and then used my mental skills to deaden my own sense of pain. "How bad is it?"

Her mask made it difficult to tell what she was feeling, but her eye glared accusingly. "A lot of stitching needed but your back will be fine in a couple of days. Lucky you heal fast even for a magus."

I kept my hand hidden as she waited for a medically-trained warden to bring her bag and patch me up like an old coat so I didn't bleed out.

"That plan went far better than I thought it would," Vincent said, still grinning from his earlier misadventures. He dusted ash and charred bits of daemon from his robes. "Dozens of daemons dead at our hands and Scarrabus destroyed. Not even a scratch on me."

I glared up at him until his stupid grin vanished.

I've said it before, and will hopefully never have to say it again, but I fucking hate shadow cats. Almost as much as I hate people.

CHAPTER 18

If you've never been carried on a stretcher downhill through slippery ice and uneven clumps of snow, feeling every step and bump like a knife to the back, and then had your gaping flesh sewn back together by ham-fisted butchers, well, I can assure you it is far from fun. It was downright humiliating – especially when you are meant to be this fearsome and powerful magus in charge of a whole army. Balls.

I concentrated on making the pain go away. It was not mine; it belonged to some other unlucky wretch. The stabbing pains faded to a dull ache but I didn't want them gone entirely. Pain was the body's way of warning you something wasn't right and I didn't want to start leaping about and burst my stitches and then have to go through it all over again.

Inside my tent, I lay face down on soft furs and cursed all gods, spirits and daemons. Fuck the Arcanum. Fuck the druí. And fuck the Scarrabus with a hot poker! All I wanted was some peace and quiet but oh no, they all had to go off and play their world-conquering games of fuckwittery. Was a single evening relaxing by a crackling fire with good food, good beer and good company really too much to ask for?

My brooding was interrupted as the tent door flapped back and let in a gust of chill air. I turned my head to see Eva enter, armoured in full war plate. "How are you feeling now?" she said.

I grunted and buried my face back into the fur. At least being a magus I didn't have to worry about plague spirits rotting the wounds.

Her freezing gauntlet planted itself on my bare back. I yelped and flinched away, then yelped again as my stitches pulled.

"It's just a little kitty scratch," she said. "Don't be a baby."

I bit my lip to stop the insults flying. What complaints could I possibly hurl at her? Not without getting a slap on the back anyway. To her this really was just a flesh wound. "I hate you so much," I growled.

"Hate you more," she replied. "You might be annoying but I admit that was a decent plan. Now I can head on out and we can start slowing them down without getting picked off by hordes of flying daemons. It is a better start to the campaign than I had hoped for."

I turned my face towards her, groaning as my back pulled tight. "Give me a hand up."

"Not a chance," she said. "If you rip those stitches open out in the field then you might bleed to death. It would be a shitty, pointless death for the magus who took down the Magash Mora and killed a god, wouldn't you say? And more pertinently, you would be a great inconvenience to me if I had to drag you back here again. I don't have the time or people to spare on being your nursemaid."

I hated it when she spoke sense. "But you might need the mighty Edrin Walker to haul your sorry arse out of the frying pan."

Her single eye just glowered at me, packing in a surprising amount of disdain despite the mask.

I cleared my throat. "Ah well, arrogance aside, who knows what else is waiting for you out there. It sticks in my craw that I'll be laying here like a butchered hog while you are off fighting for your life."

She shrugged, oiled steel whispering. "Things are as they are. If we cannot change something then it is best to accept it and stop complaining. Nobody wants to hear our whining. We must meet this challenge head on."

I grimaced. "I can't just loll here like a drunken lord, I need to do something useful."

She cocked her masked head, green eye flicking down across my wounds. "Well, do you have to be there physically? I know you can communicate at a distance. Could your magic serve as a secure and swift method of communication?"

I suddenly had a far better idea than mere communication. I reached out to my one remaining thrall and entered what was left of his mind: an empty burnt-out hall devoid of all independent thought and personality. I had done a thorough job and it made him an empty ale cup just waiting to be filled by my particular brew of foamy goodness. I ordered him to come to me, and as he walked towards the tent I concentrated on feeling the pull of his muscles and blood pumping with a slow and heavy thudding. I poured myself into his brain and body…

Light flashed in my eyes and I stumbled in the slush, almost falling onto the beaked axe hanging from a loop on my belt. I was dressed in rusty chain and matted furs and the rancid stench of months-old sweat was in my nose. I stared at my large and filthy hands, the fingernails long and black, then around the makeshift camp we had formed on a rise now almost free of snow. Everything was subtly different, the colours a shade duller and hazier than usual. I reached the tent and much to Jovian and Vaughn's surprise, said: "Good job with all the guarding," then entered before they got over their shock at the mute thrall suddenly speaking.

Eva turned, hand darting to the hilt of the blade at her hip.

"It seems I really can do better than that," I said, my voice deep and gruff and manly. This body was that of a warrior's, not a skinny bony thing like my own, and it only took a trickle of magic from my own body to sustain my presence.

Jovian peered through the tent flap, looking first at me and then the real me. I winked with both bodies and he swiftly retreated, looking a little green about the gills.

"Walker?" I heard the hesitant note of horror and disgust in Eva's voice.

I nodded, greasy shaggy hair falling around my bearded face. This body itched all over, hunger gnawed its belly, and one broken tooth throbbed with raw pain. I had forgotten just how weak it felt to be merely human, with all their bodies' weaknesses. Physically I wouldn't be any more use than one of her wardens but I wondered what else I could do. From inside this body I reached out to Eva's mind.

She flinched back. *Out!*

"I guess that works too."

She was not exactly impressed. "The next time you do that without my permission I will hurt you so badly you will be screaming for a week. You can touch my mind in an emergency, but try anything else and whatever trust we have built together turns to ash. If you want to play the tyrant then I will treat you like one." Her gaze dipped to the sword at her hip.

I swallowed – in two bodies at once – and nodded. "I apologise. It won't happen again."

"It better not," she replied. "You have abused my trust once, when you opened yourself to me and touched my face. I am not the forgiving and forgetting sort."

I fled my thrall's body and slunk back to my own brutalised flesh. "Nor should you be," I groaned. "I'm sorry. I fucked up. I've spent ten years alone only caring about myself, and it's been… difficult adjusting to being back home. It's not an excuse, but there it is."

She remained silent for some time. "It is not my job to educate you."

"No," I agreed. "It's all on me to become better, not on everybody else to tolerate me and tell me when I step out of line. I'm not a child. I am trying."

She grunted. "See that you continue to. Well, let us say no more about it." She edged around my motionless thrall, disgusted as much by what he was as the rancid stench.

"Stay safe," I said. "I'm not sure how far or for how long I can reach out to help you."

"I'm sure I can manage a few smelly, bearded heathens," she replied, stepping out of the tent and preparing her parting shot. "Hopefully they will all prove as foolish as you."

Thanks, Eva. Still, it was not undeserved.

She left to lead a small chosen force out onto the icy rock to blunt the nose of the Skallgrim advance. Me, I got to lie here under guard until my wounds closed enough that I was no longer a liability.

I slipped back into my thrall's mind and decided to join her for as long as I could. But first I needed to wash this stinking barbarian body before it made me throw up. I left the camp to locate an icy stream and peeled off my furs and mail, layers of congealed grease and mouldering skin coming off with it. Had I been in my own body with a nose not used to the stench I might have gagged. This one was not in the best of health, but that wasn't terribly surprising given he hadn't washed since Black Autumn.

I stepped into the water and gasped as the cold burned against my ankles. As I hastily began scrubbing with water and grit, the stream darkened with filth. While washing, I couldn't help but think of Eva and Jovian's reaction to what I was doing. The perverse morality of wearing another human body was not lost on me, but nor did I really care if I was brutally honest. He had attacked Setharis and paid the ultimate price. If this body could help protect Eva then I felt no guilt about riding it to destruction. I knew I was sliding closer towards the monster that the Arcanum always feared I would become, but needs must, and like me, any Docklander would put pragmatism far above morality. Morality and ethics didn't fill your belly with food. Which is not to say what I was doing was not creepy as all fuck…

I dunked his head into the water and frantically scrubbed at the greasy hair, but moments later I couldn't take the cold any longer and ran for dry clothing. I dressed, hefted my axe, and then went to join Eva's expedition north.

She had decided to leave the heavy infantry here while taking thirty wardens armed only with bow and spear and fifty local Clansfolk warriors who knew the lay of the land and all the secret cattle rustling paths. Cormac, Granville and Bryden were to accompany us, though after our battle with the daemons none looked especially pleased about leaving the safety of our camp. I had to admit, Cormac did look rather fine today. Had he trimmed and oiled his lovely bushy red beard?

That brought me up short. I looked over the men and women readying to march north – but mostly the men. Then it dawned that this particular body I was wearing had a beard fetish. As much as I wore this body, it seemed to also influence my thinking in return. The flesh remembered pleasure and pain and movement of the muscles, but precious little else as fluids gushed about and the various organs did all the things I had no real knowledge about.

An untidily-bearded warden blocked my path as I sought to approach Eva. "Piss off, idiot mute. Head on back to your own degenerate magus."

My fist slammed into his face before I could think about it, sending the warden sprawling in the dirt with a split lip. He lay dazed and bleeding.

These muscles remembered exactly how to punch with maximum force, and were far more proficient than I had ever been. Apparently this body was used to reacting to aggression with extreme violence, and the merest twitch of muscle had set it off. Magic influenced the body and the body and its Gift influenced the magic, that much was common knowledge, but no magus had truly explored the role of the mind on the other two – how could they without slipping on a new suit of meat?

Eva's wardens closed ranks around her. The spearman nearest me levelled the point at my chest.

Fuck off, I told him.

"Righto," he said, and wandered off as the other wardens looked on in disbelief.

Eva turned and grimaced. "Leave me; this one is Edrin Walker's aide." The way she emphasised that last word left me in no illusion that she would be most displeased if I horrified them by revealing who was really behind this face. These people had no real need to know about that, and if they already thought my mental trickery was worrying then this would be an utterly nightmarish situation for them. They would not be in the right mind to do their job.

"Hello," I said cheerily as I wandered over to her. "I'm here to watch your back."

She sighed. "Yes, because you have proven so good at watching your own."

I pouted. "Unfair."

"But accurate," she replied. "If you are sticking around then you will be polite and obey the orders of the magi, as befits an unGifted warrior."

I smirked.

She pinched the skin on the back of my hand between two steel-clad fingers. "Can you feel that?"

"Ow! Yes!" I was so deep inside this body it felt every bit as painful as if it were my own.

She looked shrewdly pleased. "Good… good."

"Ah. I will play the part."

"I thought you might." She looked me up and down, noting dirty furs and rusted mail. "For the sake of the gods, go find a helmet or…" she shook her head like I was an imbecile.

I took her advice and using my particular skills of persuasion, acquired a spare pothelm and arming cap from a quartermaster only too happy to please, donned the cap and then stuffed the slightly overlarge helm on top. I didn't much like my vision being restricted to slits and holes in a faceplate but it wasn't as bad as I'd been led to believe.

With the foreplay over with, Eva proceeded onto the main event – war. Bryden, fifteen wardens and twenty Clansfolk headed towards a small goat track climbing up towards the hills on the east side of the valley. Sadly Cormac and his lovely lush beard went with them. I grimaced and bit my own… his… no, this body's cheek. This was all wrong. I didn't. Like. Beards. Like. That.

Eva, Granville, myself, the other fifteen wardens and thirty angry Clansfolk headed up a steep and slippery escarpment leading to the west side of the rise above our camp. The assembled warriors kept glancing at me curiously, until I realised that none of them currently wore their helms. After all, we were not in combat or anywhere near the enemy… I flushed and removed it for now, tying it to my belt with a leather thong. Much better.

For a day and night the Clansfolk led us along their secret paths either side of the valley – time was far more important than sleep or safety. It was a gruelling and dangerous hike navigating narrow moonlit ridges across rocky crags by the meagre light of shuttered lanterns. Two of our men slipped down scree slopes and broke their legs. We had no time to spare and were forced to leave them behind to crawl back to camp on their own. My borrowed body grew weary and slow with shocking swiftness – this crushing tiredness was what it was to be a mundane human. Eva and Granville powered on until dawn as the rest of us flagged. How did normal people cope with this fatigue on a daily basis? I dared not try to work my small talent with body magic on this borrowed flesh – or even if that was possible. I didn't yet know it well enough to try to tinker with it, and it was far, far less resilient than my own Gifted form. Exploding it might prove bad for morale.

As we drew closer to the advancing enemy snaking through the valley we shed men at key narrow points suitable for ambushes. They began to work on the boulders, digging their bases free from earth and stone ready to be shoved down to crash on any people and daemons passing below, and with any luck start a small avalanche to block the pass for a time until they dug it free.

Just before dawn we took position at the narrowest point between Dun Bhailiol and Kil Noth. We secured armour, pulled on helms and gauntlets, readied weapons and waited beneath a jagged ridge for the enemy to march right into our trap. Eva kept watch on the skies for daemons, a heavy war bow ready in her hands. One eye or not, she was still the best shot we had.

I nodded to a scarred woman next to me dressed in Dun Clachan plaids. She grinned back, feral and furious. "I'll take six heads afore we send them scurrying back to their ratholes. What about you, big man?"

I thought about it. "Couple hundred I reckon."

Her grin widened and she clapped me on the back. "That's the spirit! Good to have a goal right enough."

I was being deadly serious.

A light blinked on and off from the other side of the valley. Eva signalled back, flicking her lantern shutters open and closed in a pre-arranged sequence. We were ready to strike from both sides of the valley. Granville rolled up the sleeves of his fine robe and placed his hands on the stone to allow his magic to gain a better feel of it. He smiled and I knew we were ready to wreak havoc.

CHAPTER 19

From our safe vantage point, we watched the Skallgrim scouts moving through the narrowest point of the entire valley – a mere ten paces wide and fifty long – their keen eyes scouring the way ahead through a thin morning mist that coiled around them like a living thing. They paused to listen at every scuff of foot on stone, bird cry and crack of ice and rock, as if they too had heard chilling tales of entire armies disappearing into the misty depths of the Clanholds. Although knowing what I did about the Scarrabus they undoubtedly feared failing their masters more than fighting us. It would be wise to learn exactly what they knew and it occurred to me that I should probably see about capturing one alive without burning out their mind and memory.

"Knowledge is power," Eva whispered to me with eerie synchronicity. "And knowledge of terrain has won many a battle against superior forces."

She glanced to Granville, his eyes closed and fingers sunk deep into solid rock. "We have knowledge, terrain, and magic all on our side. This will be a slaughter." She waited until the Skallgrim scouts had passed and the armoured vanguard were halfway through before flashing another signal towards the far side of the valley.

Down on the valley floor one of the Skallgrim noticed the blinking light and pointed up, but it was far too late to do anything about what was coming.

Never fight a geomancer in the mountains, and always, always flee from two. The ground thumped like a giant had punched it, and I watched in awe as Granville, and Cormac over on the far side of the valley, caused the entire rock face on either side to shatter and slide down in an inexorable mass towards the Skallgrim advance. The enemy found themselves trapped between two oncoming waves of rumbling rock, ice and snow. Their terror was a sharp knife twisting in my gut as they fought and climbed over each other in desperation to escape forward or back. Only a few made it out before the avalanches hit, their relief a fluttering thing with heavy wings of guilt.

It crashed down on the heads of the enemy, killing the lucky ones outright. Others were buried alive, broken and bleeding and gasping for breath as rock squeezed hard on cracked ribs. I shuddered and looked away, remembering my own entombment beneath the earth only too well. Unlike me, I doubted anybody would spend the time to dig them out – they would probably perish of thirst or frostbite after a long and drawn-out ordeal. It was a horrific way to die.

Back in the city I used to think that water and fire were the two deadliest elemental affinities a Gift could boast, one swift and deadly, the other capable of massive destruction and fear. I was now reassessing that opinion.

Eva shoved me back from the icy ridge. Fire bloomed across rock with an angry hiss. "Halrúna," Eva stated. "Two-no, three, coming up to examine the rockfall."

My breath rasped loud inside the helmet. I grinned and patted my axe. She shook her head. "Not here, not now. We are to delay them and bleed them dry from many cuts. A pitched battle would be…" She trailed off, then cursed. "Bloody idiots!"

Clansfolk were descending the opposite side of the valley, nimble as mountain goats, while others perched on the very edge and began loosing arrows and screaming about revenge for Dun Bhailiol. The Skallgrim that had made it through before we blocked the pass bunched together and linked shields, arrows tinging off helms, only a few finding flesh.

Before Eva could stop them the Clansfolk on our side leapt to their feet and charged, not willing to be shown up as cowards by their kin.

"At the craven blood-drinkers!" the woman next to me cried as she launched herself down the slope, sailing downwards on a wave of snow and loose rock. Glory called to them and they answered eagerly.

Eva and Granville exchanged glances. "This blockage will not delay their army long," he said. "Not with shaman and daemons to call on. The Clansfolk here will not withstand them."

The Setharii wardens shifted nervously, awaiting the command to fling themselves into battle. "We stick to our plan and retreat to the previous position," Eva ordered. "Walker, you stay and help these bloodthirsty fools – every sword you save here may prove vital later. It's not like you will be in any real danger down there after all."

I groaned and for a moment Granville looked bewildered. I wasn't here as far as he knew.

I slapped a fist over my borrowed heart. "As you command, lord knight."

Granville's cheeks bulged and his face paled at the realisation of what I was doing. He knew I was incapacitated and had also known this body was a witless thrall of my magic's making. His cheeks reddened and his bushy eyebrows shook with fury.

"This is an abomination!" he roared. "How dare you treat the lives of others so cheaply. By the gods, are you even human anymore?"

"Fuck off, Granville," I said. "This body is a casualty of war so I might as well make use of it. And watch your tongue from now on. I am done with your derision and stuck-up attitude. If I have to hollow you out and wear you like a cheap tunic then that's fine with me. I don't really need you intact to use your Gift."

Eva hauled me up and over the ridge like I weighed no more than a sick puppy. "Fight the enemy, not each other." Then she let go and I was sliding downhill on loose stone and pebbles, heart pounding, screaming, arms flailing for balance.

It was a terrifyingly swift descent before I thumped into snow drifts in the crevice between cliff and valley floor. I rose bruised and scraped but with my axe in my hand and ready to fight. The air was dusty and earthy, seasoned with the metallic tang of spilt blood.

I surveyed the blocked pass and the boulders already rolling free of the rockfall – the magic of the halrúna would not allow us much time to play with the enemy on this side and a pack of dog-like daemons were already clambering over it.

The Skallgrim were in a tight and disciplined defensive circle, mailed axemen at the front with shields raised and a few spearmen in the centre thrusting out and over at the raging Clansfolk thundering into the shield wall in waves, swords up and stabbing down trying to pierce Skallgrim eyes and hands or slashing down to sever toes. Screams of rage and pain echoed through the valley.

Their battle-blood was up and infecting me, making me want to fling myself into the fray. I waded through deep snow towards the circled warriors and drew deep on my Gift. The linkage back to my real body was an imperfect thing and it felt weak and strained by the distance. The Gift-bond to my old friend Lynas had also thinned with distance on my travels through Kaladon so this came as no great surprise. Still, it would prove more than enough to deal with these crude heathens.

The battle ahead was frantic and fragmented, confused and split into moments of panic and pain. The conscious mind closed down in such times, making it easy for me to slip in and wreak havoc.

I infiltrated a Skallgrim spearman's mind first: in the fog of battle he noticed a Clansman break through the shield wall so he stabbed him through the belly. His Skallgrim friend fell with a spear through the kidney, skewered from behind.

The warrior next to the fallen man turned and saw a plaid-clad warrior with a spear behind him, the one that had killed his friend. He swung his axe and the spearman went down clutching a ruined face. It was a joy to take them apart from within, a glorious song composed of notes of misdirection and sleight of eye. Lost in the moment they were mere actors in a play of my devising, and they would all die when the curtain closed.

The defensive circle collapsed as Skallgrim butchered each other, allowing the Clansfolk to cut them to pieces.

I picked a man in finer mail clutching an expensive rune-etched axe and called him to me. "This one is my prisoner," I said to the Clansfolk. "Harm him and die. He is magically bound to obey me now." His eyes were wide and terrified as I slithered in and out of his mind, nailing orders and restrictions of behaviour in place. He dropped his axe and shield and stepped close to me.

"You a druí?" the woman I'd met atop the ridge asked, the blood of her enemies spattered all over her face. She eyed my clean axe and the warrior I'd taken, and kept well clear of me.

"Something like that," I said.

"Next time I'd prefer to beat them myself without yer help," she chided.

I shrugged. "Kill faster then."

That earned a chuckle.

However, all of a sudden I didn't feel quite as jolly. Something was coming towards us from the north side of the avalanche, beyond the pack of daemons and the halrúna trying to remove the mess we'd landed on them. Whatever it was, it made my stomach churn, the sort of might that reminded me of the time I'd stood waiting for the god Nathair, the Thief of Life to come and kill me. My Gift screamed for me to leave and if it was one thing I was good at it was knowing when to run away.

"We had best get the fuck out of here," I said. "Death will be on us shortly." I didn't wait for them, I took to my heels with my prisoner jogging along behind me. After a confused moment of watching the druí fleeing as fast as his legs could carry him, the Clansfolk followed, casting fearful glances back as boulders began exploding from the blockage.

They whooped and hollered and screamed prayers to their spirits, glutted on the blood of their enemies and exalting in victory. It was infectious and I felt my lips twist into a grin and my body flush with the joy that only people who have kicked death in the face and then legged it can know. Humans were bred to fight and win, to take joy in proving themselves better than others, and to strive for ever-greater knowledge, skill and power. I wondered if the magic present in our race had gifted us this basic human drive to succeed. It certainly heightened that desire in us magi when we used it. It felt so damned good to wield power.

We didn't try to climb back up the steep side of the valley via secret paths and hidden tracks – that would be slow going and make our exposed backs prime targets for Skallgrim archers once they broke through. Even a city-boy like me knew not to try that. Instead we sprinted past abandoned farmsteads and still hamlets and puffed and panted along the cart-rutted slushy track leading south towards Kil Noth. I hoped Eva and the wardens would be at the next position ready for the next ambush.

A series of booms echoed down the valley, shaking stones and ice loose from the cliff walls. I glanced back to see the pass opened once more and the army squeezing through the narrows. A halrúna was rising into the air accompanied by a dozen bone vultures and one of those large, scaly lizards.

I stopped to catch my breath. Even with my power weakened by distance from my real body, if I could see that halrúna then I had every confidence I could kill him. I reached out for his mind.

Oh shit. I flinched back before touching him, barely avoiding the notice of whatever great power was back there. The Scarrabus were inside that halrúna and he thrummed with power both human and of their making. Something with immense magic was currently looking through his eyes.

Two hulking serpentine forms shoved the Skallgrim aside and squeezed through the pass, each creature twelve foot tall and at least thirty feet long, with six golden slitted eyes burning below jagged crowns of black iron. All along their bodies small claws opened and closed, and in their two main limbs they held huge, black saw-toothed blades capable of cutting through almost anything. A ravak daemon was almost a match for an elder magus, and here were two of the fucking things.

The massive daemons flanked a silk-covered palanquin carried on the back of some great iridescent armoured beetle inlaid with gold and jewels. Once through the pass the creature lay down and folded its legs away out of sight. Their leader wore ornate robes of the most ancient design, voluminous enough to hide any physical sign of male or female and dyed the rare blue of lapis lazuli from the desert of Escharr. On their brow, above a bald scalp, sat an ornate crown of twisted red gold and rubies. To me they appeared like a dark abbot of a perverse heathen religion. The ravak bowed before them as they waited for the army to filter through the narrow pass and form up in front.

I felt queasy as the flush of previous victory dropped away like the onset of a bad case of dysentery. Whoever or whatever that was, they were the great power I had sensed within the halrúna aeromancer and I wanted nothing to do with it. Fortunately their attention was still fixated on the halrúna in the sky, studying the lay of the land.

A howl was taken up by throats that belonged to no hound ever born on this world. A pack of scaled canine daemons with blood-red eyes erupted from the enemy lines and ploughed lines in the snow towards us. They would probably catch up with us in a worrying short space of time.

"Run for your lives," I shouted. The chances of any of us surviving this, never mind holding them for long, had dwindled to almost nothing.

CHAPTER 20

This body tired so easily compared to my own, and that scrawny thing I called home was more unfit than any magus' body had a right to be with magic to call on. My calves burned and a stabbing pain under my ribs suggested something was ready to burst out in a spray of blood. The back of my throat seared with bile and my breath rasped in and out of the helmet, the restricted airflow suffocating. This whole body ached like I was too big for its skin, and maybe I was at that. The prisoner kept pace with me against his will, but was having a far easier time of it than I was.

Most of these locals were fitter and faster than this underfed body that had spent time in the depths of the Black Garden, but others faltered and fell by the wayside due to wounds taken in the fight. They doubled over heaving for breath or limped along clutching bleeding thighs. I left them to it and kept on running, terrified that what was behind us would catch up – and I didn't mean that stupid pack of dog-daemons.

The slowest among us screamed as the creatures reached them, although fortunately the pack of daemons seemed to prefer hunting individuals, bringing them down and savaging until their prey was dead, before moving onwards. It bought us time to reach the next ambush point.

Five or six had fallen before the valley narrowed once more. I ran through and then stumbled to a stop among the gathered Clansfolk, my legs like a newborn colt's and my bearded face and back drenched in steaming sweat. My stinging eyes scanned the icy cliffs on either side but saw no trace of Eva or her wardens.

The Clansfolk formed a battle line as the daemons howled towards us. They readied swords and shields and roared their defiance. The daemons were faster and would cut us to pieces if we kept running, so a pitched battle it was.

I joined them with my axe in hand, the freezing steel biting my fingers. The Skallgrim prisoner I kept out of the way behind us, sat in the snow and unable to move.

They came at us in a disorganised mass of slavering fury – teeth bared and bloodied. Ten paces from us I loosed my magic, a battering ram of unsubtle power that pitched three scaled snouts down into the dirt and left them dazed and drooling.

I winced as my skull throbbed with unaccustomed pain: this body could not handle so much magic roaring through it. My guts churned as their temperature rose. Muscles twitched and bone creaked inside me as changes began with fearsome swiftness.

No time to dwell. I swung my axe but mistimed the blow, gouging a trench in the daemon's shoulder rather than smashing the scaly canine's brains in as I'd intended, but it proved enough to knock it back a step.

The man to my left went down with a daemon gnawing on his throat. The woman to my right brained one with the rim of her shield and rammed a blade through its eye to finish it off.

The enemy was fast and vicious but no match for the ferocious hillfolk and their cold steel. I roared as my axe came down again, this time cutting off a paw and caving in its flank. The fangs of another beast fastened on my left forearm and it wrenched me to one side. My axe fell.

No choice but to use more magic, tweaking fleshy bits and reinforcing muscle. My heart thundered, straining to burst from my ribs. Blood gushed down my beard and bubbled across metal eyeslits. I punched the fucker in the eye, right-handed hammer blows that reduced scaled face and knuckles both to bloodied scraps of flesh and bone.

A hand on my shoulder – the woman from before staring at

my hand. "Yon beastie is dead. Best see to your wounds a'fore the plague spirits get in." She shuddered. "Too late – already turning black, so it is. Those things must be venomous."

It wasn't venom. My bloodied right hand was darkening as black plates began spreading across it – my spiritual taint had followed me here to this body and was feeding on the bloodshed.

Then the internal pain hit. I pulled back and distanced myself a little from this body; losing some fine muscle control was a small price to keep it to a dull and ghostly ache. This thrall could not last much longer. The heart would soon burst under the strain, and if not I would have to see it burned myself. An overdose of magic was flooding its blood and bones, far too much for any unGifted body to cope with. The Worm of Magic was gleefully twisting its insides and I didn't want to wait and find out what monstrosity would be left behind when it was finished.

"Run on," I gasped. "Take this prisoner safely back to camp and straight to Magus Edrin Walker to interrogate." I went into my captive's head and made the necessary adjustments to his orders. My skull was being pounded like an anvil.

"That black-hearted tyrant?" she gasped. "I want no truck with the likes o'him."

I grimaced and clutched my right hand as the blackness oozed up the wrist. "Oh, it's far too late for that. You see, you've been palling about with me all this time. I did say I was *something* like a druí."

She hissed and stepped back, clutching a small charm bag tied to her belt. Fat lot of use that superstitious nonsense would be against me.

I doubled over and vomited blood. "Cockrot. This body is coming apart at the seams but I can still buy you time. Maybe I'll even get to a hundred."

She backed away, pale and terrified.

"Take him with you. Or else."

She swallowed and nodded, grabbed the prisoner and ran.

I watched her go as nausea warred with pain in a three-sided battle with a rising ecstasy. The pain was turning to pleasure, a sure sign that the Worm was almost done making a monster out of a man. I was so deep inside this body it might as well be my own, and it was beginning to dawn on me that inhabiting it came with mental and magical dangers I hadn't considered.

As the Clansfolk retreated I staggered to my feet and found my axe again. Blood ran down my arms and made the grip slippery, but this body would soon be dead whatever I did. Its soaked clothing was beginning to freeze and it shivered uncontrollably, so even if it survived the battle, it could not survive the cold.

I spat blood and bile and scanned the cliff walls. Still no sign of Eva. Where were they? I was in no state to find out using magic. This body's best use was facing the enemy to learn what I could before it expired. It would certainly hurt, but they couldn't kill me… or so I hoped. It was all guesswork at this point.

I didn't have to wait long. With the two ravak in the lead, the giant beetle-borne palanquin lumbered down the valley towards me. It was followed by a long tail of Skallgrim warriors blowing horns and thumping shields in a savage, rhythmic beat. What a fool their leader was to come at the head of their army. Eva's ambush would hopefully destroy them.

An enormous magical presence brushed my mind. The fuck? That was… that was my magic! Except, it was far weightier than my own, strong as I was.

Oh.

Fucking.

Shite.

I suddenly needed to piss. Badly.

That dreadful presence inside the palanquin could only be one thing: another tyrant. And an elder magus at that.

I greet you, Edrin Walker. The voice blasted against my mental defences like a signal-horn held to my ear.

The thoughts were shaped in Old Escharric with inflections of superiority of power and position, the way a master would speak to a servant. It also dripped with Scarrabus stain. I had felt this mind once before, back when I delved into the Scarrabus mindscape through the unfortunate Rikkard Carse's mind.

He, and it was a he apparently, was an infested tyrant, and the very host of the Scarrabus queen too. It was nightmare fuel for the rest of the world.

Sod the risk, I had to warn Eva. If I could find their minds up there then so could the enemy. It didn't matter to a tyrant if they couldn't see with eyes, but I had the advantage of knowing they were there already.

My skin burned all over, and something burst with a wet pop inside my chest, but I found my allies' minds as masses of nervousness hiding out of sight.

The enemy leader is an elder tyrant, I projected. *Run now. The greater the distance the more ground they have to search for you – run before they take you!* After a moment of panic Eva leapt into action, signalling our allies on the far side of the valley and then fleeing with her wardens.

Can you hold them? she asked.

I shrugged in my mind. They wouldn't get far if I didn't, so we were about to find out. *Oh hello there,* I said to the enemy tyrant. *Are you the big blue bugger I spotted earlier? The one too lazy to walk?* I swallowed and gripped my axe tight. The weapon would be useless here, but its solid presence did comfort me.

<Shock> <Anger> <Disdain> You dare talk to me in such a manner you ignorant wretch?

If he knew my name you would have imagined he might have known what to expect from me.

Sure I do. You Scarrabus-vermin have the mind of a gnat if you thought I would be polite about it. In what world would I ever give a crap about being polite to parasites?

There was a moment before realisation kicked in. *Ahhh, no, ignorant one. Your thinking is false. You have the highest honour of speaking to the great Abrax-Masud. Bow before me and I shall let you serve me.* That name was supposed to mean something, dripping with expectation. *If you do not bow you will serve me all the same, as a slave.*

I scratched my gore-crusted beard. *What, old Abrax from Masud Lane? Pretty sure you were a cobbler, so why are you here in fancy robes? A little old to be playing dress-up are we not?* All I could do was still him and keep his attention on me to buy time for the others to escape.

He slapped me with immense power and my mind rocked from the blow, almost torn from this dying body entirely. And yet I could feel that for him it was a mere tap. I burrowed in deeper and held on tight.

I am Abrax-Masud, the last living magus of immortal Escharr, the greatest seat of learning this world has ever known.

I could feel the sincerity in his thoughts. Bollocks on a hot plate, he really was an elder magus, the oldest in existence if he spoke truly, and would be capable of wielding godly power by any reckoning. He would likely be an adept of most known magics, and perhaps a few other arts lost in the fall of Escharr. Oh well, if you dip a toe into cold water you may as well jump right in and get it over with.

Escharr, what those crappy old ruins with architecture that look like children stacked a bunch of blocks? It was about as immortal as my stinky old boots. Pah, greatest seat of learning? You are badly out of date. The Great Library at Sumart in Ahram holds more lore than your shitty little empire ever created. I hear they even have an entire building full of woodcut illustrated sex manuals. I mean, really, did your lot of crusty old farts ever boast anything like that?

And then he killed me.

I looked down at the smoking hole through my chest, confounded and confused. Fucking elders and their fucking magic. He howled with incandescent rage – quite literally igniting the silk palanquin around him.

As this body pitched forward into the snow I tried to flee back to my own, but his power grasped a trailing part of me and held on. He came for me; a raging inferno. The world grew dim and dark as the body I currently inhabited slid towards death, heart stopping, brain starved of blood. Black tendrils of nothingness reached for me, trying to drag my mind down into death along with the flesh.

The cliff above Abrax-Masud exploded, showering the army with massive boulders. Granville stood proud at the jagged edge of the cliff, bushy eyebrows lowered in concentration as he pierced the ravak and Skallgrim with spikes of stone. The proud fool had stayed behind to cover the retreat. Men died screaming, punctured and crushed by stone. The entire valley trembled as more debris hurtled into the path of the army. Even as I danced with death it was awesome to behold. A spear of stone shot towards the burning palanquin.

Abrax-Masud was not afraid of mere fire or stone, but he didn't care to test his immortality against the death overtaking this body. He let go of me. Granville screamed as the air ripped him from the earth and tore him limb from limb, scattering the spurting pieces all over the army. Me, I escaped by a whisker, with only the chill of oblivion in me and death's dank breath caressing the back of my neck.

I sat up gasping for air and drenched in cold sweat, back in camp and back in my own body, stitches and all. That had been far too close for comfort. I wrapped my clumsy gloved hands around myself and rocked, trying to forget that cold, dark embrace.

Eventually it dawned on me that if the Scarrabus Queen and its host were here in the Clanholds, then just what the fuck did they have waiting for the Arcanum army at the enemy's supposed stronghold of Ironport?

CHAPTER 21

As the human mind is wont to do in order to protect itself, the razor-edged panic of my nearness to death quickly blunted and began fading to a rusty memory. We are so very talented at fooling ourselves. I took deep, regular breaths. When I calmed down, I sensed I had company. A quiet presence had been waiting outside the tent for what I suspected was quite some time. The Eldest of the ogarim had travelled all the way from its weird black pyramid inside Kil Noth for an audience.

I dressed carefully; every movement an agony. My hands were clumsy and nigh-useless things, one a lump of tainted iron and the other taken by fits of twitching and trembling at the slightest movement. I found it immensely frustrating, especially after enjoying the use of two working hands again, borrowed though they were. It occurred to me that we didn't realise how much we took things for granted until we lost them. A missing leg or hand would make you look at the entire world differently when a step or a door posed a challenge, and it made tying my gods-damned belt an exercise in choking down anger.

Talking about choking, my mouth was a desert and my belly rumbled angrily – of course, I hadn't been in this body for a day and a night so I hadn't actually had anything to eat or drink save whatever Jovian might have poured down my throat, if the mad little Esbanian had even thought of it.

I exited the tent and winced against the afternoon sun, sinking low and red over the half-frozen and shadow-wreathed valley. The looming bulk of the white-furred ogarim was stood waiting right out in the open and my coterie guarding the tent were completely oblivious of either it or myself. The Eldest was in their minds fogging all memory and perception with the casual ease afforded by millennia of practice.

Come with me to a place of power, it thought. *I must show you more. You must make an informed choice.*

That did not sound good.

I shook my head. *I need to warn them about the elder tyrant and Scarrabus queen. Can't you just quickly dump all I need to know into my brain as you did before?*

It exhaled, its breath sharp with the scent of raw onion. *They can do nothing until your other humans return. The full understanding of this ancient knowledge is more important and will require a period of reflection. You have time enough to do both.*

Its urgency pressed on me like a lead weight, so I nodded my acceptance.

It led me through the camp, past men and women busy preparing wooden stakes, sharpening blades and fletching arrows. Their mood was nervously buoyant – they had no idea it had all gone to shite in the north and our forces were fleeing for their lives. I spotted Secca in her black and white hood and she paused, brow furrowed, eyes scanning across the camp as if for a second she had sensed something was amiss. I thought about passing on a warning of what was happening to the north, but the ogarim warned we would be revealed and delayed. Everything that could be done was already being done. She blinked, shook her head and moved on.

How far away was Eva now? Could I contact her?

I opened myself up and reached out across the valley, speeding north as far as I dared, as far as I could without straining my Gift, but it was a big place and I found no sign of her mind, or any of her wardens. It was as futile as looking for a handful of raindrops causing ripples somewhere on the surface of a lake. Hopefully that meant she would also be safe from that smug shite Abrax-Masud as well.

We took our time climbing a gentle incline above camp. I

didn't think the ogarim kept a relaxed pace out of consideration, and thought it more likely it was never in a habit of rushing anywhere. At the peak of the hill a stone circle had once stood proud, the great slabs worn down by age and element until only stumps remained jutting from the bones of the hill. Nearby lay the crumbling ruins of an ancient temple of human design, the remaining vaulted arches and tumbled granite blocks only hinting at the vastness of some ancient clan's long-vanished halls and forgotten gods.

The Eldest entered the stone circle and planted its great hairy arse down in the very centre, heedless of the snow. I had to kneel, and even that was an ordeal, the wounds in my back pulling tight. It said nothing and my impatience grew – Eva was out there fighting, fleeing, dying; I didn't know which.

This is a place of peace and power where the magic sings if you open yourself to it. I got the distinct impression it thought me incapable of that kind of subtlety. *Long ago the elders of my race gathered here to share their wisdom. Here we shall wait until the stars emerge and broken Elunnai rises to her fullness. <Guilt> <Regret>*

"No we bloody won't," I replied aloud through irritation. "I don't give a crap about your crusty old traditions. People are dying out there and the enemy is upon us. Why would I care about a gods-damned history lesson? Tell me what you want right now or I'm fucking off to go and do something actually useful."

A glacial, slow surge of irritation submerged just as slowly back beneath calm waters. *So be it.*

All of its race's history opened up before me. War. Ogarim fighting huge towering monstrosities crafted from flesh and bone. Winning. Always winning as their magic eventually overpowered everything and anything the Scarrabus queens could throw at them. The problem was numbers, and the towering guilt and pain of causing such bloodshed. The ogarim were so pitifully few compared to their enemy, and they could not be everywhere at once. The war required nine tenths of their entire population to leave their home realm, with only the very young and a few ancient guardians left behind free from the suffering of war.

Over hundreds of years – not so long to a race of Gifted immortals like the ogarim – realm after realm was cleansed of the Scarrabus presence, until finally they came to a lush tropical world that had been turned into a breeding pit for those vile creatures' abominations. The ogarim had never seen anything like the scale of it: an entire world's resources bent towards a single horrific purpose.

The Eldest witnessed this for itself as a youth: a group of ogarim advancing on a great beast rising from the largest of the pits. This beast was formed from the bodies of countless thousands of other creatures, including their own kind captured or killed in the wars. As they had every time before, the ogarim set the unrivalled might of their awesome magic against it, expecting total victory.

I shuddered inside the vision. I knew this creature. It was the Magash Mora, the beast that devoured all magic. It fed on their magic, engulfed the ogarim and absorbed their flesh and Gifts into itself.

The Eldest's pain was raw despite the passage of millennia. *Formed from a seed taken from their god-beast and grown in a pit of flesh and blood.*

How did you defeat it? I asked.

We could not. We destroyed that world by pushing it closer to its sun. All life burned.

Sweet Lady Night. *They had that kind of power?*

Yes. Which is why the Scarrabus desired to possess our flesh at all costs. With our magic they would reign unopposed for all the tomorrows yet to come.

With their greatest breeding pits destroyed, the long war among the Far Realms was all but done and won, and what few Scarrabus remained were scattered and in hiding, slumbering in the deep dark places beneath minor and forgotten realms. Without the Scarrabus their great god-beast was lost, blind and starving in the void between realms. The home of the ogarim – here – was finally safe. Nine tenths of the ogarim race had left their home to wage war in alien worlds, but after centuries of battle only two broken remnants of the nine returned alive, expecting to experience an age of peace and rest, and to rediscover the joy of dancing under the stars with their innocent kin who had never known that abomination called war.

What they found waiting for them was… us. Humans. Broken Ones.

The infested Eldest they left behind to die had mastered their magic and somehow slowed its inevitable death. It had broken free, with only younglings and a few decrepit guardians to oppose it. Ogarim did not kill ogarim, but the Scarrabus had no such compunction. It slew the guardians and used the younglings as raw material in vile flesh-crafting experiments. It broke them apart and bred a lesser form of being, one with a more restricted access to magic that the parasites could safely tolerate. That Scarrabus queen had succeeded in creating their perfect host. And then it had hatched its eggs.

We humans thought ourselves so vitally important and so very unique. We were the rulers of this world, the strongest and most intelligent of beings ever to grace any realm. Hah! It turns out we were made things, mere hosts designed by a perverse Scarrabus mind. The Arcanum and the pompous priests would love learning they were originally naught but tools.

My world rocked only slightly – after all, had the great Archmagus Byzant himself not interfered with my boyish mind to serve his own needs? Had my beloved old mentor and father figure not twisted my personality into this bone-headed sarcastic fool that I was, with an aim to getting me killed before I ever achieved any real power? However, as any parent knows – look at my old friend Charra and her daughter Layla for example – children do not always follow the path their parents lay out for them.

What then? I asked.

Magical war like we had never experienced. Beyond a few other powerful but isolated races pitifully few in number, notably the ravak, what you call daemons lack that connection to the sea of magic. We were exhausted and not prepared for… you, and your enslavers. It felt reluctant to elaborate on its interactions with those ancient humans. *But that was not what broke the spirit of the ogarim.*

I could suddenly see the second moon in the sky, a baleful red weeping wound that was growing larger with every second that passed. The ogarim's fear washed over me, never forgotten and never to be diminished. The surviving Scarrabus had called their starving god to our home to eat and to breed more of their disgusting kind.

I gasped aloud from shock. "What did you do?"

<Shame> We chained and twisted our oldest ally, a great and honourable elder spirit, and crafted it into the most dreadful weapon ever forged by our race. We had learned much about death over the course of the war. The ways to burn, to freeze, to burst the blood inside, to call lightning, to drain all the magic of life and to kill the mind… many others you would not understand. All of our skill and power combined into one last great working of magic that claimed most of what was left of our race.

I watched through its eyes as they threw the moon at the god-beast of the Scarrabus. What is now the broken moon, Elunnai, slammed into the red stain in the sky, and the last of their magic exploded through it in mind, and body. A magical apocalypse was unleashed that shattered the moon and turned the night red as blood. The spirits of this realm screamed; most perished.

The Scarrabus shrieked in rage and pain all over the world as their god-beast fell to earth, burning and unconscious, its vast mind a fragmented thing drained of all magic. The elder spirit fell with it, forever chained to the enemy. They slammed through the skin of the world and its fiery blood spewed into the sky.

We had thought to kill it. We failed. It cannot be killed and would rise again in time.

I watched as seasons flickered passed and molten rock solidified into a great plug of black rock, a scab sealing the beast deep below the earth – this then was the birth of my home, Setharis.

What of the infested Eldest? I asked.

The ogarim shrugged. *Legend suggests it was slain by its own spirit-bound weapon, turned upon it by a mere human free of*

Scarrabus control. I think it did not foresee danger from their own slave race as a possibility.

Their queen on this realm destroyed, the Scarrabus were thrown into disarray until another could be hatched. Much to the parasites' shock, their tools, their pit-bred hosts, rebelled en masse, and turned magic upon their masters.

This was unexpected, the ogarim commented. *Never before had we witnessed a creation of the Scarrabus exercising free will. They had built you too well. Or perhaps it was due to magic affecting your twisted minds. We shall never know for certain.*

I had to ask. I had to know, and would likely never get another chance. "The thing, the idea, we call the Worm of Magic – is it real? Is magic alive? Why does it twist us?"

As alive as all life is. Magic is life. You question the changes wrought upon your human minds and bodies, the corruption as your thoughts call it. The Worm of Magic is not at fault. Your bodies are. Your Gifts are not natural, and they still remember that which was ogarim. Magic does not corrupt you – your Gifts flail to blindly fix that which was broken long ago.

A shiver rippled up my spine. Sweet Lady Night…

Indeed. Time marched on and black pyramids and soaring towers rose from the rock of Setharis. *We could not kill it so we built a prison, and then the remnants of my people left this realm of pain and regret to find a new home elsewhere. Some few stayed on as wardens, however the task has proven beyond our ability to endure for eternity.* The very first gods of Setharis… the hair on the back of my neck rose as I studied the five raising vast towers and found I recognised one of their number: a slender human woman in a silver mask: Lady Night.

Not human. Not ogarim. Its thoughts were filled with shame and abject gratitude. *An elder spirit now eternally chained to this place by our magic. Never again will Elunnai watch over us from the night sky with an eye of shining silver. Weep for her broken one, weep as we do.*

Tears rolled hot and heavy down my scarred cheeks.

With her assistance, the ogarim wardens ripped the half-digested hearts of stars from the belly of the Scarrabus' god-beast and placed them within their own breasts, granting them inconceivable power. With it came chains that bound them to their captive, most of that power used to keep the thing drained and deep in slumber.

And one of those crystals had only recently been sitting in my coat pocket…

I felt its curiosity piqued at why I had turned down my chance for greater godhood. *There is so much more. Let me show you–*

I pulled away. "Blah blah blah. I don't have time for history lessons." It was all very fascinating, if totally beyond me, and currently pointless. "Why am I here?"

It reeled back, shocked at my shortsighted attitude, though to my mind the sands of time were running far too low to dally with this sort of thing. *Your hand,* it said. *It consumes you. Angharad has foreseen that you will die unless you form a binding pact with the Queen of Winter. Though I have not her foresight, I have seen enough signs of the coming danger to sense the truth in her words. You will die if you do not gain the power of being greater than yourself, and in your failure loose the imprisoned upon all realms once more.*

I licked dry lips. "What choices do I have?"

Form the pact. Or all will die.

It abruptly stood and walked away.

"Wait! I have more questions."

Then find one that can offer something other than history.

Snow swirled and it was gone, leaving me alone on a deserted hillside with a wet arse and a sore head. Just… what the fuck had I just seen? I… fuck. How could I even begin to wrap my head around seeing the entire history of my world spread out before me? I had witnessed the birth of my race.

The answer was simple. I couldn't. I had to ignore it. Prepare to fight. With two useless hands, a dodgy back, and wounds that would take at least another day or two to heal I was no good to anybody. Not without help.

I rubbed my chest, where I still bore silvery scars from my

grandmother's nails. After witnessing the enormity of what would be unleashed if we failed, I had no choice but to bite my tongue and beg her to work that damned ritual again. I supposed that was the whole fucking point of the Eldest's history lesson, that manipulative hairy arsehole.

CHAPTER 22

I had plenty of time to think as I limped down the hill, my back on fire from the movement. Dwelling on serious topics and coming up with detailed plans was not my strong point, I was far more of an on-the-fly kind of guy.

Those stinking bard's tales all featured a wise old mentor spouting cryptic nonsense to manipulate the brave young hero of the story, but this was just taking the piss. That history lesson had been about as much use as knitting gloves for a fish. Was I supposed to be so dazzled by the big hairy fucker's age and knowledge that I threw all sense into the sea and did exactly what it advised? Probably; it did call itself the Eldest, and the old always thought themselves so much wiser than the young. Nah, I was too cynical for all that gullible shite. I knew something it didn't – a truly wise person had to change with the times, not grimly clutch onto the past. Which begged the question of why of all folk I knew that.

I also knew that we pitiful few stood almost no chance against what was coming for us. And just where was that bastard army promised by the Free Towns Alliance? Not that I held out much hope there; however well-armed they were, they would only be mundane humans with a few relatively untrained Gifted to provide magical muscle. Against an elder tyrant infested with a Scarrabus queen they would either die or be taken over and forced to serve in their army.

All I could do was wait for Eva to return, and my prisoner with them. Then I would have to make some hard decisions. I glared at the rocky snow-capped peak of Kil Noth and shivered. The last thing I wanted to do was allow my grandmother to get her claws into me again. I wanted nothing to do with her bloody spirit.

Then a thought struck. Yes. YES! The druí dealt with spirits, which would be immune to the enemy tyrant's powers. Sweet Lady Night, this could be the answer to everything! The druí would have to use them or die. But knowing my grandmother as I did, it wouldn't be easy. If the worst came to the worst then I had the leverage needed to force them into it, but I really, really didn't want to have to deliver myself up on a platter to her.

I tore down the hill… briefly, then slowed to a limp again when I ripped my stitches and the back of my tunic grew wet with blood. Great. Could that great hairy heap of ancient history not have sat and had a chat right there in my tent? Sod it and its nostalgia trip. I was a magus. I could do this. It was only pain. I limped downhill with all the stubborn determination of a cat fleeing a bath.

Jovian stared at me in confusion as I wandered towards my tent, blood-soaked and drenched in sweat. As far as he had known I had been safely sleeping inside. He scampered over and grabbed my arm, guiding me in and back onto the furs. I groaned with relief as I lay face down and rested my aching back.

"How…" he began, then shook his head and thought better of asking as he stripped off my sodden tunic. "Have you fought cats once again?"

"A know-it-all giant ape this time," I replied.

He sucked air through his teeth and prodded the wound. "You heal as fast as you drink."

"Not fast enough. I need to get to Kil Noth with all speed." My belly chose that moment to rumble.

He eyed my wounds and my shaking hands. "You need food and wine and more rest. A man who was dead to the world this morning is fit to fight nothing greater than mice. Or perhaps small, slow, and especially stupid children."

"Being dead will hamper that somewhat, which is exactly what we will all be if I don't get back there."

"Vaughn has his pony, Biter, and a small cart," he said. "Travel as glorious as a sack of grain perhaps, but you shall get there all the same."

I nodded and he stepped outside to have a word with Vaughn. The big man whooped with joy. "Bring me my war pony!"

Jovian returned bearing a water skin and a lump of hard cheese. "He should have been a stablehand instead of a murderer. A happier life for all, I feel."

I unstopped the skin and smiled at the unexpected sour aroma of cheap wine instead of water. "I'm more afraid of that evil pony than I am of him."

Jovian's expression was entirely serious as he made his way back outside. "As you should be."

A deep swig of wine warmed my belly as I waited for them to gather the pony, cart and pack up our weapons and supplies. Coira and Nareene helped me up and settled me down atop furs on the back of the cart. Nareene was oddly tender about it. She leaned in close to whisper in my ear, "Thank you for Vincent."

I took a peek inside her mind and found it a pit of flaming death and overly-sexual dancing. Everything burned in there, everything but our resident pyromancer who was naked and, well, engorged. Whatever this was between them, it would likely explode in our faces. Or perhaps the enemy. Gods help that poor boy if he ever decided to leave her and shack up with somebody else.

We were off, and as I passed Secca, who seemed to be heading for my tent, she looked up in surprise and caught my gaze. She paled and a conflicted and unreadable range of emotions flickered across her face. "Where are you going?"

"Eva is in trouble. The Scarrabus queen is here and it inhabits the body of an elder tyrant. I go to fetch help."

She stared at me open-mouthed. And then a few moments later the cart turned and she was out of sight. It was a lot to drop on somebody but there was nothing any of them could do but wait for Eva to return – it wasn't like they had any defence against an elder tyrant.

I suffered a half-day of bone-rattling as Biter pulled the cart along the rutted track heading back south towards Kil Noth, my coterie walking alongside. I could swear that the vile creature took us over every single bump it could possibly find. And if it farted one more time I would not be held accountable for my actions – I'd have Vaughn hitched up to the cart instead if needs be!

It was mid-afternoon when we finally trundled into the town that squatted below the ancient holdfast and I found Angharad and seven druí there waiting for me. Unlike how the pompous Arcanum might have done it, there was no formality here – they were sat around a table outside a tavern with horns of honey-scented mead in their hands and bowls of gnawed chicken bones in front of them.

"I knew ye would be here," my grandmother said, taking a gulp of mead. "Have ye made a decision?"

I shrugged. "You must summon your spirits and set them on the enemy leader. He needs to be kept away from the battlefield at all costs."

"No." She took another drink, taking pleasure in my shocked expression.

"You must be mad. They will kill you all and destroy this place just as they did with Dun Bhailiol." My coterie spread out and their hands settled on the hilts of their weapons.

She ignored the implied threat. "So? It is just death. You Setharii may not believe that humans becomes spirits after the flesh dies, but we druí do."

I looked to the other druí to knock some sense into her. "Are you really going to sit here on your arses and do nothing when you could all be aiding the defence of your own people? How many of your children will be slaughtered if you don't act?"

An old woman met my challenging gaze with a pitying look. "Angharad of the Walkers speaks fer all o' us on this matter. She has the second sight and has foreseen the need fer a great spirit to tread this realm in the flesh. You will have no aid without following the true path laid out before you."

"Are you all cracked in the head?" I demanded. "What makes you think I won't just walk away and leave you to die of your own stupidity?"

They declined to answer.

"Don't make me force you to do it," I said, changing tack.

"Ye may be able to control them," Angharad said. "But ye cannot control the spirits they have a pact with. The spirits will know what ye have done and will refuse ye."

I ground my teeth and reached out for her mind. I didn't know enough about spirits to know if she was telling the truth. Her mind was open and brimming over with ironclad certainty. I pulled back with great reluctance. It would have been so easy to break in there and mess her up.

"Then fuck you all." I turned and walked away, stewing in anger at the depths of their stupidity. Why would they refuse to save themselves? It made no sense to me.

"Ye will be back by dusk," Angharad spat at my back. I glanced back to see her staring at my tainted hand hidden within its glove. "Ye will bow to the wisdom o' the spirits."

I stalked off, too furious to even feel the pain of my back. My coterie slipped into formation around me.

"No luck, Chief?" Coira asked, scratching a scarred cheek with a blackened fingernail.

"Want me to crack their stupid heads?" Vaughn added, ever hopeful. "After the first few the rest will listen real good." Baldo nodded in agreement, and leaned in close to whisper in Andreas' ear. They both glanced back at the druí and licked their lips unpleasantly.

I sighed and put a hand behind my back to support it as I limped over to a shoddy ale house for a seat. I fumbled money out of my pouch and slapped it down. Turned out it was a fat Esbanian gold coin bearing one of their merchant princes' noble profile. I couldn't even marshal the strength to take it back and try to fish out another. "Bring us ale," I growled. "The good stuff."

The gold invited stares until a boy brought us mugs of drink. I doubted any of them other than Jovian, once sword-master to rich High House brats, had ever seen such money and here I was buying drink with gold enough to supply a month's worth for all of us.

"Do we leave them to their doom?" Jovian asked. The others stilled, listening.

I badly wanted to throw my hands up in disgust and head off home. I tried to rest my face in my hands but they refused to cooperate and I failed to achieve even such a simple thing.

How were we supposed to survive this if these stubborn fools refused to help themselves? It was all politics and backstabbing, self-interest and secret agendas and bloody alchemic-fuelled visions and whatnot. The Arcanum, the Clansfolk druí, and even the Free Towns Alliance were all obsessed with their scheming self-interest. I'd had a gutful of it and just wanted somebody to stand up and do the right thing for once in their fucking life – much like Eva I supposed. Despite her constant physical agony she was out there fighting for all of us more than for herself. If it were me I would have ended myself before now. I knew her will was iron but even so, there had to be a limit to human endurance.

If I ran then Eva would still stay behind and do her duty, and the Scarrabus and their hosts would overrun this hold. They could not hope to resist an elder tyrant for long. With me here they at least stood a slim chance. Which meant it was all on me to stand up and do the right thing. Again.

I groaned and downed my ale. "More!" The serving boy's lips thinned at my rudeness, but gold made up for many things in life.

Last time I trusted my grandmother I'd ended up a butchered hog atop her altar. I suspected this time around would prove no better. I could run and survive, until my taint consumed me anyway, but I'd left Eva to die once already and I refused to do so again. I would have to toss the dice and see if they could cure my hand and grant me power enough to defeat the enemy. Shackling myself to her frigid spirit would come with its own, as yet unknown, costs. Nobody ever gave great power away for free.

I sat pondering my plight as the light faded. Just before dusk a tired and sweaty Clansfolk runner arrived in a hurry from the north. I dipped into his head and what I found caused my mug to shatter in my hand. A new wave of flying daemons had appeared from nowhere, raiding our camp, killing many before disappearing back into the mist. If they attacked again Eva and her advance force might become trapped, and come the next day when Abrax-Masud cleared a way through Granville's avalanche, she would die.

I couldn't allow that. Not when I could do something about it.

Exactly as she'd predicted, at dusk I stood once again before my grandmother. She lounged back on a bench, her three crystal eyes glowing softly as she waited for me to speak the words.

I had to drag them out kicking and screaming: "I will do it. Call your spirits and send them to keep the enemy leader away. He's the greasy-locked prick in the blue robes riding on a huge beetle, in case they can't tell. Do it now and I will come with you."

She smiled, and it was that rarity of hers: genuine pleasure. "Very well, grandson, let us go and save the world." She snapped her fingers and the other druí leapt to carry out their part of the deal.

CHAPTER 23

They made me wait in an antechamber of the Hall of Ancestors until night had fallen and the broken moon was directly over Kil Noth. Elunnai's pale light bathed the hold's sacred standing stones atop the mountain that reared above it, granting power to their spirits, or so these heathens believed. I sat on a bench with only a single small candle for company, my eyes closed, using my Gift to follow their stray thoughts and flickers of emotion.

The robed druí and the sky-clad painted warriors waited in silence atop the snowy peak until the first of Elunnai's tears fell streaking and sparking across the sky. They gathered ice and snow in baskets of bone and sinew made from their own ancestors before beginning their descent back into the hold. Their faith was a silvery light in my mind, burning and unshakable as the procession travelled secret paths back down the mountain and wound down the spiral staircase into the Hall of Ancestors.

I heaved myself to my feet, groaning with pain as I faced the doorway. They would see no more weakness from me. The stone door ground back to reveal a blaze of torchlight that stung my eyes.

"Come," Angharad said, body naked, black and blue tattoos dancing across her pale skin. Her eyes were bound with a strip of black cloth sewn with stylised eyes, but she knew the way with a familiarly bred from centuries of ritual and habit.

The procession shuffled to the end of the hall where two doors awaited us. To the left was the black pyramidal chamber of the Eldest of the ogarim, but this time my grandmother placed her hand on the polished silver circle to the right. The doorway slid back to reveal the holiest site of Kil Noth, the place where they communed with their great spirits.

I had been in this sanctified place only once before, on the horrendous night my grandmother tried to crack my chest open and carve symbols into my heart with her fingernails. Until the Magash Mora, it had been my worst nightmare, forcing me awake and drenched in sweat, pawing at phantom chest pains. Now, it didn't make me terrified, it made me angry. I had sworn I would never set foot in Kil Noth ever again unless it was to cut out the bitch's eyes.

I was in no condition to put up much of a physical fight if my magic proved insufficient, and that had already failed in the face of Abrax-Masud's overpowering might. I was weak and broken and needed both healing and more power if I was to face the Scarrabus queen again and hope to survive. To go in unprepared would be suicide, and if I didn't go through this damnable ritual all over again everything was at risk. My grandmother had won, but then she usually did. Those amethyst eyes of hers allowed her to see further than anything human ever could.

Angharad gloated, knowing exactly what was going through my mind, that I had no other choice but to do as she demanded. My young mother had been right to run from this evil creature that shared our blood. That raised her. Tortured her. It was no wonder that she had grown up hearing strange voices and seeing things that were not there. It was a gods-given miracle she hadn't ended up a raving madwoman.

Of course, once I had all the health and power Angharad promised me, I wouldn't need her any more. The thought of gutting her kept my mood buoyant. I expected her beloved spirit would complain when I did, but I didn't give a rat's arse what it wanted.

The natural cavern was vast, lit by roaring braziers and smouldering bowls of incense arranged in a wide triangle around an altar of black stone. Every inch of space was carved with depictions of the great spirits of the Clanholds. There were many that I, not being native, could not identify, but the far wall bore a depiction of a woman holding sheaves of grain – Summer – holding court over the other spirits of growth and life. On the right among many different warrior spirits, was the Skathack, the lady of swords herself with outstretched crow's wings made of blades. On the left were the nameless great spirits of the animals, with the horned head of cattle in place of prominence. On one side of the ceiling was Sun and its attendant spirits of rain, wind and lightning, and on the other, Elunnai of the broken moon, her tears falling across cracks and crevices towards the black stone slab in a place of honour in the centre of the cavern. That altar was dedicated to the Queen of Winter and made of the same slick organic-looking stone that comprised the room of the Eldest, and also the gods' towers back in Setharis. It was carved all over with stone icicles and frost patterns so intricate it almost appeared to be a chunk of black ice. Angharad had placed a white wolf's pelt across the top, still fresh and bloody from the skinning.

The Eldest of the ogarim was already here, sitting in a time-worn hollow in the shadows. Its three dark eyes reflected the dancing orange and yellow light cast by the braziers as Angharad led me into the room and closed the door behind us.

"Disrobe," she commanded.

I fumbled at my coat and tunic, both hands nigh-useless.

She sighed, exasperated and impatient, and then assisted me none-too-gently to remove my clothing. My scarred and bony body was not a pretty sight but neither she nor the ogarim seemed to care. To one I was a tool to be used, and to the other all humans were broken and half-formed creatures that evoked feelings of pity.

The ogarim studied my right hand, and the hard blackness that was now rising past the elbow. Its white fur stirred though there was no wind in this isolated underground chamber. I felt its mind reach out towards my hand and then recoil a moment before it touched, wary of whatever dwelt within.

Angharad directed me to stand before the altar and offered me a silver cup retrieved from a niche underneath.

"Not going to fuck it up again are you?" I asked, eyeing the half-frozen dark liquid it contained.

She did not deign to answer my taunt and instead rammed the cup against my lips. After a moment's hesitation I managed to clumsily take it in both hands and drank deep. The thick slush seared a trail down my throat to numb my belly. Whatever was in her alchemic elixir, it tasted like ice and blood mixed together – sharp and metallic but not entirely unpleasant. I suspected this was what pumped through the veins of the callous creature.

She reached for the cup again but I tossed it aside to bounce and clatter across the floor until it came to rest by a pair of huge furry feet. The Eldest tilted its head, studying me with its three eyes in both the physical and magical, not entirely comprehending my ire. They were strangely calm and uncomplicated creatures.

She opened her mouth to rebuke me but I got there first: "Just get on with it. I don't have time for pointless ritual and pathetic prayer."

Her eyes blazed with fury as she shoved me onto the altar and pressed my wounded back down hard onto the wolf pelt. The coarse fur prickled my bare skin like little knives but any pain felt distant and woolly as the world began to stretch and spin around me. Angharad's crystal eyes swirled and pulsed with purple light. Pungent wisps of blue smoke rose from the incense to dance across the room and caress us, the scents changing with every breath. Half-heard whispers filled the room, almost on the edge of understanding.

She took a small flint knife to her fingertip, slitting it open with a deft cut. The blood welled up and she began to draw runes in arcane patterns across my chest. This time I paid very, very careful attention to every single thing she was doing. Some of those runes I had seen before, used by a halrúna blood sorcerer to summon a daemon during the attack on Setharis.

My heartbeat sped up until it thudded in my chest. I had been here at my grandmother's mercy once before, a naive lamb on the butcher's table, and had escaped her rage with only horrific gushing wounds down my face and neck. If I failed to willingly form a pact with the Queen of Winter then I doubted I would be so lucky a second time.

"Close your eyes," she demanded. I did, and she ran bloody fingers from my forehead down across my eyes, whispering the many names of the Queen of Winter as she went.

"My lover and my beloved queen," she said, her voice dripping with reverence. It was strange to hear her of all people talk of love in such a voice. "Angharad o' Kil Noth calls ye. Come to this ancient holdfast where the Shroud is thin as paper and the Far Realms but a stone's throw away. Come, Beirraa, great Queen o' Winter! Come to Kil Noth. There is one here who has drank o' your essence. There is one here who offers his essence to ye." She repeated it a dozen times before I felt a vast presence squeeze into the room.

I shivered as the temperature plummeted. Colours flickered and danced at the edge of my vision, red and blue bleeding in, faster, faster, spiralling in towards a black centre. My flesh refused to obey me, as if asleep.

She placed a hand over my heart, sharpened nails pressing in to draw beads of blood. Her touch was cold as death, cold as the heart of winter.

"Open yourself to the magic," she ordered. "Relax and wait for her touch. Follow the prepared path into the heart o' her realm o' ice and snow. Be at peace, for your journey will be over soon. The Queen o' Winter calls ye, Edrin Walker."

The moment I flung my Gift wide her hand pressed down and the runes on my chest began to burn. "I open the ways between realms!"

Ice filled my heart and stabbed into my mind.

"Go to her – I set ye free of this realm o' flesh and blood and bone!"

I plunged into absolute darkness, screaming and spinning for an eternity.

Light exploded all around.

All was now as it had been once before. There was no prepared path and no gentle descent into the Queen of Winter's realm. Instead I tumbled into a maelstrom of magic and madness. Unnatural worlds and strange skies flickered and faded all around me. Realms without number clamoured to claim the spiritual traveller in their midst, hot and moist winds billowing around me, warring with frigid arctic gusts. Strange air no human could breathe seared and scalded and boiled in my lungs. For a moment I felt icy fingers wrap around my ankle – but then my tainted right hand spasmed and reached out through the void to seize a flickering red light, one small realm among the many.

My body convulsed as if I'd touched lightning, causing the taint of black iron to writhe up to engulf my whole arm. The hand latched onto something solid and yanked me free from that endless fall, flinging me into a realm that was not my own. I fell burning and screaming until I hit land…

CHAPTER 24

I lay face down in cold red sand until the swirling flashing lights faded. When I was able to rise to my feet and brush the crud off my face I found myself in a ruddy, blasted hollow of sand, bare rock and desiccated scrub. The ground was pitted with holes and littered with shattered fragments of bone and gnawed shell.

Ahhh shite. I was back.

This was where I'd ended up when the previous ritual had gone wrong. I'd fled it screaming. This was not the home of the Queen of Winter, this was a death world populated by monstrous daemons living only to kill and eat, and not necessarily in that order. The last time I had thought it all my fault, that somehow I had messed up the ritual, but now it seemed my incompetent and vindictive grandmother had ballsed it up all over again. It wasn't like I'd any say whatsoever in where I'd ended up.

This realm was old and sickly, the sun a dull, swollen red orb covering an entire third of the jaundiced sky. The air smelled like a bad case of arse gas after a heavy meal, one liberally seasoned with boiled cabbage. The air was probably deadly poison to a human. Had I been here in my actual body rather than in spirit, or mind… or whatever the fuck I was currently… I had no illusions that I would survive for long.

Despite the grotesque size of this sun, my breath misted in the chill air. I was all alone on this alien world. I shivered and wrapped arms around my naked body, dearly wishing I had Dissever once more. It was times like this where I missed having an incredibly lethal spirit-bound blade in my hand – being able to cut through anything with ease is very comforting. That dark spirit's presence in the back of my mind had been silent for some months, only waking when blood flowed and it was time to feed, and to take more of my arm. I might not have been in my actual body, but my right hand had not changed – it was still black and hard as iron, the taint sticking to me like flies on shite, yet more evidence of it being a magical as well as physical affliction.

My ankle throbbed, misshapen red welts like finger marks encircling it. I remembered the feeling of something trying to grab me during my fall. At least here, away from my real flesh, my back did not pain me and my left hand worked properly. The fingers opened and closed on command, as obedient as they had been before I'd been forced to burn out a tiny part of my brain to permanently destroy knowledge so the traitor god couldn't uncover my devious plan to end him. And now I had a new powerful being that I needed to contend with.

After my last fucked up foray into trying to make a pact with a great spirit of the Clanholds, I knew I did not have time to stand around scratching my head and gawping at everything like a lackwit. The daemons would sniff me out soon. I searched the ground and found a bleached bone the length of my arm and then chopped the end with my iron hand, snapping off a knobbly chunk to form a sharp point.

I once ran from here naked and screaming, hunted by hideous creatures that I had tried so hard to forget. Even now I wanted to piss myself, but I'd had more than enough of living in fear and being pushed around by others. This time I was stronger and far more vicious. I was no longer prey, and I had seen far worse than anything this realm could possibly offer.

I opened my Gift and let magic flood through my mind and pseudo-muscles, preparing to kill. Fear and uncertainty washed away, leaving a burning knowledge that I was the baddest, boldest bastard in this whole miserable place. I would survive and I would find this fucking Queen of Winter and bend her to my will.

When the first burrower burst from the sand, red carapace gleaming and mandibles clacking, I was ready for it. As its segmented centipede-body swung round to face me I thrust my makeshift spear right through one of its large compound eyes, wincing at the high-pitched squealing as it flailed and gushed thick orange blood all over my hands. My right hand burned and itched as the creature fell at my feet, legs twitching. It stank worse than rotting meat, and I was drenched in its thick and cloying coppery putrescence.

I sprinted to an outcrop of red rock and climbed atop it, wincing as it crumbled to sharp edges beneath my bare feet. In the distance mounds of sand shifted and sped towards my location, but the burrowers seemed more interested in squabbling over the remains of their own kind than in me. The sand churned as the daemons fought one another. I was safe for now, but they were just one of many monsters in this alien desert. Wind swept dust and sand up into the arid air, forcing me to squint as I surveyed the blasted lands around me. Clusters of fungal stalks reared like a forest from the cracked earth, shedding spores like autumn leaves. Smaller furry creatures moved through that forest's nodules and frills, eating and being eaten in turn by things that looked like iridescent armoured snakes, those themselves being sucked up by armoured behemoths with horns and razor-tipped teeth on the end of a long fleshy protuberance.

This realm was kill or be killed for whatever scant resources it had to offer, a world consisting only of eat, fuck and fight.

"Show yourself, Queen of Winter," I shouted. "We have a war on and I cannot afford your tardiness."

I waited and listened, both with my ears and with my Gift. The great spirit was coming, her chill creeping across the rock I stood on. A struggle of wills was about to take place, and I refused to let her win. The Arcanum did not rule me, nor did the gods of Setharis, and I'd rather cut my cock off than bow and scrape to anything, especially not the inhuman spirit my vile grandmother worshipped.

Unfortunately, the Queen of Winter was not the only entity to hear my call.

In the fungal forest, immense stalks of growth cracked and

fell squealing as something huge crashed through, charging right towards me.

Just what I needed. I awkwardly hefted my spear in my left hand and held up my right to serve as a crude shield – it was mostly iron at the moment after all.

The smaller creatures fled the forest in a tide. The tusked behemoths trumpeted and lumbered off. Burrowers hid their heads and dug deeper into the sands. I discovered why moments later as a massive, fearsome ravak daemon emerged from the gloom.

Normally it would be more than a match for me, but this one bore gaping wounds all down one side, and half the smaller claws were severed oozing stumps. I didn't fancy meeting whatever monster had chosen such a powerful daemon as its prey. Perhaps it had been wounded in conflict with its own kind.

I tried to spit on the rock at my feet, but this spiritual body boasted no spare moisture. "Hurry the fuck up you accursed spirit," I snarled as ice slowly encased the rock below me. My bone spear was a pathetic threat to such a powerful daemon, but then my mind was a far more potent weapon.

It spotted me and surged in my direction faster than a horse at full gallop. I drew in as much magic as I dared hold and prepared to assault its mind before it could attack, but that was not its intention. It slowed and studied my arm instead; the iron a match to its own blade and crown.

Three eyes remained fixed on me while the others slid across its head to look back at the forest it had come from. "Fight with me, small deformed ravak-spawn, or it will devour us both," it hissed, and somehow I understood its daemonic language though it was nothing I had ever heard before – the one I had encountered previously had spoken the Old Escharric of ancient humans.

Part of the fungal forest exploded and I felt its fear. Something even larger was approaching.

I swallowed and licked dry lips, for all the good it did in this body. "What hunts you?" I demanded, my voice coming out in its own sibilant tongue.

"The Old One comes," it replied, looking at my two legs far less suitable for sand than its serpentine form. "Fight the Severer with me or I will flee and leave you to delay it alone."

I eased back on the mental blow I was preparing and extended my senses into the surrounding area.

From the ravak by my side, terror and pain and Scarrabus stain shot through its mind. This daemon was infested by the enemy. My knuckles whitened around the spear.

From the forest, bottomless hunger and unquenchable bloodlust. And, oddly, vast and almost-human amusement. This thing loved the hunt and kill.

From the frigid air around me, a hiss of stray magic as the Queen of Winter manifested in physical form. She had found me.

The ancient god-spirit constructed a human female form from sparkling ice. Unlike my slight and slender grandmother, she had opted for a functional beauty with thighs like tree trunks, arms like a blacksmith's and a face plain as an anvil. I supposed that back in ancient days, when the first humans to wander the Clanholds had been armed only with their wits and weapons of wood and stone, that this might have been their idea of beauty. Her head cricked and cracked around to stare at me with eerie blank eyes.

"Edrin Walker," she said. "I have come for you."

The ravak attacked immediately, its black blade whipping out at the spirit's head. An arm of ice rose to block it and the blade bit half-way through before sticking. Those weapons could cut through almost anything, but it seemed the Queen of Winter was made of sterner stuff.

The spirit drew breath and exhaled a storm. Spiritual body or not, I felt her chill nip at my naked flesh as it stabbed into the serpentine coils of the ravak. The daemon screeched as frigid winds ripped it from the ground and flung it through the air, ice crusting its black iron scales. Ravak were hard to kill, but the spirit merely flicked it away like an unpleasant bug.

I felt the Scarrabus' terror as the spirit sent its daemonic host plunging right back into the fungal forest it had only just escaped from. Then red pain bloomed as the hidden presence engulfed it. An almighty crack echoed through the forest and its thoughts snuffed out.

The spirit's blank eyes turned to me and she stretched out her arms to welcome me into her embrace. I felt a compulsion to obey wash over me. "Give yourself to me."

The spirit's blatant attempt to coerce me only served to piss me off. I was a tyrant for fuck's sake, did she really think mental manipulation would work on me? Or pass unnoticed? Anger began building inside my breast and my right hand itched to punch her in the face. "Nah," I answered. "But we can thrash out a deal of some sort."

There was a moment of silence, perhaps confusion. It was hard to tell from her lack of expression. She had no human tells. "Give yourself to me," she repeated.

"This is a pact, pal," I explained, as if to a particularly stupid child. "I don't give myself to anything. What do I get out of this? What do you get?"

"I get?" she repeated as if puzzled. "Angharad has already given of her blood and magic many years before now. You are mine to wear when I walk in the human realm." Oh shite. That treacherous little bitch had lied to me. It was only a small surprise she was stabbing me in the back. This was no pact, this was a blood sacrifice.

She reached for me and I backpedalled, heading towards the forest. Better to risk whatever was in there than let the spirit touch me. "I am an independent sentient being, Queen of Winter. Angharad does not own me and has no authority to promise you anything." She did not deign to reply as she floated towards me, fingers of ice reaching towards my heart. Reason had been worth a shot but I hadn't expected it to work. Now it was time to kick her fucking head in… somehow.

My mental probing had nothing to latch onto, no brain and no real body to invade so I snarled and poured magic into my muscles, such as they were in this current body and in this place. It seemed to work as normal, unspeakable strength flushing through me, ready to fight. No crusty old spirit was going to wear me like a cheap tunic, and my grandmother would suffer for this if it was the last thing I did. I kept backing away. There was something horrible in that forest that even the mighty ravak had feared, a monster that had eaten it if I was to guess. Perhaps I could introduce it to this piece of crap spirit and watch them murder each other.

The icy form darted forward in a streak of mist. I batted her arm away with my hard right hand and thrust my bone spear into her face. The point splintered on impact. I ducked a swipe and rammed my iron fist right up into her jaw.

I convulsed and sparked from the impact, like I'd punched lightning.

The spirit reeled back, her icy jaw riven with cracks. My hard black fingers dripped with water, and drank it in like blood. Stolen strength flooded through me.

I shook off my surprise and took to my heels, speeding towards the looming trunks of mottled fungus. I was brimming with energy as I leapt over rock and dips, feet pounding the sand like a drum.

My hand burned and the blackness crept up past my shoulder to caress my neck. An unbearable itch under the skin like thousands of insects trying to bite their way free. *Hungry*, came that old familiar voice in the back of my head. Dissever! I had hurt the Queen of Winter and her watery magical blood had fed the taint. Fuckity fuck fuck.

Frigid wind swept past me and my foot stuck fast to frozen sand. I ripped it free, leaving skin behind, and continued running, each step burning agony.

Shelter was so close! I could smell the forest's musty aroma, and feel a dark presence watching from somewhere among the trunks.

A drop of white bloomed in the treeline directly ahead between two trunks, and from it an icy form grew in the space of two heartbeats. The Queen of Winter opened her arms and I could not stop. I slammed into her and bounced off like I had charged headfirst into a stone wall. I sprawled on my back at her feet, shivering as ice enveloped my legs and arms. All my magical might could not free me.

"Give yourself to me," she demanded, bending to place a transparent hand over my heart, right where my grandmother's hand had been. By give, she meant to take.

I screamed at her touch. Ice bloomed inside my heart, reverberating with that back in my real body. I could feel both, and the pain was almost overwhelming as they began to merge into one. I screwed my eyes shut, desperately trying to think of a way out of this. I refused to let them have my body – I would die first.

Thunk.

A weight in my lap. The pain in my chest fled.

I opened my eyes to see the spirit's severed head in my lap; impassive features already melting. The body fell back and shattered on the sand.

The swollen red sun was blotted out as an enormous shadow pulled itself free of the forest and reared above me.

Just my luck.

CHAPTER 25

Looming above me was another ravak daemon, but easily twice the size of any I had ever seen or heard of before – almost as tall as the sodding walls of Setharis itself! Its armoured coils and barbed tail belonged on a monstrous siege engine rather than a living creature. Above shining slitted golden eyes, all staring down at me, the black crown was a forest of spikes, eldritch purple energy crackling between them. In one long six-clawed hand it wielded a wicked black barbed blade identical to my own destroyed spirit-bound weapon grown to gigantic proportions.

I was beyond fucked. My stomach dropped away as I wrenched at the melting ice pinning my arms and legs. It was useless, I was stuck fast. All I could do was lash out with my mind, panic driving me to attempt to kill it if I could, or stun it until I could free myself.

My magic slammed into it. The huge daemon let me in with a warm welcome.

What are you doing, you odious little cretin? Its hissing voice came from the back of my own mind, not from its great maw with fangs like swords. In my shock I stopped the attack on… on myself!

I knew that disdainful voice only too well. My tainted right hand burned with the need to rejoin its progenitor.

"Dissever?" I gasped. This was the monster that had been bound inside my enchanted blade before Nathair shattered it?

The huge blade stabbed deep into the ground beside me. Enormous armoured coils gathered under it as it settled down next to me, lowering its crowned head until it was level with me, golden eyes sliding this way and that across black iron scales. Several long forked tongues flicked out to stroke and taste my naked body.

"You wear a magically constructed body instead of true flesh. Disappointing and disgusting," it said, not in its own tongue or in Old Escharric, but in modern Setharii with a guttural hint of Docklands an exact match to my own; not surprising since it learned it from me. Then it laughed, a hissing mockery of human mirth. "You are even smaller than I had thought from inside my cramped prison." *Did I not say a great war was coming?*

I grimaced as I finally worked my arms free and started on my legs. "Bloody spirits and scum-sucking Scarrabus! Every fucker out there seems to want to try and own a piece of me." And yet, in this huge daemon's presence my terror was swiftly draining to be replaced with its own fury and bloodlust. I should have been terrified of the daemon but it was a part of me, linked by the taint consuming my arm. Which should have been worrying in its own right. Meddling with spirits and daemons and blood sorcery was an abomination... except when I did it. I wasn't like all the rest, but then I supposed that's what all the bad and the mad told themselves, and I had never been entirely stable in the first place.

"They cannot have you, flesh of my flesh, blood of my blood," it said, repeating the words and feelings of the original pact we'd made when I had been a mere pup in the ossified depths of the Boneyards below Setharis. "I require more sustenance."

I kicked off the last remnants of ice and got to my feet. "Your concern warms my heart, you vile old thing. That spirit, you killed her?"

"The frozen spirit–" the word dripped with the daemon's derision of all things ephemeral, things it could not devour, "–circles this realm even now, and this time it returns with more of itself. It will prove a far more difficult foe, especially for your breed of magic, but you must fight. You cannot run from that which lies within."

I swallowed and looked down at my breast, where a crude handprint had been cold-burned into the skin. That bitch Angharad had pierced my flesh with a solidified part of the Queen.

No wonder she had found my mind as it tumbled between realms.

"I came here instead of the Queen of Winter's domain," I said, realisation dawning. "Because I already had an existing pact with you? It was your fault the ritual went to shite both times?"

"Yes," Dissever replied. "This realm belongs to ravak. Ravak belonged to me before the Scarrabus came to enslave us."

I studied its eyes, unable to fathom just how unutterably old this being was. "They belong to you?"

"All ravak are spawned from my flesh. We are not divided as absurd, fleeting humans and insipid ogarim. Once there were many ravak that were not of me. I devoured them all."

I stared at it, feeling its bottomless hunger and lust for bloodshed. It lived to fight and eat, and in the end it had devoured all on this realm that could possibly oppose it. "And then the Scarrabus came."

Its rage ignited. "They did not fight to prove themselves fierce and strong. They are a disease, and when I discovered how many of my spawn had been taken and turned against me even I could not prevail. They buried my body and bound my essence into a weapon. Me! A slave used in their infection of the ogarim."

My hand itched, remembering holding that blade where the daemon had spent uncountable thousands of years imprisoned. During the Black Autumn I had leaned hard on its anger and hunger to prop up my own fear and failings. I held up the useless lump of black iron that was my right hand. "Speaking of disease, what the fuck are you doing to me?"

Membranes slid across its golden eyes and then opened lazily. Rather pretty eyes too I thought, now that I was close to a ravak without soiling myself in terror. I shook my head, aware of its unnatural influence on me.

"I do nothing," it said. "You do that to yourself."

"Oh piss on that," I snarled. "Humans don't tend to come covered in iron plates. I can't even bend the damn thing. Fix it."

Its pupils widened like a hunting cat's and its head lifted, bearing its fangs. "Were you not my pet I would devour you." It reached out and ripped its blade from the ground, leaving a deep cut right through bedrock. The barbed and jagged edges of its blade softened and turned fluid, and the blackness flowed up its hand and merged into its own flesh. "I am not a tool, you brainless bald ape. And I am not an infection."

I swallowed, feeling the anger and hunger warring in the back of my own mind. I dared not step back. Showing weakness was a stupid idea when faced with a vicious predator, which Dissever most certainly was. But then if the hard black plates were still part of it, a living thing rather than a spiritual taint, then…

The fingers on my right hand trembled, flexed.

The daemon slapped me, a contemptuous blow that sent me sprawling. "Feeble little creature. Your weakness is laughable. You let all those humans die in their hive at Scarrabus hands."

I shot to my feet, red rage igniting.

Dissever laughed, hissing mockery. "You let your fat little friend be skinned alive."

I lost it, flinging myself at the huge daemon, roaring, the knife in my hand plunging deep into its armoured hide.

It shifted serpentine coils, knocking me onto my arse with the merest nudge, then rested its crushing weight atop me. Its great head came down to my own until we were nose to nose. Two golden eyes slid across its face to study the knife in my hand. Wait – what knife? I stared at the jagged black knife currently gripped in a bloodied hand of fresh pink and unblemished human flesh.

I gaped first at it and then at Dissever looming above me, utterly unharmed at being attacked with a part of itself.

Your fear of yourself was consuming you, the voice in the back of my head said. *True ravak know no such feeling. If we are threatened we fight, we kill, and we devour our foe to grow ever stronger. Be more ravak.*

It was all my own fault? That made a twisted kind of sense. I had been so afraid of myself and focused on resisting my own power that the confused remnant of Dissever buried in my own flesh had seen me as an enemy and had been trying to eat me.

What a fucking idiot! The Arcanum and my old mentor Byzant had twisted my mind in against itself all those years ago and I was still dealing with the aftereffects. One way or another I would have to pay that pain back.

"Get off me you big lump," I growled, shoving ineffectively at the bulk of daemon atop me. It shifted and I crawled free. I kept glancing at my right hand, at smooth human skin. It had been a while.

A sharp pain stabbed through my breast. The air suddenly chilled and my breath misted. Snow began to fall, dirty orange in the dull red light of this alien realm. The Queen of Winter was returning to claim her prize.

I had come here seeking healing and power to use against the Scarrabus. And I had found it, just not in the way my beloved grandmother wanted. Dissever was right; I needed to fight. "I must wake," I said. "Don't suppose you have an idea how I go about doing that?"

Oh yes. It smiled as much as a daemonic serpent can.

I knew enough of what amused Dissever to be afraid, and I screamed as its jaw yawed wide to expose nightmare fangs. It swallowed me whole. A few moments of struggling in darkness against hot wet bone-crunching convulsions and then searing pain.

I stabbed upwards and felt my blade bite, punching hilt-deep through muscle and bone. A woman grunted in shock and hot wetness spilled across my chest. My eyes opened to see Angharad fall to the floor, flesh ripping from Dissever's black barbs. Blood pished wildly from a gaping wound in her belly.

My chest burned from the cold, but I was alive and free. I slid off the altar dedicated to her septic cunt of a spirit and stood on wobbly legs. I was back in my real body and rediscovering a hundred human aches and pains, from my lacerated back to broken bones that had never healed quite right.

The Eldest ogarim sat motionless, watching this turn of events silently and without visible expression, but emanating emotional turmoil.

"I'm back, o'beloved grandmother of mine." She was a vicious, heartless beast, so I did what Dissever had taught me. I fought what I feared, my power ravaging her unprepared mind as I stepped forward. "You murderous bitch. You meant me to be a sacrifice to your stinking spirit – well guess what, your vision of the future has come true, except it turns out I already had a pact with something far more powerful than your weakling spirit. Pah, ice and snow and winter winds? What use are they to me? I am blood and fury. Come now, let me show you."

She clamped hands to the wound that passed right through her body and her three amethyst eyes flared bright with power as her Gift fought to resist my intrusion. She was old and strong but not quite an elder magus, whereas I had bathed in the blood of gods and monsters. I was going to win. Why had I lived so long in dread of this pathetic creature?

"Queen o' Winter," she screeched. "Protect me!"

Frost rippled from her, flowing along the walls and floor towards me.

I sneered at her. "You murdered thirty-six of your own children for your mad rituals, and who knows how many others. You are finished." I turned and hammered Dissever's point down into the altar. It sank in and I wrenched it out sideways, gouging a deep trench through the stone.

"No!" Angharad cried as her ancient altar cracked and fell in two halves at my feet. The frost stopped, white tendrils writhing blindly and building crystals in unnatural shapes. The spirit could no longer see me here in this place so deep below the earth. My grandmother's blood kept flowing. Even such a vicious wound wasn't fatal to her, but it would slow her down.

"Yes!" I snarled, advancing on her with bloodlust burning away the chill she had placed within my heart. I intended to feed my big daemon friend.

I was aware of the ogarim clambering to its feet and backing away. It could feel exactly what I intended as my Gift used a torrent of magic to crack open her mind, and it wanted nothing to do with it.

"Will you fight beside me when the time comes?" I demanded of it. "You are ogarim, and you wield magic potent enough to turn the tide."

<Regret> <Disgust> <Fear> I no longer have the fortitude to endure war. I will not kill a sentient being ever again.

"Your fucking inaction dooms us all," I said. "That's right, run away and hide and do nothing. That's what your kind do best these days! You would have let her destroy me before lifting a finger of your own to help. Hah, and you call humans Broken Ones? Magically that may be true, but you are the real Broken Ones. Once you were the great defenders of the Far Realms – well where are you now when we need you most? Pathetic."

It bowed its shaggy head and fled through rippling stone walls, consumed by guilt.

It had been through so much, enough to break down anything with a conscience, but I wasn't inclined to pity it. My disappointment was vast and all-consuming and I was the type that held grudges. I turned to my grandmother, still struggling against my mental power, and forced her mind open. I nodded gravely to the silent skulls of my dead kin lining the walls and then I got to work with my knife.

As I emerged from the hold's most sacred place and stepped back into the halls of the ancestors, the other druí looked up from their meditations and flinched at the sight of the bloody footsteps I left behind me. They rose unsteadily, having knelt from nightfall until whatever time of the morning it was now.

"Catch," I said as I passed, tossing them parcels wrapped in strips of white-wolf fur. There was a war on and I had one fully working hand and Dissever again – and no more fear of what I was, or what I was becoming. If it took a monster to save those I cared about then I would be that monster.

The ogarim's mistake was, ironically, being too human. Had they been human then I had no doubt the Scarrabus would have been wiped from existence, likely along with everything else that stood in their way. We had been built for war but the bugs did their job a little too well to have any hope of controlling us.

I smiled as the screams erupted behind me. I don't think they appreciated the gift of my grandmother's hands and feet, but they do say to take pleasure in the giving, and I most certainly had. Her crystal eyes clinked together in my coat pocket, a little souvenir.

"Best keep your spirits busy with the enemy leader," I shouted. "Or I will be back for yours."

She had yearned to sacrifice her own flesh and blood to the great spirit she worshipped so that it could walk by her side among humanity. My mother had been only a tool to that evil creature and I was very glad she had the sense to flee her fate. As for me, my grandmother had intended me to be a prisoner in my own body, if any part of me survived at all. I was just returning the favour. No hands or feet or eyes and locked inside the festering darkness of her own mind.

Perhaps I would return some day and end her torment, but let's be honest, probably not

CHAPTER 26

A number of Clansfolk warriors tried to challenge me as I passed through their halls with my newborn blade writhing eagerly in my hand, lusting to feast on more blood. "Follow me," I said, and they did. My magic twisted in their heads and gave them no choice. Even a few druí tried to stop me but their relatively untrained magic was nothing to me now, and their pacted spirits were busy elsewhere.

I was no longer afraid of what I could do if I let myself go.

I was the monster.

I left the stone doors of Kil Noth with a small army at my back, found my coterie and acquired yet more warriors from the town below. Once I boasted enough swords and spears the recruitment carried its own momentum and most followed me by their own choice – people saw the swelling numbers and felt that irresistible call to glory. They were sucked in as if I were the very centre of a whirlpool. I had manipulated crowds before but this was something deeper. My magic mixed with their feelings to form an army burning to fight. It was a heady thing to know that my will would be done without having to say a single word.

The Worm of Magic reared its ugly head inside me and shouted YES! This was what it had always wanted for me, but I was in total control of my magic. Instead of giving into it I was bending it to my will to open up my true potential as a tyrant. This is what I was born for: not to be a sacrifice for my grandmother's goals, not to be used and disposed of as troublesome trash for my old mentor

Byzant. Oh no – I was meant to lead armies and save the world of humans.

It felt a little like being a god.

A warband of ritually scarred and heavily tattooed warriors from Dun Clachan and a few other Clansfolk from all over met me at the edge of town, having just arrived after hearing of the fall of Dun Bhailiol. They were spoiling for a fight, especially if it was not on their own holds' doorsteps. They shoved into the crowd to marvel at and mock the weak-kneed warriors of Kil Noth for accepting a thin-blooded Setharii as their war leader.

"I'm half Clansfolk," I shouted back. "And boast the black-hearted bastard halves of both our peoples. Follow me if you want to take some heads, or stay and whine like those toothless elders and mewling babes cowering in their hold."

That sort of bravado seemed to tickle their fancy. I subtly encouraged that: a prod here, a suggestion there…

The Free Towns Alliance was still three days off if their last report was accurate. If we could hold the Skallgrim until then we had a chance of survival and it would offer us breathing room to figure out what to do about Elder Magus Abrax-Masud, the ravak and whatever blood sorcery-using halrúna accompanied them. The human warriors and daemons I would leave to Eva's superior knowledge and skills.

We loaded up every cart and pony with food and supplies and marched north towards the Setharii camp. I'd learned a lot about leadership simply from watching Eva, but I couldn't always rely on her martial prowess to pull my arse from the fire, so I spent the time learning to become a warrior by dipping in and out of people's thoughts. Sword techniques, the use of shields as lethal weapons crushing faces and throats, small squad tactics, ambushes, using terrain to your advantage… some of it was useless to me, things that had to be learned more by muscle repetition than by the head. Others were now safety nestled inside my mind, borrowed memories integrating with my own, more than I had ever tried to absorb before. My head began to ache and I was forced to stop. It seemed there was a limit to how much my brain could absorb at once.

By the time we reached camp my head was pounding with a knowledge-hangover, but I felt almost competent now. I surveyed the forces at my disposal, at least a thousand added to the Setharii forces left in the camp. We were outnumbered by five to one at best but our magi were worth far more than haphazardly-trained halrúna. Secca and Vincent were there to meet me, their coteries closed around them until they realised that it was me in charge of this horde of Clansfolk. Then they closed up even tighter, shields up.

"Has Eva returned yet?" I demanded, as I strode right on past them and into the camp.

"Not yet," Secca answered, seeming surprised to see me. She ordered her wardens to stand down, which they did with great reluctance. "We thought you had fled this place for good."

"None of us are that lucky," I replied, distracted as pain spiked in my skull and then subsided. The worst was over with, and now it was time to concentrate fully on the war ahead. "The terrain is rough but she should be back from the front shortly, everything going well. Then we can begin to form a battle plan. Oh, and Granville is dead."

Vincent hissed. "How?"

I paused. "Best we discuss this in private."

I took them into my tent and told them everything they needed to know of recent events. I left out any mention of my exploits within the daemonic realm and the foul rite, Dissever, and what I did to my grandmother. Best not to terrify them completely.

They sat in appalled silence. "How do we deal with an elder tyrant?" Secca asked, staring at me with wide eyes.

"Luckily you have a tyrant for a leader," I said. "We will find a way, even if it is fucking petrifying. Abrax-Masud is everything that the Arcanum always feared I would become. Granville and I bought Eva and Cormac enough time to get out of there, or so I hope. We–"

A distant voice cried out and a rumble of chatter began to rise from the army gathered around us. Jovian poked his head in. "Clansfolk arriving from the north. They ask for you. They have a prisoner."

I rubbed my hands together. "Excellent. Bring him here." He caught the malevolent look in my eye, grinned and nodded.

Secca and Vincent seemed less pleased. "What will you do with him?" Vincent asked.

"What I have to," I replied. "It should be painless and far more productive than any alternative."

They shifted uncomfortably on their seats but couldn't think of any reasonable objection. The naked prisoner was ushered in and shoved onto the bed. His hands were bound tight enough to turn them purple and he looked far more worse for wear than I recalled. His flesh was mottled with bruises, eyes swollen and black and his lips split like a log, red and puffy and sore. It was more or less what I had expected of the folk I'd put in charge of him. At least he was alive.

I cut his bonds with Dissever and stepped back. "Have no fear, you will not be harmed." I massaged his thoughts to put him at ease and place him into a compliant frame of mind, then I slid deep into his brain like a knife through the eye, and just as deadly if I wanted it to be.

"What do you wish to know?" he asked in guttural Setharii. He was an educated man of some influence if his surface thoughts rang true. Certainly his fancy helm and clothing had been indicative of that when I chose him.

"Why did you attack Setharis?" Vincent demanded.

"We were forced to," he answered honestly.

Secca's gaze flicked to me and I nodded. "He cannot lie, or withhold information."

"Explain," she continued. "Tell us everything."

"Since beyond my great-grandfather's time the honoured halrúna have paid well for salvage from ruins of a vanished empire far to the south across the Cyrulean Sea."

I winced, knowing exactly which ancient magical empire they had in mind.

"Some ships go and are never seen again. Others return with clay tablets, trinkets and pots. Thirty years ago my grandfather returned with a wise man dark of skin and black of hair, an ancient ruler of that old empire."

"This must be false," Vincent said. "Ancient Escharr was destroyed and the last of their magi sought refuge in their outpost at Setharis. They all died far too long ago to be here, now."

"Nay," the man said. "It was the aftermath of a great storm and new ruins had been revealed to brave Skallgrim explorers long of limb and sharp of eye. He was dug from an undisturbed tomb buried below mounds of rubble, a place only the snake and the scorpion had entered for untold years. They found him alive and waiting."

I swallowed. He had been buried alive for as long as my home had existed. How could he have survived and stayed sane for all those years? Not even an elder magus could endure over a thousand years without proper food and drink. He must have already had the Scarrabus inside him keeping its host body alive as it waited patiently for the world to change once more.

It seemed that Secca had reached the same conclusion. "If these parasites were around in the days of Escharr, could they have caused that empire's fall?"

"Why don't you ask him when you see him?" I snapped. "What matters is he is no fake and possesses ancient knowledge we lost in the fall of his empire. That's not going to work out well for us."

The Skallgrim continued, his eyes glazed. "It took him only two years to become the chief of all halrúna across the land and be worshipped as a living god. In eleven he had forged all far-flung tribes into one."

"How did he manage to seize power so thoroughly?" Secca asked. "Your people were riven by blood feud."

Our prisoner simply stared at me.

Secca winced. "Ah. Understood." She avoided looking at the tyrant in the tent.

"What has he been doing in the years since then?" I asked. "Seems to me he's been a bit of a lazy git."

The man shuddered despite my mental control keeping him immobile and compliant. I glimpsed the answer in his mind and felt bile sear the back of my throat.

"Not lazy," he said. "Waiting for their eggs to mature and bless our chiefs with more of its kind. Now there are hundreds of Scarrabus among us, and among the leaders of this land."

That was not all I had seen. "Tell them about the pits."

The poor man wanted to throw up. He licked cracked and swollen lips. "That was not all he did in those years. He had us build… workshops, to breed unnatural beasts crafted from flesh and bone."

I sat down on the bed beside him, head in my hands as I shared his misery.

"Walker?" Secca asked. "What is wrong?"

"During Black Autumn a halrúna said something that puzzled me at the time. He said 'They have our children!' These Skallgrim we fight are not evil – they are desperate."

The prisoner continued. "He bred monsters from those who angered or failed him and their children went into the pit to be twisted into things other than human. Some were forged into unholy beasts that fed on magic. We dared not disobey."

"Magash Mora," Vincent gasped. "How many?"

"Dozens," the man replied. "Much smaller than the one grown in the belly of your corrupt and degenerate city, but still unkillable, or so the war leaders of the Skallgrim believed."

We three magi exchanged horrified looks. I cleared my throat. "We have seen none in the Clanholds. If Abrax-Masud is here, where are they?"

"The town you call Ironport. They will feast on your Gifted and then make their way towards your undefended city."

Secca clutched a hand to her mouth. "Sweet Lady Night…"

The Arcanum army had marched right into the jaws of a trap and we had no way to help them.

The tent flap opened allowing Eva, Bryden and Cormac to enter. Each was scuffed and caked in dust but otherwise intact.

"What goes on here?" she said. "I am told you have a prisoner."

We looked at them, each of us brimming over with despair.

"We are beyond fucked," I said. "The Arcanum army will not be coming to save us. They will be lucky to save themselves."

I told them everything he had relayed, and all that I knew of the Scarrabus.

We slumped there, threatening to cry for some time.

"Then we fight," Eva said, finally.

We looked up in surprise.

"What else can we do? If we fight, we die; if we flee, we die. At least if we fight we have a chance. The Free Towns Alliance is three days away. We can hold for three days, and then their numbers will turn the tide."

"What of the elder magus and the two ravak?" Vincent cried. "How can we hope to prevail against that?"

She shrugged, steel scraping. "Maybe we can't. Maybe all we can do is buy Setharis and the Arcanum some extra time, and pray that will be enough for our legions in the Thousand Kingdoms to cross stormy winter seas and arrive in time to reinforce the city's defences. What I do know is that if we stand back and let them wander right on through, then our world falls here and now."

"A maybe is better than nothing," I said. "We have jumped into worse with less hope."

"And look at the price that was paid," Vincent cried, nodding to Eva.

She stiffened. "What was paid is not regretted. I would suffer it all over again to save thousands of innocents."

Her honour and iron will stiffened my own spine. "We fight."

"This is suicide," Vincent said, shaking his head and edging towards the door of the tent. "Granville is already dead and I will have no further part in this madness. I am heading home."

"Sit down, lad," Cormac said. "You are better than this."

"Die if you want," he spat. "Fools." He moved to leave, then gasped as I speared into his mind. It was a morass of panic, his defences pitiful and disorganised. I felt sad doing it because I agreed with him, it was suicide, and half a year ago I would already be several hills over fleeing as fast as I could.

"Stay," I said.

He choked and turned back to us.

"Walker," Eva snarled. "Don't you–"

Bryden cut her off. "Walker is right. If he won't fight then he must be forced. We have all sacrificed enough over the last few months and we will again. This is what it means to be a magus. We protect the weak and ignorant against the perils of blood sorcery. Is… is that not right?" He faltered and looked to Cormac.

The red-bearded magus stroked his chin and grimaced. "Needs must."

"This is not right," Secca protested. "You cannot simply enslave him and force him to do your bidding."

I sighed. "Would you sacrifice everything in exchange for one coward's free will, Secca?"

Her mouth opened and closed, then her head drooped to look at the ground.

"When he wakes, say nothing of this to him." I twisted his thoughts and memory around and constructed a new course of action. He was a weak man who envied the brave and the strong and bitterly wished he was built of stronger stuff. Well now was his chance. I set that urge in place and heightened it to a burning desire. He would become the hero he always wished to be.

Vincent blinked and then turned to me, eyes full of deep sincerity. "You have indeed jumped into certain death on less before. That was a truly heroic deed and I aspire to nothing less than that. We fight to the last."

His brows fell as the rest stared at him.

"Let's fuck these bastards up," I said.

"We need only hold for three days," Cormac reminded Vincent. "Then we will be reinforced by more Gifted and thousands of warriors."

Secca laid a queasy, disturbed look on me. "We fight."

"We are agreed," Eva said.

CHAPTER 27

I stepped back and let Eva lead the interrogation of the prisoner. She winnowed all the necessary military details from him and it was apparent that even with all my recently stolen knowledge I still boasted only a pale shade of her skills. She gathered information on the types of forces we would face, their morale, and details on the halrúna and daemons that came with them before formulating a plan. She was not happy that among the halrúna opposing us was a noted geomancer.

"This complicates things," she mused. "We collapsed what rock we could while fleeing the elder tyrant, and with any other army this would bottle them up for days, weeks even. With a geomancer of such skill they will be able to clear the paths ahead and reach us before the Free Towns Alliance army do. With their advantage in numbers they will overwhelm us and then destroy our allies piecemeal."

"We could hole up and fortify Kil Noth?" Cormac suggested.

"They cracked Dun Bhailiol open like a rotten egg, using elder magic and what I can only assume are alchemic bombs," Eva replied, nodding to me. "I see no reason to think that Kil Noth would not suffer the same fate."

"It is to be a pitched battle then?" Vincent asked.

"That would be the last resort," she advised. "If the spirits are able to keep the elder tyrant at bay then I want to hit the enemy hard and fast and fade into the mist before their magic and bows can turn on us. They must be made to fear every step and cringe at every shadow. We can only slow them, not defeat them."

Vincent pursed his lips. "What about wards? I am, dare I say, quite the prodigy in that field. Given a day or two I could create quite a number of crude wardings containing flame that will explode if trod upon with any force."

I smiled at Eva. "You did say you wanted them to fear every step. I have some experience there too."

"Do it," Eva commanded. "Both of you see to that while we figure out how best to use our other skills." She was the most skilled and knowledgeable among us so she took the lead, as it should always have been – the best thing I could do as a leader was to take a step back.

"What of the prisoner?" Secca asked.

"He fights for us now," I advised, reaching in to influence him. "He will be on the front lines when we face them. See that he's armed."

Secca looked sick and the others were none too happy about it, but said nothing – we needed all the numbers we could get.

Vincent and I left them to it, retreating to the rocky northern edge of the camp to find suitable material for creating wards. I sighed in relief as we left that tightly packed morass of humanity behind us. Even a little distance between us reduced the pressure inside my head to a dull roar. I'd been trying to mute them but my Gift was cracked and I couldn't keep them out for long. So many churning emotions and nervous thought that sometimes I feared it would wash me away entirely.

The wind picked up, its chill nipping at my nose and ears until I pulled up my fur hood. Distant thunder rumbled across the valley. Not so far to the north, the mountains were obscured by a heavy blizzard, black clouds boiled and lightning flashed. The spirits of the Clanholds were angry and venting it on Abrax-Masud. I hoped that his metal crown called all the lightning down on his head, but suspected that would not be enough to destroy an elder magus, never mind whatever else he was now as the host of the Scarrabus queen.

We made our way to a scree slope and examined the material we had to work with. "What do you think?" I asked Vincent.

The pyromancer scowled and picked up a wedge of sandstone. Flames licked around it and it crumbled. "Not terribly impressive. We need harder rock, something that can withstand the heat and magic I pour into it."

We continued along the bottom of the cliff, eyes scouring stone and patches of ice until Vincent crouched next to a large deposit of granite that had tiny quartz crystals sparkling in the light. He picked up a flat sliver of stone the size of his palm and examined it carefully, flames licking his fingers. "Now this I can work with. A perfect size and density with a face ideal for carving, but thin enough to break if stepped on." He looked around the boulder and sighed. "If only we had more like it."

Dissever's hilt crawled into my hand, leaving little pinpricks of blood behind. It wanted to be used.

I examined an edge that could slice through steel like rank cheese. Then I cut off a thin slice of granite and held it out to Vincent.

He stared at me for a moment and then took it to examine the smooth flat face. "It would seem that we have more than enough material. May I use your weapon to carve the wardings?"

Dissever liked that idea.

I drew it back. "Er, that would not be wise, not if you want to keep your hands." The weapon grumbled its disappointment into the back of my mind. "I'll do it. Wards were the one thing in the Collegiate that I was fairly decent at."

It was stupidly quick and easy for me to cut basic capture-and-release warding glyphs into the granite, but back as an initiate many had failed to even grasp this much of the art of warding. They were physical frameworks built to contain simple single weaves of magic until the ward was broken and it released its contents. In our case that meant Vincent's pyromancy would explode beneath the unfortunate bastards that stepped on it.

Something I would have spent hours on as an initiate with hammer and chisel took me no time at all with Dissever, if I was being careful. I think perhaps I should have gone into stonemasonry instead of dabbling in magery. I did two dozen of the things in quick succession before Vincent put a hand on my shoulder. "Just how quickly do you think I can construct and embed the weaves into the glyphs?"

I grinned. "Who says these are all for you? Just imagine the fun I'm going to have with those bastards."

He flinched, contemplated wiping his hand on his cloak, but thought better of offending me. I let him get on with his warding while I pondered preparing my own. Hmm, choices choices: I knew enough aeromancy now to cause some serious slashes to exposed legs, but that was weak compared to what Vincent could achieve. I could instil fear, but that would wear off and they would be back. Much more effective to go for blind rage and panic. But what to anchor the emotion to…?

I started with my own pain. I had plenty of that to go around. I found those old feelings of being a half-starved street rat cornered by a much older boy, his fists cracking into my belly and face, again and again until I was soaked in blood and realised he was not going to stop. The boyish panic and fear that I might die… the need to escape, the moment of rage as I lashed out with whatever I had to hand… I bound it all up within the glyph. Every one of those warriors would have their own moments where they feared they were about to die. Then I topped up the fear with something fresh and raw – my rage at my grandmother. They would lash out in a fear-frenzy

It was slow-going cold work without moving our bodies, so Vincent maintained a magical fire nearby. My crafting was a far more harrowing and personal experience than Vincent's wards, all he had to do was place a crude dump of magic into it with nothing more complex than turning his magic into flame. I managed four to his ten and thought that perhaps there was a more effective way to be useful.

"I know a little aeromancy," I ventured.

He paused in his work. "You wish to try combining our magics?" Air magic would feed his fire and heighten it into a blazing inferno – if we were successful. Every warder did things in their own particular way, whatever worked for their own unique Gift. Not all were compatible, and some proved to be explosive opposites. Weaving separate strands of magic from two magi into a ward glyph was an order of magnitude greater in difficulty than a single magus doing it all themselves, and I hadn't tried it since my last dismal failure during my Collegiate years. But back then I had been only a mere initiate…

I nodded. "Doesn't feel like we have much choice at the moment but to push the boat out and hope for the best."

We moved our completed wards to a safe distance, careful not to drop one and then we began. We held an incised sliver of stone between us and Vincent traced the glyph with a finger, leaving a path for his magic to follow. He concentrated and began to summon his fire, then he stopped and held the magic half-formed inside his Gift, resisting the instinctive urge to follow it through to completion. It was unnatural, like half-swallowing a whole rasher of bacon and leaving it dangling down your throat while you fought the urge to swallow.

I quickly traced the glyph myself, finding it oddly warm despite being icy cold when I handed it over to him, and forced my Gift to twist my magic into awkward aeromantic forms atop his. The foreign magics writhed around each other slippery as eels. I had to hammer mine down atop Vincent's like I was pounding steel on an anvil to weld the aeromantic magic to his pyromantic base, and difficult though it was our Gifts proved not entirely incompatible. Then I had to grit my teeth and hold it there while he resumed his own weavings, laying down yet more pyromancy around my magic to encase it within his own, trapped, only to be released when his magic was.

By the time he sealed off the wardings inside the carved glyph I was panting and sweating from the unaccustomed effort. He was fine, given he was using his Gift-given elemental affinity and I was forcing mine into forms that did not come naturally.

He smiled at the warded sliver of stone in his hand. "This will make quite the bang when it goes off. We should make more." I groaned but we got to work on it.

I only managed five in two hours before my Gift started to suffer under the stress. Vincent was disappointed, no doubt wanting to show off as much of his flamework as possible when the time came. He went back to creating his lesser wards while I rested and watched parties of three leaving our burgeoning camp heading east and west up treacherous hidden paths, each composed of two wardens armed with long war bows being led by a Clansfolk guide. Eva's eyes and ears on the ground would skewer any Skallgrim scouts they came across.

In the distance Bryden rose on wings of air, robe swirling around him as he flew straight up until he was a black dot against grey cloud. He drifted north to get an overview of enemy movements. Eva must have been envious of his Gift on some level – she loved watching birds flitting across the sky. What she wouldn't give to be among them swooping and diving on the air currents, free from this dreary earth-bound existence.

Perhaps many of us magi envied the Gifts of others. What I wouldn't have given to be a naturally skilled healer like Old Gerthan! He had tried to teach me some of his techniques during my time in the hospital but my talent with body magics still only extended to the crude basics. My aeromancy was coming along only a little better. As yet all other forms of magic eluded me. Any great improvement would take years I didn't have.

Vincent sat back and wiped his brow. "I think perhaps we are done for now. We must keep ourselves fresh for facing the enemy in hand to hand combat. My power will devastate the ignorant savages."

Pffft. He was still as arrogant and clueless as ever. The only hand to hand he would be seeing would be from Nareene before any battle. That was what wardens were for. They fought and shielded and died for us so we could focus on using magic.

We carefully wrapped each warded sliver of stone in cloth and nestled them into Vincent's pack before heading back to camp – I was not stupid enough to carry those things and walked a safe distance from him.

Between us we had managed to produce five air and flame

wards, five of my own special breed of bastardry, and fifteen of his basic flame traps. All were crude and leaked minute traces of magic, likely only to last five days or so before decaying to uselessness. Fortunately, or unfortunately as the case may be, we didn't have to wait that long.

Bryden dropped from the sky to join me and I noted that his robe bore a few singes. "It's a little wild out there," he explained, sighing at blackened cloth. "This was bloody expensive too. Wards held off the worst of the lightning though."

"How does it look?" I asked.

"Not good. They have already cleared narrow paths through all but the last rock fall." He swallowed nervously. "No sign of their leader though, thank the gods. He's keeping his head down in the back somewhere trying to fight off all those spirits."

"Couldn't happen to a shittier man," I replied. "We have a few crude wards, so there is that."

He nodded ahead to Eva's wardens forming up in ranks and Clansfolk gathering in their separate warbands, checking weapons and shouldering packs. "Looks like we are moving out." Both then looked to me.

Bryden and Vincent were younger, not long out of the Collegiate, and were looking to their supposed leader of this expedition for some kind of reassurance. I knew this was the moment I should step up and deliver a stirring speech. I had none to give. I knew more than them and I was shitting myself

CHAPTER 28

With Abrax-Masud temporarily indisposed, our hopes lay with Cormac, whose skills as a geomancer were our only real way of slowing down so large an army – ambushes and arrows could only do so much, and against the numbers we faced they were no more than insect bites to an angry giant's ball sack.

While Eva, Secca and Vincent prepared for the inevitable running battle, Bryden and I went north with Cormac, taking along an escorting force of warden archers and sneaky locals who would try and keep the enemy as off-balance as possible. Some of our best shots would wait to strike at night, hidden by darkness from the eyes of their archers and halrúna. A warrior warming his hands around a campfire was a tempting target indeed. If we could gift a large number of them sleepless nights fearing an arrow in the back then we would be doing well.

Cormac got to work sending massive boulders tumbling down to block the path. He grinned and made me watch the valley floor as he forced shards of rock, narrow and sharp as a knife, to stab through the half-frozen earth into the snowfall. The stone caltrops were barely visible beneath a thin layer of snow except for when the sun was directly overhead and the path out of the cliff's shadow.

"Think that will slow them down?" Cormac asked while taking a piss, his robes bunched up around his waist to expose extraordinarily hairy legs.

"Some," I answered, imagining my own trepidation if faced with such a thing. "I suspect they find that which drives them on far more terrifying."

He grunted, waggled his cock northwards and pulled down his robes. "Well let's make this even more fun then." Much larger jagged spikes erupted all around where the enemy would have to pass, a forest of razor edges rising to eye-height that would tear anybody trying to squeeze through to bloody tatters.

I left him to it and got on with my task. I was there to keep watch for anything coming our way, not to fight. I sat on my arse with my Gift open, sweeping the surroundings for hints of thought.

Bryden was our eyes in the sky, and our best defence against the winged daemons that periodically swooped in to try to eat our faces and make nests out of our bodies, or whatever the bloody things wanted. After seeing the insides of that frozen farmstead I wouldn't put anything out of bounds, and I took great pleasure in every one he plucked from the sky and sent plummeting to its death.

Every so often I stood and gave early warning that the enemy were approaching. We packed up and fled south to the next narrow, uneven bit of path to repeat the process. Some of our archers stayed behind to harry the enemy, and if they got very lucky, to put a halrúna face down in the snow before they too were forced to retreat under a hail of arrows or worse, magic.

There was never enough time. The enemy had one or more geomancers and while they might be slower removing the obstructions than Cormac was in constructing them, they would still be able to take apart the worst of what we were able to throw in their path as their army approached. We took pleasure at hearing distant howls of pain as men stepped on spikes, and we were successful in slowing down their march to a full day of grinding, gruelling pitiful advance that tired out their Gifted for little gain. Of course Cormac was left exhausted as well, but the grumpy bearded git could take it and bounce back the next day.

At dusk I began a roaring argument with Eva. She had ditched her heavy armour for soft, quiet snow-white cloth covering her from hooded head to toe and was determined to go in under the cover of darkness alone to kill as many of their leaders as she could.

I thought that was fucking stupid and told her so with none of my usual charm. She finally had enough of my squawking and started walking away and I had to grab her arm to stop her. Or I tried to. I might as well have tried to stop a whole team of enraged oxen. She dragged me stumbling along behind her, slowed not at all.

I didn't let go. "I won't let you do this."

She stopped and used two fingers to prise off my hand. Her two fingers were stronger than my hand and arm combined. I winced as she bent my hand back. "They are two days from our camp. We need at least three before our reinforcements arrive. I need to buy us one more day. What else would you have us do?"

I shook my head. "I don't fucking know. Something that doesn't get you killed might be a good start."

"I came here knowing that I would sacrifice myself if it proved necessary."

"I know that, but I'm not going to let you. I'm in charge here, remember?"

She snorted and her single eye studied me from behind her steel mask. "Why do you care so much?"

"Because I just do!" I shouted. "Not everything has to be complicated. Sometimes you just bloody well care about someone." I looked her right in the eye. "And probably far more than I have any right to."

She was silent for a time but I felt her yearning for something normal in the middle of this battlefield so far from home. "There can be no future for us."

I shrugged. "Never said there was. I'm no great catch."

She coughed, choking on her own surprise. "You? I meant me."

For a moment I couldn't wrap my head around it. "Oh. I hadn't even considered your burns." I had only been thinking about her personality and her mind. She was brave, loyal, hardworking, intelligent, sarcastic, drank like a fish and boasted a sharp tongue. What more could a man want?

She did not know how to reply to that, shocked and unsure if she was angry or not. Instead she shoved it all aside and focused on her goal. "You cannot come. You would only slow me down. If I can kill my targets and retreat to safety then I will."

She was right, I would not be able to move quick enough to get in and out in one piece and all my mental trickery could not take on an entire armed camp at once. "Then I will ride along inside your head. I can do that now."

She groaned. "As long as you stay quiet and let me get on with my work. I have nothing to hide."

I knocked on her thoughts and she grudgingly let me into the courtyard of her mind, but her innermost thoughts and feelings were locked away tight behind thick keep walls. "Stay where you are put," she said. "I am in charge here."

Sure thing, my lady. I will try to keep you safe.

My body stood senseless and vulnerable once again. I reached out to Jovian's mind and ordered him to take it to safety and guard me as I rode along in the back of Eva's mind.

That lanky, good-for-nothing wastrel of a man is beyond infuriating, she thought. *He needs a few good kicks up the rear to keep him in line.*

I can hear you, I said indignantly. *You do know that right? Oh, wait, of course you do. Bitch!*

Bitch? she snorted. *Weak. Then than makes you a gangrenous, dog-faced, leper-fucker!*

I had to admit to being impressed. Another reason why I liked her.

Eva reached up and undid the buckles that held her steel mask in place and carefully set it down where she could find it again if she returned. This was no place for metal reflections.

For the first time in months she walked out in the open without her mask. She tried not to think about that hideous sight. The chill air bit into the holes in her ruined face and nipped at exposed sensitive teeth.

I said nothing. It wasn't like my usual uncouth and inappropriate self, but I knew if I said anything at all about it then she would immediately kick me out of her thoughts and never trust me again.

Eva took a deep breath and let her magic seep into every part of her body, granting strength and hardness beyond anything human. Armour was not necessary for anything less than a direct hit by a war hammer or spiked axe swung by a giant of a man, and even then it would be more likely to scratch than kill. Magic was a different matter, and speed was her best defence. Might rose inside and with it the urge to rampage among the enemy like a god of war.

Enveloped by darkness, she ran swift and nimble towards the enemy camp. Her magically-enhanced eyesight was superior to theirs and she could see every sentry they had placed: around fires warming frost-bitten hands, and also those huddled in the shadow of icy rocks waiting to see if anybody would attack the visible guards. Eva avoided them all with ease, laying low when their eyes swept across the area and then flitting past, silent as a spirit.

Insectile daemons with luminous green eyes and armoured carapaces stalked the snowy night where humans dared not tread, sniffing the air as Eva drew close, antennae twitching. A swift punch through the head silenced them as she passed, barely slowing as they slumped down dead. She flicked gunk off her fists and sped towards the lights and tents.

There were three tribal standards in this camp, the boar, the eagle and the sea serpent. All should have separate war leaders here in the larger tents.

Careful, I advised her. *I feel halrúna in these two large tents to your right, and we are in luck – one of those is a geomancer. Take her out and they won't be able to counter Cormac. To your left is a fancy tent with an eagle emblem on the side; it's a ruse, the war-leader of the Eagle Tribe is actually in the smaller one just to the left of it and his sub-chiefs in the large one. The war-leader of the Boars is absent but the Sea Serpents' chief is on the far north of the encampment. I doubt you can make it there and back unseen.*

Her sensitive eyes and my mental senses worked well together, and Eva was only just discovering the joys of having somebody along for the ride who could read minds and steal information.

Oh yes, you are a joy alright, she thought. *Now cease your prattle and let me do my gods-damned job.*

I did as she asked and got up to no good by infiltrating Skallgrim minds in the vicinity. Sooner or later a distraction would probably come in handy.

The halrúna were her primary target, the closest war-leader with the eagle banner was the secondary objective and his two sub-chiefs a tertiary goal. She wanted to cut the head from the body and if everything went well, have them thrash about mindlessly for a good few hours until somebody else took over.

Eva wasn't one for lingering about and wasting time. With my Gift for detecting minds guiding her path, she ducked and dived and crawled through snow and dashed through the camp until she was right outside the tent of the halrúna. The snoring was thunderous, deep in sleep after a day's exertion removing Cormac's geomantic handiwork.

She slit a doorway up the side of the tent and slipped through, drawing another knife ready to impale the first skull.

Wait! I said, drawing her attention to a perfect circle of dog's teeth on the floor by the beds, each tipped red with human blood – some sort of crude heathen ward.

If you give me a little time I can unpick those, I suggested.

There was no time for that, she thought. All wards had a very short delay before activating and these heathens were no Arcanum experts. She palmed a knife in each hand, and considered throwing them. No, there was no certainty of a one-hit kill against Gifted that way and she wouldn't have time for a second. She filled her muscles with as much magic as they could stand and then dived forward over the first bed, knife crunching through the centre of the sleeper's forehead. She let go and rolled, launching herself over the next bed, the second knife punching through the orbit of an eye and up into their brain as she passed over it.

The earth exploded in vicious spikes behind Eva as she burst headfirst through the canvas wall, already running towards the war-leader of the Eagle Tribe as the tent was torn to pieces. There was a guard outside, reacting sluggishly as she blurred towards him. A fist to the face sent his corpse flying. She was into the next tent, found the bearded war-leader unarmoured and in his blankets with a book open. His eyes bulged in shock as she grabbed his head and twisted. His neck snapped like kindling. She dropped him, exited, did the same to his sub-chiefs in the next tent, and then sped north towards the war-leader of the Sea Serpents.

What are you doing? I howled. *Are you cracked in the head? You are done here.*

She could not let the war-leader live and take charge. All of them needed to die here and now; she was not likely to get another chance. The camp erupted into yells as she sprinted north, keeping pace with the cries of shock and anger. Keep them confused. If they didn't know where she was and what she was then she might yet survive.

I fell silent, feverishly working on something dark and devious, warping the minds of outraged Skallgrim warriors.

Magic flared above the camp, a burning white magelight turning night into day. Men pointed and lifted weapons as Eva charged past them. Arrows and spears began raining down around her. One or two struck home, staggering her but not anywhere near to penetrating a knight's iron-hard skin.

There! Right ahead, the leader of the Sea Serpents emerging from his tent with a glowing axe clutched in a meaty hand.

Two guards got in her way. Eva blasted through without slowing, sending them spinning and broken. Then it was their leader's time to die. Her fist flashed towards his face. He dodged, slipping aside with unnatural grace. A mageborn with enhanced physical abilities! Moving too fast, she skidded in slush and plunged into the tent behind him, momentarily caught up in a tangle of goatskin and canvas. She ripped free and found herself facing three armoured warriors, their mageborn leader with an enchanted axe and… shit, a wizened halrúna festooned with bone charms and beads.

Eva was in a sticky situation but she didn't let that stop her. She made for the leader of their clan, dodging two axe blows from his guards. A single punch sent one to the snow with a crushed sternum. Their leader scowled and twirled his axe, saying something in their guttural language as he stared at her ruin of a face.

The halrúna lifted his bone wand and flames burst from the end to curl around it. Eva flinched back. Fear and self-loathing filled her as she cursed her fatal moment of hesitation. She wouldn't reach her target in time.

Fortunately for her, all my hard work had paid off handsomely.

The war-leader staggered as the head of a spear burst through his chest. He pitched forward as ten men bearing eagle crests on their shields charged in howling vows of revenge. One of the newcomers hacked at the mageborn's neck, then lifted the severed and dripping head aloft by the hair, screaming in victory. The rest went for the halrúna. Flames devoured three of the men before he went down, axes rising and falling in bloody arcs above him, lines of red painting the snow.

The magelight went out, plunging the area into darkness once again.

Get the fuck out of there! I shouted in Eva's head. *I have them believing the Sea Serpents betrayed them and killed their leaders. It will be mayhem. Abrax-Masud may have forged the Skallgrim into an army but the old blood feuds run deep.*

You scare me, Eva thought as death screams filled the night.

You scare me! I protested. *But damn, you can fight.*

She smiled, burnt cheek and jaw protesting. I was her silent companion until she escaped the camp and retrieved her mask. The night felt too quiet and she was alone and miserable in drenched and freezing clothing. Such was the comedown after a battle.

I returned to my own body, grabbed a blanket and wrapped it around me as I waited for Eva at the edge of camp, worried that despite everything she was still in danger, or wounded, or worse. Her steel mask floated towards me, shining eerily in the darkness, a wraithlike vision of death. Then I could make out actual arms and legs, all soaked and dripping with sweat and blood and brains.

I was furious and relieved, a heap of emotion all rolled into a tight ball of stress that thumped in the centre of my chest. I tossed her the dry blanket.

"We bought a day," she said. "Don't say another word about the risk. I'm hungry. Be a dear and fetch me meat and drink."

I bit my tongue and did just that. Whatever relationship we had was a tentative thing always teetering on outright disaster, and my tongue tended to run away with itself in all the worst ways. That and her battle-blood was still high and she could crack me like an egg with only a single finger.

She had butchered men and was in no mood to talk. Unlike older magi, she still cared about people of no personal importance, though it would not stop her doing her duty. I felt a fleeting sense of regret for what I had lost, but only for a single moment.

CHAPTER 29

Dawn arrived. All the Setharii and Clansfolk warriors sat on their half-frozen arses spooning down lukewarm porridge while staring at slices of salted bacon sizzling on upturned metal shields placed above the hot embers of last night's fires, every grumbling belly willing the salty mouth-watering meat to cook faster. Skins of ale were passed around as we toasted the fall of the Skallgrim camp. The valley echoed with the distant clang of steel and the piteous wails of the dying as tribesman butchered tribesman, not that they saw each other as any kind of kin at all of course. Forced allies were no allies at all, just enemies temporarily working towards the same goal.

As for our side, their death cries were beautiful music to many of our ears. Some found that thought macabre, even evil, but others had seen friends hacked to death by Skallgrim invaders right in front of them and took a great deal of satisfaction from our enemies gutting one other. To my mind, it was better them than us.

With the rising of the sun, word must have spread about the betrayal of the Sea Serpents, we saw smoke from other camps to the north. That was a damned good sign for us and a satisfying personal victory for me. A few whispered words into the right minds were worth far more than a hundred swords.

Storm clouds still boiled to the north and lightning flashed periodically, thunder rolling down the valley. With Abrax-Masud busy surviving the fury of the Clanholds' great spirits, his mind-controlling magic was unavailable and it would take the Scarrabus time to regain control of their human forces.

We had no idea how many Scarrabus existed in this realm or how many of them inhabited humans of influence, but they had their work cut out for them getting all those feuding tribes to work together again after such a vicious outbreak of bloodshed. Old grudges had come to the fore and now new ones were being birthed into the world even as we sat here and admired our handiwork.

I enjoyed the results and wished to heap more on them. Our three youngest magi – Bryden, Secca and Vincent – felt conflicted: killing daemons was one thing, but humans quite another. Cormac was an older magus and as jaded about such things as I was. As for Eva, she might have been young but she had seen many a battlefield and many more deaths than all of us combined. She was a veteran and was already planning how to kill more of them.

Under Eva's guidance Cormac returned to work growing spikes of stone in irregular patches across the valley, partly to discourage a night assault, and partly to break up and hamper any enemy charges come the morrow. Diodorus took Baldo and Andreas with him to paint the spikes with a grey paste he called the screaming death. It sounded delightful to me.

Bryden and Vincent, assisted by Nareene, combined on more exploding wards. Bryden was a skilled aeromancer and I a mere dabbler. There were better ways I could be of use. I found myself a quiet hollow to relax and open my mind, drifting through the thoughts of our army to dampen fears and where necessary induce fierce courage. We had to be ready and I had no qualms about seizing whatever advantage I could create. So many secrets dropped into my lap: scandals, murders, plots and plans, theft and unrequited love, all manipulated to make them fight harder and longer. The faces of murderers, rapists, betrayers and everything dark and disgusting were linked to the enemy, old angers and grudges ready to be resurrected and all those feelings set to come to the fore when we faced them in battle – they would not break.

The Skallgrim thought their berserkers were fierce – ha, those ignorant heathens hadn't seen anything yet. It kept me busy and out of Eva's way while she directed the defence preparations.

Over the course of the day, Bryden undertook a series of scouting flights over the valley to look for sign of enemy movement in the hills. He reported on the progress of their self-slaughter as it slowly petered out, one tribe or another proving themselves victorious. It finally died all together when a group of halrúna accompanied by their daemons and a powerful war-leader bearing the boar banner arrived to put all who resisted his orders to the axe.

Come nightfall we knew the enemy would resume their assault, and they had the numbers to keep it up until they exhausted us. I took the task of carefully placing a few wards at key points amidst Cormac's forest of razor-sharp spikes. I kept half of the wards back to deal with a future assault, and I took two of the most deadly crafted by Vincent and Bryden for myself – a little backup plan if everything fell into the crapper or a fucking huge daemon got a hankering for a tasty haunch of Walker-meat. Even a ravak would be hurting after one of those wards to the face.

We prepared as best we could with such limited time and resources. Rest and recuperation would likely prove as much a boon as any devious plan we could possibly come up with.

Darkness fell swiftly, and my coterie gathered around me, grim and ready to dish out pain. With the last of the light our archers uncoiled waxed bowstrings from around their bodies to keep them from freezing and snapping, and strung their weapons. We strapped on damnable cold armour, readied weapons, took up position on the foot of the hill and began listening for the first signs of trouble. Eva had abandoned all subtlety for a massive war hammer almost as tall as she was. Its haft was thick ridged steel, and the head shaped into a spiked corvun beak. Only a knight had the inhuman strength to wield such a brutal weapon, and only such a weapon could hope to withstand a knight's strength for long. I couldn't wait to see it put to good use.

It wasn't long before the enemy reached Cormac's forest of pain. We couldn't see their advance, but at some point a number of them must have cut themselves on stone spikes. Any muffled cry of pain quickly escalated to unearthly agonized screams that gave away their position.

Diodorus nodded in satisfaction. He appreciated a job well done.

With the screams came a feeling like we were being watched from afar, a nebulous itch at the back of my head that said somebody, or something, was paying me attention and that it didn't much like what we were doing.

In deep darkness, Eva was the only one capable of seeing the enemy creeping through the snow towards our defensive position on the hill, shredding themselves against razor-sharp stone and spikes. She leaned on her war hammer and kept up a steady narration as the enemy came onwards, relentless and grimly trampling over the fallen bodies of their own side.

An hour passed, two, and then Bryden and I both stiffened and looked up at the same time. "Flying daemons!"

Vincent threw a burning ball of flame into the night sky to reveal a swarm of them. A dozen different breeds plummeted towards us, including two-headed bone vultures, chitinous insects with razor-sharp limbs, a single large flying lizard and a bunch of flitting translucent things I could barely catch a glimpse of.

With enough warning our bows and spears were readied and Clansfolk slings set whirling. A barrage of death met the first wave. Daemons fell across the valley: eyes and carapace shattered by stones or pierced by arrows. Dead or dying. Of those that reached us, many were impaled on spear tips, claws and beaks snapping in futile attempts to kill even as they squealed their last.

Diodorus and Adalwolf took aim at the largest target, both arrows striking deep into the flying lizard's soft belly, bringing it down with ease. The impact of its fall shook icicles free from the hillside.

Some made it through, steel and talon clashing as they went for eyes and faces. A single strange daemon made to attack me, a thing akin to the giant mantis found in the hot damp forests of The Thousand Kingdoms far to the south. Jovian and Coira leapt up to meet it, spear and sword bringing it down at my feet, crumpled and leaking fluids. I looked into its bulging green eyes and saw a measure of intelligence there, enough at least to know fear. I plunged Dissever through its armoured head, killing it instantly. It wasn't their fault they had been ripped from their home realms by blood sorcery and forced to serve this vile bunch of bastards. I supposed the same could be said of many of the Skallgrim themselves.

The flying daemons were no match for a forewarned and heavily armoured foe. We finished them off and then turned to meet the first ragged remnants of the Skallgrim advance arriving in disorganised groups, their clothes and bodies torn and bloodied by Cormac's traps.

A few stepped on wards and were blown to bits, body parts and blood showering those following them. And having your friend's intestines hitting you in the face wasn't great for morale.

It was not a fight, it was more like casual slaughter, or a drove of human cattle that kept walking headfirst right into the abattoir. If their only goal was to wear out our sword arms and chip spear tips then they were doing a great job of it. Eva didn't even bother using her great hammer – her fists were more than enough. At first I thought them stupid, but then I began to think the Skallgrim's plan was to blunt Cormac's defences by sheer numbers alone, stone tips and jagged edges breaking off against armour and bone, allowing the next warrior to get a little further each time until more and more reached us without wounds. It was working, but at horrific cost. A cost they could easily afford to pay.

At first light we stared in silent horror at the utter carnage all their stumbling about in the darkness had left behind. The valley floor was red ice, dirty brown snow, and carpeted with corpses. Hundreds of men were dead, some impaled on stone spikes and gently swaying in the breeze, others still feebly moaning at the head of red trails of gore smeared along the frozen earth.

With the coming of dawn the situation changed in their favour. The war-leader of the Boar Tribe arrived accompanied by a strange pack of six halrúna walking in step like they were one. They were still well out of bowshot but Vincent lobbed a hopeful ball of fire anyway. They countered and caused it to fizzle out long before reaching them.

Utilising a combined assault of fire, air and water magics their Gifted reduced the field of spikes to cracked rubble. I tried to interfere but the moment I touched the mind of one I found all six huddled behind a shared mental defence like layers of a spiked metal onion. Somehow they had found a way to join their minds together to resist me. Or more likely, Abrax-Masud had linked them with the Gift-bond, as I had once been linked to my old friend Lynas. Their Gifts might be weaker than mine, but six Gifted linked together was almost my match.

I could break them given time, but the effort would be enormous and straining. After a quick discussion of tactics, Eva decided I was best keeping my strength in reserve. At least this way I was kept fresh while their Gifted used themselves up against mere rock instead of human flesh. If we could push them into succumbing to the Worm of Magic then they would turn and ravage those closest to them.

The Skallgrim came on in a long shield wall, beating axes against wood, hide and steel. Horns blew and war drums began their ominous beat, booming faster and faster as they approached our lines under a hail of arrows and slingshot. Eva hefted her war hammer and I almost pitied the corpses about to face her.

Their war-leader and his halrúna stayed back to watch how we dealt with this first attack. Vincent and Cormac took a dreadful tithe of their warriors, blowing holes right through the shield wall, but more grim-faced Skallgrim stepped forward to link shields and take their place. Bryden and I kept ourselves fresh for bigger prey like the halrúna themselves, while Eva took charge from the front line.

The first clash began with a bang like a hammer hitting an anvil; sparks flew along with blood and corpses and shattered shields as Eva's war hammer demolished the vanguard of their left flank. A vicious melee erupted as she waded through them. Never, ever get into hand to hand combat with a knight. Somebody should have warned them what the fearsome woman with the steel mask was capable of – and if they had heard then they still wildly underestimated her. The left flank of their shield wall immediately buckled before her fury. Axes and spears clanged ineffectively off Eva, and they appeared clumsy oafs compared to her dance of death, every movement crushing skulls or sending two or three broken men to the snow with a single brutal blow.

A horn droned thrice and the enemy began an orderly retreat. We could do little but let them go. If we broke to give chase then some might slip through our lines, and with their numbers we couldn't afford any disruption.

While sweat-drenched wardens caught their breath, I nipped ahead and laid a few more wards, including some of my own unique creations. Cormac grew another line of stone spikes ahead of us. A scant defence but better than nothing.

The next assault came on quickly and it was a scramble to ready ourselves to meet the charge. Vincent laid down a barrage of fire. I grinned in satisfaction as wards detonated, ripping off legs and opening holes in the charge, the disruption growing wider as my own wards broke. Men went mad and started slaughtering their allies. Despite the confusion, their shield wall was long and the enemy were many. After another vicious, exhausting melee the enemy again retreated, dragging their wounded with them.

Healers rushed to our lines to do what they could and Clansfolk boys ran past handing out fresh skins of water. The wardens in heavy armour lay down in the snow to cool themselves – battle was hot and thirsty work even in this frigid weather.

Another wave of Skallgrim charged, their fresh warriors facing ours who were cold, quickly tiring and thinning in number. I was inside the heads and hearts of our army, feeling muscles burn from swinging steel, the mounting bruises and burning wounds, and with it the rising fear that we were going to lose. The enemy sensed a moment of weakness and pushed hard.

It was going to be a long and fraught day. I took a deep breath and got to work on our tired wardens and wounded Clansfolk. It was time for me to become what I was always meant to be: a tyrant.

CHAPTER 30

Eva plunged into the centre of the shield wall, her huge hammer smashing through shields and the men behind them, launching warriors through the air like they were nothing more than dolls. Axes and spears bounced off her armour and the magic-reinforced skin beneath, earning their wielders an early grave as elbows, fists and feet staved in chests and shattered bones even if they managed to avoid her hammer. She opened a hole in their line and her heavily armoured wardens took full advantage, shields up pushing through, swords swinging in the front, spears stabbing from behind. The gaps widened as more Skallgim fell. The enemy began to waver as casualties mounted and men pulled back from facing Eva.

Vincent loosed a roiling fireball into a clump of Skallgrim. It exploded to consume half a dozen men in an instant, and set as many more alight, their screams echoing across the valley. Their army's morale crumbled, axes drooping, feet shuffling backwards in what would soon turn into a rout.

Horns sounded and a war-leader armoured in mail and a cuirass inlaid with a golden boar pushed forward to hold their line. His rune-etched axe trailed purple sparks of arcane energy as it destroyed swords and split shields. A warrior behind him thrust the boar banner into the air and roared. All resistance stiffened.

"Fight harder!" I shouted. "Push! The Free Towns Alliance will be here in only a day. I expect them to be greeted by a carpet of Skallgrim corpses."

At my words the wardens and Clansfolk I had influenced threw themselves forward, heedless of personal safety, swords hammering down, boots lashing out, and teeth ripping out throats. I slipped into the minds of some of our wardens, directing them to attack where the enemy morale was weakest. Their fury and fear flooded through me.

"Kill them!" I snarled, sending my warriors into a frenzy fiercer than any berserker the heathen Skallgrim could offer. The snowy battlefield was a churning mass of heightened emotions. Bloodlust. Panic. Rage. Pain. Fear. I rode the swell, experiencing it from behind the front lines while resisting flinging myself right into the midst of it. The rising exultation of our approaching victory was intoxicating. Every mundane human I touched had a Gift, and small and stunted as they were, each of them seeped a little magic into me – I took it as my own and threw it against the enemy. My power was swelling.

I gathered all the additional magical might offered by my army and struck at the six linked halrúna. My blow smashed into the mind of the nearest like a charging bull. He reeled back clutching his head and the others followed. These fools thought the Gift-bond was a strength, and it could be, but what hurt one also hurt the other. I burst him like rotten fruit and the other five fell to the snow drooling and senseless.

I laughed and lifted my arms wide. With one wave of my left hand a line of wardens smashed through the enemy, and my right sent maddened Clansfolk charging to their deaths, taking three times their number down with them.

I stood there directing the battle with my coterie guarding me, being strong where the enemy were weak and inflicting them with panic wherever I desired. I saw through every eye and directed every hand. In that moment I was the greatest general who ever lived – because I cheated. "Victory is mine!"

Behind me: killing intent!

I spun, Dissever clutched in my fist. My guards shifted around me and Jovian peered back to see what I was looking at. There was nothing there. It had to have come from my own people. They were taut and ready for a fight, hearts hammering as they watched the conflict below. I shrugged it off, obsessed by the play of life and death enacted on the fields below me.

With the halrúna dead, or as good as, this battle was as good as won. Eva made it certain by blasting through another knot of axemen to reach their war-leader. His guards might as well have been cloth, and she swung her war hammer upwards into his cuirass. His chest crumpled. Blood exploded from his mouth as she launched him clear across his battle lines to land on one of Cormac's spikes, stone piercing through metal. He hung there impaled, his heart's blood spurting across his own men as they looked on in horror.

The boar banner fell into the snow and the will to fight vanished. The dam burst and thoughts of flight flooded the panicked minds of the enemy. This battle had been won. I was already plotting how I would control my forces in the next one.

I didn't see the knife until it plunged between my ribs. I felt a punch to the chest, and looked down to see a horn hilt jutting out just below my heart.

"Fuck a pig!" I cried, staggering back. The front of my coat was already darkening with blood. "Who…" My coterie were all around me and scanning the area, but we were totally alone. Nobody else had been close enough to stab me, and I had enforced the former prisoners' loyalty when I chose them.

That killing intent…

I searched. Again, I felt that distant attention watching me, but that presence withdrew before I could seek it out. The presence didn't seem directly malevolent, so I disregarded it and instead searched for minds in my immediate area. I discovered somebody right in front of me despite the area looking clear, their thoughts quiet and calm as a mouse. "No you fucking don't," I gasped. They were disciplined and highly trained but not truly prepared for the likes of me. Few were. I hammered my way through their defences and started to crack them open.

Light wavered and shattered right in front of me. A line of

footprints appeared in the snow, then Secca's oddly familiar face, her black and white hood pulled back and a feral snarl twisting her lips. A second dagger was in her hand, raised and ready to plunge into my chest.

Secca? I… I had thought she liked me.

Jovian intercepted her with a shoulder charge and slammed her to the ground. He sat atop her, the point of his sword pressing into the soft flesh beneath her chin. Blood welled up in the hollow of her throat.

"Hold the traitor there!" I gasped as the pain suddenly hit like a red hot poker to the chest. "You maggoty cunt! Why the fuck did you do that?" I was deep in her head and I would rip out why she had betrayed us before I killed her.

"Monster!" she hissed, squirming in Jovian's grip. She was stronger than she looked and Coira, and then Vaughn, had to pile on to hold her down.

My Gift was stronger than hers, and with her discipline and defences broken I cored her like an apple and held her secret seeds up to the light. A man's face was forefront to her thoughts. It took me a moment to recognise the heavily built older man wearing a flat cap, a clay pipe clamped between rotten brown teeth. Her father was the man I had left mindless in a ditch outside a gambling den in the Warrens while investigating Lynas' murder.

"The fucker tried to rob and kill me!" I protested. "And you stab me for that?" By The Night Bitch, it really hurt… ah shite shite shite, it was getting harder to breathe. The bitch had punctured a lung. I dampened down my sense of pain and tried to ignore the length of sharp steel in my chest.

"Liar!" she snapped. "My father was no murderer; at most he would have demanded his coin back. After cheating him at cards you burned out his mind! I know you were there. You were seen, but as usual nobody cared about what happened to a poor dockhand. Especially not with you being some kind of big deal now." She spat at me, but it only landed on my boot. "You left him drooling and pissing himself on the street." She sobbed and tears glistened in her eyes. "You did worse than murder him."

Visions of her father blankly staring at a wall in a room that reeked of piss. Secca trying to feed him porridge and it dripping down his chin. The pain, the loss, the rage as her investigation found the culprit. Her coin drained away by the costs of constant care and helpers, her from a background as poor as my own…

Oh fucking Night Bitch, had he really not meant to kill me? I remembered that hard calloused hand wrapped around my throat, the panic of being caught unawares and then lashing out. Was it murder or was it self-defence? I… I wasn't sure.

I shivered, then grimaced as the knife grated between my ribs. Best not to remove it just yet. "You could have snuck into my tent and stabbed me while I was defenceless, lying on my face and healing up. Why didn't you?"

She glared up at me, brimming with fierce regret. "I wanted to. I had to know first. I thought maybe you'd have a reason, an accident… that you weren't what they all said you were. But look at what you've done."

I rocked back. "Are you mad? I'm trying to save everybody here!"

"By enslaving them all yourself?" she shouted. "You are the monster they all said you were, and every bit as bad as the enemy."

I am the monster… my own words echoed back at me with a shock like I'd dunked my head into a barrel of ice-water.

A flock of bone vultures descended from the sky.

Jovian and Coira rolled away from Secca to fight them off. I didn't move, because I knew they weren't real. I sensed no thought or life from the illusions flapping around us, and inside her head it was full of deception. She tried to veil herself in light and then run for it.

"No," I said. She flopped down to the snow and her magic cut off. "I am in your head now. It is pointless to try to resist."

"Do we kill her, Chief?" Coira asked, a knife in her hand. She didn't look entirely happy about it.

I sighed. "No. She is a magus and while this battle might be won they will regroup and be back with more daemons and who knows what else."

"Never leave an enemy at your back," Jovian said. "Especially one you wronged."

I glared at him. "She is no enemy. Or rather, she won't be when I am done with her."

Secca's mouth snapped open and her eyes flew wide as I opened her up to alter her memory. I burned away old links whilst forging new ones between thought and feeling and image. Most think of memory as something chiselled in stone, but really it's far more like squishy wet clay. It was always easier to take what really happened – or at least what they thought really happened – and sculpt a few minor details to create an entirely new narrative based on the same old structure.

What she would now recall was investigating her father's attack and finding out that her father was robbed outside of the gambling den. All sorts of scum loiter in the alleys in the Warrens so it could have been anybody. A blow from a club had rattled his skull, addling his mind (I added some lovely images of extensive bruises all over the back of his head). Nice, simple and entirely believable, as all the best excuses were. I tied that memory to all the pain she had revealed to me and made sure it was not one she would ever wish to examine carefully for minute discrepancies.

Say nothing, I advised my troops. *Vaughn, you big lump, get off her.*

The big man stood, and moments later Secca shuddered and blinked, then rose to her feet and frowned at her sodden robes. "What was I saying?" She stared at the knife jutting from my chest, then winced as she discovered the cut under her chin caused by Jovian's sword. "Sweet Lady Night! What happened here?"

"You don't remember?" I said, wheezing for breath. "Two enemy scouts attacked us. Fortunately I managed to take their minds and send them off to attack their own side before they did more harm." It was a crap excuse, but I massaged her mind to accept it and forget it and then I carefully withdrew.

Her eyes remained glazed for a few moments, then she looked at me in horror and ran to place both hands on my chest as she studied the knife. I remained very still, fighting the urge to kick her the fuck away.

"We need a healer," she said. "This is bad, yes very bad indeed. You mustn't move! You, Esbanian fellow, go fetch a healer!"

Jovian looked at me for permission, his expression flat and lacking any of his usual energy. Everyone was silent.

I nodded and he hurried off to find a warden handy with needle and thread.

What was wrong with them? I peeked inside their heads and did not like what I found. What trust we had forged together was dust and ashes now. They would still do their duty because I magically forced them to do so, but for a short time there they had also wanted to. We had been, if not friends exactly, a team.

Now they saw me as the monster I was, the tyrant the Arcanum had always feared. Killing somebody was something they understood and could deal with, but this forced each of them to look inward and pore through their memories looking for my manipulations. Paranoia bloomed unchecked as their realities came unspooled in my hands. They feared they were puppets dancing on my strings.

How could I claim otherwise? It was all true.

I'd taken them from the cells of the Black Garden and bent them to my will.

I'd taken the Clansfolk.

I'd taken the wardens.

And I controlled them all, forcing them to obey my commands.

I considered making changes to their minds, to force them to accept what I had done, even approve of it… but no, they were totally correct. I looked downhill to the wardens mopping up stragglers, and at all the bodies scattered across the bloodied snow – witnessing my handiwork. What would my old friend Lynas have said about my actions? I had enough of a conscience left to feel… not ashamed, because I still thought what I did was necessary, but regret. I had lost control and drifted into the whirlpool of tyranny. Had Secca not shocked me out of it I might have been consumed.

I tried to take a deep breath and gasped with pain as the blade shifted. Pink bubbles frothed around the wound and caused Secca to fuss over me. Coira was eyeballing me, her scarred smile seeming more like a scowl. *She's alive isn't she?* I said to her. *Would you rather I had killed her?*

She turned away rather than answer, but I felt her fear and disgust all the same.

I could not continue this way. My Gift was cracked and leaking and it was impossible to keep people out. It was growing harder not to meddle in their minds as my powers grew – with but a thought I could change their memory and correct my mistake. It was so very tempting. I knew my weaknesses and I was deeply selfish. It would begin with small things, necessary things, but that was a slippery slope and what was merely convenient now would eventually become necessary. What did it matter? It didn't really hurt them after all…

I was a monster.

They had made a grave mistake giving me an army. If by some miracle we survived this I would need to take myself away from people and live in the wilds. I could not be trusted.

When Jovian returned with the healers I welcomed the pain of them drawing out the dagger. It was a quick and hasty battlefield surgery and less than neat, but I was a magus and this little prick would not be enough to put me down. As long as I didn't try to run or fight I would be fine – I laughed at my own joke. I would never be that lucky.

If the enemy didn't get me then somebody else would stick a blade or arrow in my back if they realised what I had done to them.

CHAPTER 31

After the savaging we had given them an hour ago, the Skallgrim were far more cautious with the next attack. The hulking mailed forms of their biggest and best advanced under shields painted with emblems of many tribes. Their more numerous halrúna fared better against Cormac, Bryden and Vincent. Our stronger and more refined magic still slipped through here and there, flame torching and stone skewering screaming men. Aeromancy was less suited to offence but it was terrifying to see your friends go down gasping for breath that would never come and wondering if you would be next.

The Skallgrim approached to ten paces from our line before dipping shields and unleashing a hail of throwing axes. The lighter-armoured Clansfolk took the brunt of it, but didn't break. If anything it only served to further infuriate them as the Skallgrim charged, trying to buckle our lines and push us back to allow more of them to flood through the narrows and bring their huge numbers to bear.

A trio of mageborn war-leaders in exotic Esbanian plate cuirass, gold-chased helms and mail stepped forward to challenge Eva. They exchanged a flurry of blurred blows, their half-formed Gifts offering magical strength and speed that allowed them to fight her evenly. Almost. She wore one down and a kick launched him through the air to come to a crunching stop behind their lines, his steel breastplate bearing her footprint. He didn't get back up. The other two had their hands full trying to dodge Eva's mighty war hammer. Their physical prowess was impressive but a single hit from her would end them.

I clutched my chest and wheezed for air while studying the vicious melee below, every breath accompanied by burning pain. I refused to control our forces this time. Secca had been right about me; I had been using them as tools instead of people with hopes and dreams of their own. Instead, I spread myself through the army, feeling their pain and panic, and their gasping last breaths. I saw through their eyes, everywhere at once. Instead of forcing them into a brutal killing rage I concentrated on saving their lives, on aiding rather than controlling. The human eye sees more than the brain can process all at once – but that did not apply to me, I was in them all, the centre of a buzzing hive of angry bees borrowing from one to give to another. The strain of my presence in so many minds was like being tied to a thousand horses pulling in all directions, with some whining entitled highborn idiot whipping the frothing beasts to get them to pull harder.

Fuck those guys, and fuck these Skallgrim pricks with a hot poker!

An axe swung toward a warden's head. I bid him duck and had the woman next to him stab the exposed hand, severing fingers.

A knot of Clansfolk fell back before a heavily armoured Skallgrim war-leader with an enchanted axe, the runes flaring bright as it cut through swords and spears. A woman slipped on ice; opening a gap in our line. He roared and stepped forward, axe raised. Then he paused, befuddled as I fogged his mind. The woman's hand found her way to her sword and it bit into his knee. He fell screaming and the woman rose, her boot kicking in his teeth.

Block right – cut left!

Parry and riposte! A bearded warrior reeled back gurgling on blood.

Lean backwards! Steel whipped past her face.

Slip your foot back! Just in time for a blade to miss the knee…

I flitted across the battle, an invisible ally with a thousand eyes and hands, coordinating the defence with unnatural efficiency. The army began to fight with the precision of an artificer's machine. I could still feel the magic dwelling inside them even if they couldn't – tiny sparks of life and power reaching out to me, begging to be used. The Worm of Magic urged me to take it, but I would not be what Secca had tried to kill me for, not again. Our forces steadied and pushed them back towards the narrows.

A flight of arrows fell on our forces as the Skallgrim sought to break our momentum. Some bore great war bows and took aim at Cormac on the hill to the left of the valley and loosed at me on the right. Vaughn hefted a shield in front of me and grunted as arrows thudded into it. "Safe as Coira's virginity, chief."

She scowled, and thoughts of bedding him or stabbing him flitted through her mind, undecided as to which she would prefer. Maybe both.

The enemy line split in two to let an abomination though – a fleshcrafted creature bred for war. It advanced on all fours like a beast and then rose up on two enormous cloven hooves, a hairy giant three times the size of a natural human, with legs like tree trunks and skin covered with hard plates of chitin like an insect. Instead of hands it bore spiked steel balls embedded into bone.

The Clansfolk froze at the sight of the thing, but the wardens levelled spears and swords and charged. After the attack on Setharis they knew they had to put it down in the dirt hard and fast. A few arrows struck home but might as well have been bee strings. It bellowed and lumbered ahead, a swipe from its spiked steel fist rending a warden into red raining bits.

Vincent? A little help here?

He heard me and a second later the hairy man-beast erupted into a pillar of flame. A spray of water suddenly doused the flames as a halrúna ran up behind it. The creature shook its scorched head and roared in anger. Ah shite, aquamancers were deadly even half-trained. A warden clutched his chest and fell, then another, their hearts ruptured.

Eva was still engaged with the enemy vanguard of elites and Vincent and Bryden were locked in magical battle with another two halrúna. Cormac was… I couldn't find him for a moment.

Then I found his corpse. Through his shocked guard's eyes I looked at the arrow jutting from his eye socket. A shitting lucky shot! The halrúna aquamancer turned his eyes on Eva. Magically hard as her knight's body was, it would be little defence against her heart bursting from the inside out.

I took matters into my own hands. The great fleshcrafted brute had been twisted from its origin as a Skallgrim child, but the structure of its pain-addled mind had changed little. I directed its anger onto its own side. Its spiked fists took the aquamancer's head off, then began wreaking havoc on its own lines before being felled by a dozen wounds. The enemy fell apart and retreated in disarray back to the narrows.

We clustered around the fires, and had some breathing room to bandage wounds and stuff food and water down our throats. They would be back, and we were all but worn out.

Eva climbed up to meet me, drenched in blood and dripping unidentifiable shreds of her enemy's flesh. Her armour was dented and gouged and the steel haft of her great war hammer had a distinct bend from its brutal work. Even the finest and heaviest of weapons could not endure her enormous strength for long. She removed her helm and breathed easier, despite the steel mask she wore underneath.

"What do you make of that?" she asked, nodding to the storm clouds to the north. They were dissipating and turning grey. Lightning flashed only rarely now, the spirit-storm swiftly draining of ferocity. Even the great spirits of the Clanholds could not keep that level of violence up forever.

"We're running out of time," I replied. "But we only have to hold until tomorrow morning and then those glory-seeking bastards of the Free Towns Alliance will haul our arses from the fire."

"It will be close," she said. "How are you doing? You look like shit."

I laughed, then gasped from the pain thanks to a hole between my ribs. "It's no more than I deserve."

"Perhaps," she said, tapping her forehead. "I know what you did."

I hung my head and hid my face behind unruly hair.

"This is war, Walker. Atrocities happen. In the past I have ordered dozens of wardens to their certain death to win battles. This is little different."

"It's very different," I protested. "I took away their choice."

She shrugged. "None of us have any choice here and now. It's fight or die. If any wished to run I would cut them down myself."

I lifted my head. She meant it.

Horns sounded.

Eva sighed and slipped her helm back on. "There will be no more rest for us I think. Prepare yourself for a long and gruelling wait for dawn. Let us hope that the spirits can hold Abrax-Masud and his ravak off for a little longer."

As the battle wore on until evening the Skallgrim came at us in relentless waves of hacking steel, sometimes accompanied by those swift and ferocious daemons shaped like dogs, or brutal tusked boars with barbed quills jutting from their backs – boaram if I remembered the sketches in Byzant's old scrolls correctly. One wave was accompanied by another huge flying lizard, but Bryden took great pleasure in clipping its wings and sending it head first into a cliff. I could grow to like that boy. High up on the snow-bound hillsides, Clansfolk played lethal cat-and-mouse games with those few Skallgrim scouts able to find their way to the top of the treacherous icy slopes in one piece. Sooner or later some would return to their leaders with details of safe routes up. It was only a matter of time before we would be forced to retreat under a hail of arrows from on high.

We were being ground down by constant attack while the Skallgrim warriors could switch out and rest between assaults. Our lines bent and buckled under the pressure. Secca's illusions distracted and blinded, muddling their attacks each time, buying our soldiers time to rally and for Vincent's fires to fall where most needed. Without Arcanum magic we would have broken quickly.

As the sun dipped behind the Clanholds, the burning light pierced through the storm clouds gathered by the spirits, heralding the end of their aid. Abrax-Masud was once again free to come forth and conquer. The assaults slowed as night descended, but we all knew this was temporary.

I eased myself down onto my knees in the packed, bloodstained snow next to Eva and Bryden, swigging stale water and trying to wash away the taste of blood. It was pointless; the scent of bloodshed filled the entire valley and tainted everything with its metallic taste. I took the wooden box from my pack and counted my remaining wards. "Is it time?"

Eva looked up at the night sky. The broken moon, Elunnai, was visible through drifts of thickening cloud. It looked like a blizzard was imminent. "They'll use the blizzard for cover," she said. "Their war leaders will seek to break us and open up the route south before Abrax-Masud reaches them and shows the depths of his displeasure. He does not seem the forgiving sort."

"Flames in the night will reveal them to our archers," I said.

I sensed Eva smiling on the inside, looking forward to surprising them.

I summoned Adalwolf and Andreas from coterie guard duty with orders to set our remaining wards down in the narrows where they would do the most damage.

Eva noted I'd kept three behind, including a ward I made with Bryden. If I could see her face behind her mask – if it had still been intact – I was sure she would be quirking an eyebrow at me. "Always keep something back for an emergency," I said, shrugging. She seemed to think it sensible.

As the blizzard blew in and fat flakes began to swirl around us, war drums began to beat again in the night. Eva stood, offering me a hand to haul my broken and bloodied body back to its feet. My back and ribs were agony but it was far less that she suffered every single day, so I kept my mouth shut instead of complaining.

In the darkness and snowfall we wouldn't be able to see much of anything from the high vantage offered by the hillside so we slid down the hill onto the valley floor.

A short while later Adalwolf returned alone. He shook his head.

"Arrow."

I grimaced and felt strangely sad. Andreas was nothing to me really, to nobody truth be told. Just a dull-witted murderer. And yet he had been one of mine.

Wardens and Clansfolk limped into a defensive line and waited for the enemy, weapons dragging or thrust into the snow to save strength. They didn't have much fight left in them.

Pillars of flame bloomed in the night as somebody stepped on our wards. Men screamed, set alight to run and roll, illuminating their advancing forces. Arrows thrummed through the air as our archers loosed. The Skallgrim slowed to a crawl but kept coming as the Clansfolk let their sling stones fly.

We only had to last until dawn and then the Free Towns Alliance would march in to save the day. I was more than happy for them to steal the glory of victory from under our noses if they had brought enough Gifted to face down Abrax-Masud and his Scarrabus-infested ravak allies.

Eva lifted her war hammer. "No rest for the wicked or the wanton, eh."

I snorted. "I doubt I will ever find peace again. One day I swear I will hunt down that hidden valley where that God of Broken Things is supposed to dwell and disappear into it to get away from everybody and everything that wants a piece of me."

"I would like a sleep devoid of nightmares," she replied, wistful. "Still, until then I have a bloody huge hammer and a purpose." She examined the bent haft with a critical eye.

If I survived this I vowed to dedicate myself to a life of peace and quiet. And drinking, barrel-loads of drinking. I took a deep and painful breath, gripped Dissever tight, and then we slowly walked through the blizzard towards the enemy.

CHAPTER 32

Our personal coteries were fresher than the Clansfolk warriors or Eva's more numerous bloodied and battered heavily armoured wardens, so they moved forward to stiffen the line. Each of us kept only three by our sides to defend us – there wouldn't be much hope if the line broke and the Skallgrim numbers were able to swarm us. I kept the most reliable of my people with me: Jovian, Vaughn and Coira. Diodorus and Adalwolf stayed back with their bows and poisoned arrows. Even a scratch would take something down frothing and spewing blood. Their task was to hunt for daemons, halrúna and fleshcrafted monstrosities rather than mere men.

Another explosion rent the darkness as the last of the wards we had set out detonated. Men burned, but the enemy advanced regardless, axes raised as they charged from the blizzard.

We threw them back the first time after a brief but vicious melee, the ragged holes in their lines telling of the death our wards had wrought. I felt a spear take Baldo in the gut and somebody dragged him back out of the way. His innards spilled between his clutching fingers like bloodied sausages as he tried to stuff them back into his belly. I slid Dissever into his skull so he didn't linger in agony. It was all I could offer in return for his service.

The second time the Skallgrim came at us they had two halrúna behind them: a powerful pyromancer and a weak geomancer. I broke the geomancer's mind before he could do too much damage and Vincent killed the pyromancer in a gruelling, protracted contest of magical mastery that lit up the swirling blizzard. With our magi distracted, their infantry managed to push our line back, breaking it in several places. Only Eva rampaging among them stopped the flow and allowed me to urge our exhausted forces to push them back once again into the neck of the valley.

It was three hours from dawn, and in a pause between assaults we remaining magi gathered on a rise. I slumped atop a rock and squinted through the swirling snowflakes. Secca and Vincent were on the edge of succumbing to the Worm, their Gifts badly strained from casting their magic across the entire battlefield. Bryden was faring only a little better. Eva and I were still in decent shape and good to fight on for a while yet. Knights' Gifts seemed to require less magic to affect their bodies, and I… well, whatever I'd been through had apparently made me something between magus and elder.

"We must concede the field," Eva said. She had finally voiced what we all knew to be true, but it was a bitter thing to swallow. Our camp to the south was burgeoning with wounded that now outnumbered the living. The dead now numbered more than both added together.

"One more attack may end us," I conceded. Morale was about to break. Even I could not change so many minds in the face of reality, not unless I reverted to what I had been doing before and forced them into it.

Their war drums started up again, and the next wave of warriors began marching towards us.

Eva turned to two of her wardens. "Prepare for flight back to camp. We will throw them back at the narrows once more and then we run." They sped off to organise it.

We all reluctantly got back onto aching feet. I was not built for war; I was made for soft beds and supping cold ales by crackling fires. Even Eva seemed wearied of slaughter.

Vincent grunted, falling backwards, staring in dumb shock at an arrow embedded in his knee. Another whooshed past my head.

Eva blurred and batted one, two, three from the air, all aimed at me with inhuman accuracy. "Up on the hill! Bring me my bow!" A warden peeled off to fetch it

I sought out the enemy minds and found nothing. Even my small skill at body magics that sharpened my vision proved insufficient in the dead of night during a blizzard. I dipped into Eva's mind and saw shadowy shapes through her magic-enhanced eyes: several bowmen on inaccessible rocky ledges above us.

I reached out to them through her eyes and found Abrax-Masud wearing them like hollow shells. The dirty bastard was copying me! His control was strained from distance, but growing stronger all the time. I struck but he fended me off, albeit with great difficulty as he was trying to control several at once. We bit at each other's magics, and finally I forced one of his men to step off the cliff face. He fell silently to splatter on the rocks below. Somebody handed Eva a strung bow and then two more fell with arrows in their chests.

Eva loosed another half dozen arrows in as many heartbeats, all but one finding purchase in Skallgrim flesh. Fleeing its dying hosts, Abrax-Masud's mind snapped back northwards and I loosed a sigh of relief. He was so very strong even at this distance.

Vincent clutched his knee in agony. The flesh was swollen around the embedded arrowhead. There was no time for surgery so Eva wrenched the shaft free. The wood came loose leaving the head behind. She paused, and lifted the end to her mask, sniffing. "Ah."

"What is it?" the pyromancer hissed, writhing in pain.

"Poison. Magically enhanced from the swiftness of reaction and probably daemonic in origin."

The wound was an angry red threaded with black even in the dim light of torches. He panted and looked at it with fury, tried to stand and failed. "Fetch me a stretcher."

"There is no point," Eva replied. "We have no healer able to deal with this. You will die unless we take the leg off." She did not wait for permission. Her axe fell, cutting through flesh and bone. He screamed as his leg rolled free, severed a foot above the knee.

I deadened his pain. He looked up at me with gratitude and Eva with disbelief.

"Cauterise it," she ordered, and Vincent obeyed, his flesh sizzling and smoking.

There was no time for feelings as another arrow zipped towards us. "How are they getting up there," I snarled.

"I see huge wings through the snow," Eva replied. "Two of those large flying beasts ferrying bowmen to the rise above us."

Bryden stepped forward. "Where? I cannot see."

I went into Eva's mind, and Bryden's too, linking them together. He gasped as he looked through her eye. "Your vision is incredible."

An unearthly screech in the darkness signalled a large shape plummeting from the sky bearing screaming men to their deaths.

"It is done," he said. "Though I imagine more will be on the way."

I broke the connection and he gazed at me with wonder. "That is an incredible Gift you have been given."

I scratched my chin, stubble rasping. "Most do not think so, and for good reason."

He shrugged. "Depends what use you put it to, same as with anything else."

That was a rare opinion. One he likely wouldn't have if he knew everything I had done with it.

Glinting mail and weapons appeared at the edge of my vision, and with them came three of those hulking fleshcrafted monstrosities with spiked steel balls for hands. Bows sang and peppered them with arrows but they continued unperturbed. One stumbled, then collapsed as poison coursed through its veins. The others broke into a lumbering jog on legs thick as tree trunks.

"Time to fell some timber," Eva said, tightening her helmet strap. She dashed forward and swung, her hammer shattering an ankle and bringing one of the things down. Then she engaged the second, enemy arrows bouncing off steel and magic-infused skin like pine needles off a rock.

"Get me some help," Vincent said, staring at his stump. "I can still fight!"

I summoned Nareene from the front lines. At least they would enjoy the company. She arrived with only a shield, her other arm a bleeding mess. "What have those evil bastards done!" she demanded. "You burn the fuckers, you hear me, my love?"

Vincent's spine stiffened at her words and I left them to it. Who was I to stand in the way of insane arsonists at a time like this.

I reluctantly stood with Secca, and between us we managed to have the enemy attacking each other in the confusion of snow and night-fighting, assailed by illusions until the entire front was a churning mass of Skallgrim flailing at anything that moved.

Then I felt the elder tyrant's power rolling over the battlefield, searching for me as he drew close to the front lines. He was coming for me, and so it was time for us to engage in the better part of valour.

Under the confusion caused by our trickery, our forces took the opportunity to flee back towards camp, an organised retreat that swiftly became a rout as Skallgrim and scaled dog-daemons finally gave chase. The wounded were left behind; slow in the panic.

Secca bravely stayed by my side, putting my arm around her shoulders as pain spiked between my ribs with every step. If only she knew it had been her that had shoved a length of steel into me, and why.

Eva was guarding our retreat, assailed on all sides, parrying, blocking, and killing too quickly for me to follow. Finally a lucky hit with a heavily enchanted axe evaded her guard to pierce her helm and knock her onto her back. She lay dazed as axes rose around her. Flame bloomed and they fell back shrieking, clutching burning faces.

"Get her out!" Vincent shouted. He had wrenched his Gift wide open and was pouring sheets of burning power all across the enemy front. He had gone too far. His Gift ripped asunder and he began to change, his flesh crawling with too much magic for it to handle. Nareene was at his side, shield up as arrows and axes thunked into it. She had no intention of leaving him to die alone. Vincent had always dreamed of being a hero, and now he was going to get his wish.

I summoned my magic and flooded muscles with power, more than I should have in truth. I shoved Secca off and ran for Eva, trying to ignore how close I too was coming to succumbing to the lures of the Worm myself. If I reached for more power I could turn the enemy upon themselves: *Do it…. do it… do it…* I grimaced and resisted the urge.

The inferno raging all around granted me time enough to haul Eva up onto her feet and lead her away.

Vincent and Nareene laughed as the narrows burned around them. Men and beasts and daemons were all consumed by their lust. This was why the Arcanum feared magi losing control, and this was also a display of how Setharis conquered almost every other city and nation it had come across over the centuries – what were mere mundane humans before such devastating magical might?

Eva regained some of her senses and we broke into a run, creating as much space as possible before Vincent really lost it. My wounds made it difficult. Eva wrapped a steel-clad arm around my waist to support me.

I risked a glance back. The flames raged on and Vincent now stood on two legs, his missing limb replaced with molten fire, and the other covered in bubbling blackened scales. A huge dark shape loomed through his inferno, a crown of dark iron atop a serpentine head slithering through the flames. Abrax-Masud had sent one of his ravak ahead of him.

We ducked our heads and ran into the safety of a snowy night, hoping that Vincent would prove strong enough to grant us enough time to escape. Ravak were fast and hunted by sight – this time darkness was our ally. Explosions thumped and light flashed behind us as the twisted magus unleashed his magic.

We ran on before the night sky caught fire, two pillers of incandescent flame rising, entwining in the moment Vincent and Nareene were butchered by the mighty daemon. Were we far enough away?

Again, I felt the distant presence that had been watching the battle unfold. With it came a blizzard howling across the valley, hiding us from any pursuit. I reached out to it but whoever, whatever, it was, they were not interested in communicating.

Then all was black, blind stumbling southwards towards Kil Noth.

We enhanced our night vision; about all our strained Gifts could manage. We fled until I collapsed; clutching my chest and heaving for breath. Eva slung me over her shoulder the rest of the way south back to our camp on its steep and defensive rise. Even without magic she was far stronger than me.

It took the Skallgrim some time to reorganise. We grabbed some vital food and rest while they prepared whatever new vileness they had in mind. As dawn arrived the blizzard eased off into a soft snowfall and the enemy were on the march again, and this time the elder tyrant himself was in the lead.

The sun was a burning red sliver rising above the hills as we few remaining defenders wearily prepared for another sortie. The wounded joined us, or were carried south to the perceived safety of Kil Noth, their absence replaced by a stream of new Clansfolk choosing to fight with us. Mothers wielding hunting spears and crafters with hatchets and barrel-top shields moved up to stand beside us. We all knew what was at stake here.

I sent Vaughn riding south on his damnable pony, Biter, to seek out the Free Towns Alliance. All we could do was hope our help would arrive first.

The air was charged with strange energy as we formed a ragged line in the snow. Again I felt something I couldn't identify, that felt like the Shroud itself was straining and twisting in the whole area around us. Small crackles of lightning snapped from hair and steel, and the earth rumbled softly and rhythmically, a giant's soft snore.

A dozen druí accompanied by a small warband arrived from Kil Noth and spoke only to Eva. They ignored my existence entirely; flinching from my gaze when they accidentally met it. They took up position on the right flank and readied to do battle. At this point anybody with a broken bottle and a bad attitude would do.

As the sun rose higher, the snow lessened to a few drifting flakes. My gut churned and my arse clenched at the sight of the enemy: a river of steel flowing down the valley behind a line of those huge fleshcrafed monstrosities, all led by an enormous glistening beetle accompanied by two huge ravak. Their magical presence was growing stronger, a dark miasma that threatened to choke us and force us to our knees, begging forgiveness.

A drumming of hooves from behind made me turn and I saw Vaughn riding his pony like a madman towards us. "They are here! Ten thousand men running at full speed only half an hour behind me!"

Yes! Fucking YES! All you bug-fucking bastards are about to burn!

The Free Towns Alliance army would arrive before Abrax-Masud. We were going to win this battle and ram a rusty spike so far up his ancient arse he would choke on it. I nicked my thumb with one of Dissever's barbs and it eagerly sucked up the blood.

Feed me his heart's blood, it demanded.

Wouldn't that be a sweet, sweet thing.

CHAPTER 33

We were a sorry lot of mangy curs compared to the shining mailed soldiers of the Free Towns Alliance in their laundered green and yellow tabards, who hadn't seen the fighting we had. Even their conscripted militia in padded linen gambeson and crude iron pot helms were clean and uniformly armed with sturdy spears and slingshot.

Their robed Gifted, eight in all, and their general in his mirror-bright harness and red crested helm, rode towards us on sturdy Clanholds ponies, looking ill at ease atop such short, vicious mounts. They trotted over to us and sat there surveying our ragged forces with a critical eye before turning their gaze to Eva and the robed magi. As always, without robes and with these facial scars I was dismissed as unimportant. One day I should get a silver badge made that said 'Magus' on it. Probably followed by another saying 'Yes, really.'

The general removed his helm and dropped it into an attendant's waiting hands. His luxurious moustache and neat beard quivered as he scowled northwards. "My goodness, it is cold here. We shall handle this mess and be back in warmer climes before the week is out."

I laughed at him, which earned myself a glare. "You face an elder magus and two ravak daemons," I said. "How exactly do you intend on handling that?"

"With discipline and steel," he replied. "And of course, magic enough to shame your Arcanum."

I bit my tongue and skimmed his mind, finding it full of pride but dwelling on solid military tactics for the coming conflict. He appeared to be a pompous bore, but adequate at his role. His Gifted dismounted but hung back, their minds clamped tight as a gnat's arse as they stared at us with eyes dripping with mistrust. Any overt mental intrusion would be detected, and given the force surrounding us I thought it better not to provoke a violent response.

"We shall form the vanguard of the charge," the general stated. "You may take the centre with our militia bringing up the rear."

I looked to Eva, and I didn't need to see her expression to feel the anger bubbling up inside her. "With all due respect," she said. "You have no knowledge of the enemy."

"Be that as it may, we have every confidence. We also have ten thousand men and eight fresh Gifted. This field is ours."

With the paltry numbers left to us and the state we were in, there was no disputing that.

It was taking some time for the entire Free Towns Alliance army to filter into the wider space where we had set up camp. Their heavy infantry formed up in the snow ahead of us, all dressed in half-plate that was lighter than our wardens' heavy Setharii battle plate, but also a lot cheaper too – typical Free Towns penny-pinching. They were all armed with long spear, shield and short stabbing swords hanging at their waist.

Our wardens were exhausted, battered and wounded, and mostly running on guts and grudge. They were happy to let these newcomers form the vanguard and take the brunt of the charge. The militia formed up behind us, their captains barking orders about placement.

We four remaining Arcanum magi were quietly hopeful now the numbers were on our side. I glanced at my weary guards. Vaughn had brought his vile pony with him rather than leave it in Kil Noth with their many wounded and hungry mouths to feed. I would have objected but its teeth and hooves looked more vicious than many of our wardens.

The Skallgrim drums beat faster, the rhythm alive, ominous.

I edged closer to Eva as Abrax-Masud came over a rise standing proud atop the back of his great beetle, blue robes flapping in the chill morning wind: dark skin, bald head and an oiled beard, his full lips twisted into haughty disdain as he surveyed our army. Snow danced around him, the air itself agitated.

I frowned. "I can't sense any attempt to get into our minds." My Gift was open and watchful. The Free Towns Alliance were calmer than I might have expected, but a few probes revealed nothing other than they didn't like Setharis much and would much rather be home in front of a warm fire instead of stuck in this dreary frozen valley.

Abrax-Masud was up to something. The air crackled with stray magic. A stiff breeze began to blow and a blizzard formed from nowhere.

Our ranks swelled with reinforcements while the Skallgrim warriors were forced to advance towards us in a thin column. The Free Towns Alliance baggage train arrived, packed with far more water barrels and sacks of grain than they needed, and oddly, the heavy wooden beams of siege engines.

"Something is wrong here," Eva said.

The Skallgrim ceased their advance. Instead of charging as I'd expected, they pivoted right and began to ascend the hill to our left, heading up towards the ruined temple and the stone circle where I had conversed with the Eldest.

NOW – Abrax-Masud's mental voice reached every mind.

Something twisted inside the brains of the Free Towns Alliance leaders, and the general's mind unlocked like a box of secrets to reveal plans for our death. That bastard tyrant had hidden his manipulations from me! Their Gifted opened wide and the thoughts stank of Scarrabus-stain.

The Free Towns Alliance heavy infantry did an about-face and levelled spears – not at the Skallgrim, but at us. Behind us lines of militia stood their ground, the anvil ready to receive the hammer blow and us the metal. Their slings began to whirl.

Eva grabbed Secca's arm hard enough to bruise. "Hide us from their sight." The air rippled. Eva pointed to her head and I opened a mental link to all of us. *Head further up the hill immediately,* she thought. *It is too late for anything else. Be silent!*

A thousand sling stones crunched into the rear of our forces, aimed at the unarmoured Clansfolk and druí, many going down. They were lethal weapons at short range. A stone slammed into Adalwolf's temple and he fell face first into the snow. Diodorus went down with a shattered jaw, bubbling for help. Coira leapt onto a charging heavy infantryman and her sword found its way through his mouth out the back of his neck. For a brief moment she was a fury of slicing death before a spearhead burst through her breast.

We left our people behind and fled, covered by Secca's illusion. I mentally commanded Jovian and Vaughn to run for their lives, if they could. They leapt onto Biter to gallop south through a storm of snow and stones trying to hit a fast moving target. His evil pony trampled two militiamen to death and I had the blind hope that somehow they might make it out. *Good luck!*

Abrax-Masud and his army reached the ruins atop the hill. The air seemed to tremble. It ripped open to reveal rolling green hills – somewhere not here. Wind began to howl through the doorway. Men and monsters marched through. No wonder he was not attacking us – all his energy was working on opening this portal to elsewhere.

Surrounded on all sides and with the elder tyrant's strange Escharric magic; despair took hold.

It was a short and inglorious end to our campaign: butchered by our supposed allies. The Free Towns heavy infantry cleared a route to the hilltop for their baggage train. That explained the siege engines. They were never meant for battle at Kil Noth.

Secca's Gift faltered. *I am not sure how long I can hold this.*

You must, was Eva's only answer.

"Find those accursed Arcanum sorcerers," the general shouted to the militia. "A hundred gold to those who take a head!"

What do we do? Bryden thought, pulsing with panic.

We fight, Eva replied. *We try and take Abrax-Masud with us.*

Walker, keep us hidden from mental probes. Secca, keep your illusion up if it kills you. To the top of the hill!

We picked our way up the icy slope, avoiding the roving gold-hungry forces searching in vain for our heads. By the time we made it up the hill every breath came in a wheezing gasp and my tunic was soaked with blood after the stitches in my chest ripped open during the climb. The Free Towns heavy infantry and the supplies were already halfway through the portal.

Abrax-Masud's mind dredged the battlefield, searching for us. *Where are you, ignorant vermin?* We were mice, quiet and not worth noticing in all this mayhem… The edge of the portal wavered, his distraction compromising it before Abrax-Masud diverted his full attention back to steadying it. I was glad that for the moment most of his power was directed into keeping that portal open.

Creeping closer in the snowfall, little mice with sharp teeth, closer and ready to bite. Secca was drenched in sweat and struggling to hold on. The ecstasy of magic lit up her eyes. As we approached I recognised the hillside beyond the portal, and the inn where I had once spent a night. That hill was only two days march from Setharis.

The air tasted like metal. My hair hurt and lifted into the air, crackling. The Shroud around our world was straining to close the wound, and the enemy's power could not hold it open forever. His two ravak were already through, along with all his fleshcrafted creatures, daemons, and most of his Skallgrim. Only the rearguard of the Free Towns Alliance remained, scouring the hillside for us.

We were moving through the ruined temple, closing in and readying to strike when Secca's Gift gave way and ripped wide open. She screamed, half joy and half agony as magic roared through her flesh. The air rippled in heat-haze around us as her illusion failed, our tracks in the snow revealed to all. Cockrot!

I stiffened as a spike of mental power slammed into my defences. Strong. So fucking strong. Once, twice, and then piercing through the outermost layer. I threw everything I had left into pushing him back. I could not keep him out for long and the

Worm of Magic was rising inside me as desperation took over.

"You will not thwart my glory, little magi," Abrax-Masud shouted from the centre of the stone circle. "No more than great Siùsaidh and her vaunted high cabal could. They had to destroy Escharr and bury me alive to thwart us. You are but ignorant children compared to her. Now I head to Setharis to unleash my true power."

The portal shuddered and contracted. He hastily stepped through mere moments before the hilltop was engulfed in a lightning storm striking the soldiers caught outside the stone circle. Snow began to fall harder, coating the corpses with a white death shroud.

"At least that shut him up," I said, clutching the throbbing wound in my chest. Nobody seemed to appreciate my humour.

Secca was down twitching, her eyes leaking red tears. She was being twisted by the Worm of Magic. I sank Dissever in her heart before she mutated further.

A few of the Free Towns men left alive after the lightning began to stir, dazed. I limped through the ruins leaving a trail of my own blood in the snow behind me, and fed my hungry blade on the storm's survivors; its joy singing in the back of my mind.

We approached the ancient stone monument and stared dumbly at the circle of smoking earth on the icy hillside. The air smelled sharp and clean in the aftermath of the lightning storm. I spat blood on a fallen stone and leaned heavily on Eva, shaking with my Gift on the edge of ripping. She steadied herself on her war hammer. She and Bryden were in no better shape. We had fought four days straight. Even the unnatural vitality of magi had its limits.

I dulled their pain. Eva nodded her thanks. Bryden didn't seem to notice, his eyes glazed with thoughts of a home and family he would never see again.

We watched the green and yellow tide of soldiers race towards us. I exchanged looks with Eva and calmness descended as we accepted it.

Abrax-Masud was far beyond our reach, taking his ravak and the bulk of his army with him. The remnant of the Free Towns Alliance he left behind trampled our fallen into bloody slush as they ascended the hill intent on finishing us off. I sensed two fresh wholly human Gifted amongst the soldiers. Two others with them wore the blank expression of the Scarrabus-infested. The nerve of them, thinking themselves the match of Arcanum-trained magi.

Bryden managed to stand. He wiped sweat from his brow and managed to look vaguely hopeful. "Four, eh? Can you still fight?"

My back hurt. My bones ached and the wound in my chest was pishing blood – my boots squelched red with every step. I groaned and pushed myself to stand on my own two feet. I would rather die standing than be skewered sitting on my arse. "I can fight but I won't survive it. I'm so close to giving in to the Worm." It was at the forefront of my mind, urging me to do so.

"Should we?" Bryden asked blandly, as if we were discussing a second slice of tasteless pie instead of one of the most horrific and dreaded things a magus could ever do.

I looked to Eva, who was also seriously considering it. We were going to die, but the question was, should we give in and lose ourselves to the magic and let it twist us in order to take as many of these bastards down with us as we could? Or die here wholly as ourselves?

"We take these betrayers with us," she said. "Setharis might still find some way to survive. Maybe they have managed to recover some of our ancient weapons from the collapsed vaults below the ruins of the Templarum Magestus." None of us believed that was possible. The vaults had been buried so deep, and falling stone alone was not the only threat. Some wards and protections were still in place and the whole area was magically damaged and deadly to all intruders.

The militia were almost upon us, their boots a rhythmic tramping through the snow, steel jangling and mouths boasting. I extended a hand to Bryden and then clasped hands with Eva. "Never let it be said we did not resist as much as humanly possible. What more could be asked of us." Ah, her single green eye was pretty as an emerald.

I smiled at her. "We should've gone for that drink when we first met. Imagine where we could've been."

Her hand tightened. She chuckled mirthlessly, "Really? At a time like this?"

"It's not like there will be another," I replied.

In the face of death her thoughts made it clear that she too regretted we hadn't gone for that drink – and she had fully intended on going much further than drinking with me!

"Filthy bitch," I gasped.

I sensed her grinning behind the steel mask.

Bryden rolled his eyes. "Death cannot come fast enough if I am to be stuck here with the both of you."

I had grown to like him. Shame. We readied our weapons: Gifts and steel. It was time to fuck them up.

This shall not be. The Eldest of the ogarim's mental voice was quiet but the sheer certainty of it brooked no disagreement. It had been the unknown presence that I had sensed during the battle.

It appeared from nowhere, stepping out of empty air to stand in the burnt circle of stone beside us. Its three eyes were bloodshot, its shaggy white fur unkempt and its decorative beads in disarray or missing entirely. Eva and Bryden panicked but a gentle touch of my thoughts stayed their hands. Its three eyes fixed upon me and I felt its turmoil and torment. It still would not kill; it could not kill again even faced with its race's ancient enemy rising once more.

I refuse to let this world end without struggling to the last. This was once the womb of the peaceful ogarim. Now it is yours, our broken kin. You are not ogarim, but you are of us. You deserve a chance to live. I will give you that chance.

It placed a hand on an ancient stone and poured its magic into the circle. The air thrummed. For a moment I thought it about to unleash the sort of godly power I had seen in its memories, but it was weary and its life worn thin as paper by the passage of thousands of years. It was no longer able to summon such strength. All of its kind that had stayed behind to guard this world had long since lain down in their black pyramids to take the final sleep, their essence returned to the magic that spawned all life. It had been yearning to do the same for over three thousand years, but instead had stubbornly hung onto its duty as the final guardian of its race's mother realm. It was not here to fight, but to open the portal to elsewhere and offer us one last chance.

The Free Towns Alliance army howled and charged. A spear flashed through the snow to thud into the Eldest's shoulder. Their Gifted flung their power at it, fire and earth burning and rending its flesh. It ignored them all to lift a huge hairy hand in farewell.

The stones shuddered around us as the Shroud began to warp at its original builder's command. It was created from ogarim lives and magic and it recognised its own, and it did not require the brute force of Abrax-Masud and the Scarrabus queen to hold it open.

I will transport you as close as I am able. I wish you success.

"There is still great honour in the ogarim," I said formally.

Its third eye looked up at the sky. *Should broken ones survive, free and thriving, and ever travel to other realms, speak well of us to those you meet. My kind still walk those realms, in the quiet places. <Peace> <Hope>*

The Free Towns Alliance swarmed the stone circle and fell upon the last of the guardians. Weak as it now was, it could still have killed them all with ease, but instead it chose to die, a soft relieved exhalation of all life and magic.

The icy hilltop near Kil Noth faded to swirling grey. We were transported to a different stone circle on a sun-drenched hilltop somewhere else. Three exhausted magi and a Free Towns Alliance solider. He must've dived through the portal with us.

Yet he stood his ground.

Brave fool. Eva ripped his shield away, snapping his arm like a twig in the process. She disarmed and dropped him with one punch. He flopped down like a sack of shite, his skull cracked like an egg.

"Where are we?" she asked, using his tabard to wipe brains and blood off her fist.

We were near a coastal town surrounded by orchards, the masts of several small ships swaying in the bay. I recognised a tavern with outside seating laid out in a yard shaded by apple trees. "Port Hellisen." We were on the southwest coast of Kaladon.

Bryden whistled. "Imagine if we learned to use these portal stones."

Eva began walking towards town. "We must reach Setharis before Abrax-Masud."

Bryden and I limped after her, bags of broken bone and bloody cloth. "They are two days march from our home," I said. "We are three by ship at best. We are still too far away." I'd learned a few things in my ten years of exile from Setharis, and knew details of most of the common travelling and trade routes.

She looked at Bryden.

He paled and wrapped his arms around himself. "You expect me to control the wind and fill the sails all the way to Setharis? That would kill me."

"Probably," she replied, then resumed her descent.

I followed, and after a moment's hesitation so did the aeromancer, nervously chewing on his lip.

We drew stares as we entered the wide straight streets of Port Hellisen with its ivy-wreathed picturesque stone buildings. It was a quiet rural town with a peaceful and industrious population tending orchards that produced the sweetest cider in all the land. They were not used to seeing bleeding people in armour on their streets clutching weapons. A portly big-busted woman hurried over to Bryden and proffered a damp cloth. Ah yes, he was the only one of us that wore Arcanum robes, torn and filthy as they were.

"M'lord magus," she gasped, eyes wide at the state of him. "How can we be of assistance? Have you been set upon by brigands?" Though filthy, Arcanum robes came in handy.

"We need a ship to take us to Setharis immediately," I said.

Hand held over her heart in shock, the woman eyed Eva and me askance. "Well… we could ready a suitable ship by tomorrow if necessary. We only have one with the whole crew in town and half of those are drunk already."

"You will ready that one now," Eva demanded. "We leave

immediately."

"They haven't finished unloading the trade goods," she snapped, drawing other townsfolk towards us, curious to find out what all the noise was about. "She's heavy and sitting low in the water. This is winter and the winds are picking up – we will not risk travel unless the weather is more favourable."

"You are done now," Eva stated. "Toss your trade goods overboard and ready to set sail immediately or I will burn this town to the ground."

I tried the truth. "The Free Towns Alliance has allied with the Skallgrim and they are marching on Setharis as we speak. If we don't leave now then all is lost."

The woman goggled at me, then her pig-headedness drained away to be replaced with furious determination. "Dyrk! Ashton! Get your crap off that ship. Somebody haul those scurvy sailors out of the tavern. I won't be having no heathens dirtying up my streets with filthy swords and foul language. Port Hellisen are proud Setharii and we will do our bit!"

In an hour the ship was raising anchor with a full crew and three bone-tired passengers. I was slumped on the deck, too tired even for seasickness. Eva was talking with Bryden. He railed against it for a time, then grew quiet and morose as he accepted what we all knew had to be.

The sails swelled, catching a rising wind that pushed us east towards Setharis. Bryden stood looking out towards home, already under strain. I prayed he would last long enough to get us close before his Gift gave out. I didn't expect any of us would survive this.

We had a few days to get our affairs in order, and to use quill and ink to say goodbye to those who mattered. I started writing a letter to Layla, then decided that I may as well also write a few more to various people. I had a surprising amount to say. Bryden scrawled a letter to his family and gave it to Eva for safe keeping. Eva didn't bother. Everybody she really cared about was either here or already dead.

She was far more interested in learning all about me, all the mistakes I had made, the suffering, and also the joyful moments too. On learning that I had fled into exile for ten years to keep my friends safe, she wanted to know all about my time spent with Charra, Lynas and their daughter Layla. Her own upbringing was worse than mine in many ways: more privileged but devoid of love and appreciation. She let me into her mind to experience her parents' manipulation. I returned the favour and our minds entwined, exploring our pasts. It felt good to open up to her and leave myself bare of all pretence and sarcastic quips. I didn't trust easily, but with Eva everything was different. She was the third person in my entire life I trusted with everything I had.

It was far from the worst way to spend your last few days alive.

CHAPTER 34

Our ship crashed through choppy waves. Its taut sail was tearing at the seams, the second to be driven to destruction by Bryden's fearsome winds. The aeromancer was drenched in sweat and teetering on the edge of losing all control, of giving in to the Worm of Magic and allowing the magic to roar through his Gift without restraint. He was perilously close to becoming a monster. I had almost succumbed to that fate before, and I knew how urgent the need was, how tempting it was to give in. Somehow Bryden found the will to hold on, dancing with the fate of the world borne on his young shoulders. He would see us home in time even if it meant we had to kill him afterwards.

Salty foam sprayed across my face. I fought down my seasickness as I longed for Old Town's high walls to come into view. I prayed we were in time.

Eva's magic-enhanced eyesight noted a pair of storm-battered carracks anchored in Westford Docks – the first two ships to brave the treacherous winter crossing of the Cyrulean Sea to bring Setharis' legions back from our colonies in the Thousand Kingdoms far to the south. The sight of reinforcements was welcome, but it wasn't enough. Militia archers lined Setharis' outer walls. The few magi who had not marched north with Krandus, and those that had just returned from the war overseas, stood with them.

A few ballistae had been cobbled together by Arcanum artificers and raised on stone platforms, taking aim at the approaching daemons and hideous fleshcrafted monsters now crashing through outlying villages and warehouses on the northernmost outskirts of city-sprawl beyond the walls. The enemy forces were a black stain flowing towards Setharis, one that drank up all hope and exuded despair.

"We face so many with so few," Eva paced at my side, dressed in what was salvageable of her dented battle-plate, helm on and visor up over her mask. I tried to pick up her war hammer, and failed, so she held it to her back with one hand so I could lash it in place.

"We only have to kill one enemy here today," I replied, fumbling the leather cords into tight knots. "If we are successful then his army will disintegrate and the daemons will flee or turn on each other."

"Let us pray we arrive in time," she said, looking up at the gulls screeching and flapping above us, ever hopeful of a cargo of fresh fish being unloaded.

My mind reached across the sea to Cillian and found her burning bright atop the outer wall. At first I felt her terror, and then her relief on realising that it was me and not the enemy. She already knew what kind of magus was coming for them.

Hurry, Edrin. Already their power saps our will to fight. The defenders are untrained, with only a handful of magi and wardens to lead them. If the enemy are able to compel us to open the gates then all will be lost.

I pulsed reassuring feelings of my proximity. *Here we live or here we die, but we will do it together.*

How many are you? she asked, images of an armed fleet with seven magi in her mind.

Fuck. I eyed Bryden's mad, burning eyes. *Only Eva and I. Everybody else is dead, or will be soon.*

She covered her despair well and rallied. *With you we now stand a better chance.* She was not hopeful. If what Abrax-Masud said was the truth then he was the oldest elder magus in existence, a god in power and knowledge. And worse, he was a tyrant enslaved by the Scarrabus. I was Setharis' only defence against his type of magic but he was far more powerful than me.

I took a deep breath to steady my nerves, and stroked Dissever's hilt, allowing my dread weapon's bloodlust to seep into me and bolster my confidence. I was afraid. I knew exactly what to expect now. Every bone in my body shouted for me to flee as soon as we hit land. But that was the old me raising its ugly head. On this day Eva stood to my right, the most stubborn magus I ever met, and the memories of Lynas and Charra stood on my left, the bravest and most wonderful fools of friends I had ever met, or ever would. I was doing the right thing for once. I would do them proud or die trying. Their daughter Layla was behind those city walls, a piece of both my best friends, and I would not let anything lay a stinking claw on her if any drop of blood or magic remained in this broken body.

The sinuous towers of the gods were dark against the cloud. They coughed and spluttered and spat magic as the immortal guardians of the city fought to return. Even this far from the city I could feel them frantically straining against their chains, becoming desperate. It felt like the fabric of the world was being stretched taught around us, and yet not quite ready to burst. They were not going to be in time. It was up to the city's mortal wardens to stop the Scarrabus queen from freeing the dread prisoner from its tomb deep beneath the city. Our gods would be late, but I was uncharacteristically right on time, sober, and spoiling for a fight. I slung my pack over my shoulder, containing my letters and the wooden box with our remaining wards.

Eva gave my hand a reassuring squeeze before letting go. Some of my terror subsided. Behind the steel mask her eye creased in a smile. Together we had faced the Magash Mora and killed that mountainous beast of stolen flesh and blood sorcery. Nothing we faced here could possibly be as nightmare-inducing as that.

"Thank you," I said quietly, my words almost carried away by sea spray and Bryden's howling wind.

She nodded.

"No, I mean, thank you for everything. For saving my life time and again, and for… for being good company."

She snorted. "You have done the same for me. Don't go getting all weepy on me now, big man."

"Hah! No, it's just that I may never get a chance to say it again."

She clutched the prow as the keel scraped hidden debris beneath us. We were close to land now and the bay was filled with charred wreckage of ships torched during the beginning of Black Autumn.

The ship collided with something heavy, forcing me to grab her hand to keep my feet. "Maybe it doesn't need to be said," I added. "But sometimes I like to."

This time she did not let go of my hand as the ship drew into Westford Docks. We picked up speed and the sailors started to look worried – we had not, after all, told them we would not be slowing down. Eva and I readied ourselves for the impact. She locked her visor in place, then let me jump onto her armoured back and wrap my arms around her gorget and the hilt of her war hammer. We nodded gravely to the brave sailors steering us directly into death. Bryden was finally succumbing to the torrent of magic flowing through him. His skin rippled from the inside and I could see the uncontrolled exultation in his eyes. His forehead bulged and broke in a welter of pus as a third eye pushed through bone.

"You had better be victorious after this," he said through gritted teeth. "May the gods watch over you." He lifted a fist in final salute.

The docks grew from a misty distant line into a thick, barnacled solid stone wall with alarming speed. The sailors panicked and tried to turn the ship. Bryden threw them overboard with gusts of wind.

I tensed every muscle as Eva braced to run. The prow of the ship crunched into stone, timbers rending.

Eva leapt, carrying us up and over onto dry land as the ship crumpled and shattered behind us, accompanied by screams of tortured wood. Bryden's magic snuffed out as the mast fell and shattered his skull. It was a quick death, and better than the pyre. He might well have saved the world with his sacrifice. I just hoped somebody would still be around at the end of this to tell his tale.

Eva landed in stride running, a heavy bruising thump that had my teeth rattling. For a moment I worried about the wards being jostled, but if they'd broken I'd already be dead.

Cobbles cracked beneath her steel-shot feet with every long, leaping step that carried us faster than any horse towards the city walls. Warehouses and workshops blurred past as I held on grimly, praying I didn't fall.

The streets were thankfully deserted – if Eva had collided with anybody then they would have died instantly, their bones shattering against her armoured body. Thankfully it seemed they had all fled for safety behind the city walls, which grew ever higher and more intimidating as we sped closer. Not that it would help much if the enemy had more alchemic bombs like they had used on Dun Bhailiol and the Templarum Magestus.

I could feel the enemy as a mass of human fear and daemonic stench. The daemons were being driven ahead of the enslaved humans. Being this close to Setharis had to be paining the daemons already, but once inside the city walls they would soon die off, consumed by the daemon-toxic air of the city itself. Then it would be left to human slaves to carry out the will of the Scarrabus and their pet tyrant.

I would not allow that to happen. "Hurry," I snarled.

Eva didn't answer. She was already moving as fast as only a knight could. Finally the walls loomed above us and she skidded to a stop in a spray of stone cobbles and sparks. She put me down and I cut the lashes holding her war hammer in place. She gripped it in both hands, ready to wreak havoc. I could feel the eyes on us from above, the people on the walls squinting down, curious to see two insane warriors out in the open facing the advancing horde. I held Dissever tight, but everything going well Eva would see to my safety and it wouldn't see much use. One more knife, however deadly, could achieve little here. It disagreed and demanded I create an ocean of blood.

The ground before the walls was already littered with corpses, blown apart by magical or physical missiles. Green and yellow tatters of the Free Towns, Skallgrim fallen shields, and horrific daemons. A single halrúna lay sprawled on the earth. His magical charms and horned stag-mask hadn't preventing the crossbow bolt from puncturing his heart.

They must've been the first wave sent to take measure of Setharis' defences. The enemy tide came on, apparently unimpressed. Even from this distance Abrax-Masud's power was at work on the city's defenders, a diffuse miasma sapping strength and sowing despair. Soon he would begin taking minds and then the gates to the city would swing open to welcome him in.

Skirmishers swarmed ahead of the orderly shield wall of Skallgrim, who beat their axes and spears against wood as they advanced with the spearmen of the Free Towns Alliance behind them.

Fewer bone vultures and giant flying lizards filled the air than in the Clanholds. Countless smaller daemons loped and crawled and scuttled towards us, a bewildering array of everything I had ever seen in Arcanum scrolls. Those annoyingly swift dog-daemons, glinting shard beasts scuttling on legs made of crystal knives, snake-men, tusked boaram, and in the lead his two ravak, each ten foot high and twenty long, bearing dark crowns and long jagged swords a match to Dissever. One alone had managed to severely injure Elder Shadea before she had dispatched it.

Dissever pulsed in my hand, hungry and happy. *Oh what fun! Shall we play with them, you and I?*

I patted its hilt and chuckled nervously. "Won't that be a fun surprise for them."

They have used my spawn for years beyond number. No more will these so-called lords of the flesh rule the great devourers. I have consumed the rest of the infected left behind in my realm, and these are the last of the enslaved. Prepare the way, my pet.

"Pfft. You are my pet," I muttered, much to its scorn-filled amusement.

Cillian stepped up onto the battlements in her blue robe, golden wards glimmering and curly hair billowing like a mane. She pointed and her voice boomed out proclaiming for all to hear, "There stands Evangeline of House Avernus and the tyrant Edrin Walker, slayers of the Magash Mora, the destroyers of the traitor god Nathair, the Thief of Life."

Hope swelled, and the combined will of the people erupted like an inferno in my mind's eye, temporarily burning away Abrax-Masud's despair. More and more strands of his magic focused on me, all crushing power and devious will.

Distance be thanked, I held him off and bent over the corpse of the Skallgrim halrúna. I had paid careful attention to my grandmother's runes as she opened the ways through the Shroud to send me tumbling into the realms. I had a very different use in mind.

With the two ravak speeding ahead of the horde, I carefully set my pack down and then pricked a finger on Dissever's barbs, drawing blood to trace those same runes on the splayed corpse of the shaman. No one on the walls was close enough to see me practicing blood sorcery.

If the Scarrabus wanted to play with ravak, then so would I, and mine was bigger and badder and madder. The magic-rich blood of the shaman would provide enough power to pierce the Shroud and summon Dissever here. Angharad had correctly foreseen the need for a daemon ally here in the flesh to prevail – she'd just got the wrong daemon and the wrong flesh.

It was yet another thing the Arcanum wouldn't forgive. A tyrant and blood sorcerer? Even if we survived, I would burn for this. The city would never tolerate yet another monster sticking around to plague their sleep.

As I readied myself to activate the ritual, a grey, masked figure flung a length of rope from the wall and slid down, walking towards me with knives out and ready.

I glared at Layla in her nightfang assassin garb. I was about to order her back to safety when the rope was cut from above and it piled up in a heap behind her. Nobody was willing to risk that left dangling. It was too late. Lynas and Charra's daughter was exactly where she wanted to be.

"I know what comes for us all," she said. "You are the only hope we have. I am here to watch your back, Uncle."

Eva had been moving to block her but I waved her off. She looked at me curiously. "Uncle?"

I nodded. "Uncle through friendship not blood," I said. "Eva.

Layla. Great, now we're all acquainted." I removed the wooden box of wards from my pack and tossed the rest to Layla. "There's a letter in there for you if this all goes to the pigs. Keep it safe will you?"

She nodded and set it down next to the wall.

"Hey Eva," I said, grinning evilly at Dissever. "You were asking about how I got this back? Well, here we go. Try not to piss yourself."

I reached out to warn those whose minds I had touched before, Cillian, Layla and her guard Nevin, the leader of the Smilers gang, Rosha bone-face, and a hundred other scum across the city. I didn't want them panicking and attacking us. I said the only thing that could possibly give them hope after feeling the despairing touch of the enemy: *Tell all that can hear you that Edrin Walker has returned. The tyrant of Setharis fights with you! And he has brought the biggest and baddest fucking daemon they will ever see to fight the enemy.*

The two ravak would be here in a hundred heartbeats. I shed my blood in a circle around the corpse and pushed magic into it. I reached out to that spiritual part of Dissever that always lurked in the back of my mind: *come!* At my feet the body twitched. Its belly burst to reveal six-clawed scaly hands and an ornate black crown rising on sinuous coils far too large to be contained by a mere human corpse.

Eva and Layla backed away in a hurry. People stared from the city walls, overwhelmed by awe and terror as it kept coming.

Over twenty foot high and forty long, Dissever was a monster even among daemons. And I was patting its tail like a proud parent. I couldn't exactly reach much else.

I waved my jagged knife at them. "This here in my hand is only a little part of Dissever, and this is the rest."

"Sweet Lady Night," Eva and Layla said together. "It's huge."

An enormous black blade slid from Dissever's flesh and settled into its hands. "Mine is much larger that this fool's weapon, and I know how to use it."

Before I could process that Dissever was making a distinctively human dirty joke, the enemy began to charge.

With Dissever at my side, at least we now stood a chance.

CHAPTER 35

Abrax-Masud began forcing his will upon the populace. Every human mind was different and it was an astonishing display of skill and power for the elder tyrant to split his attention in thousands of directions all at once. Atop the city walls, bows drooped and eyes glazed over. He would take them and turn them upon the Setharii gods, intent on storming the pit where the Scarrabus' god-beast was chained. He was willingly dooming this world, and their damnable queen even had him convinced that this whole thing was his idea. It had turned his overblown pride into chains that he could never escape, not without admitting that he had been entirely wrong for well over a thousand years – and if I knew one thing about magi it was that as we got older and more powerful, so did our arrogance. There would be no last-minute change of heart.

Magic thrummed through me, hot and heavy as a drunkard's kiss. Though I had to be subtle for as long as possible instead of charging in like a drunken bull.

I did what I could for Layla, Eva and myself, keeping our minds shielded from his probing as we hid out of sight behind Dissever's huge serpentine coils. He knew I was here, somewhere. If he found me too soon then all that power would fall on me like a hammer and pound me into mush.

Dissever shifted and fidgeted like an impatient child as it waited for the enemy. The ravak as a race were, I think, not built for defence and waiting. Its hatred of its two enslaved offspring was stifling. The daemon intended to ignore everything until it obliterated them.

The human forces advanced towards the city gate with packs of howling daemons running before them, the two mighty ravak in the lead and shambling fleshcrafted monstrosities of claw and fang on either wing.

At a thousand paces, I opened my wooden box and removed the warded stones, sliding them into my coat pockets for easy access.

At nine hundred paces, Eva's magic-enhanced sight picked out a blue-robed figure in the rear.

At eight hundred paces, a single ballista bolt launched from the city walls, the very extent of its range. The swift ravak it was aiming at was gone by the time the heavy bolt arrived, and instead it punched a small hole in the Skallgrim shield wall, two or three skewered on a length of wood as long as my leg. They didn't slow and the hole was filled immediately.

As the elder tyrant and his monstrous horde advanced to only five hundred paces from the wall, only a handful of ballistae loosed, the operators of the others standing motionless and dazed. Bolts punched through clusters of scaled daemons, lines of Skallgrim warriors, and thudded into the misshapen chests of Scarrabus-crafted monsters, felling some but serving only to slow others. Dozens died but the ballistae shots did not come close to hurting the elder tyrant at their rear – any that almost reached him burned to ash in mid-air. The shots slowed, then ceased as a moan of despair rippled through the city. Abrax-Masud's power seized the defenders on the wall.

Fuck him and the bug he rode in on! This was my home. I struck back, freeing as many as I could on the walls and filling them with defiance. Anger was easy, and it built on the same emotion in others around it. Single-minded anger could help them fortify their wills. Bows lifted again and more ballistae bolts plunged into enemy monstrosities.

I could feel him focusing on finding me, the pressure building as we cut and raged at each other in invisible combat. If his attention was fixed on me then I wasn't sure how long I could survive, but if I didn't distract him the city gates would swing open at the hands of unwitting dupes – I was playing with fire.

The horde broke into a run heading straight for the city. Bolts, arrows and incandescent stabs of lightning lashed down from the walls, followed by billowing balls of flame erupting among the charging daemons.

Dissever ran out of patience. "Fight me, Scarrabus! I will be your end." It surged forward to meet the two infested ravak in a flurry of crackling purple energy and clashing blades, claws and fangs ripping into each other. Their thrashings reduced a dozen nearby daemons to gobbets of steaming flesh, while others more magical in nature dissipated into mist blown away on the breeze.

I grimly fought to keep Abrax-Masud from the magi and ballistae operators, and from ourselves. Fighting and slaughter erupted at several points atop the walls as he turned friends to enemies. Sooner or later he would manage to break a magus and then it would be carnage up there.

I patted Eva on the shoulder plate and stepped forward to go on the attack. I lashed out and speared into the enemy tyrant's mind, rocking both man and Scarrabus queen with the ferocity of my blow. Their defences held but they did feel it, and now they knew exactly where I was.

"We are Setharis," I shouted loud enough for the defenders on the wall to hear. "And we are humanity. This world is ours, Scarrabus scum, and you are ancient garbage fit only to be scraped off our boots. I piss on your queen, just as I have with your so-called god. Seriously, I actually have pissed on your god, and it seemed to enjoy it." I had details from the visions of the ogarim, and sent Abrax-Masud that image mixed with a steaming flow of yellow.

The answer was exactly as I had hoped. In a rage, the Scarrabus queen took control of its host body and the full force of Abrax-Masud's mental power fell on me like a landslide, doubled in power but lacking the magus' more dangerous finesse. I gritted my teeth and endured it, feeling like a sandstorm was scouring the flesh from my bones; I had to so the city remained free to act. I could not stand against it for long, but to scream and show weakness to the city's defenders was to destroy the world.

The first wave of daemons reached us, a pack of eight lithe and swift crimson-scaled canines with razor fangs. Eva leapt amongst them, her war hammer a blur of remorseless skill, crushing heads. Layla watched her back, throwing knives at any that survived Eva's initial attack and finishing off the fallen.

Up on the walls, the populace felt the elder tyrant's grip on their minds dissipate, and with renewed fury they bent their bows and loosed a rain of death upon the enemy. The Skallgrim shield wall took the shots, a few at the front falling. A few long shots took down the lighter-armoured Free Towns spearmen behind.

A huge fleshy abomination reached for Eva with four twisted arms ending in steel pincers. She spun her hammer and knocked its deformed head clean off its body. As the monster fell she vaulted it to butcher the next in line, the steel haft of her hammer bending badly from the force of her blows. She tossed it aside, raging among the enemy with her hands, a whirlwind of death crushing anything that came close. Layla wisely left her to it, and focused on slaying anything that managed to get past merely wounded rather than pulped. She lacked Eva's extreme magical might but was quick and precise, each strike a kill. Even so, they kept coming.

Dissever shrieked in victory as it reared above the battlefield with another ravak's head in its jaws. It swallowed, then began cutting limbs and body parts from the next. Its savage victorious glee bolstered my own mental fortitude.

For a moment it looked like we were winning, and the will and hope of the people of Setharis focused upon me. I had learned an unpalatable lesson about my own weaknesses from trying to enslave an army, and instead of commanding I opened myself up wide and held out an open hand saying *I am here.* Their minds willingly took that offered hand and flowed towards me, and with it the magic offered by hundreds of thousands of stunted Gifts. It was a lesser version of the Gift-bond I had once shared with my friend Lynas, an imperfect linking of our Gifts. From an entire city of people intent on destroying the enemy, those individually insignificant raindrops of power fell on me and joined to become a raging river.

Sweet gods, it was glorious! THE POWER!

I was a fucking god, a weapon of war worshiped by an entire city. It was ecstasy. And it was agony – I was no elder magus and this body did not boast a crystal god-seed to help channel so much raw power. It was burning me up from the inside out, but it felt divine.

My skin shimmered with golden energy as I stood tall. I was on fire with the flames of their righteous fury. It was as endless as the sun. Wings of air lifted me from the ground to hang over the city, glorying in my people's adoration and worship.

Eva and Layla looked up, staring at my change.

I lifted my arms wide to encompass the army intent on ravaging my home. "Die."

Thousands of Skallgrim warriors, Free Towns Alliance soldiers and Scarrabus-infested shaman screamed and dropped, their minds blown away like autumn leaves in a storm. Daemons and fleshcrafted monstrosities died in their hundreds, their alien animal minds uncomprehending as burning power overwhelmed and crushed their feeble thoughts.

I was so far beyond what the Arcanum had feared I would become that I had to laugh. I recalled my old landlady calling me Setharis' nightmare, but in this moment I embodied the entire world's worst fears, but also their most desperate hope. "I am a god!" I cried, voice thundering across the sky.

The Scarrabus queen wearing the flesh of an elder magus was now the only threat. It did not seem overly concerned. "A small god, and half-baked at best," it said, then pointed at Dissever busy flaying the last of the infested ravak.

The Shroud cried out as it was rent asunder. Cold yellow skies belonging to another realm engulfed my daemonic ally and it was gone, the Shroud scabbed over. They struck at me with all they had.

Filled with the power of a city, I contemptuously swatted it. Or I tried to. I found myself not as irresistibly strong as the magic had convinced me. For a moment the stalemate held. They pincered me – two separate incredibly powerful wills trying to burrow through my defences. Human tyrant and Scarrabus queen attacked with bewildering speed and irresistible might. I drew deeper on the magic of the populace, causing some atop the walls to collapse from the strain.

I dropped to the earth, forced to concentrate only on keeping them out of my mind as Abrax-Masud's robed form approached us. The city's defenders attacked while he focused solely on me. Arrows and magic alike bounced off an invisible sphere.

Eva and Layla charged. He waved a hand, disdainfully flinging them aside. They bounced off rocks and daemon corpses and rolled to a stop. Layla was dazed and out of the fight, mask torn, blood welling up from underneath.

I slid a hand into my pocket and drew forth a ward, flinging it at the bastard's face. It detonated in a ball of churning flame, but succeeded only in singeing his warded robes. His body had been changed and reinforced with magic for over a thousand years and it seemed the wards would have little effect.

The moment he came within reach I slashed at his throat. He tried to block it with a bare hand, and hissed as the blade bit deep. Power and bloodlust sang inside me, only to be cut off as his other hand wrapped around my wrist and squeezed. Bones shattered and Dissever fell from numb fingers.

My mental resistance faltered, and so did the belief of the entire city watching. The power flowing into me dried up as they lost faith.

I was going to die. We were going to lose, and with us the world. Humanity would become a slave race if it survived at all. He started to crack open my mind.

A dark hand wrapped around my throat and pulled me close. "You too will be Scarrabus." I was all out of luck.

I glimpsed Cillian on the battlements. She lifted a hand and the elder tyrant stumbled, choking as his bodily fluids tried to burst free of his body. He spat blood and laughed as his flesh settled once more. "Good try, girl." With but a thought he caused Cillian to scream and claw at her eyes.

With the last of my strength I kicked him right in the balls. His eyes bulged and that moment of distraction was all it took for Cillian to drop out of sight, unconscious but alive.

I flailed in panic as they penetrated my mind and pushed deeper. There was only one option left, something incredibly stupid, and so very me.

Eva staggered upright and our gazes met. She started to come for me despite knowing it would be the death of her.

I slipped a hand into my pocket, wrapped my fingers around the remaining slivers of warded stone, and then I let the enemy in. I let them win. They burst through my shattered defences, exulting in their absolute victory.

Then my trap descended. Walls slammed down to keep them inside this body. In their shock I had a few heartbeats to act before they broke me and escaped.

You fool! Abrax-Masud sneered as I pulled out the wards. *That will not be enough to destroy my body.*

"Not yours, no." I'd always said heroism could get a man killed, but I never said I'd go alone.

I smiled at Eva, stuffed the wards in my mouth, and bit down hard.

CHAPTER 36

I stared in horror as Walker smiled at me and then broke the wards between his teeth.

Light.

Burning heat.

Roaring in my ears as the shockwave ripped me from my feet, tumbling and bouncing and screaming until I slammed into the wall of a ruined building in a tangle of bent armour and fallen beams. I rolled in the dust and rubble, screaming, frantic to put out the flames until a moment of clarity pierced the terror. I was not on fire. I was fine. Fine. I had been far enough away to escape the worst of the blast.

It took me a few tries to get to my feet, the world and city walls spinning as I blinked away tears and tried to focus on Walker.

A huge crater in the earth smoked where he had been locked in dreadful mental battle with the enemy, their hand around his throat. I could not see anything moving. The defenders on the walls grew silent, expectant and watchful.

What was left alive of the daemon horde started screaming. Some began choking, vomiting up dying Scarrabus before perishing themselves. Others turned tail and fled in terror. Had… had Walker won?

The defenders atop the walls stared in silence, bows and magic at the ready as the billowing smoke gradually cleared. Ballistae cranked round to take careful aim.

I limped towards the crater. I had no weapons left but then I didn't need any; I willed magic into my hands, making them hard and strong as steel. If anything but Walker moved I would punch its accursed head right back into the Clanholds.

Metal crunched underfoot, shards of black iron. Fragments of bone and blood splattered across the churned earth. Tattered ribbons of cloth, the rich silken robes of the enemy and grey wool from Walker's coat…

The smoke thinned, cleared. Walker was nowhere to be seen. Nor was the enemy. A groan of relief erupted from the walls.

I searched in vain for any sign of life, expecting at any moment to see Walker rise from the earth to spit mud and make a bad joke. Instead, in a pile of jellied flesh and blood, I found a finger bearing the darker skin of Abrax-Masud, ripped free by the explosion.

Nausea rose as I spotted something else in the crater.

I fell to my knees in the red baked mud, staring at the partial remnants of a man's jaw with white bone and broken teeth. Ragged scars ran down through the stubble.

There would be no more bad jokes.

Edrin Walker was dead.

CHAPTER 37

Two months after the end of the Scarrabus war and the death of Edrin Walker right before my eyes, it was strangely unsettling to be standing alone before a newly raised Archmagus. Krandus had been a constant and reliable presence in my life, one far more understanding than my conservative and disapproving parents for whom even a sip of alcohol or flash of leg and cleavage was a scandal, and I a constant disappointment. After the mistakes made during the war he had been forced to resign his position by the magi that had only barely survived the trap the Scarrabus had set for the Arcanum army, despite being largely responsible for disposing of the monsters laying in wait for them. He did not seem entirely sad to be relieved from that responsibility, and I did not blame him in the slightest.

The gods had finally returned and their towers flared with magic once more, though it seemed to me that they were still greatly weakened. Reconstruction of the city advanced at a pace only gods could maintain, but many streets were still choked with rubble.

Cillian Hastorum now sat at the huge desk in front of me, haggard and sleep-deprived and partially hidden behind piles of paper and stacks of scrolls. Despite all the power and prestige, I did not envy the enormity of her new role. Administration and scrollwork had ever been my bane – I was a creature of conflict. Such dry detail bored me half to death. Or I had been that way once. Now I craved quieter moments away from people's pity, of being one with nature.

Underneath the steel mask my cheek ached and the softest of tunics rubbed against my shoulders like rope and grit with every movement. Phantom searing burns flitted across what was left of my skin. Nothing more to be done, the healers of the Halcyon Order had said. The pain was relentless and exhausting and I prayed for it to end. There was no more need to endure it, no great cause required to be fought.

Cillian too bore wounds, self-inflicted scars from when Abrax-Masud demanded she claw out her own eyes. It was only thanks to Walker's intervention that she could still see. She pinched the bridge of her nose and squeezed her eyes shut for a moment, willing the stress headache to leave her. "I am sorry it has taken so long to see you in person. I have read the reports of course, but I would like to hear it for myself. How did Edrin Walker die?"

I felt a twinge of loss. Odd, that. He was a fool… and yet if things had been different… "He died well. He died a hero."

A smile flickered across Cillian's lips, quickly vanishing. "Who would have thought it of him. Of all the people in this city I think we alone suspected he could be greater than he was. A shame it cost him his life to realise it himself."

I cleared my throat, "We confronted the Scarrabus queen and its tyrant host. I could do nothing, it was all Walker. He spoke to us, and all Setharis rose behind him. Ah, if only you could have been by his side in that final moment, Cillian. He glowed as golden and proud as any god as he threw off the other tyrant's yoke. Did you see that from the wall?"

Cillian nodded, eyes dropping to study her desk as she chewed on her lower lip. "Sadly even that was not enough to survive an ancient Escharric tyrant and a Scarrabus queen."

"He already knew he could not possibly win, I think. The look in his eyes said it all." I chuckled, making Cillian look up, curious. "It's not in the formal report, but in that final moment he grinned at me. You know the one – when the sneaky bastard comes up with a dirty trick. When he knows more than you do and is so fu- ah, that is, smug about it."

Cillian snorted. "Oh yes, I know the one only too well."

"They tried to enslave him. I watched the Scarrabus queen seize him by the throat. Then, just for a moment, peace overcame him."

"Peace?" Cillian repeated.

"Exactly like he did with the traitor god, Nathair, he let them win. This time he trapped them all inside his own body and sacrificed himself to save all of us – I don't think that option could ever have occurred to such selfish creatures as they were. With his last shreds of willpower he held up the wards and..." I struggled to get the words out from a throat gone dry.

"And then he died," Cillian whispered. "And dragged them down into oblivion with him."

We were silent for a long time.

Cillian drummed ink-stained fingers on the desk. "How certain are you that you witnessed the death of the enemy tyrant? They possess such a devious magic, and we only found a finger."

"I am certain," she replied. "They were locked within Walker's body and had no opportunity to affect me before the end, or they would have. He managed to destroy them in body and mind. We would not be having this discussion were it otherwise."

Cillian sighed and nodded. "What now for you? I have so many tasks needing done. There will be great need for a knight of your prowess in the coming days. You are a hero to the people you know."

I shook my head. "I am done." My voice rasped, hard and harsh even to my own ears.

"I could order you to stay," Cillian replied. "But I know you would just ignore it. A little of Edrin Walker seems to have rubbed off on you. Sometimes I think the Arcanum could use a little more of that. Still, you have sacrificed enough, Evangeline." The Archmagus grimaced, and forced out her next words, dripping with pity: "I know you suffer greatly from your wounds, and I know that will never change. If you wished, I would end it quickly and without pain?"

I considered it, feeling little emotion about dying. It would be a relief from the relentless pain. She could do it in an instant – burst my heart and stop my blood. "No," I answered, surprising myself a little. "I would not ask that of you. There are still mighty daemons lurking in the hinterlands. I shall venture out alone, find these remnants, kill them, and eventually die at their claws. I will go down fighting."

Cillian rose, came around the desk and put her arms around me. I stiffened, but then just put up with it. "May the gods go with you, Magus Evangeline Avernus."

I snorted and eyed the mass of scrollwork on her desk. "I think you need their attention more than I do. I have all that I need."

With that I left the Archmagus and the Arcanum behind and descended from the Old Town into the Crescent. I stopped and looked back up at my home for the last time. The gods' towers were lit and their temples glowed with renewed life. The war was over and the world was safe. Setharis would rebuild. I was no longer needed. I could finally rest.

I did not consider saying farewell to my parents, even with their newfound desire to reconcile now that I was thought a hero. Funny that.

I set off to obtain a mount and supplies. I would set forth for one last glorious fight. Peace could wait. Filled with resolve, I turned my back on the Old Town and visited the supply stores and stables. While a boy saddled my horse, I watched the people passing by on the street. For a moment it seemed like the old Setharis, if you didn't look down to witness the devastation of the Docklands. Even here in Sethgate, the richest area of the Crescent, the clothing was old and patched, and weapons worn on every hip. The jugglers, illusionists and wandering bards were mostly gone from the street corners, replaced by weapon carts and sword masters touting for business, offering training for sons and daughters at reasonable prices, promising spectacular results.

I stiffened, noting a face I had been seeing entirely too often over the previous weeks, too regularly to be mere coincidence now that it occurred to me. I had felt eyes upon me but until now I had not managed to locate the watcher. She was very good indeed if it had taken me this long to notice such close scrutiny.

The woman smiled and nodded a greeting, then crossed the street towards me. There was something oddly familiar about the way she moved…

She was young, pretty and dark skinned, and up close I realised that she was known to me through the memories Edrin Walker had shared before the end. I looked to her hand, noting the distinctive callouses and small scars from weapon-work, and then imagined her wearing a mask. "Layla," I said. A vague protective emotion washed over me, the ghostly memories of Walker.

"Hello Eva," she said. "He said you would know me without the mask if I came too close."

A moment of confusion, and quickly quashed hope. I did see the sneaky bastard die, after all. There was no faking that or the recognisable fragments of his body scattered across mud and grass. Even Dissever had broken into jagged shards upon his demise.

She held out two folded squares of parchment sealed with blobs of red wax. "Uncle Walker left these letters for you among the pile entrusted to me."

"And it has taken until now for you to deliver them?" I growled, snatching them from her.

She shrugged, not concerned in the slightest about angering me. "He told me to wait and watch, and only to hand them over if you decided to leave on a stupidly suicidal quest. His words of course, annoying bastard."

I opened the first letter and began to read aloud. His handwriting was atrocious.

Dearest Eva,

If you are reading this then I am dead, which sucks arse. Still, surprise! Just because I am dust and ash does not mean I am done annoying you just yet.

If you have this letter then it means you are determined to go off and get yourself killed. I get it. I have felt your pain. I know that only duty kept you going. You fought to save Setharis in its darkest hour. You fought to save the world. It was a worthy cause to endure agony for. Now you no longer have any reason to.

If you want to die then go right ahead. I'm dead so I can't exactly stop you. You might want to try something first of course, a way to find peace and freedom from your pain. Do you recall I said that there is supposed to be a sacred valley deep in the Clanholds, a place that only the despairing can find? There, the God of Broken Things dwells. Apparently he cannot heal, for that is a rare talent indeed, but they believe that those wounded in body will feel no pain, and for those wounded by the past, they are gifted with forgetfulness.

Worth a trip to check it out, right? Do it for me – one last request. If it doesn't work out, have a drink for me and then go pick a fight with something big and nasty. There will be plenty of such things loose up here for years to come.

I have also sent you a map. Apologies for my artwork. It's about as grand as my poetry. Note to self – leave a letter for Layla to burn the contents of that damned box.

Well, I guess this is farewell. I hope you find peace, one way or another.

–Walker.

PS – Did you see how fucking awesome I was at the end? At least, I hope I was. If everything went to plan then that should be worth an epic tale or two from those bloody bards.

I opened the map and stared, then showed Layla. She burst out laughing at the uneven scrawls and child-like drawings of trees, mountains and towns. I couldn't help but smile. It was truly, truly awful, but it would serve.

I looked to Layla, who was studying me intently. "Did you burn whatever was in that box?"

She grinned. "Oh gods no. He's a hero don't you know, and it might be worth something one day." She handed me another slip of paper, old and yellowed at the edges. "Have a read later and you will see why he wanted it burned. It really is that bad. So, what will you do?"

I instinctively liked her. We might have been friends in different days. "I'll go; I owe him that. One last request to try and find peace… hah, I expect it to prove superstitious nonsense, but there is nothing lost by taking a look, and daemons roam the Clanholds as well as the rest of Kaladon. That place is as good as any other to die."

Layla stuck out her arm and I clasped it. "I hope you find your peace," she said. "I will help look after this place, and Cillian is not a bad choice of archmagus."

"She will do well," I said, as the stable boy brought my readied horse over. I mounted and lifted a hand in farewell. "I wish you well, Layla. May life treat you kindly." With that I rode down into Docklands, past new housing being built and rubble being cleared. One day all of this would be a distant memory. A horror recorded only in crumbling scrolls and weather-worn statues, read only by scholars and remembered in inflated tales told by bards on dark and stormy nights. That was no bad thing.

Walker's memories offered me conflicted feelings as I left Setharis behind and made for Westford Docks to take a ship north to the Clanholds. He had been forced to leave his home once, with no intention of returning, and now I too had no expectation I would ever set foot here again.

Somebody was waiting for me at the docks, currently deserted with all the sailors cowered in their ships' holds. They'd had more than enough of magic and monsters, and even gods like Shadea. She was clad in flesh of shining bronze with a golden skull, steel wires and pulsing human veins.

"Magus Evangeline Avernus," she greeted me.

I dismounted and offered her a hand, a huge breach of etiquette when facing an Elder, never mind a god. She had always been good to me and I think some of Edrin Walker's boldness bid me to treat her as human one last time.

She took it, careful not to crush even my knight's body to pulp. "I would heal you if I could, but I do not possess the skills required. If you do not wish to wait the years necessary for me to learn then I could construct you a new body immediately?"

I ran my eyes across her body of brass and blood and shook my head. "I am tired. I think I would rather rest than become something inhuman. No offense meant, elder… ah, my god."

Shadea smiled, cogs turning, wires pulling. "Then I hope you find the rest you seek."

Behind me the sky flashed purple and the ground trembled. One of the gods towers shook and spat a stream of fire into the clouds – the one belonging to the Hooded God.

Shadea laughed, a tinny, unnatural sound but no less filled with undisguised glee. "That sly boy! He was always trouble. He had a letter delivered to a certain group of scribes along with a bag of gold. Copies of it have spread all through the city."

"What did this one say?"

"It truthfully detailed every single illegal act, every murder and machination that Archmagus Byzant once carried out when he was in charge of the Arcanum, or asked young Edrin to do on his behalf. The boy has spilled every last one of Byzant's dark secrets, and placed the guilt at the foot of the Hooded God's temple. All now know who that god was before he ascended, and what he did. I suspect, however, that the additional stories of Byzant's dalliances with a pig might have been false. It would seem in line with Edrin's perverse sense of humour. False claims or not, the god is now a laughing stock and utterly reviled."

Laughter erupted from my mouth and my eye burned with tears. "Couldn't happen to a better piece of shit." Shadea joined me in my mirth. It was a lovely shared moment, but passed all too soon. She had so much to see to, and never enough time.

As she sank down into the stone below her feet, frightened faces peered out from portholes and cabins, gazing on me with wonder. I turned my back on the rage of Edrin Walker's old mentor who had tried to have him killed, and made my way aboard my ship with a wide smile under my mask.

This was goodbye.

CHAPTER 38

The Clanholds on a sunny spring day was quite a sight. The endless white snow-bound valleys and frozen streams had given away to lush grass and budding trees. Sheep dotted every hillside and long-horned cattle with shaggy red hair had been put out to pasture, barely even noticing a horse and its steel-masked rider winding through the valley. It was serene without hordes of screaming daemons and bloodthirsty warriors trying to hack your head off. Hawks circled lazily overhead and small blackbirds flitted through trees and bushes, singing their hearts out. I was in no great hurry.

Banks of vibrant yellow blooming gorse bushes lined the path on either side, prickly and fragrant. A riot of small white flowers, delicate as single drops of snow, bloomed outside the squat, drab farmhouses and atop picturesque rises.

As the light began to fade I came to the only inn for leagues around, two storeys of grey stone and lichen. An old man was sat outside weaving a length of rope, smoke rising from a clay pipe jutting from cracked lips. He looked up, shading his eyes against the sunset as I approached and dismounted. "Lad!" he shouted. "A customer!" A small, surly boy scurried out to take the reins and led my mount to a small stable around the back.

I looked at the valley ahead, the route growing increasingly steep. "I need a private room and a hot meal." The mask was itching and my legs were burning, the skin cracked and weeping from all the riding.

The old man leaned forward, took out his pipe and cocked his head, looking me up and down. "Room and meal? Nae bother, but you don't wanna be headin' up those parts. There's tell of monsters lairing in the hills now. O'course you have a big sword strapped to yer mount. Any good?"

I shrugged. "There will not be monsters for long." I collected my pack and sword from the stables and was shown to my private room. After undressing to treat my wounds and slathering a mixture of herbs and grease across burning, itchy scars, I replaced my mask and clothing and went back out to sit at a table by the hearth in the common room. A young girl brought me a cup of ale and a wooden platter of bread, cheese and a bowl of mutton stew. She shied away from me, afraid of the mask.

The old man was not so bothered, quite the reverse. "Wounded in the war were ye? Didn't mean no offense. You folks fought a'side our young'uns against the Skallgrim and their monstrous beasts is all."

I nodded. His expression slumped into gratitude. "Did you know 'im? The tyrant as was called Walker?"

"I did. He was a good man."

The old man sat opposite without asking and bellowed for ale. "That must be a story and a half."

I looked down at my food forlornly. An audience was not welcome, given I would have to lift my mask to eat and drink.

"Have you ever heard of a being they call the God of Broken Things?" I asked instead. "Is it real?"

He paused, then slowly nodded. "So I hear. Certain to be strangeness on the path ahead through those there hills. Folk vanish. Folk go in with food and goods and come back with silver and no idea where they've been."

I unfurled my map, set it on the table and tapped a crude drawing. "I am looking for this valley."

He squinted down at it, then back at me, then at the map again. "The rock there looks like the maiden stone. Said to be a legendary druí bard with a silver tongue as was turned to stone in a storm, struck down by great spirits who didn't like her telling tales better than themselves. It's a little off the track. A way's up the rise and then left through a tiny pass right by a shrine to The Queen of Winter. Horses refuse to go there so it's said. Nothing more to see, it's just a barren hunk o' rock and scree down that way. Whole legend is a crock of shite if you ask me."

I was almost at my destination. "Keep the horse. Where I am going I will have no need of it. Have your boy lead me there in the morning. Now leave me to eat in peace."

The next morning the surly boy led me to the entrance of the pass. He seemed nervous to go any further, muttering about curses and dead spirits of evil druí stealing away and eating the hearts of wayward children. I imagined any such being might spit this sour child right back out.

I slung my pack and sword over my shoulder to squeeze my way through the small pass, a crevice in the side of a cliff really. On the other side another, hidden, valley began. A crooked stone pillar, like an old woman with a hump, guarded the route ahead. An old shrine to the Queen of Winter lay in ruins, kicked into a ditch.

I began to walk, and at my pace I would be at the mark on the map within the day. It was disappointing to only be attacked twice, once by a half-starved bone vulture, and once by a strange demon that was half-dog and half-monkey. I enjoyed the diversion of beating both to death with my bare hands.

After a few hours, rock gave way to soil and grass. I came across farmers tilling small plots of land, and tending sheep and cattle. I didn't see what all the fuss was about. This was no hidden valley, and was surely no secret if people lived and farmed here. A few of them waved as I passed by, and I hesitantly returned it. It was certainly not a place of daemonic terror and they didn't seem scared to see an armed stranger with a steel mask. It was a little odd so soon after a great war, and yet none of them bore any weapon beyond hoe and shovel.

It was a pretty place, and sheltered from the winds that scoured some of the other places in the Clanholds. Swallows flitted and danced in the sky and I found myself enjoying the walk. For a time it distracted me from constant pain and the rubbing of clothing.

After another league or so past a number of occupied dwellings, and others still only half-built, I realised that something was bothering me. I had not seen any children, and a number of the inhabitants bore nasty scars. Old limping warriors and women with faces lined with grief laughed and smiled without care as they worked the land. Phantom hairs on my arms rose.

This place was not right. I kept my blade close to hand.

Splitting from the main path up ahead, a gravel track led to a wide circular tower made from dry stone that loomed above every other building I had seen in the valley. Smoke trailed from gaps in a circular slate roof, and people were coming and going from the tower's single and very defensible doorway, some laden with building materials and others hefting sacks of grain. As I approached the door leading to a large and smoky central room, a man on his way out stepped aside and with his sole arm held the thick oak door to allow me to enter. I stepped through and tried not to stare – his face was a disfigured mass of burn scarring.

"Good afternoon," he said cheerily in a Setharii accent hailing from the cultured middle classes of the Crescent. "The ale here is cold and the food is hot. You will find what you seek, of that I have no doubt." He pointed to her mask. "You will not need that, Eva. We are all friends here. None will judge a person on such superficiality."

I went for my sword, but he turned his back on me and wandered away, humming merrily. I stood inside the doorway, hand on sword hilt and heart hammering.

"Are you coming in or not?" a dry, male voice said from a chair by the fireplace in the centre of the room. "It's a little draughty with that door open."

I advanced slowly into the room and let the heavy door swing shut behind me. The place appeared to serve as the tower's great hall, with huge wooden beams and tables and chairs set around the central fire pit while other doors led off to side rooms and steps up and down the tower. The man's back was carelessly exposed to the doorway, as if he was not in any way afraid of being surprised or attacked. His stockinged feet were up and resting on a padded stool, and next to him was a small table with two foamy mugs of ale.

Smoke curled in the air like dragon's breath, drawn from a clay pipe held in his left hand…a dark and weathered hand missing a finger.

"How do you know my name?" I demanded. "Are you the one they call the God of Broken Things?"

"I am," he said. "As to how I know your name…"

He stood and turned. My sword was up and ready to strike in a horrified second. The ancient Escharric tyrant Abrax-Masud stood before me. The enemy lived!

I flashed forward, magic singing in my veins as I cut at his neck.

He lifted his right hand and my sword clanged into it, like I'd struck iron. I stared at the enchanted black iron plates enveloping his hand, and then at the cheeky, foreign smile twisting Abrax-Masud's lips. His bald head had grown to stubble and the oiled beard shaved off entirely. On his tunic was pinned a badge that said: "A god. Yes, really." This… this was…

"Walker?"

"Ta-da!" he said, ignoring the blade so near his throat to fling his hands wide and grin at me.

"Walker?" I repeated, stunned. I had to be sure. I fumbled for the scraps of terrible old poetry Layla had given me and began reciting it.

He cringed. His face reddened and he snatched the paper from my hands, crunched it into a ball and lobbed it into the fire. "I will kill her!"

"It is you!" I gasped.

"Course it is. Do I look like an arrogant piece of shit with a bug pulling my strings? What other bloody sneaky little bastard do you know who could pull this off?"

He must have sensed my rising anger: "Uh, we have ale. Or I have a flask of whisky somewhere…" he fumbled at his clothing, searching.

"Walker?"

He looked worried. "I… uh… I thought it would be fun to surprise you once I sorted myself out. I guess seeing me in my new meat suit might have been a little terrifying now that I think about it."

I snapped and punched him full force in the face. It sent him spinning to crash head-first into the far wall. I choked with sudden fear that I'd killed him.

I got back up and dusted myself off, without so much as a scratch to show for the truly impressive blow I'd taken. I smiled ruefully at Eva. "I have an elder magus' body now. Just as well really. Sorry about the bad joke. It honestly sounded far more fun in my head."

Her sword clanged to the floor and she rushed me, wrapped her arms around me and squeezed hard. "Bastard. Utter bastard."

"Did I ever deny that?"

"How did you survive? I saw you die. You both died. You…"

"Like all bullies I gave them exactly what they wanted, and exactly what they expected. When they used their full might to force through my defences they found a simulacrum of myself waiting, and then my trap slammed down to keep them locked inside my flesh. My true self was already slipping into their body, leaving only a few physical movements for my own to finish the job." I looked down at the new flesh I inhabited. "As for this, you never did see it destroyed. You all remember only what I wanted you to. In fact, all I did was turn and walk away from the city.

She shook her head and cursed my weird magic. "What of the Scarrabus inside you?"

My face twisted in disgust. "Let's just say that after I killed its mind what was left made its own way out of my body in a very unpleasant manner – now there was a shite I can never forget."

Both of us could have done without that lovely image, but as usual my mouth was running far ahead of my brain.

"What brought you to this place?" she asked.

I held up my new, darker skinned hands, and examined them. They still felt utterly foreign. I willed the black plates covering my right hand to slide forward and form the vicious barbed blade of

Dissever and then back again. The daemon grumbled in the back of my mind, complaining I wasn't feeding it enough. Not that there was enough blood in all the realms to sate its thirst.

"I came here searching for the legendary God of Broken Things," I said. "I hoped it could bring me peace. What a crock of shite that was. Maybe once there was such a being, but no longer. Instead I sat in this ruin alone with my thoughts, trying to put all the broken pieces of myself back together and overwrite all the remaining inclinations this body's previous owner left behind. All he knew is still inside this old brain you know, good and bad and ratshit insane. While I worked out the issues I thought I'd take the time to write a great saga for the bards to tell, but one that tells how it really was, full of pain and panic, sacrifice and bloodshed."

I sighed and shook my head. "The world had other plans for me. I can still feel them all out there, the wounded and the despairing, the ones who had once prayed I might save them from the Scarrabus queen and gifted me their will and power. I invite them here to rest and to heal, and eventually return to their old lives if they want. And if not, they can stay and forget their pain and turmoil and have a second chance to be happy. I can offer them that. There was no God of Broken Things when I arrived, but there is one now."

I narrowed my eyes. "Say, how do you feel right now?"

It took her a moment. Then she gasped with the sheer bliss of suffering no pain. "Thank you."

"What are friends for?"

"Is that what we are?" she countered.

I sensed her malicious glee and realised I must be flushing with embarrassment.

Then that glee died, utterly, replaced with a barren yearning. "Walker, there can be no future for us. I cannot offer you anything physical. With my wounds we can never… you know…"

I chuckled. "The pleasures of the flesh are overrated, Eva. I'm more interested in your mind. The things I can do will surprise you."

My magic wrapped around her. I opened myself up and invited

her into my mind, our thoughts entwining, pleasure exploding.

She drew back, panting. "I will stay, to rest and heal in mind if not in body. Besides, a big, ugly, idiot like you needs somebody with some sense to watch his back, and to stop your damned saga from making you sound far worse than you really are." She punched me in the arm hard enough to crack stone. "I'm glad you didn't die."

I handed her a mug of cold ale. "I've always said that heroism could get a man killed; luckily I am more thief than hero."

She removed her mask and knocked the ale back. "I hope this fancy new body of yours is not as much of a lightweight as your old one."

"Challenge accepted."

For the first time in a long time, it was going to be a good day.

ACKNOWLEDGEMENTS

Despite the image of the solitary author toiling away late at night, I've found that writing and publishing a book is really more of a team sport.

I'd like to thank the good folk at Angry Robot for making the process of writing and publishing this second book as easy and fun as possible: Penny Reeve, Nick Tyler, Marc Gascoigne, Gemma Creffield, and my editor Paul Simpson – you have all been amazing and it's been a real joy working with you. Thanks also to Jan Weßbecher for another kick-ass cover.

Dawn Frederick and everybody at Red Sofa Literary, you have been as wonderful as ever.

My deepest of thanks to all the readers, reviewers, and the fine people at Fantasy Hive, Fantasy Faction, The Fantasy Inn, Reddit r/fantasy, Grimdark Fiction Readers & Writers, Fantasy Focus, Absolute Write, and many others who have all helped to spread the word about The Traitor God and God of Broken Things. Your support has meant a lot!

As always, the science fiction and fantasy author community has been a welcoming place, with people like Anna Stephens, RJ Barker, Edward Cox, Gavin G Smith, Ed McDonald, Sam Hawke, Peter McLean, Dyrk Ashton, Anna Smith Spark, Stephen Aryan, Jen Williams, Cat Hellisen, Ruth Booth, Rob Adams, Neil Williamson and many more making sure I am hard at work. Seriously, no distractions and amusements at all. Nope. None. *sidles off*

And finally, to Natasha, Misty, Mum & Dad, Billy & Lisa, Paula & Michael, Craig & Mary - thanks for your unwavering belief in me, your support has been invaluable.

By the same author...

SILENT HALL
N.S. DOLKART

AMONG THE FALLEN
N.S. DOLKART
The Gods are drawing battle lines

A BREACH IN THE HEAVENS
N.S. DOLKART
The end is nigh

THE BULLET-CATCHER'S DAUGHTER
ROD DUNCAN

UNSEEMLY SCIENCE
ROD DUNCAN

"ELIZABETH BARNABUS WILL ENTICE READERS FROM THE FIRST PAGE."
– STEPHEN BOOTH
THE CUSTODIAN OF MARVELS
ROD DUNCAN

PAIGE ORWIN
THE INTERMINABLES
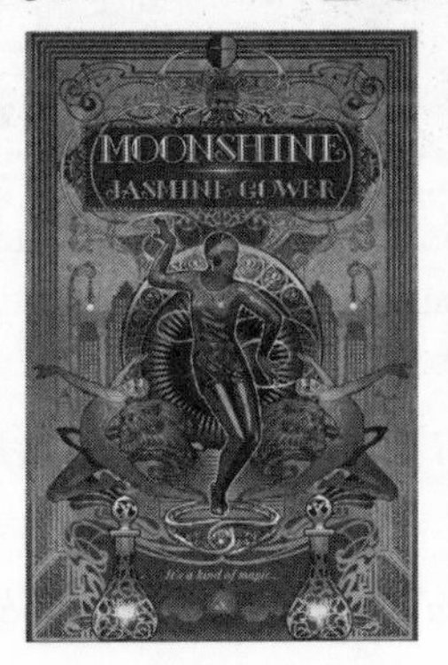
MOONSHINE
JASMINE GOWER

"RARE AND PRECIOUS... COMPELLING AND TRUE."
AN OATH OF DOGS
WENDY N WAGNER